YO AMO ♡

Not Everything Should Come in 3's

THREE
TWO
ONE

Everything should come in 3's!

Not Everything Should Come in 3's

THREE
TWO
ONE

USA Today Bestselling Author
JA HUSS

Edited by RJ Locksley

Copyright © 2015 by J. A. Huss
All rights reserved.

ISBN: 978-1-936413-79-9

Formatted By Tianne Samson with E.M. Tippetts Book Designs

Other Books By
J.A. HUSS

Rook and Ronin Books
TRAGIC
MANIC
PANIC

Rook and Ronin Spinoffs
SLACK: A Day in the Life of Ford Aston
TAUT: The Ford Book
FORD: Slack/Taut Bundle
BOMB: A Day in the Life of Spencer Shrike
GUNS The Spencer Book

Dirty, Dark, and Deadly
Come
Come Back
Coming for You
James and Harper: Come/Come Back Bundle

Social Media
Follow
Like
Block
Status
Profile
Home

ABOUT THIS BOOK

ONE GIRL

Battered, barefoot, and huddled under a bookstore awning in the pouring rain, Blue only knows one thing. After fifteen months of captivity, finally... she is free.

TWO FRIENDS

Self-made millionaires JD and Ark are not out to save anyone when they stumble upon a wet and shivering girl one early Sunday morning. But when you sell sex for a living and salvation rings your bell... you answer the call.

THREE SOULMATES

After years of searching, love lifts the veil of darkness, and three people—with three very big secrets—find themselves bound together in a relationship that defies the odds.

Or does it?

Love. Lust. Sex.

This trinity might be perfection... but not everything should come in threes.

For JD,

*Because he puts up with me three nights a week and I'm a total
bitch to him. He really should fire my ass from his gym.*

ONE

Denver Federal Center
Lakewood, Colorado
Present Day

"WE can't help you if you don't help *us* help *you*."

I just stare at the guy. That's his angle? *Help us help you?*

"Ark—" He hesitates and gives me a sidelong look, like it's just now occurring to him that Ark might not be my real name. I let out a small snort and a smile breaks. He does not appreciate the smile or the snort, because he rubs a hand down his face and huffs some air into it.

"Ark," the other suit says, taking over. I guess this is when they do the good-cop-bad-cop thing. "Come on, man, we know, OK?"

Now that intrigues me. "What do you think you know?"

"We know people are dead," Bad Cop interjects, warranting a feigned exasperated sigh and an upheld hand from Good Cop.

"People die every day," I add, just so Good Cop doesn't have a chance to play his card. It ticks him off too, because he has to take a deep breath.

"Ark," he tries again. "We need to know what's happening. People might still be in danger. More bodies might turn up. Bodies who might not be just bodies if we can intervene in time."

"Nothing's *happening*," I say, stressing the word. "It's over."

Bad Cop slaps down a stack of eight-by-ten photos and they skid across the stainless steel table with a whoosh. "This," he says, tapping one of the photos, "is more than nothing. This is a dead woman. And this—" He points to another photo, one I'm not sure I can look at and not be affected by. So before he can say anything I clear my throat like I'm gonna talk. It shuts him up just long enough to let Good Cop change the subject back to me.

"Ark, come on. We know there's more to this than you're saying. It's clear that you were working with this guy. We've found hundreds of contracts in your office." He taps another photo and sucks some air through his teeth while he lets me think about that. "Just start from the beginning. If you explain, I'm sure we can make things easy for you."

I give off another snort. "Make things easy, huh?" That's what they always say before they fuck you. I know. I've been fucked lots of times.

"Just tell us how you met her." I look over at Bad Cop, who is surprisingly calm now. His façade is slipping. Or maybe he just knows I can't be had that way. I've been on the streets too long. I've seen too much. I've done too much to be lured into talking with a fake promise. "Just start with this one," he says, pointing to the dead woman in the photo, "and we can get to the other stuff later."

I stare at him.

He stares back at me. "You're gonna have to tell someone."

"Eventually," Good Cop adds. "I mean, come on, Ark. There's

bodies. You don't walk away from this, understand? You don't just get to walk away. We can't cut that kind of deal and you know it. So just start at the beginning and we'll take it one step at a time. We'll put all the pieces together and write the report and then we'll talk about your options."

I already know my options. I glance down at the photos again, then flick them with a fingertip, making them slide across the smooth metal table.

Blue peeks out from underneath the ones on top. Her face in this picture is just the way I saw it that first day. Innocent, but stoic. Scared, yet strong. She was cold and wet. Her long hair was hanging down the front of that drenched summer dress that was too skimpy for summer, let alone late in the fall.

"You can pick it up," Bad Cop says. "Go ahead."

I can't stop myself, so I reach for it, but the chain on my cuffs is too short and it jerks taut. Bad Cop slides her photo across the table so it's directly below me.

"Start with her. The girl you're calling Blue. When did she turn up? Where did she come from?"

I can see it all so clear in my head. It started out like any other day. JD and I were up early to do business…

My fingertips can't help themselves. They reach for her photo and I hold it up. The silence in the room drags on for what seems like minutes, but it can't be more than a few seconds. Time just… stops. That's how it was from the first moment I met her.

"Ark," Good Cop finally says, breaking the stillness. "You have to start somewhere. We're not gonna judge you, OK? We're just here to get the story. You gotta trust us. OK?" When I look up at him he gives me a sympathetic shrug that comes off too real for me to chalk it up to FBI interrogation techniques. "You gotta tell someone, man. It might as well be us."

"It's a long story."

"We've got all day."

"It's"—I look at the picture for a moment, and then look up at Good Cop, AKA Special Agent Matheson—"complicated."

"I got a degree in logic, man. I can follow. And Jerry's heard and seen it all, OK? He doesn't judge." Matheson jacks a thumb over his shoulder at Bad Cop, AKA Jerry. "Hell, he's been involved in some fucked-up shit too. So just… take a deep breath, man. Just take a deep breath and start with the girl you're calling Blue."

I do take a deep breath. Not because he told me to, but because I really need one. And then, because I know there's no way I'm getting out of here without telling them something, I begin on the exhale…

"I saw her first, OK?" I look up at Matheson and he nods. "I saw her first and that's all you need to know."

It was last October. It was raining—pouring like a waterfall rushing down a mountain in the spring time. And the 16th Street Mall was empty because it was six-thirteen AM on Sunday.

My hands were in my pockets, my shoulders were hunched like that would keep the rain off me. Church bells were ringing. A weird time for the bells, I remember thinking. But it's burned into my memory of her. The church bells ringing. Every time I heard them I saw her in my head. Just like she looked that first day.

She was soaked, huddled under an awning over a bookstore, crying. She was shivering and her teeth were chattering uncontrollably. Her eyes—a striking, almost surreal aquamarine—tracked me as I walked by. Last night's makeup was streaked down her cheeks, black and gray stains that mimicked the sky above.

I stopped walking. Like mid-stride. And stared at her. She had on a short dress and no jacket. She looked like she'd been dumped there after a one-night stand gone wrong.

"You OK?" I asked her.

And then her eyes darted behind me and I knew that this

was not going to turn out well.

Now I look up at Matheson, maybe because he reminds me of someone I don't want to think about right now. Or maybe because I already know the whole thing is over, so the secrets don't matter anymore. But either way, I start talking.

"I saw her first…"

TWO

Late October
6:13 AM
16th Street Mall, Denver, CO

MY teeth are chattering so bad, I can't seem to take a deep breath. And I really need a deep breath. I draw one in, but it's not enough to stop the dizziness left over from last night's party and the sobs come pouring out like the rain that floods over the top of the bookstore awning. The alcove is only two feet deep, and with the wind, any shelter is minimal.

A cry escapes before I can rein it in. I look down at my bare feet and wonder if it's possible to die of fright.

Because I'm so scared right now.

Voices. Men, at least two of them. They are loud, a little ways off, and they are running. Their boots thud as they come closer.

I slink down to the ground and wrap my arms around my knees, trying to shrink into nothingness. Trying to be invisible. I duck my face down so my hair falls forward. The men come closer and I know—I just know—they are coming for me.

I scramble to my feet, because fuck this. I'll be damned if they're gonna take me back. I'll fight back this time. I will.

The boots stop, like they know I'm here, and they start talking in hushed whispers. I imagine they are planning how to capture me, but it won't be hard. I'm half naked in this summer dress that's soaked through so that it's clinging to my skin. My limbs are shaking. I doubt I have the strength to face one man, let alone two.

The boots start again. Coming closer and closer.

A man comes into view from the right and takes two steps. Two steps where I'm hopeful that he will not look to his left and see me standing here.

But I used up all my luck last night when I escaped. Because his head turns in my direction and he stops. Mid-stride. And he just looks at me for a long moment. I bite my lip and hold in another sob, but it escapes as a whimper.

His eyes narrow into slits. He's wearing a black bomber jacket with the hood pulled up over his head and he's got a large duffel bag slung over his shoulder. He looks scary as fuck until those eyes rest on mine. I let out the breath I was holding. Those eyes tell me everything. They are dark, but they are deep. And they are not the cruel eyes of the men I am running from. "You OK?" he asks.

Before I can answer the second pair of boots is running towards us and another guy appears behind him. My eyes shoot to the face of the newcomer and again I'm surprised at what I find there.

"Who's this?" he asks in a playful tone. "My, my," he adds, pushing the first guy out of the way. His eyes are light blue. Mesmerizing. Like the sky of a summer day. His blond hair is cropped short and he's got some blond stubble to match. He's soaked too, but he's not dressed for it either. He's wearing a tan flannel checked with red that looks so old-school, it might actually be from the Nineties. It's hanging open, not even buttoned up, and underneath is a faded red t-shirt with the Rolling Stones tongue on it. "You look cold, darling. And wet." He winks at me as he takes a step to close the few feet of distance between us.

I shrink away from Grunge and look back at Deep Dark, desperate for some way to get past this moment. His eyes latch onto mine and never let go as he speaks. "You need some help?"

I shake my head at him.

But then Grunge is right up next to me, pulling my cold body into his. "You're freezing," he says, rubbing my bare arms. He wraps his hands around my waist and laughs into my neck like we've been friends our whole lives. "Me too. Wanna keep each other warm?"

I struggle against him and Deep Dark puts a hand on Grunge's shoulder. "Stop, JD. You're scaring her."

JD puts his hands up in the air, a 'my bad' gesture, and steps away so Deep Dark can move in closer.

He scans my body, seeing pretty much all of it since the dress is wet and plastered up against me. My nipples are perked up from the cold and pressing so hard against the thin fabric of my dress that every shift of my body rubs across them, sending a chill through my body. "Do you need help or not?" Deep Dark asks again. "Because we're losing money here."

"Hey," JD interrupts. "Calm down, man. We've got time. That last bitch bailed."

"Yeah," Deep Dark says. "Which means we need another bitch fast."

"Well, lookie here," JD says, gesturing to me. "She's got potential." He looks me up and down now, the same way Deep Dark just did. But he smiles. "She's perfect, actually. Hey, darling, you need to make some money today? Get yourself out of this, ah… situation you find yourself in?"

"Money?" I manage to squeak out.

He moves up close to me again and his hands find the same place on my waist they had a few moments ago. "We'd like to take some pictures of you, darling. Right here," he says, motioning to the alcove we're all squished up into.

I shake my head no, but he ignores me and turns to Deep Dark. "Go over there, Ark," he whispers and points to an empty bus stop across the pedestrian street where only the mall busses run. "Your camera will be dry in there, right? And you got a long lens?"

Ark nods his head, but he's looking at me, not JD. "This what you want?"

"What kind of pictures?"

Ark opens his mouth to speak, but JD beats him to it. "No nudies, darling. Just like you are is fine. OK?" He reaches up and swipes a strand of wet hair away from my eyes.

"What do I have to do?"

JD smiles. "Depends on how much you wanna make."

"How much do I get for standing here and doing nothing?"

JD leans in and kisses me. I'm so shocked I don't even pull away. His lips brush against mine, lingering for a moment. His hot breath caresses my cold face. Then his hand is behind my neck as he slips in some tongue—twisting us together in a way that sends a chill of heat through my entire body. When he pulls away I almost reach for him.

"Stand here looking lost and cold… I'll pay you a hundred dollars. Let me kiss you like this, and you get two hundred. Get on your knees and suck my cock, and that's five hundred. So it's your call, darling. You tell me how much you need."

I lean back and stare up at him. His head is bent so he's looking down on me. His smile is easy and those eyes are still mesmerizing. They're like the water on a tropical beach.

"Where did you get those eyes, darling?"

I huff out a small laugh and my body relaxes a little. "I was just thinking the same thing about yours."

He traces my lips with his finger, so softly I have to swallow to stop myself from sucking on it. "So you wanna make a deal?"

"Let me see the money." When I stop talking he takes an opportunity to slip his finger into my mouth. Ark is already inside the bus stop, camera ready.

JD pulls out a wad of cash and starts counting. "We're gonna kiss, I know that much," he says with a laugh. "So here's two hundred right now."

He holds the money out and waits for me to take it. As soon as I do he thumbs up Ark and the camera shutter starts clicking. And then…

I am kissed like I've never been kissed before in my life. His lips are magic. His hands brush against the back of my neck in a way that makes me tremble, and the cold ceases to exist. He presses his knee between my legs and lifts it slightly, rubbing it against the wet v of fabric that defines my pussy. His kiss continues. We're twisted together again. He's probing into me, deeper, on so many levels. His knee, his tongue, his hand as it grasps my nape.

I'm losing myself in him. I've never had a man affect me this way before in my life. I've never swooned over a kiss. I've never felt weightless from a hard body pressed against mine. I've never wanted something to go on forever quite like this moment I'm having with a complete stranger.

My knees begin to buckle and I find myself sliding down the hard-edged brick wall until I'm sitting down, looking up at his beautiful face as he unbuckles his belt. "Five hundred more, darling. You want it?" He finishes with the buckle and unzips his pants, pulling out his fully erect cock. The head is round and thick, and the length is long. "Just put it in your mouth and let Ark get some shots—"

A shrill whistle cuts off his words and he immediately stashes his dick away and pulls me to my feet. "We've got company." He opens his flannel and pulls me into an embrace. He's as wet as I am, so we become bonded together by our clinging clothes.

A few seconds later a mall security vehicle passes by.

Ark appears. "He's on to us. We gotta go."

JD hugs me tight. "You wanna come back to our place and finish this off, darling?"

I look down at the two hundred dollars still clutched in my fist, then notice my bare feet.

JD notices my predicament at the same time and turns his back to me. "Hop on, baby. I'll carry you." He shoots me a wink over his shoulder and I can't help myself.

I laugh. After everything that happened last night, I can still laugh. And this stranger did that for me. He did that for me and he's offering to do something else for me. He's giving me a way out if I want it.

Seven hundred dollars can buy a thrift-store outfit and a bus ticket. I could stop all this. I could leave Denver and forget.

I look over at Ark and he shrugs. "You wanna suck his dick for five bills, that's your choice. But you can take that two hundred and leave. And if I were you, I'd take that option. Because he's not as charming as he looks. Neither of us are what we appear to be right now."

"Jesus Christ, Ark. No wonder you can't get a girlfriend. Fuck him, little darling. I'm guessing you don't have somewhere better to go, otherwise you wouldn't be out here in the rain on Sunday morning."

He's right. I have nothing. Literally nothing but the dress and panties I'm wearing and the two hundred dollars. That's not enough to make a difference. But five hundred more can. Five hundred more changes everything for me.

"I don't," I admit, ashamed. More ashamed of how I got here

than I'll ever be after sucking the cock of this man for money.

"Then let's go." JD pats his back and I grab his shoulders and jump. His strong hands clasp under my knees and he hikes me up, rubbing my already throbbing pussy across his wet flanneled back.

And the three of us run out into the rain.

THREE

ARK

I MET JD four years ago when I first made my way into Denver via the Greyhound bus terminal. I had money. And I had a contact. One contact and that was it. So I basically started this new life alone. Just me and my camera.

But JD was there that first night after I got off the bus.

It was a fight, but not a fight. It was a breakdown, that's for damn sure. His life was over. The very moment I stepped outside the terminal was the very moment he learned he lost everything.

And he was getting his ass kicked. Which I didn't realize then is a pretty big deal. Because JD is a dangerous guy. He's no stranger to fights, but he is a stranger to losing them.

It was four on one that night and even though I was brand new in town and my business was so many shades of shady, I stepped up.

Because that's what I do. I step the fuck up.

We didn't quite win that fight. But we didn't lose either. And after I told him I was new in town and was just on my way to find a hotel, he offered me a place to stay.

And this friendship grew out of that first night. His story was a blessing and a curse. A reason to stay and a reason to leave. We are polar. I am north and he is south. We are equal and opposites in almost every way imaginable. We are this and that. Black and white. Rough and calm.

And yet there is this straight line that connects us. One to the other. No matter what, we are bonded together by some law of the universe.

And now he is a brother. A best friend. A business partner.

But back then JD was making money as a stripper for some company who specialized in bachelorette parties. So it was not hard to convince him we could do better on our own.

And that's how Public Fuck America was born.

We approach women in public venues. Clubs, festivals, concerts—shit like that. And we make an offer. Very nice offers. Because I had that start-up money when I blew into town, so we could afford to set this shit up so it was legal.

Once we have the girl spinning with dollar signs in her eyes, we bang out a contract and set up the testing with a local clinic. We pay up front for that and take it out of their contract pay. So this girl who ditched us today was a hundred-and-twenty-dollar loss because she never worked. Once we get them tested and on board for the first shoot—which is always outside, early AM, and in a recognizably public place—we typically get them to do more.

That's where the clubs and concerts come in. And those get the online hits like nobody's business.

But a few months after we started, a guy approached us. Asked if we'd like a steady paycheck. We could keep the Public Fuck America name—which was not even negotiable, since we bought the domain name for it on day one—and just upload our videos to his boss' aggregated site. We have a quota of three videos a week and we make money per view on the site once it's live.

We make bank.

Bank.

Like we make more money in a month than my old man did in two years back when I was a kid.

But it comes with a price. Three vids a week is one of them. That's three girls you gotta have set up and ready to go to work each week. They do it a few times, most of them. And then they're out. Either onto bigger things—porn is everywhere. Why stay loyal to us?—or we find out they can't pass the STD testing. Or they have a drug habit, that's an automatic, *Get out of here.* Or whatever. But they never stay long. So this week, man, we are fucked. Good and royal. Because we are two videos short.

But now JD has this girl in his sights and we're taking her back to our place. There's no way we're doing a movie. She's got no contract, no test, and no ID because from the looks of it, she's got a dress and some panties to her name and that's about it.

Panties I'm staring at right now. Her ass bounces along JD's back as he jogs through the rain and my dick grows a little as I imagine what that might feel like. Both for her and for him.

Dammit. This is not going to work. She's good for some gifs on my Tumblr blog, but not a whole lot else.

JD runs faster, making the girl give off a little squeal of surprise.

I walk. Fuck that shit. They round a corner and disappear. My jaw is clenching hard and the anger inside me is building as I think of all the ways JD just refused to take the hint. And why? To meet our quota? We're too far behind this week. Even if she was legit, and she's not, this one girl sucking his dick is not enough to keep the boss happy. We need her, plus one more, to break even. And one more to stash away for when the Public

Fuck America site launches on Christmas Day.

We have been making four videos a week for four years—three for our boss, Ray, and one for us. That's two hundred extra porn videos, give or take, which is just barely enough to launch the site and start our own aggregation business where we have other dudes do the legwork. And even though this is the whole point of the last four years, I'm stressed, man. I'm stressed bad. I do not need this girl complicating things this week. Especially when JD refuses to acknowledge that she was mine first. That shit just pisses me off.

But fuck it. Fuck her too. He can have her. I saw some bruising on her arms and she looks strung out. Beyond the fact that she's half naked and sobbing, I mean. She looks like she just came down from some goodass shit.

And that's something we do not fuck with. No druggies. They steal, they lie, and they don't eat enough to make them curvy.

By the time I round the corner JD and the girl are gone. Already inside, I suppose. I walk a little faster. I don't want him to get her home with too much lag time. Fucker.

We own the top floor of a building on California Street. When we bought that place with cash, the shit got real.

We are fucking rich.

I press the button on my electronic key and open the thick wooden door to find JD and the girl sitting on the steps. She's in his lap and he's kissing her.

"What the fuck?"

JD laughs. "I was waiting on you, dude. Ready?" He stands up, the girl sliding down his legs as he does it, then grabs her by the hand and pulls her to the elevator. She stumbles after him, dead on her feet. She probably won't make it through a shooting. What a waste.

We get in the elevator and I press the top floor, because JD's hands are all over this girl. Pressing up against her breasts and sliding around her neck as he continues to kiss her.

I shake my head as the doors open and head across the hall to the only loft up here. Ours. The penthouse.

When I open the door, I let JD go first. He walks the girl backwards, still kissing her like his life depends on it.

"Wait," she whispers against his lips. "Wait, what are we doing?"

"Taking some pictures, darling. Remember?" He knows she's stoned from the night before too. "You still got your money?" She looks down at her clenched fist filled with twenty-dollar bills. "Good, baby. Don't let go of it, OK? It's yours. And we're gonna give you more. Just let me take care of things so Ark can get the photos, and then you can have the rest. OK?" He kisses her and then turns back to me. "Where do you want us?"

We are all sopping wet so I point to the terrace. JD kisses her one more time to stop the whimpering protests, and then walks her backwards a few more paces before twirling her around and pointing her to the terrace doors. He slides them open and drags her through.

"Up against the glass," I call out when he looks back at me. "You two, leaning up against the glass so I can get a good view of the city in the rain. I'll set the camera up in here with a long lens."

By the time I get it set up on the tripod JD is ready to tear her clothes off. What the fuck has gotten into him? He's never like this with the girls. He can take or leave most of them, and most of them are cute. But this one, she looks homeless. She's skinny. She's dripping wet, and not only because he's fingering her pussy through her panties. Her lips are practically blue, she's so cold. And yet he acts like this girl is the love of his life.

I don't get it.

"Leave her clothes on," I call out to him.

"What?" he laughs, looking over his shoulder at me.

"Leave her clothes on. I want her in the wet dress. I'm the

photographer and I say leave her fucking clothes on."

He draws in a long breath and stares at me for a moment. "OK, dude. Whatever you want."

Fucking prick. I'm not sure why, but the thought of JD taking off that dress and palming her bare breasts just pisses me off. "Turn to the side," I call again. The rain is coming down good and hard now and I zoom in on their lips. The water trickles over the curve they make as they press together. His tongue. Her tongue. Lick. It swipes over her top lip to catch the rain running down her nose in a stream. Her eyelashes are clumped together and the makeup from last night has left dark gray streaks down her face.

Her head turns into the light—not a ray of sunshine exactly, but some play of light from somewhere unknown to me—and her eyes sparkle. They are blue, but they are not just any blue. They are like the ocean water in the tropics.

They are the most beautiful color I've ever seen.

"Just like that," I call out. But she's distracted by JD's mouth. And he is groping her now. He fists her breast and yanks on her hair until her head tilts back. The light catches her face again, but this time her eyes are closed. She moans.

My dick swells.

JD's hand slips under the short dress. It's got a yellow flower pattern to it with a little ruffle along the hem, a hem that's barely long enough to cover her panties, which are white. White cotton panties. All stuck to her, showing off her pussy and, if I look through the lens and zoom in, her little button of a clit. All swollen and ready for JD's fingers to do their magic.

I draw in a breath as he makes his move. My anger is mounting. I cannot believe he stole her right in front of me. And I don't give a fuck if she's drugged up from a wild night out. Or that she's cold and shaking all over from fear. I saw her first. That's the rule. We've had it for years, and we've never broken that one rule.

Until today.

And fuck that. She's mine.

I'm about to charge out there and start shit when the girl's legs buckle and she slumps down to the ground. JD follows her, effortless, seamlessly, like the actor he is, and then he's pulling her into his lap. I adjust the camera just as he opens up her legs, pulling her panties aside. She's shaved bare, which makes me pause for a moment. But then his fingers dip into the v of her legs and slip under those perfect pink lips, and that's all I can take. I reach behind my neck and pull my shirt off, then walk out there to set his ass straight.

Because she's mine.

FOUR

ARK

AS soon as I step out onto the terrace, JD stops what he's doing and shoots me a look. "What's up?" he asks with a smile.

I ignore him and walk to the other side of the girl and bend down in front of her. Her head is lolling to one side, that's how out of it she is. "What's your name?" I ask her.

She straightens her chin and shrugs JD's hand off her shoulder as he tries to get her attention back. "Fuck you," she spits. "I just want my money." Her words come out slurred and her head drops down towards her chest.

"Well," I say back calmly, "I'll call you Blue Eyes, then. How's that?"

"You can call me whatever—"

I lean in and grab her face, my fingers wrapped along her jaw and my thumb pushing into her cheek. "Do you want your money or not?"

She slaps my hand away and tries to get up, but her legs

buckle underneath her again and she falls into JD.

"Jesus, Ark. Just go back to the camera and let me handle this."

"Fuck that," I say back, my eyes never leaving the girl. "I want in on this one."

"What?"

I look over at him, logging his surprise, but not caring much. "Why?"

"Why not?" I say back, settling down next to him, my back against the clear wall that separates us from the Denver city streets eight floors below. "Is she even conscious, JD? Look and see."

He leans down to try to see her face through the curtain of long hair and the drooping slope of her neck. "Fuck, I don't know."

I reach for her hand and she's suddenly all arms and legs as she tries to push me off. "Get away," she growls. "Get off me. If you try to take my money—"

"Quiet," I snap back at her, forcing her face close to my mouth. She's panting, and the hair falling over her face puffs out with each breath. "You're on something. We don't film girls on drugs. So we're gonna have to cut this short. You can take your two hundred and go."

I start to get back up to my feet, but her small hand darts out and grabs my wrist. "Wait." She pushes her hair out of her eyes with her other hand and tries to look me straight on. "Wait, please. I'm not a druggie. I swear. I'm not. They shot me up with something last night. They got me high and I don't know what happened next. I just…"

Her words trail off and I look over at JD and shrug. "Dude, this is bad news. She's not good for anything. We've got no contract, we've got no test, and there's no way we can sell anything we're doing here. Why bother?"

JD opens his mouth to say something, but the girl beats him to it. "Just, please. One more chance. I'll sign anything you want. I'm not underage. I'm not on drugs. I just got caught up in something bigger than me. I just need money to get home."

"Ark," JD says. He takes a deep breath. "Maybe we can't use her for business, but we can make some good memories trying." He laughs a little and that smile he's famous for breaks through. "Right?"

The girl turns to him now, realizing he's her ticket to the promised money. "Please." She places her palm flat against his stubbled cheek. "Please, JD."

The fact that she knows his name is what does it, I think. Because he slips a hand up her thigh, grabs her leg, and hikes it over his, spreading her halfway open for his pleasure.

I see red again. But instead of putting a stop to it, I pull her closer to me so her ass is straddling both our legs, and I slide my hand along the soft inner skin of her thigh. She moans out, and I'm not sure if it's JD's kiss or my fingertips pressing against her wet cotton panties that makes that noise come from her mouth, but it's the sexiest fucking thing I've ever heard.

"Dude," JD says, pulling his lips away from hers. "Get back to the camera. We're missing the moments."

"It's shooting right now," I say. "It's gonna keep going until it runs out of battery." And then I turn the girl towards me and lift her chin. Her eyes are closed and her mouth is open. "Look at me."

She struggles to open her eyes, heavy from whatever drugs she was fed last night, but she manages to get them to half-mast. *Help me*, she mouths. No sound comes out. Just her lips move. *Help me.*

I look up at her to make sure I'm seeing what I think I'm seeing. "What?"

But instead of a silent *Help me*, she says, "Take me. Please, just take me."

JD's hand wanders down the inside of the thigh draped over his leg, softly caressing her. Just then the sky lights up with the crack of lightning and the rain pours down so hard, the noise drowns out all the questions.

Her words.

My thoughts.

She wiggles against me as JD's hand crashes into mine, which is still cupping her cotton panties. And then he's past me, his fingers underneath the soaked fabric, searching for the release she wants. I can feel his movements, just the thin fabric between us. He plunges inside her and she buckles her back, shifting into my lap. I grab her throat with my other hand and she tilts her head my way. JD goes down on her tits, biting her through the dress that clings to her hard nipples. And then he yanks the front of her dress down, making her breast spring free, and he devours it.

I take her mouth at the same time. She moans into the kiss. Little mewling whimpers. Slight squeaks as JD reminds her whose fingers are between her legs. And then a hard grunt as he pushes another finger inside her.

My hand is still over the top of his and I feel all this like it's me spreading her folds apart, and suddenly I can't stand the fact that he's inside her and I'm not. I rip the crotch of her panties and seek out her warmth.

JD laughs. "Fuck, Ark. You're possessive today, dude. If you wanted in, all you had to do was say so."

"Fuck you, man. I saw her first and you know I did."

He shrugs and withdraws his hand from her pussy. "You take the front, I'll take the back." His hand dips deeper between her legs, seeking out her asshole as I push my fingers inside her pussy, taking his place. Blue Eyes moans, turning her face towards me, her tongue licking my lips as we fill her up. "Kiss me," she begs.

"Kiss me."

I tighten my squeeze on her throat and pull her forward so she's at an awkward angle. She readjusts the leg still draped over JD's leg, her knee coming forward towards me, closing her legs. But it's too late for that move, because we are both deep inside her.

I bite her lip as I kiss her and she opens her mouth wider. I picture what it would be like to stuff my cock down her throat as I add another finger to the party between her legs. JD does something to her ass that makes her gasp, and then she's moaning, and writhing, and panting into my mouth. My thumb finds her clit and I strum faster and faster until her muscles clamp down on our fingers and she explodes between us.

She comes so hard, both her arms spread wide, one around each of us, and we hold her like that.

It's just the three of us.

Our uncontrollable lust for a lost girl.

The rumble of the city waking up.

And the rain.

FIVE

ARK

MY cock is so hard, all I can think about is getting this girl's mouth all over it. JD grabs her hair and pulls her head back. "She's gone, man. Dust."

And she is. The little bit of action she gave us is officially over. Her eyes are closed, her mouth is open, her breathing is deep, and her body is limp. I slip my arms around her waist and get to my feet, bringing her with me, then slinging her light body into my arms like I'm cradling a child. "She's cold, too. She's shivering like a motherfucker."

I look over at JD as he gets to his feet. He squints at her and then puts a palm on her upper arm. "Yeah, she's way cold. We probably should've done this inside. What do you want to do with her?"

I take a breath. Because it's a good question. One we didn't think through.

"We should warm her up before we kick her out."

THREE TWO ONE

Fucking JD. I shake my head and laugh at him. "We're not throwing her out, asshole. She's way too out of it. Let's just go inside and get her out of these clothes."

"Put her in the tub, Ark. She can warm up that way."

I carry her through the living room. My feet and clothes are soaking wet, so I leave a trail of water across the dark gray polished concrete floors as I take her to my bedroom. I've got the only bathtub. The other two bathrooms only have showers. JD pushes past me and gets there first so he can turn the water on. It blasts out as I hold the girl and look at myself in the mirror.

What a strange day.

I've never had a girl up here in my room. I don't like to date. It just complicates things. Plus, almost all the girls I know do porn and I'm not interested in that kind of girl.

I turn back to JD. "I'll hold her up, you take off the dress."

JD turns back to me as I set her on her feet. She does not stand on her own, so I really do have to hold her up. JD grabs the hem of her dress and pulls it up so he can pass her arms through the skimpy straps holding it on. It's such a thin dress. Something you'd wear on a hot summer day. Not something you spend the cold October night in.

As soon as JD pulls up the dress up over her head, we see the bruises. "Fuck," he says as he maneuvers her other arm through the last strap of fabric. "What the fuck?"

I turn her so I can see them in the mirror. One is a welt across her shoulders, another branches off and climbs up her neck, half hidden by her wet hair. Underneath the yellowish hue are the faint remainders of scabbing.

On her back are the healed ones. Long gashes. Dashes of scar tissue that cross her back like stripes on either side of her spine. And between those are the knifeplay scars. They are scattered between the stripes like so many broken pieces of glass.

"She was caned and cut," I say. "Pretty hard and deep from

the looks of it. And for a pretty long time."

JD just shakes his head and walks back over to the tub to check the water. "Just put her in here. It's deep enough now." She doesn't struggle when I pick her up and set her in the tub while JD strips down, throwing his wet flannel and t-shirt on the floor, and then dragging his soaked jeans down his legs.

His cock is hard and he pumps it a few times before he climbs into the tub and positions himself behind the girl's back before sitting down, holding her close to his chest with his legs on either side of hers. "Go get your camera, Ark. I want pics."

"Why?" I ask. "We can't use them for Ray."

"For me," he says as he leans into the girl's ear. And then he ignores me as he talks softly to her. I've seen JD in action. I've filmed him getting hundreds of blowjobs. I've seen his cock more than anyone on this planet. I've heard all the dirty talk he's got in his repertoire, time and time again.

And that's not what this is.

He whispers nice things to her as I stand there watching. Calming things. She struggles a little against him when he wraps his arms around her, but he talks her down and she stills.

"Get the fucking camera, Ark."

I let out a breath and walk back out to the living room where the camera is still clicking away. I pick it up and stop the shutter, then change the lens so I can take pictures close up.

When I get back to the bathroom the girl's eyes are open and she's looking up into JD's face as he talks in that low soothing voice I never knew he had. He must ask her something because she nods her head. I zoom in on her face, catch a tear streaming down her cheek as she listens to him tell her things she needs to hear, and then I lose myself in her sad beauty.

She's so skinny. She looks like someone has been starving her or feeding her drugs to make her forget to eat. Her hair is a true dark blonde. Not dyed, because her lashes are light now that the makeup has been washed off, leaving that trail down her cheeks. Her lips are full. Fuller than they probably should be with her skinny body. Her breasts are full too. And they don't look fake, so she must be a nice curvy girl when she's got some weight on her.

JD stops talking and the camera shutter startles her. Her head turns in my direction and I capture the heart shape of it. Long strands of hair are plastered against her cheek and trail down her neck to the tips of her nipples that hover just above the rising water line.

I watch her watching me. Those blue eyes studying the camera. Logging my intentions.

And even though I expect the same hostility she gave me outside, that's not what I get. She tries very hard to smile, but she can't do it. Her chin quivers and then she's sobbing again.

I get all this on film.

She's so pathetically beautiful.

JD comforts her again, his words drifting up to my ears. "Sweet thing. You're safe now," he says. "They won't get you."

I wonder what I missed in the few minutes I was gone getting the camera.

"You can stay here," he says.

I raise my eyebrows at him, but he does not look my direction. Like what I want doesn't matter. It's been settled.

"I need money," she says in a voice so low, I almost miss it over the rumble of water still pouring out of the tub faucet. "I need that money."

JD goes back to murmuring in her ear as I set my camera down and unbuckle my belt, unbutton my still dripping wet jeans, and pull down my zipper and free my thick, hard cock.

I grab the camera and walk towards the tub.

JD just stares at me. "What the fuck are you doing?"

I ignore him. This girl started out as mine and that's how she's gonna stay. "You want that money, Blue Eyes? Suck my cock and I'll pay you double."

"Hey, asshole," JD says. "She's not—"

But she is. Because her hands are already reaching for me. I step into the tub and the water laps against my jeans as I get close enough for her to grab me.

And the second her tiny hands wrap around my dick, I fucking groan. She squeezes it a little and then her mouth is coming at me. Her lips are parted, her tongue flat and ready to take me in.

"You better fucking film it then," JD says.

I smile at him and point my camera down at Blue Eyes and capture the moment her lips first wrap around my head. "Oh, fuck, yes," I whisper, palming her head with my free hand. I glance down at JD and he's looking up at me with an interest I can't quite gauge. "What?"

"You've never filmed yourself before. Ever."

It's not true. But I've never filmed myself in front of him. "So?" I say, taking my attention back to Blue.

"So why now?"

"She wants it, that's why."

And she does. Because she sucks my dick like it's delicious. Her tongue twirls around my head like she can't get enough. Her hand pumps along my shaft with an intoxicating twisting motion that tells me she's done her share of blowjobs. I close my eyes, hoping like fuck that the camera will stay steady as I try to enjoy the attention.

But then a hand comes up underneath my balls and I open my eyes back up to make sure I catch it on film.

JD's hand has hers and he's urging her to cup me.

"What the fuck, dude?" I ask him. But then he squeezes her hand and she squeezes me, and holy mother, that shit, combined with her sucking and twisting, just obliterates my mind.

"Take him, Blue," JD says, mimicking the name I've given

her in my head. "Take him all the way in." And then he pushes her head towards my groin and forces her mouth to open wider. Her tongue to flatten down even more along my shaft. And her throat to open up.

I watch this all play out from the other side of the lens. JD and the girl. Me and the girl. JD's hand making sloshing waves under the water as he plays with her pussy.

And then it's too much. My balls tighten up and I shoot my come down her throat. She chokes and it runs out of her mouth and plops into the water, but she keeps sucking on my cock, like she's been trained how to end a blowjob properly, her blue eyes upturned to look at me as I film her, the streaks of makeup still staining her cheeks. And when I'm done she pulls back. Slowly. So very, very slowly.

And she silently mouths, *Please help me.*

I put the camera on the counter nearby and kneel down in the tub so I can cup her face with my hands. "What kind of help do you need?"

"Keep me," she says through her sob. "Please. Just keep me. I can't go back."

"Go back where?" JD asks, turning her away from me in a way that makes me think he's jealous. "Who is after you?"

The girl shakes her head and starts to cry again. "I can't say. I can't. I need to go home, but I can't go home, either."

"Where's home?" I ask.

"Montreal."

"Where's your passport?" JD asks.

She just shakes her head.

JD looks up at me. "She can stay here."

I stare at them both for a second, wondering what this is. Something is off, but I can't quite figure out what. "Of course," I say, nodding. I need more time with this girl. More pictures. More talking. More everything. I place my hand on her cheek and turn her head back to me, tipping it up at the same time so she has to meet my gaze. "You can stay here until you sort it out."

And then she collapses back against JD's chest and sobs. "I'm sorry. I'm so sorry."

"Hey," JD says as he pets her hair. "Shhh. Forget it, OK? Just relax now."

I'm about to tell JD to get the fuck out of the tub and give her some privacy, but I can hear my phone ringing out in the living room. "Fuck. I know who that is."

Ray.

JD looks at me as I step out of the tub and peel my jeans the rest of the way off, leaving them in a soaking heap in the corner as I wrap a towel around my waist and go looking for my phone. It's still inside my bomber jacket pocket. And it's wet when I take it out, but it's ringing again, so at least it's not ruined. I tab the accept button. "Yeah."

"Please tell me you're on track."

"The bitch we were gonna film this morning never showed."

Ray lets off a long sigh. "I need to see you, Ark. Today."

And then I get the hang-up beeps.

Fuck.

I walk back into the bathroom and find JD making out with the blue-eyed girl. "Who was that?" he mumbles through his kiss. I can tell his hand is between her legs, and she's whimpering from the stimulation.

"Asshole. That was Ray. He wants to see me today."

"Well, have fun. I'll hold things down while you're gone." JD stands up. "Hey, darling, it's my turn now."

She looks up at him and nods. Her mouth opens and I turn around and walk out.

Fuck.

I dry off with the towel and then dress in some clean clothes. Jeans and a white dress shirt. Blue tie, loose. Dry pair of boots.

THREE TWO ONE

And then I grab my leather jacket and leave them to do whatever they're gonna do before I get too pissed off about it.

Because it's pretty clear. JD thinks he's entitled to this action and that's a conversation for another time.

SIX

ARK

RAY'S business is in lower downtown, not very far from our place, but I never walk there. It's got a sketchy approach because you have to bypass the trendy part of LoDo and weave your way into the more industrialized area on the other side of Union Station. And even though it's probably only a mile or two to walk, I just don't do it. I'm not afraid of a fight. But why start one if you don't have to?

The assholes who work those corners, either with bitches or drugs, are strung out. They have no business sense. They just don't get it.

I mean, look. I make porn, but I don't *do* porn. Hell, I don't even *watch* porn. I get enough dirty sex in my daily life. If I want to see a guy get his dick sucked by a whore, I have JD for that.

That makes me laugh, even though that asshole is upstairs fucking my Blue Eyes right now, I just know it. Normally he doesn't fuck the girls, but I can feel this one-upmanship going on between us today. I just know he's gonna fuck her.

But these wannabe thugs down here by Ray's place all double-dip. They sell the girls and fuck the girls. They sell the drugs and do the drugs. It's not good to get attached to your product.

So I drive.

I pat my red Dodge Viper as I pass her by. Poor baby gets no action around here. I drive her to Vegas or So Cal, when I need to do business out of state. But to rumble down to Ray's, I take the Jeep. It's got a few small rips in the soft top that make it loud as fuck to drive, and scratches all over the body. The wheels are still muddied up from the last off-road weekend JD and I had up in the mountains, and she's old. Nineteen ninety-eight.

There is nothing about this Jeep on the outside that makes the dealers and pimps want to steal it. And that's just the way I like it. She's got a nice lift kit on her, I have to have that. But that's about it. So this is what I drive around town.

JD has a bike and a similarly under-equipped Ford F-150 for his daily travels.

We might live flashy upstairs, but down here on the streets we are scum.

I get in and start her up. She might not be much to look at, but she purrs nicely in the engine department. And then I head out and take a left on California so I can go hear what Ray has to say. I already know he's gonna try to cut a deal. That's just his style. I mean, look. Reality is, I could pull two videos out of my ass. I have enough saved up for Public Fuck. But I'm not going to. And the only other way to get these videos in on time is to pay a visit to my old contact.

And I'm not sure I'm ready to do that. I like this life I've built for myself, and I don't want to have to justify it to anyone. Least of all her.

We're behind. End of story. And since money means nothing to him—or us, really. I could give a shit about losing out on this week's money—there's gotta be something else in mind for this summons.

He always does this when we fall behind. And he never deals with us together. It's always, *Come see me, Ark.* And then we make a deal and on my way out, he says, *Send JD over tomorrow.*

JD never tells me what he does for Ray and I never tell him what I do, either. But I know. I mean, it's simple deduction. I run the cameras, so that's what Ray usually wants from me. And JD gets his dick sucked by wannabe porn stars. And that's usually what Ray wants from JD. Acting.

I make him a movie. JD acts in one.

That's how we break even with Ray.

So I'm expecting that today when I pull into the private security garage of Ray's lifestyle club. Don't let the fancy name fool you. While I'm sure there are plenty of sex clubs doing legal business, Ray's is not one of them. In fact, this club in LoDo is not even open for membership. It's an ancillary business to the ranch, which is located up in the mountains. This club here is just a place for friends of the ranch to have sex during the workweek. We keep the online stuff on the up and up because the Feds are all over that shit. But this little local stuff is all about greasing the right palms. You can take a lot more risks.

Oh, and he makes porn in the building next door. He's got production going five days a week.

Sex. It sells like a motherfucker.

The security waves me through as the gates open and I drive around the twisty entrance ramp until I get to the top level of the garage. I park in a spot that says PFA—Public Fuck America—and don't bother locking the door.

The rain is still coming down, but this top level is like a carport and has a roof, so I take my time walking to the elevators. I punch in my code when I get there, and the doors open for me.

I punch in my access code to Ray's office, one floor below,

and the doors close.

A few seconds later they open again into what looks like an elegant living room. But Ray doesn't live here. I actually do not know where he lives, but it's not here.

"Hey, Ark," Silvie says from behind the bar. "Wanna drink before I tell him you're here?"

"Ah, no, thanks, Silvie. I'm good." I smile at her. She's been Ray's better half for as long as I've known him. I'm not sure what their relationship really consists of, seeing as how she looks to be my age—twenty-seven or so—and Ray is easily in his forties. But whatever floats her boat. She's always friendly, always smiling, and never had a bad day in front of me for as long as I can remember.

"OK, then go right in. He's expecting you."

I give her a little salute and head to the back of the room where two ten-foot-tall double doors made of hardwood stand guard between me and the boss.

I knock first, just to let him know I'm coming in. I don't have to, but you never know when the guy's gonna have a girl on her knees and I'd rather not surprise him.

He's at his desk, his eyeglasses that he only uses to read financial statements perched on the bridge of his nose.

I mutter, "Fuck," under my breath. Because that means I'm gonna get a lecture about 'the bottom line' today.

"Ark," he says in that stern fatherly voice he's always used on me. His hair is not gray—I'm not sure if he dyes it or what, but it's a rich medium brown. And his build is still solid and trim, just like he was twenty years younger. I guess that's what Silvie sees in him. But you know, the guy's a porn mogul so… "I'm not happy about your latest failure to provide."

I have to stop the eye roll. "Ray," I say, taking a seat in one of two leather chairs in front of his desk. "The last time we failed to provide was a year and a half ago."

"I know, Ark. But it took me months to recover from that. It's still fresh."

Such bullshit. But if this is his angle, I can play. "How can I make it up to you then? Hmm?" I just want to cut this short. I know that JD is screwing that girl at home right now and I'd like to get back there before he marks her with piss and my chances of keeping her for myself are blown out of the water.

And then Ray does what he usually does when he knows he's gonna get what he wants from someone. He steeples his fingertips under his chin and leans forward. "I have a movie."

"When do you need me and what kind of shots will it require? Location or studio?"

He smiles. Like big. And that's when I know he doesn't want me to run the cameras. "I have a cameraman, Ark. I need an actor."

"OK, so call JD."

He shakes his head. "They don't want JD. They want you."

"Who?" What the fuck is this?

"A couple from the ranch. They want to make a sex tape and they want you to join in. They saw you a few weeks ago and the wife thought you were exactly her type."

"Well, you better let her know she's mistaken, Ray. I'm not participating in any movies."

He smiles again.

Fuck. "What?"

"I told them you'd say that. So they said they don't need cameras. Just a…" He struggles for the word. I'm about to fill in the blank with *whore*, when Ray says, "Date."

What the fuck is this? "No. I don't do dates and I don't do guys."

"Oh, he just wants to watch, Ark." Ray gets up and walks around his desk to take the seat next to me. It's a ploy to make me feel like he's not the one in charge here by sitting behind the desk. He wants us to feel like equals. "It's a personal favor, Ark. For me. You owe me two films and I need this. She wants you. She gets you."

"You don't own me, Ray. I'm not a whore you can pimp out. I make movies and give them to you in exchange for money. That's all. If you'd like to cut our business short, I'm happy to sell my holdings, my loft, and get the fuck out of here so you can run your porn site all by yourself. I'm not your whore."

He sighs and gets up to pour a drink. "Scotch?"

"Fuck, no," I say. He knows I don't drink that shit.

He shrugs and helps himself to three ice cubes and three fingers of the golden oak-colored liquid. "Look, it's one day. Today, in fact. One afternoon. They've got the hotel room booked and everything. All you have to do is show up, fuck her senseless, and that's it. The husband will be in the other room, he'll walk in on you at some point. He'll slap his wife around a little, and then you get to finish her off."

The whole time he's talking I'm shaking my head. "No way."

"I'll tell you what, Ark." He stops to take a sip of his Scotch. "I know you're all set to launch Public Fuck America in December. I know you need start-ups to get you off the ground. Just like I needed you when you came to me four years ago. So if you do me this favor, if you get this asshole off my back, I will personally hand you ten of my best producers to give you one video a week."

"What?" I must be hearing things. He thinks I'd sell myself out to get producers?

"Not all top-tier, of course. I can't give you all my earners. Plus you and JD are number one, so I only have nine left after you leave. Make that eight, if you take this deal. So one producer from the top ten, one from the top twenty, and the rest from the top one hundred."

I say nothing. But I'm still thinking about the implications of him asking. What am I to Ray? An asset? That word in my head sends a chill up my spine.

"It's a good deal, Ark. A great deal in fact. It sets you up just the way you wanted. No more camera work. No more legwork. No more hustling girls every week. You get ten videos a week coming in, that's a nice easy start to a billion-dollar business. You know none of my guys are gonna walk with you. You know you'd never get a top-ten producer to make films for you once a week. This is gold. And all you have to do is fuck a pretty woman to get it."

Even though my head is shaking no, I can't stop my mind from racing with the possibilities of what this might mean. More money. More power. More excuses to stick around and talk myself into thinking this life I've made is my destination.

"Ark, it's an easy out."

"No." I laugh. "It's an easy in. And I'm not doing it. I'll have your movies by the end of the day." And then I stand up, ready to walk out, when he grabs my wrist. I look down at it and he lets go. When I find his face, it's got a look I'm not sure I like.

"Why, Ark? Just give me a good reason why you're too good to let a woman suck your dick. You watch JD do it every day. You let him sell himself every single day. And yet you're always too good."

"I'm not too good, Ray. In fact, I'll be back with three movies of lips wrapped around my own cock. But you're not my fucking pimp."

"You're JD's pimp."

I stare down at him. He crosses his legs like he hasn't got a care in the world. "What the fuck is wrong with you today? I've never said yes because it's not my job. It's JD's job. You don't see him running the camera. He likes getting his dick sucked in public. Me, not so much. So that's why I do what I do and he does what he does."

"And there's nothing more to it than that? I mean, what?

You have a girlfriend? Is that who's gonna suck your dick on film today?"

Alarms are going off in my head right now. "That's none of your business, but no, Ray. I don't have a girlfriend."

"Then who is your go-to girl, Ark? And why don't you have a real name? I've known you four years and never a real name."

I laugh now, but it's a nervous laugh. "What the hell is going on? If you've got a problem with me, say so. Otherwise I'm outta here. I'm gonna go make your movies and be back tonight with the product. On time. Fully edited. Ready to be uploaded. And we're gonna be settled until next Sunday. Got it?"

He stands and walks back around to the other side of his massive desk. He shuffles some papers, making me wait for an answer. I huff out a breath and turn to walk out, with or without his acknowledgment, when he talks. "There's something about you, Ark."

Where is this coming from?

"There's something strange about you. There's always been something strange about you. You blew into town from… where again?" He lifts his eyes up from the desk and trains them on me. "Where did you come from?"

"You know exactly where I came from, Ray. Miami."

"But you weren't born there."

"You know what's funny here? I've worked with you for four years and now that I'm getting ready to break ties—a legitimate break that you've known about since the day we started business—you're turning into an asshole. I was born in Nebraska, Ray. I ordered my birth certificate online right in front of you and had it delivered right here. To you. You fingerprinted me. You scanned my retina, for fuck's sake. You paraded me in front of every criminal you knew at a party in LA. And none of them knew me. And no dirt ever materialized. And I've worked for you for four years and nothing ever happened. So what is going on? Because from my end it looks like you're out to screw me over now that JD and I are making this move."

"Now you see where I'm coming from."

"No, Ray," I shake my head. "No, I actually do not see where you're coming from. I make porn videos. I made a shitload for you and now I'm gonna make a shitload for me. And maybe, if I'm lucky, in a year or two I'm gonna be set just like you are. Have I ever fucked with your business? And as far as that goes, when it comes to the movies, we run a legitimate business. All of us. We're one hundred percent on the up and up. So why this is even coming up, I have no idea. Because I've got nothing on you. You're an open book as far as I can see. We're friends. More than friends. I'd never fuck you over and I expect the same loyalty back."

He takes a deep breath and sits down in his chair. He nods to the chair in front of his desk one more time and I can sense we're gonna set this right, so I walk back over and take a seat.

"OK," he says after a few seconds of silence. "I get it. I'm just being paranoid."

"Why though? I mean, if something's happening and it involves me and JD, we need to know."

He shakes his head. "No, I'm just worried that I've made mistakes. And I've relied on you two for years and I won't have you anymore. Just… nervous, I guess."

"Dude," I laugh. "Ray, man. You're one of my best friends. I'm not going anywhere. And if you need anything, just ask."

He stares at me for a moment. "You can get the films for this week?"

"I can."

"And it will be public?"

"They always are, Ray."

"You have some secret go-to girl for this?"

"I might."

He stares at me some more. "OK, good. Thank you. I need the Public Fuck stuff, Ark. It's good shit. I'm sure this won't be your best, but you'll get me some good movies—good club movies—before you go?"

"We've got girls lined up for next week. All three are repeats and we got the clubs on board too. We'll bring you in some good shit next week, I promise."

"All right, then. If I don't see you tonight—"

"I know the drill, Ray."

And then we shake hands and I walk out.

SEVEN

BLUE

I DON'T know why they are being nice to me. Especially this one. The one called JD. He's got me wrapped up in his arms against his chest. The hot water is running again, because we've been sitting in the tub for so long it's gone tepid. He's stroking my hair and his lips are pressed up against my head.

We say nothing. We just listen to the water as it barrels out of the faucet.

I start to think about things and then shake my head a little to make it stop.

"What's wrong?" His voice echoes through the large bathroom.

I can't say. So he gets silence.

He waits to see if I'm just taking a moment to think, and then decides I'm not. "Too much, huh? The marks? Whoever it is you're running from did a nice number on you."

If he only knew.

"We'll pay you for the photos. So you don't have to stay if you don't want to."

Like I have many options.

"But we won't mind if you do stay." His fingertips continue to play with my hair as we both think about that.

What would it mean to stay here? They can't possibly be offering up a temporary home with no expectations.

"I think Ark likes you."

I let out a long breath. "I don't think so."

"Ah, she still speaks." JD peeks around my face and flashes me a smile. He's very good-looking. His blond hair is wet and tousled, and a little darker now with the water. His eyes are a bright blue and they look—well, not quite kind. Neither of these guys look *kind*. They are rough in all the ways I need to avoid right now. But this one's eyes tell me they are understanding, at least.

"Believe me." JD's voice rumbles across my neck, sending a chill through my whole body. He reaches down to cup my breast, then squeezes the nipple. "I know Ark better than anyone. But he's never walked in on a job before."

I narrow my eyes, glad he can't see my annoyance and confusion. "What's that mean? A job?"

A half-hearted laugh resonates from JD's chest. "We make porn, darling. That's how we live in this place. That's how we pay the bills. We get girls like you to suck my dick in public. Occasionally I fuck them in public too, but most of the time it's just a blowjob. Ark is the cameraman. He's done some videos in the past, but in all the four years we've been working together, he's never walked away from his camera to join in." And now JD laughs for real. "You know what he said before he left?"

I can't help myself. "What?"

"Some shit about you being his since he was the one who saw you first."

Did Ark see me first? I think back. My mind is weary and my body is aching in all the wrong places. But now that I remember, he did see me first. He asked me if I was OK and that was when JD walked up behind him.

"What if I don't want him?" The words spill out before I can stop them and then, expecting the slap or the hair pull for mouthing off, I twist and turn, trying to get away from JD before he can hurt me.

I stand up, sway and fall sideways into the wall. Strong arms reach out and grab me just a little too late, and my head connects with the hard tile.

"Shit! What are you doing?" JD is standing now, holding me steady as my weak legs struggle to hold myself up.

I slap him away. "Don't, please!" I cover my face with my hands to shield myself, but the blows never come.

"Shhh," he says, wrapping one arm around my waist as the other one pries my hands away from their defense position. "I'm not gonna hit you. And Ark's not going to do anything if you don't want him. If you say no, I can guarantee you, he'll never ask again."

I don't know what to say to that. I don't even know what to think about what's happening to me. I'm standing naked in a tub with a complete stranger who I just sucked off. I let them both get me off outside in the rain and film the entire thing. My eyes dart to the camera on the bathroom vanity. It's still recording, I think.

And I'm not even coherent enough to come to grips with what has happened to me over the past fifteen months. The marks on my back aren't the only things that linger. So does the fear. The pain. The consequences of my actions. But if these two guys are my only options for salvation… I'll take what I can get.

All these things are pressing in on me like walls, closing in. Trying to crush me.

"Do you want to get out of the tub and put some clothes on?"

"I don't have any clothes," I whimper into my hands. He's still trying to pry them down, but I'm not giving in. I don't want to see his face. I don't want to see the confusion, or pity, or whatever it is he's feeling right now.

And most of all, I don't want him to see my feelings either.

I don't want anyone to see my feelings ever again.

He steps over the rim of the tub, still holding onto one of my hands, and gets out. He gives me a tug. "Come on. I have something for you to wear. And then you can sleep for a while. Or eat. Or call someone if you want."

I let that one hand fall away from my face, but the other stays in place. I know what I must look like. The less he sees of me, the better.

When I step out he grabs a soft towel and wraps it around me. I tuck one end into the wrap to hold it in place, and then he drapes a second towel over my shoulders. "That'll keep you warm until I get you something to wear."

He takes a third towel from the linen cupboard and dries himself off quickly, then wraps it around his waist. I'm looking at his feet though, so I don't really catch sight of his body. I know it's athletic and strong. I felt the hard muscles of his chest and abdomen when he was holding me. And I know his cock is long and thick, because he was trying to stick it down my throat. But I haven't gotten a proper look at him yet.

That changes as we leave the bedroom, walk down the hallway, and enter the living room. He walks in front of me and I lift my gaze a little so I can see his back. He's got a tattoo covering the entire span. From shoulder blade to shoulder blade, all the way down his back are two intertwined dragons. It's shaded like a painting in black and red and yellow. Flames shoot out of the dragons' open mouths. There's a banner across the bottom with Latin words across it in some fancy script.

It gives me a shiver.

"My bedroom's across the loft. That was Ark's room. He's got the girly bathroom." JD looks over his shoulder at me and smiles so big it makes his eyes sparkle. "So if you need another soak, just use his bathroom. He won't care."

Ark won't? I'm not so sure about that.

"But if you just need a shower, then my bathroom's good enough." JD stops in front of his door. None of the walls in here actually go up to the ceiling because it's loft-style. But there are doors, and that's a plus.

The last place I was held had no doors.

He opens it and waves me forward into the space. It's large and bright and that's another thing that differs from where I came from. It was cramped and dark.

"Here," he says, letting go of my hand and walking over to a dresser. He pulls one open and fishes around until he comes up with some boxer-briefs with hearts on them. I can't help myself. I bust out a giggle as he hands them over. He gives me a stern look that I interpret as fake. "Don't judge, man. Some girl gave them to me last V-Day. I've never actually worn them."

"So you disappointed her?" I ask, allowing myself to look up long enough to catch his smile and accept what he's offering.

"Yeah," he laughs. "I guess I did." And then his laugh dies. "I usually do."

I stare at him for a few moments, our eyes locked. "Thank you," I say after he starts rummaging through his drawers again. He pulls out a t-shirt that will be monumentally too big for me and hands it over. I take it and repeat my sentiment. "Thank you."

And then I take in a deep breath as his gaze drops down, taking in my body wrapped up in the towel, then lifts back up to find my face. He reaches out and untucks the end of my towel, and it drops to the floor with a soft whoosh. Then he takes the towel around my shoulders and dries me off. First my arms.

Then my breasts and belly. Then he bends down so his face is even with my sex. His eyes linger on the crease between my legs, and then he drags the towel down my legs. He leaves the towel on the floor, standing again, and his hand slides up my thigh. He cups my pussy, a teasing finger slipping in and out for a moment, and then he kisses me on the mouth.

"You're not going to tell me today. I can see that. But I hope one day you will. Because no one deserves to be beaten like that if they say no."

My whole body starts to shake. What does that mean?

He takes the t-shirt from my hand and pulls it over my head. I hand the heart-covered briefs to him and thread my arms through the sleeves. He holds out the underwear for me and I step into them as he pulls them up my legs.

When I'm dressed he takes a step back, looking intently at me. "What's your name, darling? You never told us."

Us? He's referring to the roommate. Like they're a team. I just stare back at him, unwilling to give that last private piece of information out. "They called me Star."

He squints his eyes at me in confusion. "Who called you Star?"

My eyes dart back and forth to each of his, but I say nothing.

"It's not your name?"

I shake my head.

"You want us to call you Star?"

I shake my head once more, again wondering at his use of the word us.

"Well, then, I guess we'll go with Blue, won't we?"

We? Us?

My body is still shivering, even though I've got dry clothes on now. JD pulls on a pair of sweats and then takes my hand. "Let's go to bed. I got up way too early for the girl who never bothered to show."

I swallow hard and plant my feet in place, refusing to budge.

"Come on, Blue," he says, tugging a little harder. Hard enough so that I stumble forward with him towards the king-size bed covered in soft pillowy blankets. They are a deep navy blue, the color of the night sky. "I won't bother you," he says as he climbs in and moves over to make room for me. "I think you need some rest."

He's let go of my hand now, a gesture that says the ball is in my court. And I want nothing more than to climb between those sheets with him. I want nothing more than to be hugged and told that everything will be fine. I want nothing more than to feel safe.

But how can I be sure it's not a trap?

"Blue," he says softly. Not begging for me to get in bed. Not demanding that I give him my body.

Asking. He says my new name like he's asking.

"What?" I say back, swallowing hard.

"Just forget about it for a few hours. Those problems will still be there when you wake up."

He's right. Those problems are never going away. So does it matter if I let go of them for a little while? I swallow again and give a small nod. "OK," I breathe. "OK."

He folds the covers back and I climb in next to him. He's so warm. And when his arms wrap around me, I fall for it.

I fall for his charm.

I fall for his kindness.

I fall for his good looks.

And then I fall into the best sleep I've had... ever.

EIGHT

ARK

I MET JD when we were both on the streets. Him because of drugs. Me because I was new in town and hadn't found myself a place. I stepped off the bus from Miami at one in the morning, walked outside the bus station and the first thing I saw was JD getting rolled by some thugs.

They were winning, but he didn't need saving. He just needed help.

So I helped.

He's two years younger than me, so he was young back then. Only twenty-one. And he was fucked up. It was clear he'd been fucked up for a pretty long stretch. Not anything he couldn't be weaned off of, otherwise I wouldn't have wasted my time. But he was drunk and on something else he never copped to.

So I helped him out. And afterward, we sat on a concrete wall across the street from the bus station until the sun came up and he was able to talk in complete sentences.

THREE TWO ONE

Objective number one when I got to Denver was to procure a partner. So I procured JD. He never went to college but he's not a stupid guy. And he sorta knew the business, but he wasn't an actor.

And that was OK with me. I didn't need an actor. I needed someone real.

JD is as real as they come.

And that fucker can talk a girl into sucking his dick in the middle of a nightclub in under five minutes when he turns on the charm.

I know. He did it in front of me the first night we went out together. And that's how I came up with the idea for Public Fuck America. I came to town with money and a goal. But I didn't know how to reach that goal until I met JD.

He's my best friend. And I'd do just about anything for the guy. But this girl, man. I don't know what it is. I just want her. I want her and he's got her.

I want to go home and take her back but I can't. We're still in debt to Ray until the end of next week, and there's no way around it. I can talk big to Ray all I want, but he's a friend too. I don't want to piss him off. I don't want to fuck up what we've built here. And I don't want to set myself back any more than I have to. My life has been on hold for four years. I'm ready to move along.

So whatever JD is doing with her, it needs to wait.

I turn onto Speer Boulevard and take it up into the Highlands neighborhood, then cut through the side streets until I get up to 44th which takes me over to the west side.

Why do I like this girl anyway? She's too skinny, she's pasty white, she's on drugs—or was last night. Even if they were forced on her, that's a red flag.

But none of that matters because all I can think about is the mystery. Who is she running from? Why did they drug her? How did she escape?

I find myself needing to know the answers to these questions for multiple reasons. Is she in the business? Her pussy has been waxed bare. Her legs fell open on command. She was pretty receptive to the idea of making money off her body. And she never said no when JD and I tag-teamed her outside or in the tub.

I mean, we were just playing with her and what she did for us was not hardcore. But it was sexual. And we are strangers. And she's still at our house right now.

At least I hope she is. Because I don't care if JD has her, I want her. I want my fingers inside her again. I want to kiss her sad, pouty mouth. I want to take her to bed and fuck her slowly.

Jesus Christ. What is wrong with me?

You've been on the job too long, Ark, the inner voice says.

And it's true. Four years is way too long. I'm ready to get out of here.

The diner that Lanie works at is up in the western suburbs in an old downtown of a city that used to be more urban back when Denver was small. But now it's just part of the sprawl, a place with a few old buildings so they can call it Old Town. But really, most of them were razed so they could put up townhouses and make them look old-timey, but still give them that shiny new polish in order to charge outrageous prices for units.

Lanie works at a restaurant that held firm against the developers that took over Main Street. I'm not even sure it has a name. The sign on the front says Diner in that old neon script that used to be common in the Fifties and Sixties. Lanie works breakfast and dinner every day but Monday. Which is good for me, because I'm gonna need all afternoon to get my two movies.

I ease the Jeep into the lot, park, and kill the engine. I haven't seen her in almost a year, that's how long it's been since I needed help.

But I know she'll help.

THREE TWO ONE

She always comes through for me when it's about the job.

I jump out of the Jeep and hunker down into my jacket. The rain has mostly stopped, but it's still drizzling, so I jog the few paces to the door and let myself in.

It's busy as fuck inside. This place goes off for breakfast and dinner—which is why Lanie works those shifts. She makes a killing. She works hard for it, but she makes a killing.

I search for her familiar dark hair and when I see her joking and laughing with an older couple near the back of the restaurant, I relax a little.

Why don't I come see her more?

My smile fades when she catches my eye and there's a break in her fun. She narrows her eyes at me, then turns back to her customers.

I take a seat at the counter and order breakfast and ask for a paper. I have a clear view of the busy road outside, so I concentrate on that while I wait for my food and I'm almost done when Lanie finally makes her way over to me.

"More coffee, sir?"

I look up at her smiling face. "Yes, please."

She winces at my answer but keeps it professional. "Cream and sugar?"

"Black." I look her in the eyes for that one and she nods.

"I see you're finished. Can I take your plate?"

"Thank you," I say as she reaches for it. "It's busy in here. What time does it thin out?"

I catch the swallow as she takes in my words. "About an hour," she says softly.

I nod. "OK. Well, see you around." I throw some bills on the counter, stand up, and walk out of the diner, again huddling into my jacket to stave off the rainy mist.

Once inside the Jeep I check the time and then decide to stop by a camera store to wait her out. Because Lanie and I have an arrangement. We don't hang out for a reason. And even though I like her a lot and I'd love to take her out to dinner and show her a nice time, we can't. Because no one can know who the girl in these movies is. No one can connect her to me in any way.

Otherwise, both of us could be killed.

NINE

ARK

HEAD east to a strip mall and park the Jeep in a spot outside a hardware store and think.

About the girl, mostly. Her hair color. Blonde. But it was a dark blonde when I saw her because it was wet. What does it look like dry? What do her eyes look like when they are not puffy from tears? What does her mouth do when it's not downturned?

Who the fuck did this to her?

It's an answer I think I need. I'm not even sure why, because I have not thought about shit like this for a long time now. A year, at least. Possibly closer to two.

Money does that to you. Money changes you. I said it never would, but I was wrong. Something happens when you no longer have to worry about buying food and paying rent. It's a subtle shift. Or at least it was for me. I came to town with enough to get started, and Ray was right to be suspicious of that. He does not want to know how I got that money.

But that's not the kind of money I'm talking about. I'm talking about enough money to buy a new car every month. Enough money to pay cash for a penthouse condo in LoDo. Enough money to set up a secret bunker filled with private servers. Buy a new ID and passport. Stash a few million away in secret bank accounts offshore.

Enough money to do whatever the fuck I want, whatever way I want.

No. No one saw that coming, not even me. When I came here I had no clue how fucking easy it would be to get lost in the business.

But that question… it's nagging at me. Who the fuck is she involved with?

At first I suspected Ray. I mean, that makes sense. He's in the same business as us. But I know it's not Ray. Ray is not into the violent stuff. I know this for sure. I've seen his private collection of movies and none of them are weird. They are almost boring, that's how vanilla his tastes are.

I don't think it was Ray Blue was working for, but I know for sure she was involved with someone. And that is something I'm going to find out.

I contemplate calling JD just to see if he's gotten any more information out about her, but then decide that's a bad idea. I'm not sure how I want to proceed yet. I need to think this through. I need to know all my options before I go pissing him off over a girl I don't know. And I need to consider all the consequences of each action I do decide to take.

Plenty of risks to go around, that's for sure.

Just then I spot Lanie crossing the street. She took the bus like she's been told to, so it's good to know we're still going by protocol, even if we haven't seen each other in a year.

She walks right past my Jeep and I watch her, but she doesn't look at me. Her dark hair is red now. A wig. And her raincoat is long, reaching down past her knees. She's wearing jeans and some knockoff sheepskin boots.

I don't watch her once she's past my line of sight. Instead I check my phone, messing around on the Public Fuck Facebook page—which has two likes, JD and me, since we haven't launched yet—and exactly ten minutes later I get out and walk down to the discount cinema where I know Lanie went in, even though I didn't watch her.

Inside it's a madhouse of kids and video games as parents on a budget endure this ruckus so they can buy a little entertainment. I check the movies, choose the next show time for the last one listed on the board above my head, and pay for a ticket.

Thankfully, it's not a kids' show. It's a two-and-a-half-hour murder drama that has been playing for the better part of six months—because this cinema only gets movies just before they go to DVD—and there's only a handful of people seated when I walk in and find Lanie sitting up in the last row with her boots propped up on the seat in front of her.

I walk up the steps slowly, trying to gauge her mood as I make my approach. She smiles when I sit down and I take her hand like we're a couple. "Missed you," I say softly.

"I wish I could say the same," she shoots back with a smile.

"Sorry about this. You know—"

"I know," she says, cutting me off. "Forget it. Just tell me what you need."

She winces when I say, "Two." And I try my best to make it sound like no big deal. "One in here and one in the car once it gets dark."

"Jesus Christ, Ark."

"Lanie, it's not like I ask that often. I just fell short this week."

"Why?" she asks, turning to me. "What happened?"

"The fucking girls just bailed. We had three set up and two fell through. Look, I know this sucks, but we've got two weeks left. Two weeks."

"And then what? None of that makes sense to me. You actually plan on running a porn business?"

"I already run a porn business, Lane."

"Not like that, *Ark*." She sneers my name. "Not like what you're planning. It's apples and oranges. You're so much worse than him."

"Fuck you," I say before I can stop myself.

"Well, you've taken care of that, haven't you?"

Goddammit. I really do not need the lecture right now. But I can't help myself from asking. Because I'm not like him. "How? It's the same shit."

"Because you'll be perpetuating it. And not only that, you'll be profiting from it."

"I'm already profiting from it."

She turns her head away, letting me know this conversation is over. And before I can even defend my indefensible position, the lights dim and the previews start. When the announcement comes on for everyone to turn their phones off, a few of the scattered couples down front make a move to do that.

But I power mine up.

Because Lanie is already on her knees blowing me in the twilight darkness. And when the movie starts, I fist her hair and hold her face down on my cock as I come down her throat.

We don't leave together. She gets up as soon as she's done and I stay until the end of the movie and then make my way back to my Jeep and drive home. When I pull into my parking spot, she's already opening the door as I shift into first and turn the ignition off.

"You owe me," she says as I unzip my pants.

"I know," I tell her back as she gets me hard again. This takes longer than I'd like because all I can think about is how much she hates me. How big of an asshole I am for making her do this. How dirty my hands are for being in this business. And how right she is.

I'm way worse than Ray.

Because Ray would never take a girl against her will. That's why I need the proof of ID, the contracts, and all that other bullshit. Ray is legit.

And I can tell myself this is business all I want. That Lanie has to do this for me, per our agreement. But it's bullshit. I'm making her blow me. I'm making her degrade herself. And I'm going to drive over to Ray's, edit it, and upload it to his servers as soon as I'm done here.

I'm far, far worse than Ray.

Because I'm not legit. I'm nothing but a scammer. A cheater. A walking piece of shit. And everything that has come out of my mouth the past four years has been a lie.

IT was Janine Delgado who started me down this path. I blame her for all of it. I know, even as I lie in this stranger's bed, that I'm being irrational. Both for letting him bring me here and for blaming Janine Delgado for my problems. But I have a good argument for both.

Janine Delgado was a mama's girl from day one. Being neighbors and exactly the same age—we shared a birthday—we started out as friends from the beginning. But Janine and I could not be farther apart in personality. She was afraid of everything and I was afraid of nothing. By the time we got to middle school, kids used to taunt her about it. They called her Janine the Drama Queen because everything with her was a production. She was awkward in every social situation, so when it came time to go to parties in high school, Janine was told by her parents to try harder, and harder she did. She went overboard in every way imaginable. There is a difference between being fearless, like me, and stupid, like her. Although I do admit my decisions over the past year and a half put me squarely into the stupid department.

Janine and I stopped being friends in tenth grade because she said I was holding her back. You see, Janine found drugs. Drugs turned her into someone else. Into someone with no inhibitions. Into a slut, if I'm being honest.

Janine went from scared fifteen-year-old, to sexually active sixteen-year-old, to knocked-up seventeen-year-old.

She had an abortion. I can't judge her, but her parents did. They sent her away after that and she spent the last half of junior year and all of senior year locked up in some boarding school for bad kids.

This is where things really went wrong.

My parents got divorced and my dad got a new job. It was a government job, a very high-profile government job, and one of the perks was that I got to attend a very exclusive boarding school in the DC area. So my dad and I moved to the States.

But Janine and I kept in touch and wrote letters. She was not allowed to have a phone, so no texting or anything so this century. Occasionally she came home to see her parents and I'd be home visiting my mother over holidays, and then we were allowed to hang out on the front porch of her house and chat. Which sucked because all the holidays she came home for were in the winter, so it was too cold to be chatting on her porch. And she never came home in the summer at all. She was sent to church camp. Some Bible-thumping megachurch camp where the kids sing songs of praise and redemption.

I'm OK with that. I was raised in a moderately religious family. But Janine... I don't know. She was just never the same. She said she was doing well. And she was off the drugs, so that was a good thing. But she never convinced me.

After graduation I went to New York and attended Columbia,

and she went… I have no idea. I lost her. She disappeared. Her parents were frantic for months—posting pictures of her on telephone poles, talking to people around the neighborhood in case they heard something. Normal stuff that parents would do if their eighteen-year-old daughter went missing. And then there was a rumor that Janine was spotted working as a waitress at a topless bar in Denver, Colorado.

Her parents never mentioned her again after that.

But she was my friend and I never forgot her. So when I came home after graduating from Columbia and she called my mom's house while I was staying there, I was thrilled.

I was thrilled she was alive. I was thrilled she wanted me to meet her. I was thrilled she remembered how close we were all growing up.

So yeah. I went. I flew to Denver.

And that's why all this shit is Janine fucking Delgado's fault. Because I had lunch with her.

She filled in the missing years with information I wish I could forget. She told me things that made me swallow down the vomit. She pointed to her swollen belly and begged me for help.

And I said yes. Because after graduating the top of my class from an Ivy League school, filling out one hundred and fifty applications, going on twenty-seven interviews, and even doing a two-month summer internship with a very prominent company—I had even fewer prospects than her. No one even looked at me twice.

I said yes. I'd help.

So even though I'm playing the victim card, all of this is Janine Delgado's fault.

Because she pulled the best-friends-for-life card and said I was gonna be an aunt. And I said yes.

I'd save her.

THREE TWO ONE

But I didn't save her, I only succeeded in losing myself. Because seven months later Janine was dead, the baby was missing, and I was being held prisoner in a locked room down in a basement.

ELEVEN

BLUE

"I KNOW you're awake."

I'm not afraid of JD, even though I should be. He and his friend filmed me giving them sexual favors. But I said yes, even though I was still fucked up when I met them. I said yes.

And now, seven hours later, in bed, refusing to come to terms with my life... I still trust him more than the people who were holding me prisoner in a basement.

"You hungry?"

He's got his arms wrapped around me with my ass pulled up close to his hard-on. One arm fits perfectly under my neck like a pillow, and the other hand is lightly dragging up and down the center of my belly.

I imagine what it would feel like if his fingers slipped a little lower and then I feel disgusted with myself for thinking perverted thoughts. If I was back in the basement I'd be punished for that. Because no matter what they did to me there, they changed me.

They made me enjoy it. And once they discovered I enjoyed it, they took that enjoyment away. I was forbidden to touch myself, but my appetite for pleasure was insatiable and my fingers always wandered, just like they are doing now.

I pull back, expecting the slap, but it never comes.

Just his soft, rumbling voice. "Hey." He whispers it this time. Like he can feel the internal struggle going on inside me. "I know you're hungry. Want me to make you dinner?"

"Dinner?" I ask. Holy fuck, *yes*. I contain my excitement as I nod, and then turn my whole body to face him. "Yes, please," I whisper back. His hand drapes across my ass with the move and then he squeezes one cheek.

His fingers are almost between my legs and I let out a little gasp from the touch.

His eyes search mine. They dart back and forth between them as they try to figure me out. "Tell me your name." It's not a request, but it comes out soft. Like all his other words today.

"I can't," I say back, matching his somber tone. "I really, really can't."

"Do you want to call someone?"

"No," I say, shaking my head. "No, I can't do that either."

"Is it because you're afraid of them?" I know it's a generic *them* he's referring to, but I shiver all the same. He doesn't need me to speak to get that answer. "You're safe here. You can stay as long as you need to."

"What about your friend?" Ark is the one I asked for help. He's the one I'm worried about because he looked at me like I'm broken. Like I'm beyond saving. Too much trouble. Too few prospects.

"He likes you," JD says. "I can tell. He's pissed off that we're here together right now, I know that for sure."

"Where did he go?" I study JD's face and decide I like it. Before, when he and his friend were taking the pictures, JD was talking to me like the men in the basement did. Like I was a whore.

But right now he's just talking to me like the men in the waiting room did.

Like I'm a possibility.

I was a possibility a few times over the course of this last year. But thankfully, none of them ever took me home.

"I'm so hungry," I say.

His fingertips trace the outline of my ribs. "They didn't take very good care of you, did they?"

I have to swallow that down before I can shake my head no.

"I'll take good care of you, Blue."

I stare up into his own blue eyes. They are light, like the blond scruff on his chin. "Thank you," I whisper.

"You're welcome," he says, wrapping his arm tightly around my waist and pulling me close again. "It's my pleasure."

And then he kisses me on the head and we rest there for a few moments before he pulls me up, takes my hand, and walks me out to the kitchen.

Seven hours of sleep has done wonders for my observation skills, because if you had asked me anything about this place when they brought me here, I wouldn't have been able to tell you. It's such a dangerous situation. And after all I've been through this past year, I'm so stupid for allowing myself to be taken in by a pretty face.

It was the drugs. I was better off than the other girls, but only because I vomited up the sedative they gave me once the night was over. It was supposed to keep me subdued until we got back to the basement.

"What're you thinking about?" the guy called JD asks me. I'm standing in the middle of their kitchen. He's busy at the island counter, where ingredients for the food he's making are scattered around. "You look a little lost."

A little lost doesn't even come close.

"You can sit if you want." He points to the living room, which is open to the kitchen, so he'd still be able to keep an eye on me if I sat over there.

I walk around the island and head towards the chair he pointed to.

"You don't have to sit there, you know. You can sit outside. Or on the couch. Or go back to bed."

I just take my seat and pull my legs up so I can wrap my arms around them. I'm so skinny these days, I practically curl into a little ball.

"You like spaghetti and meatballs?" he asks. "That's pretty much all I can make." And then he flashes that grin at me. A smile that says he's charming and devious and dangerous all in one. It should set me back. It should send me running. But it doesn't. It makes me feel something I haven't felt in a very long time.

Relaxed.

I smile back at him.

His whole face lights up. "Fuck if you aren't one of the sexiest things I've ever laid eyes on. I can only imagine how beautiful you are when you're healthy."

Healthy. That's a nice sterile word for what I'm not.

"So spaghetti?"

I take a deep breath and nod.

"I have to run to the store for bread. Will you be OK here alone?"

He stares hard at me as he washes his hands in the island sink and then tears the plastic off a package of hamburger. I realize I'm still wondering if I'll be OK when he calls out softly, "Blue? Will you be OK if I run to the store for bread?"

Blue. I have a new name again. Not Star, but Blue. I nod at him because he's waiting for an answer. His hands never stop moving as he rolls the meat up into little balls.

When he's done with that, he puts them in the oven, washes his hands, and starts the water boiling.

I never take my eyes off him.

He comes around the island towards me when he's done and this is the first chance I've had—first sober chance—to see his body. He's tall and lean with defined muscles in his arms, his abs, and his neck. He's only wearing a pair of cut-off gray sweats that hit just below the knee, so I have a pretty good view. His blond hair is neither long nor short, but something in between. It's messy in a very nice way. And his face is beautiful in a way only a man's can be.

They make porn, my inner self cautions me. *They make porn and his beautiful face is the lure they use to get girls to agree.*

That's true. But for some reason I don't think I'm here to make them money.

"Blue," he says again when he reaches me. He leans down, placing one hand on the chair arms on either side of my body, and looks me in the eyes. "If you want to bail on us, let me know. We'll take you wherever you want to go. But don't just walk off, OK? Because then I'd have to go back out into this shitty weather and find you all over again. And you'd be cold, and scared, and we'd have to start all over again with the warm bath and rest. So just stay and eat with me."

I swallow hard as he stares at me.

"OK?" he asks again.

"OK."

My voice makes him smile again and Jesus, yes. That smile is even better up close.

He kisses me on the head again, and stands back up. "I'm gonna go change. The store is just a block down. So I'll only be gone like ten minutes." I turn my head to watch him as he walks away and I'm still looking in that direction when he comes back out of the bedroom dressed in a pair of jeans, a white t-shirt, and a black leather biker jacket that has zippers that jingle with each thud of his boots on the hardwood floors.

He looks a lot more dangerous in these clothes, my inner voice says. *A lot more.*

But that smile is still the same. "BRB," he says with a straight face. And then he's out the door and I'm left in this strange apartment. Alone. A state which has eluded me for the past year and a half, up until this very morning.

I sit there in the chair for a few minutes and take it all in. The penthouse. I do remember that from coming up here. Everything says masculine. The floors are dark gray concrete, but not the rough kind you see outside in driveways—the kind you see in malls, where they're so smooth you can ice-skate on them. And the furniture is all made out of steel and glass. Cables are used as a design element, making the whole place look like a mix between futuristic and industrial revolution.

There's a large sectional couch made of the light gray leather, accented with steel rivets on the arm seams. One end is just like a regular couch, but the opposite end is more like a lounger. The chairs are another shade of gray, overstuffed and accented with the same steel rivets as the couch.

There's art on the walls. Black and white photographs of places I can only assume are in Colorado. They are of mountains and lakes. Snow and ice. Pine trees and aspens.

The kitchen has black cabinets and dark gray stone for countertops. It's not something a woman would choose, of that I'm certain. The appliances are all high-end stainless steel and there is no clutter, other than JD's in-progress mess, to indicate they use it often.

And then there's the view. My eyes dart to the terrace. I get up and walk over to the massive sliding doors and open them up. It's still wet out, but the rain has stopped, so I tentatively place one foot into a puddle and step outside.

The railing is some kind of clear Plexiglas and the city is wide open in front of me. They took pictures of me here. I was kissing JD, I think. And then I was on the ground and they were both there, arms around me, hands exploring, mouths hungry.

I walk over to the edge and look down and see JD with his hands in his jacket pockets, his head darting back and forth as he crosses the street and then, just like he said, he enters a store a block down and disappears.

"He's not one of them," I say out loud. "They'd never leave me alone like this."

I stand there until he reappears, brown paper bag of fresh bread in his arms, and watch him walk. He lights up a cigarette and takes his time so he can enjoy it. They must not smoke inside. The apartment does not smell like smoke. His eyes flash up to the terrace and he waves. "Keeping an eye on me, Blue?" His yell is so loud I blush when every person on the street stops to stare at him. He picks up his pace and when he's just across the street from the building, he yells, "I'm moments away, baby. Now go back inside and get warm. It's too fucking cold for you to be standing out here." He looks both ways, flicks his cigarette, lets a car pass, then crosses the street. "Go."

He disappears before I turn around and go back inside. I'm still wiping my feet on the little mat in front of the terrace when he comes into the apartment and tosses his keys onto a small table near the door. "Spying on me now, Blue?" He grins as he shrugs off his jacket and hangs it on a hook, then walks into the kitchen. I love the way his black biker boots thud across the floor and I'm captivated by the muscles in his arms as he takes the bread out and cuts it in half. "Can you make garlic bread, Blue?"

I nod at him and walk over to the kitchen. I can smell the cigarette on him, but instead of making me sick, it smells good. Familiar.

No one in the basement was allowed to smoke. And I was not a real smoker before they took me, but I enjoyed one every now and then, when I was drinking.

JD's smoke smells like the past. A long-ago past that was far better than yesterday.

"OK," he says. "You do the bread and I'll start the pasta."

Twenty minutes later the food is done and we're sitting at the table eating spaghetti and meatballs. But even though the scene seems normal, I feel anything but normal. And after a few minutes of silence, this is painfully obvious.

"So," he says as our silverware clanks and I stare down at my food. "See any good movies lately?" I look up at the question, my mouth half full of pasta, and stare at him for a few seconds. "No?" he prods.

I shake my head no to end the questioning.

"Books?"

I don't look up this time.

"Hmm," he says after letting me stew for a minute. "What do you do for fun, Blue?"

I take a deep breath and on the exhale, I'm talking automatically. "I enjoy touring museums, traveling, and taking art classes."

"Oh," he says, surprised. And then he works out that I'm lying. Because a girl who looks like I do now does not do any of those things. "Hmmm," he says again. "Maybe we can go to the art museum or something one day."

I look up and smile, then quickly look back down. "Yes, that would be fun."

That's the last question he asks me all afternoon. And I'm too timid to ask him anything. But I have a lot of questions.

What does that tattoo mean?

Where is his friend?

What will they do with me?

But never once does it occur to me that I should get up and walk out. Not once. And now that I'm here, lying with him in his bed, with his arms tucked around me, that startles me more than anything I've been through or anything that might come.

Because even though this morning my acceptance felt a little bit like salvation, this evening it has a whole new feel.

Defeat.

It feels like I'm giving up. Like I'm giving in to what they made me. A prisoner.

It feels like the end.

And after a few minutes of pondering this as I stay still and silent like I've been taught to do, I realize I like that.

I want the darkness to take over. I wish I was drugged up again so I could stop caring. I wish someone would drug me and make the darkness cover me like dirt over a grave.

And maybe these guys are the answer to that prayer. Maybe these guys will finally do what the other ones never would.

Maybe these guys will just let me die.

TWELVE

ARK

I TURN my key in the door and let myself into the loft. There's a light on over the oven in the kitchen, but aside from that it's dark. I walk past and see the remnants of spaghetti, a sink full of dishes and evidence of an evening spent here without me.

I sigh as I hang my coat up and walk down the hall to my room. I don't even want to think about JD and that girl. I spent all day thinking about them, and now I'm done. I kick my shoes off as I enter the room, then flip the switch on the wall. The first thing I see is the bathroom where this morning that girl sucked me off and I came so fast I'm almost embarrassed.

I turn away, reach behind my head and pull my shirt off. Then I unbutton my jeans and let them drop to the floor, giving my cock a tug since just the thought of her is starting to make me hard.

Usually I sleep naked, but I'm not ready for bed just yet. So I put on a pair of faded army-green cargo shorts and head into the bathroom to get the camera.

It's gone.

Fucking JD.

I go out to the living room and look around. Maybe he was using it out here? I am rationalizing now. I know where that camera is.

A deep breath is necessary as I walk down the short hallway to JD's room. The door is open and that's a first. JD is a compulsive door-locker at night. I flip on the hallway light, because I do not want to disturb him, and spy the camera on his nightstand. My eyes track to the girl lying on the other side of JD, his arm wrapped protectively around her and the sheets only covering her lower half. Her breasts rise and fall with the pattern of her breathing.

I grab the camera and leave before I do something stupid like kick his ass. She's not mine. So fuck it. He can have the bitch. She's too skinny anyway. She looks like she's on drugs, in fact. I hate the druggies. She probably has some kind of disease. Probably sucks in bed too. Just lies there, maybe. Or complains. Or hates it.

I close the door on my way out and walk back to the living room where the sliding metal barn doors on either side of my office entrance are wide open. I flip the light on and then close the doors behind me before setting the camera down on the desk and walking around to the other side to have a seat.

I stare at it.

She's in there.

And me with her.

I can't plug that thing into the computer fast enough. The software kicks in with a familiar ding and then the images, thousands of images because the thing was on continuous shutter release for the better part of thirty minutes, download onto my hard drive.

The anticipation is killing me.

I watch the thumbnails flash by and the progress bar light up and even that gets me excited.

The program finishes the download and begins erasing the memory card inside my camera, but I stop it. Just one copy is not enough. What if my computer crashed? What if it was stolen? What if I somehow lost all these pictures?

I can't do it. Just the thought has me sweating.

So I leave them on there and unplug the camera. I have a shitload of memory cards in the desk, so I leave the card in, all the pictures intact.

And then I open up Photoshop and start going through them, one by one.

Her and JD under that awning on the mall. Jesus, that seems like weeks ago and it was this morning. Not even a whole day has passed by since I took these pictures. He's kissing her in some, and holy fuck, even though it's him and not me, everything about these pictures says sexy as all hell.

Skinny or not, she's alluring. In one picture her incredible blue eyes are wide and innocent as she looks up at JD. The streaked makeup just makes the whole thing all that much more provocative. Like she's hurt and she's looking to him for help.

And everything about JD, as he gazes down on her, his hands reaching for her stained face, everything says give in to me and I'll make it better.

A knock at the door pulls me from my fixation, and then the metal doors slide open.

"Hey," JD says, coming into my office eating a bowl of cereal. He takes a seat on the couch alongside the wall to my left. "You just get home?"

I look over at him. He's bare-chested, that's how he always sleeps. And his hair is messy, so it looks like he was in bed for a while before getting up just now. That pisses me off because I can think of a million things he could've been doing in that bed with the girl.

I shut that down so I can appear rational, even though I feel anything but rational. "Yup," I say, cutting it short.

He glances over at my monitor and then stands back up, placing his cereal on the desk so he can lean in and get a better look. "She's perfect, man."

"Not for Ray, though."

JD does a snort-laugh. "No shit, asshole. I wasn't thinking about *hiring* her."

"You wanted to hire her this morning."

He grabs his cereal and sits on the edge of my desk, spooning it into his mouth and talking as he chews. "That was before."

"Before what?" I manage not to growl. But just barely.

"Before I spent the day with her."

I just stare at him. "So you fucked her?"

He just stares back. "You got something you wanna say about this girl, Ark? Because I'm all ears, man. I get it, you saw her first. So she's yours. But I spent the day with her. And I like her too. And no, asshole, I didn't fuck her. I wouldn't do that to you and if you think I would—" He shakes his head. "Well, fuck you."

I look away and take a deep breath. Because he's right. We've liked the same girl before. That's why we have the I-saw-her-first rule. But this one feels… different. "Sorry," I mumble. "It's been a long day."

"You take care of Ray?" He's back to eating his cereal, so I guess our standoff is over.

"Yeah."

"You talk him down? Or did you get the movies?"

"I got them."

JD says nothing to that. He knows what it means, because I've had to do this before when we fell short.

"So…" I say.

"So," he picks up. "I think you need to see something." He stands up, sets his cereal down, and walks over to the doors. "Let me show you."

I get up and follow him out and we walk down the hallway to his door, which is now closed.

"Shhh," he says to me as we stop in front of it. "I don't want to wake her up but I have to show you what I found."

I give him a nod and then he opens the door and reaches into his pocket to pull out a tiny flashlight. We walk over to the bed where the girl is lying face down with her cheek pressed against his pillow.

A wave of jealousy flows through me, and by the time I get it under control, JD is moving her hair off the back of her neck.

She screams and flails out, knocking JD's flashlight to the floor where it rolls under the bed.

"Fuck." They are struggling, her still screaming and JD yelling back, telling her to calm down, when I reach for the light on the bedside table. It flashes on and JD is on top of the girl, pressing her arms above her head so she can't struggle.

"Get off me," she growls.

"Just calm down, Blue."

"Fuck you. Get off."

JD looks up at me. "Look at the back of her neck."

"No," she yells. "Get off me."

JD and I both ignore her now. He's looking up at me as he continues to straddle her waist and hold her arms still. "You need to see this, Ark. Just look."

"Let me go," she whines. But the fight is gone that quick. She starts to cry.

I lean down and swipe the hair off the back of her neck to find a raised scar in the shape of a circle.

I pull back and turn away, my hand covering my chin as I think about this.

JD gets off her, climbs off the bed, and walks up next to me. "That's it, right?" he asks. "Tell me I'm not just seeing things. That I'm not just making it up."

I nod. That most certainly is it. "I need to see her back again."

"Fuck you," she says in a small voice from the bed. "Just fuck you." I look over my shoulder to see what she's doing, but she's still lying face down. Crying into the pillow. "You have no right."

JD looks at me one more time and then walks back over to her and sits down on the edge of the bed so he can stroke her hair. He's such a player. He knows exactly what to do for a crying girl.

Me? I have no clue. I'm a one-night-stand kind of guy. I don't stick around long enough to care.

But this girl, man. Even before the mark. This girl is different.

So I walk around to the other side of the bed. The side she's facing. I climb in next to her and lie back. Her eyes search mine for intentions.

JD lies down on the other side of her, his fingertips still gliding through the long strands of blonde. "Just relax, Blue. We're not gonna hurt you."

"No," she huffs. "You just want to make me suck your dicks on camera so you can sell me in a different way."

JD's eyebrows go up, but neither of us says anything. There's a time and a place, and this is not it.

"Blue," I say calmly. She's still looking at me, but the sound of my voice makes her take in a breath of air. Like I startled her. "We're not putting those images online." I have to stop for a second. Because that's a lie and I know it. But it's not the same, so I continue. "We can't use you, even if we wanted to."

"And we don't," JD interjects. "We don't want to." He looks at me over the top of her body and I nod.

"You don't have any ID. And regardless of how it looks, what we do is one hundred percent by the book. Everyone signs consent forms. Contracts. Everyone gets tested for STD's. Everyone gets paid and everyone pays taxes on those payments. We're not about to fuck up our business just so we can use one sad girl who doesn't even have a name. So forget about the pictures. I need to know where you got that brand on your neck. And I need to know when."

She looks me straight in the eye and says, "Fuck you."

JD collapses back onto the pillow he's sharing with her. "Why don't we just pick it back up in the morning?"

"No," I say quickly. "Fuck that." I look straight at her. "You're not the only one caught in their web, you know." She narrows her eyes at me. "You know that's true. You know there were other girls involved with you. And I'm pretty sure the reason we found you this morning was because you escaped." Her eyes dart back and forth, like she's trying to decide to trust me. "We knew a girl who had that same mark, Blue."

"Another one of your whores?" she asks. But it comes out scared instead of defiant. I think the level of vulnerability in her voice surprises her, because she hiccups back a sob.

I shake my head. "A friend. She was a good friend."

JD gets up out of the bed and walks into his closet.

Blue and I just wait it out. After a minute of JD rummaging around in there, he emerges fully dressed and walks out the door, slamming it closed behind him. The noise makes the girl jump and this time she can't hold the sob in. It's too much. She starts to cry.

I reach over and place my hand on her arm. I'd take her hand and give it a squeeze, but she's got it tucked underneath her cheek. "The friend was JD's girlfriend. And she got mixed up in something bad and then she disappeared. She had a mark like that, Blue. They had a fight the night she disappeared, and ever since he's been beating himself up over losing track of her, and imagining all kinds of terrible things that might've happened to her. So if you can help—"

"I can't," she says, cutting me off. "I don't know any girls. I don't know what you're talking about. I don't know anything." And then she gets up out of the bed and walks into the bathroom. There's the distinct sound of the door being locked and then the shower comes on.

A moment later the front door slams and I know JD is gone.

THIRTEEN

BLUE

LOOK at the girl in the mirror. She's naked. I tilt my head a little to see the scars on her back. Not the long stripes from the cane, but the little tick marks from the knife.

Stars, they called them. That's how I got that name, I guess. Or maybe it was something else. I can barely remember now.

I stare at the girl until the steam from the running shower fogs her over and makes her fade away.

The shower is calling me even though this is the cleanest I've been all month. Hot water with no time limit is a luxury I will never get enough of. So I step in and let it pour down my body. I open my mouth and let the water run in, swallow some, spit some out, and then close my mouth so I can inhale deeply.

It's not enough.

I cover my face to hide my tears even though there's no one here to punish me. I want to feel relief. I want to thank someone. I want to call my parents and listen to them tell me they love me and everything will be OK.

But I can't do any of those things.

I'm not safe, so there's no time for relief. And no one saved me. These guys are bottom-of-the-barrel scum, just like the ones I ran from.

I can't even think about my family yet. No. I push them away immediately.

My hands come down from my face and when I look up, there's another mirror where JD must do his shaving. I push the little button on the side and it lights up and the fog begins to recede from the edges until I have a clear view of my face.

Which actually looks better in here. Maybe it's the dim light, or the hot water has decreased the puffiness that was so apparent in the vanity mirror.

It doesn't matter.

I look… better.

Blue, they call me.

Blue. My new name. I stare at my eyes and wonder what they say to these strangers. Do they see the pain? Or the fear? Or the longing? Or all of it mixed up like some poisonous cocktail?

Can they see through me?

I grab the shampoo bottle and squirt some into my palm and start massaging it into my long hair. My fingertips go to the branding scar that the guys were asking about. I trace the circle all the way around. I know every imperfection. Every spot where it scabbed over or got infected and needed to be scrubbed to create a new scar.

It sends a shiver down my spine.

The brand was the first thing they did and they did it the very first night. Before I was knocked out. Before I was tied up. Before any of that happened, I was claimed.

And if it's true what Ark said—that JD had a girlfriend with a brand like mine—then what are the chances that these guys are safe?

It can't be a coincidence.

As much as it scares me to go outside and face the world again—face reality—I have to. I need to leave and I need to leave tonight.

The hot water runs down my head when I step back under the stream, and I quickly finish up with the conditioner and then shut the water off.

I have no clothes, but I can find some sweats of JD's to wear. And a t-shirt. And I'm sure he has some old hoodie I can take.

Shoes are the major problem. I can't wear his shoes. My feet are small and his are not. But I'm sure I can make them work until I find a store and buy my own. I still have the money they gave me. JD stuck it in the drawer in the bedside table and the last time I looked, it was still there.

But… if he's a bad guy, why pay me?

I don't know. I really don't. So I just wrap a towel around myself and walk to the door. My hand rests on the handle, but I don't turn it. I lean my ear against the door instead. Listening. Is Ark still out there? He scares me a lot more than JD. JD is nice. He's charming. Ark is intimidating and demanding.

I don't hear anything, so I open the door and peek out.

Ark is still there, sitting on the bed with his head in his hands. "You done lying now?" he asks, slowly lifting his head and looking me in the eyes. He grabs the camera he was using this morning. "Because I need some answers."

"I don't have your answers."

"You don't even know what I'm asking yet, so how can you know you don't have what I need?" He stands and I back up, crossing the threshold into the bathroom.

He moves like lightning. His strike has me pushed face first against the wall, both hands behind my back, in less time than it takes me to realize I've misjudged him.

"Look," he growls in my ear. "I'm not used to asking twice, Blue. And people don't generally lie to me. Because I don't tolerate it. So tell me about that scar on your neck and I'll forget the fact that I had to ask you twice. And point me to these people, and I'll forget the fact that you lied."

"Or what?" I snarl over my shoulder. "You can't hurt me."

"No?"

"No," I say back with confidence. "You can't hurt me because I can take it."

He recoils a little at my words. "You can take what?"

I yank my wrists from his grip and even though a second ago he was holding me so tight it was cutting off the blood flow to my hands, they come away easily. I turn, still pressed against the wall, his body so close his hips are pressed against my own. Our chests rise and fall rapidly from the adrenaline. "Whatever you want to dish out." I tilt my head up so I can meet his gaze. He is way over six foot tall.

He backs up one step and then turns around and walks out.

I stand there for several minutes, waiting to see if he comes back with a belt, or a cane, or a whip, or a knife.

But he doesn't.

I walk over to the bed and sit down in the same place where he was while I was taking a shower. His camera rolls over and hits me in the thigh.

I pick it up and turn it on, then push a few buttons until the screen begins to show the photos of this morning.

"That's mine," Ark says from the doorway.

"Well," I say, pointing to the images, "that's me."

He covers the distance between us in a few paces and snatches the camera out of my hand. "Mine."

And then he's gone again.

I take a deep breath and look out the window as I consider my options. It's dark and raining again. I check the drawer and the money is gone.

"You asshole!" I yell at the empty doorway. "You took my money."

I grab my clothes from the bathroom and put them back on and then walk out to the living room to confront him.

But he's not there. I creep down the hallway to his bedroom and check there too. But nothing.

When I walk back to the living room I see a crack of light from under some metal doors against the far wall.

That's his office, JD said. Where they edit the films he makes.

I walk quietly over to the door and press my ear against it to listen. I can hear the clicking of a computer keyboard, then the rolling wheels of a chair. Finally soft footsteps as he pads towards the doors. I back away, afraid of being caught. But he doesn't slide them open. Instead, the lights flick off and then his footsteps retreat. I hear the crack of a beer bottle being opened, and then a sigh.

I slide the doors apart, just enough to peek inside.

There's a large monitor on the desk sitting on front of a wall of windows. And on the screen are the images he took of me this morning. Of JD and me. And of the three of us out on the terrace. They flip by, hundreds of them, at least. Maybe thousands. I look over at the couch where he's sitting with a beer propped up on his leg, staring at me.

"You can look at them if you come in here to do it."

I don't know how he wants me to respond, so I'm unsure if I want to look at them or run back to JD's room and hide.

"I'm sorry about that," Ark says, clearing his throat. "It's just... JD stopped thinking about her, ya know? It took him so fucking long to stop thinking about her. And now here you are with a clue. And..."

I step into the room.

"And he's gonna go looking for shit again, I just know it."

I take another step towards him and Ark pats the space on the couch next to him. "I love these pictures. Come look at them with me."

I take two more steps, and then I'm within arm's reach and he slips his hand in mine.

My body shivers from his touch, but I let him pull me the rest of the way, and take a seat as he lets go. My butt is barely perched on the cushion, my hands in my lap, my body on high alert in case he wants to hurt me.

But he doesn't. He surprises me by scooting away, propping his back against the armrest, and stretching out his legs behind me. They are long and in the way, so now I can't lean back.

He takes a swig from his beer. "I saw you this morning. God, has it only been one day?" I know what he means. It feels like I've been in their house forever. "And answers were the last thing on my mind, Blue. I mean, fuck. I'd given up, just like JD. I gave up a while back, actually. Just accepted that this was the way things were. The way my life was gonna go. But fuck."

I don't know what any of that means, but I take that it's not good by the way he finishes the beer and then throws it across the room, where it lands cleanly in an open-top trash can near the desk. "Get me another one, will you?"

I look down at him and squint.

He stares back. His eyes are bleary, and red, and now that I look closely, tired. Not tired like he needs sleep. But tired in a way I can relate to. The kind of tired where your body feels heavy and your mind feels empty. "Never mind," he says in a soft voice that I've never heard before. He says it, but he doesn't stop staring.

"What?" I ask, getting uncomfortable.

"Why'd you come in here?"

"I was…" I was looking for my money so I could leave. But this guy. These guys… they are pulling me towards them somehow. JD and his charm. Ark and his distance. And despite the fact that they take advantage of girls for a living, they feel very… vulnerable. It feels precarious. Like the whole thing might come crashing down at any moment. Like they are held together by some invisible thread. And not some mental connection or shared experience, either. Although I have no doubt they have all that too.

Held together by a thread that's invisible because it's nearly gone.

We are alike, then. Aren't we?

Three people brought together by the early-morning rain.

Two of us clinging together, trying to stick it out. Ride the wave until it crashes, and then help each other up to start all over again.

One of us already dead. Still walking, but not living. Waiting to be saved. Or maybe wanting to be the one who does the saving.

"I was looking for you," I finally say. His eyes have never left mine. They are pleading now. They are pleading for me to tell him something, but I don't know him. So I have no idea what that is. He remains silent as my words echo in my head, so I fill in the space with what I want instead. "Can we wait for JD together?"

Ark's eyes. Dear God. They are filled with so much. "JD might not come back for a while." And the tone of Ark's voice explains everything. Fear. His eyes are filled with fear for his best friend.

"Why?" I ask back, my voice softer than his.

Ark takes a long draw of air and then covers his eyes with his hand before he speaks. "JD's got a drug problem. He kicked it a long time ago, but he's tempted, ya know?" Ark lifts his hand away from his eyes for a moment to see if I'm getting this. "And the scar." His eyes dart to the back of my neck and my fingers slip under my hair to touch it automatically. "That scar might be his undoing."

"I don't know anything, Ark."

He smiles a little when I say his name. "They never do, Blue." He studies my reaction, which might in fact be a blush. Thankfully the light is low. "Do you like the pictures?"

I look up at the monitor and watch them as they flash by. Two or three seconds is not enough time to study them. And I feel like I look a mess in them. I'm wearing that wet and filthy dress from the night before. My bare feet and open legs. It all says… sad.

And I am sad. So I guess it's accurate. He's captured me perfectly.

A sad and desperate girl lost in the rain.

"Yes," I say, still watching the slide show. "I love them."

"Me too."

"Can I wait with you?" I ask again. He never answered me and there's no way I can be alone tonight. I'd rather be with almost anyone than be alone. But—I look over at him. Study his face. He looks hard. His jawline is straight and distinct. The stubble on his face tells me he hasn't shaved in more than a day. And his eyes… He's much better than just anyone. "Please," I add.

"How about I wait with you instead?"

I don't understand, but then he swings his legs over my head and stands up. I'm pulled to my feet and he takes my hand and leads me back down the hallway to JD's room. "We can wait for him in here," Ark says, as we enter.

I don't argue. I know there's some sort of struggle going on between them over me, so this must be his answer to keep the peace. He lifts the covers and motions for me to get in. I do. And he walks around to the other side of the bed and takes a seat, leaning over, with his hands over his face.

His back is covered with the same tattoo as JD's. A huge piece that covers all the skin. Two dragons, wrestling—and yet not fighting. Their bodies make a circle, and it feels a little bit like the yin-yang sign. Dark and light. Good and evil.

There's a sphere between the two dragon heads and I reach out and touch it, making him shudder. "What's it mean?" I ask. "The ball in the middle?"

He turns his head a little, so he can look over his shoulder. "Everything, Blue. It's everything. The world. Life. Dreams. Money. Happiness."

"Are you two fighting over it?" I don't know why I assume the dragons are Ark and JD, but I just do.

"No," he says, lifting his legs and lying back with me. He slips an arm underneath my neck and pulls me into him, a definite plea for intimacy. "No, we're not fighting, Blue. We're partners. We're in it together. There's a banner that runs along the bottom and JD has the Latin version. '*Omne trium perfectum.*' Every set of three is perfect."

"What's yours say?"

"'Not everything should come in threes.'"

I laugh. "Could you be more opposite?"

It's quiet for a while after that. His breathing evens out and matches mine. My eyes close and I'm in the twilight of sleep where my thoughts rush around like a madman's dream. "No," he finally answers. "We are the definition of opposite."

FOURTEEN

ARK

THE light flicks on and I open my eyes to find JD staring down at me and Blue. I glance over at the window and see the faint glow of the dawn. The light flicks off and he drags his shirt over his head and kicks off his shoes. "What are you doing?" he asks as he unbuttons his pants and lets them drop to the floor.

"Waiting for you."

"I'm fine," he says, climbing into bed on the other side of Blue. "I just needed time to think." He clasps his hands behind his head and stares at the ceiling.

"You find any answers?"

"No. Just more questions. Did you fuck her?"

"No, JD."

"Sorry," he says, never looking at me. "I'm tired."

Blue's hand reaches out to him and settles on his chest. I catch a smile on his face and then his hand covers hers and gives it a squeeze. He chances a look over at me and I shrug. I have no clue what we're doing. I have no idea what this girl is thinking. But she extended her hand to both of us. And she caught us in a time when we both need what she's offering.

My shrug is enough for JD. For now, anyway. She's not mine. Not his. She's ours.

He turns her body to angle her ass into his hips and wraps his arms around her, pulling her close. I go to get up so JD can get whatever it is he wants from her, but she reaches out and grabs my bicep. She gives me a squeeze and when I turn my head, she's looking straight at me. "Stay," she says softly. "Please," she begs when I don't answer.

JD's fingers slide down her body. I can feel his movements like they're hers, that's how close we are. And I know the moment his fingers slip inside her, because her eyes close and her mouth opens to let a tiny moan escape. It's so small. Just a breath of air, really.

I watch her face as JD touches her. Not jealous, not exactly. I can touch her too, she's made this clear. But I'm not sure what I'm feeling.

And then her hand is on the waist of my sweats, pulling them down. My dick is hard and it springs out. Her touch almost kills me, that's how delicate, and sweet, and sensual it is. She doesn't pump me hard, like the girls in our videos. She doesn't get busy with it, like this is a job.

No. She strokes me in a way I've never felt before.

Her breathing increases as JD reaches for her breast and kisses her neck. "Blue," he says. Her back bucks against him and then he switches positions, so he's hovering over her. So he's staring down at her. So he's taking control of her. "Tell us to stop now, or this shit's happening."

She looks over at me, like she wants my opinion on the matter. "I'm in," I say. More to reassure JD than her. Because that's who he's really asking. Me. He wants to know if we're gonna do this. He wants to know if we're really gonna share a girl.

Blue looks back up to JD. "Don't stop."

"Fuck, yes," he says back. And then he leans down to kiss her. Fisting her hair and grinding his hips into hers.

I grab her thigh and open her legs. JD's hands are no longer in the way, so I scoot down her body and slip my face right into her sweet spot, looking up to catch her expression as I tease her with my tongue.

"Ohhhh," she moans into JD's mouth. He straightens up and then straddles her, his knees on either side of her shoulders. And the moaning stops because his cock is in her mouth.

JD lifts his hips and I can see through his legs, a perfect view of Blue as she works him. She takes him like she touched me, with careful consideration. Not fast and wet, but slow. Deliberate. I finger her. First one, then two. She loses control of her work, and JD thrusts too hard, making her gag.

"Fuck, yes," he says again.

I lift Blue's legs to gain access to her ass, and when my tongue slips in to probe, she begins to beg. "Please," she says, looking up at JD. "I need this."

"Tell me what you need, darling," JD says. He likes to talk when he fucks. "Tell me what you want."

"I need you both," she moans.

"Where?" JD prods. "Keep telling us what you want, Blue."

I stop what I'm doing to her clit. My fingers withdraw from her ass. And I wait for it. Because I want to hear it too. I need to hear it too.

"Both of you, JD." She looks down to me. "Inside me, Ark. Please."

JD moves backwards, forcing me back as well. His hand reaches down to stroke himself a few times before he positions himself over the top of her. Her pussy is wet from my licking and her body is so ready, she angles her hips upwards, inviting JD in.

He lowers himself just enough for the top of his cock to enter and this drives her wild. I kneel behind JD, waiting for him to give her what she's begging for. And when he finally thrusts inside her, I almost think she'll come right then. I move off to the side and JD fucks her hard for a few seconds, pumping into her with a fury. She winces and cries out, and I place a hand on JD's back. "Easy," I tell him.

He slows. I move to the side of Blue and lie on my back, while JD pulls out, wraps an arm around her waist, and lifts her up, placing her on top of me. My dick is so hard it slides right between her ass cheeks and bumps up against JD's balls.

"Oh, fuck," he says. "Jesus. Fuck. Ark."

I reach down as JD lifts her hips up to allow me to gain access. Her pussy is so wet, dripping down into her ass, I have no problem entering her. She stiffens from the moment of pain, but I pull out a little, giving her time to get used to me. She breathes heavy, panting, as JD whispers dirty, soothing things into her ear. "Let him in, Blue," he says. "Let us fill you up, baby."

I slide in a little farther and again she whimpers. But this time I don't stop, I ease in a little bit more, and then I get past the muscles trying to keep me out and I'm fully inside her ass.

"Oh fuck, yes," JD says. "Fuck, yes. I can feel you, dude."

I can feel him too. His dick is moving slowly inside her, but when I move as well, he throws his head back and thrusts deeper.

Blue wails.

I place another hand on JD's back. "Easy, man. If you ever want to do this again, she needs to have fun too."

JD leans down to kiss Blue on the lips. "Sorry," he says. "Sorry. I'll go slow for you."

I reach under JD's arms and grip her breast, kneading and squeezing it until she relaxes. JD moves slowly now, letting her get used to us both, and then my hand slips down and begins to tease her clit.

This is when she goes wild.

Her whole body arches, her mouth is open, moaning this time, not screaming. Her legs are shaking, trembling from the pleasure and the exertion. I keep it up, and then JD is pumping hard, his cock sliding past my own as he fucks her. His arms strain to hold himself up. He's kissing her lips. Sucking her neck. Biting her shoulder.

And then she stops. Everything stops. For one moment, we are still.

She explodes. I can feel her muscles straining as she comes all over JD's dick. He bites his lip, trying to hold back so we can both enjoy her release before we finish and it has to end. She clenches twice, then three times. Once for each of us, I think to myself with a grin. And then when her wave of pleasure starts to dissipate, JD pumps her hard and pulls out, spilling his semen all over her belly.

"Yes, fuck, yes," he whispers as he kisses her face. "Fuck, yes."

I push him off her and then roll Blue and I over so I'm on top. "One more time for me, OK?" I ask her as her body, wanting so desperately to relax, arches up again as my fingers flick against her clit.

"Ohhh," she moans.

And then I'm inside her. I go to the pace of JD's heaving breathing next to me. Hard and fast at first, but then slower. He catches his breath. Blue accepts my movements and begins to match me, her hips moving with mine. I thrust deeper and deeper with each long pulse. And then I cup her face between my hands and look her in the eyes. "Ready?"

She closes her eyes in response, but I want to watch her. "Open your eyes, Blue," I command. "And watch me."

She tries, she really does. But then she's coming again. Not the explosion she had with JD inside her. But something else entirely. It's like floating on a river. It's like we are underwater and everything is slow and distorted. We come together. And I don't pull out like JD did. Her belly is still slick and sticky with his semen and it slides between us. Mixing with our pleasure and our sweat.

We are not three people in a bed.

We are not two people finding our climax.

We are one.

FIFTEEN

ARK

"WASH with me, Blue," JD says a few moments later. "You're sticky, baby."

I'm so fucking tired, I just ignore him. But then he scoops Blue up and carries her into his bathroom. A few moments later the shower starts and I find myself straining to hear what's going on.

I can guess, of course. JD is not a one-fuck-a-night guy. This much I know. He's gonna do her again, and that pisses me off.

I throw the covers off and walk across the room and through the open door of the bathroom. The steam is fogging up the mirror and the glass shower door, so I can't see much. But I don't need to. She's on her knees in front of him.

I open the shower door and both sets of eyes turn to me. JD smirks, like he knew I wouldn't be able to stay away. "You're too late, bro," he says, a small groan coming from his throat as Blue takes his dick deeper into her throat. But then JD relaxes and turns his attention back to me. "You have to sit this one out." He nods his head to the tiled bench on the far side of the shower.

I shrug and take a seat on the bench. "Makes no difference to me," I tell him. "This is my usual view anyway. Me watching while the throwaway girls suck your dick for money."

JD's smile falters and the girl pauses her bobbing head, like she might say something back. But then JD places his hand over the crown of her head and bends down, his dick falling out of her mouth like the water dripping down his back.

"Ignore him," he says. And then he kisses her on the mouth and stands up. She tilts her head up and holy fuck, I'd pay a thousand dollars right now to see her blue eyes looking up at me like that. Because I know what she's thinking. It's the same thing they all think.

He uses them. Pays them to suck him off in public. Everything that pours out of his mouth is a lie. And they know it.

But she's looking up at him like he's her king.

He smiles down at her and she resumes, placated. And then JD looks me dead in the eye. "You told me to be nice in there?" He motions to the bedroom.

I don't answer him. He knows I did.

"Now it's your turn. She might be yours, but she wants me."

"Then why am I here?" It's a serious question. He could break our rule and just take her. He knows I won't fight him over it. Not over a girl. It won't happen.

"Because I know you want her. And just once, Ark, I'd like to see you get what you want."

"What the fuck does that mean?"

He squats down again to kiss Blue on the lips. "Let's turn a little, baby. So Ark can watch." She scoots around until her body is sideways to mine as he grabs the soap.

And then I do get what I want. I take what JD gives me. Because her eyes lift and meet mine. She holds my gaze with none of the maliciousness I came in here with. She holds my gaze with trust.

I look back. Her attention is on me, not JD. But JD doesn't seem to mind that she's stopped, because his fingers are playing with her clit, making her eyes droop to half-mast. And when he says, "Jerk off, man. She's waiting for you to start," I get that feeling once again.

This will not turn out well.

But I'm caught in the spell of a trusting girl, my best friend, and a rock-hard cock. I can't help myself. I begin to move my hand up and down my shaft. My thumb slides up over my wet tip and then my palm slips back down my length in long, slow strokes.

A few pumps with Blue's eyes on my movements and I'm dying. JD's fingers are fully inside her now, and she's buckling her back as he soaps up her breasts. He withdraws his fingers, reaches under her, and lifts her up with two hands cupping her ass. Her legs wrap around his hips and he enters her with one quick thrust.

She gasps, her fingernails digging into his shoulders. And then he slows down and fucks her like that for a few moments. "You like it hard or slow, Blue?" he asks.

"Both," she whispers.

"You like it rough or soft?"

"Both."

"You like me or him?"

Blue opens her eyes and looks first at me, then back to him. "Both."

"Why?"

His question stops her and me at the same time. "Why?" she asks.

He nods. "Why both? Why not just one?"

She looks at me, but I can't help her. Because I'm interested too. She takes her gaze back to JD, who is fucking her so slowly now, it's just a barely detectable grinding. "Because I need to be surrounded. I need be held on both sides. I can't feel safe unless I'm surrounded."

I don't know what that means, but JD must, because he kisses her on the lips. It's a long, tender kiss. Not a kiss I usually see him give. If he kisses the girls we film, it's always hard and demanding.

But everything about Blue is soft.

And JD, who is normally not soft, decides in this moment that he will be soft for her. He gives in. I can see it.

I stop masturbating and just watch them.

Blue responds with a long, passionate kiss of her own. Her body, still being held up only by JD's hands under her ass, slowly moves in tandem with his hips.

I watch them make love.

And when JD comes inside her, she doesn't throw her head back and scream out her release. She rests her head on his shoulder and cries.

I get up and walk out of the shower, grabbing a towel on my way. I'm just about to walk out and go back to my own room when they start talking. Their words echo off the bathroom walls.

"Is it because we want to share?" JD asks. She must say no, because JD says, "Then what is it?"

There's some sniffling and a long pause. I walk back over to the open bathroom door and listen as her small voice tries to make sense of things. "I don't want him to hate me."

JD laughs. "Sweetheart, he's got it bad for you. There's no way in hell he's gonna hate you."

There's a few more minutes of talking. Reassurances from JD. Promises, even. And then the silence that says she accepts what he's telling her is true just as the water shuts off.

I take a deep breath and drop my towel on the floor. I'm

practically dry now anyway. So I just crawl in to JD's bed and flop over, face first on the mattress, forcing myself to push aside all the warning bells going off in my head. Because JD is right.

I've got it bad.

I want her and I'll take her any way I can get her.

A few moments later the bathroom light turns off and the room goes dark. They are silent as they climb into bed next to me and the girl's warm skin touches mine as JD pulls her close to him.

He's hogging her now because he can, and I feel the anger building up again.

But then her tiny hand finds mine in the dark and she grabs hold of it. Gives it a squeeze.

I squeeze back.

SIXTEEN

BLUE

JD'S breath is like a whisper across the back of my neck. It lingers the way a whisper does, and then he's kissing my scar.

I open my eyes. Ark is sleeping in the bed next to me. His chest is rising and falling in the same rhythm as the tiny puffs of air JD is caressing my skin with. Ark's dark hair falls over one eye, his cheek pressed against the mattress. He doesn't use a pillow, and that suits him for some reason—that Ark should prefer to sleep without a comfort everyone takes for granted. This makes the line from his neck to the dip at the small of his back more straight than it might be. One arm is flung out towards me, only a few inches from my own, which is tucked up under my chin. His palm is facing down on the white sheets and I want nothing more than to grab hold of him and never let go.

JD's kisses recapture my attention. "Hey," he says, right next to my ear so the sound gets caught in the curve of the shell. Captured. Maybe to keep Ark sleeping while JD gives me some attention.

"Hey," I say back with the same discretion.

"I'm sorry I made you cry last night."

"You didn't," I insist.

He says nothing to that. I'm not ready to talk yet, and he's not gonna push me. That's what he said last night after I cried. He's not gonna push me to talk. And that feels like a miracle. How did I find two people with more secrets than me, at just the moment when I needed it most?

I know the answer, but I refuse to believe it. I won't believe it. Not after everything that's happened.

JD's words stop, but his hands are just beginning to wander. I'm sore all over from the night before my escape. It's always worse the second day. It's like the gods of punishment are fucking with you the first day. Because you start to think it wasn't so bad. You start to think you won't be limping for a week or struggling to breathe through the bruises on your throat. Or that the open sores on your back won't be weeping with pus for days before they finally scab over.

But the gods of punishment are cruel. Because they make that first day bearable for the sole purpose of building you up just to take you back down again on day two.

My whole body hurts, but JD's touch is soft and soothing. He doesn't try to fuck me again. He doesn't even try to get me off. It's like he knows. And he must have an idea if he recognized the branding scar on the back of my neck.

"You know what it means?" he asks, his voice still very low. "That brand?"

I nod. Of course. Everything was explained the first day. "Eternity."

I feel a long hot breath on my upper back as JD deals with that. "Did you see any—"

"No."

He stops talking for a few seconds. Maybe I stunned him. Or maybe he accepts it as truth. Or maybe he knows that was too much.

We're silent for so long after that, I figure he wants to go back to sleep. But then his soft touches start up again.

A fingertip tracing up and down my prominent ribs.

His palm cupping the hip bone that sticks out way too far.

His lips caressing the welts on my back.

Every bit of it hurts. Not all in the same way. But every bit of it hurts. The bones remind me of how malnourished I am. What could these two beautiful men see in me? How could they possibly see past my emaciated shell of a body? And the kisses across my back are just painful. Putting on a shirt will be a reminder of what they did, no matter how loose it is.

And then his hands rub lightly over the curve of my ass. The hands that grabbed it with such passion last night and made me forget.

He knows I'm crying before I do. He turns me towards him, hugging me close.

But it hurts. It all hurts and I cry harder. "Please stop," I beg. "Please don't touch me anymore." I just want to lie still and forget. I don't want to be reminded of anything. Not the good. Not the bad. Not anything.

JD is still next to me for several minutes, but then he just gets up, gets dressed, and walks out of the bedroom. A few moments later the front door slams.

I close my eyes with relief and slow the crying down to small hiccups of air that cannot be rushed. They stop in their own good time and there is nothing I can do but allow myself to forget.

"I saw this golden monkey once," Ark says a few minutes later, startling me out of my blissful solitude. "It escaped from its enclosure at the zoo a few summers ago. JD and I were just getting into the groove of things with the business. And we were shooting a scene at the zoo." He stops to chuckle. "It's fucked up, I get it. But don't judge me yet, Blue. Because I'm a man of many layers. And I do things for a reason."

I turn my body, wincing and groaning as I let the pain take over for a second. "What's that got to do with a monkey?"

He smiles at me and his dark eyes soften for a moment. He's older than JD, that's clear. He's got some worry lines around his eyes. And he's got a look that makes me feel like he's in control of things. Maybe everything. "They thought it was still in the zoo, so they were telling all the patrons to keep an eye out that day. Like a public service announcement. They'd stand at all the intersecting paths leading to various animals, and talk about the missing golden monkey. They were desperate to catch it. If it got out of that park, it'd probably get hit by a car on Colorado Boulevard, or snatched up to be sold as a pet."

I eye him, wondering if they found and sold the monkey.

He smiles again, like he knows what I'm thinking. "But it didn't get out of the park. And JD, me, and the girl we were filming were the ones to actually find the golden monkey."

"Where was it?"

His smile stops and his expression becomes sad. "Just sitting in a tree. It was closing time and even though we are scum for filming a girl sucking off JD at a family park, at least we did it late at night. So when I looked up and saw it, it was illuminated in one of those yellowish sodium lamps they use all over the city to try to cut down on light pollution. So it was…" He stops. Like he's thinking. Like he's picturing that golden monkey right now. Seeing it again. "It was like a halo around its head."

"Was it beautiful?"

"No, Blue. The monkey was sick, I guess. It escaped while being transported to the medical facility and that's how it got away and we found it in that tree."

"Oh."

"They said she had cancer and they were taking her to be euthanized, because they felt she was in a lot of pain."

My attention on his story is rapt. I cannot look away even if I wanted to. "What did you say?"

"What do you think I said?" His eyes search mine for a moment. And then he breathes out a long breath. "They said she was not worth saving. The treatment would be long and the odds were not good. It was expensive." He shrugs. "So JD and I adopted the golden monkey. We donated a hundred thousand dollars to save her and buy some new machine they needed for... something. I don't know what."

"Did she live?"

"Well, first they had to catch her. She was up in a tree. She was in pain. She was not at all interested in coming down. No amount of food could coax her. They had a net and they had her keeper calling to her. But she just clung to that branch high up in the tree for dear life."

He looks at me and his expression softens again. I have a bad feeling about this story. "She died, didn't she?"

"She came down, but not until the sun came up. She climbed down. So very slowly. She was in a lot of pain. But she came down and she wrapped her little monkey hands around that handler's arm and... gave in."

"She died," I say without emotion.

"No, Blue. She gave in to us."

I can't breathe.

"She gave in to what we were offering. She let us help her. And yeah, it involved a lot of things that made her sick, and uncomfortable, and probably wishing she was dead. But she trusted us to save her."

"Did you? Save her?"

"She's still alive today. No one thought she'd make it. And fuck, after the first night, JD and I were kicking ourselves for offering up that money. We had it, but money was new for us back then. We were pulling it in, and the payoffs were big. But it still felt like a dream. Like it wasn't real. So the money meant more back then than it does now."

"That just means it was a bigger sacrifice to give it over."

He nods. "Yeah. I know. But even though it's not such a risk for us to help like that now, it's still a genuine offer."

"We're not talking about a monkey, are we?"

He shrugs.

"You made that all up, didn't you?"

"Her name is Ophelia. I'll take you to see her one day."

"Why are you helping me?"

"Why do you need help?"

I shake my head at him.

"Well, when you can admit that to me, I'll tell you why we're helping you."

And then he throws the covers off and swings his legs out of bed. He's naked, as am I, but after that conversation it feels… different. I watch him walk around the bed, turning my body to see him as he comes over to the other side and picks up his pants. His dick is erect and he looks at me as he handles it, tucking it inside his jeans, but only drawing up the zipper halfway and leaving the button undone. "You're not the monkey in that story, Blue. JD is."

And then he walks out of the bedroom, leaving me alone. And even though five minutes ago, all I wanted was for these two strange men to let me work out my conflicted thoughts on my own, I feel lonely.

And a little while later, as I work up my courage to get up and go talk to the man who told me a story, the man who wants me to tell him one, the front door slams again.

I guess wishes do come true.

SEVENTEEN

ARK

I STOP by a boutique on the mall and chat up the salesgirl about some clothes for Blue and then head over to the bus station.

It always comes back to the bus station. I'm not sure why I look here first when I need to find JD, but this is where I end up. I sit on the concrete wall where he was sitting that night I got off the bus. High on something. Starving. Talking to a girl who wasn't there.

JD the junkie.

Lots of people have asked me over the years why. Why him?

But why not him? Why only help people who are good candidates? Why bother saving the dying monkey when there are so many more deserving animals?

What does deserving even mean?

The bus station is busy because it's Monday morning. Most people are going to work, but this is my weekend. JD and I work

Thursday through Sunday. If all goes well—and most weeks it does—we film Thursday, Friday, and Saturday and then I edit and deliver on Sunday.

This week we have girls lined up for all three filming days. But that doesn't mean they will show. I'm not sure why we've had such a rash of no-shows lately, but it's getting old. I can't wait to shed this business and move on.

I spy a hooker I know coming out of the bus station and whistle. "Shadow!" I wave her over.

She takes a long drag on her smoke, probably wondering what I want. Maybe wondering if I'll pay her to suck off JD. But we don't do whores. They can't pass the health tests.

Shadow knows this, so that's why she hesitates. I don't want her for work, so I must want her for something else.

She drops the cigarette and stubs it out with the toe of her four-inch heels, then waves back as she looks both ways and crosses the street. Her short skirt is gold and barely covers her ass, and her top is sleeveless and beaded with black and gold sequins. "I ain't seen him," she says as she steps up on the curb. "I know you only come here to look for JD and I ain't seen him."

I nod. "OK. Well, thanks for letting me know."

"Now wait, sugar. I said I ain't seen him. But I heard something that you might find interesting."

I don't bother being suspicious. Shadow wants a little bit of cash and truthfully, I'd have given it to her just for crossing the street. So I'll take whatever she's got. I grab a wad of bills from my pocket and count out three twenties. "Buy some breakfast, Shadow. You're too skinny."

She smiles and I notice she's missing a tooth. Not one right in front, but off to the side a little bit. "You always were a sweet talker, Ark."

I put my hands up like I'm guilty.

"Anyways, I was just coming from Charlie's and I overheard

some men talking about you."

"Me?" Charlie is her pimp. Not some corner dude, either. A guy who knows his business.

She pulls out another smoke and lights it up, taking her time with a long drag. "Uh-huh. Someone called in while I was talking to him. They tells him there's a girl missing and do Charlie know anything about it. Then Charlie says talk to JD and Ark, because you keeps track of the street girls."

"Do you know who called him?" I ask, feigning disinterest.

"Nah," she says. "Charlie just hung up without saying names. But he was talking all polite and shit. So my intuition figures it was someone more important than him."

"OK. Well, thanks for that, Shadow. I guess he'll get in contact with me if it's important."

She flashes me her new smile. "Any time, sugar."

"What happened to your tooth?" I point to the missing one she's flashing, but her smile fades quick.

"Nothin'. Just a misunderstanding."

I smile at her. "OK, Shadow. Stay safe."

"You too, honey." But she's already walking off.

I sit on the wall for a little longer trying to figure out what that bit of information might add up to. Blue is running, that's for sure. And they were violent with her. Beatings, torture maybe, possibly rape. They've got her ID. They marked her as property. And she's afraid to call home.

Add that to JD's missing girlfriend from four years ago and that means something.

Back in the early days, before the money started pouring in, JD and I were winging it hardcore. It took weeks to clean him up and he had like two dozen relapses. Every time I took him back to rehab, they asked me why I bothered. And I always told them the same thing. Because no one else will.

Everybody's got a past. Everybody is running from some

demon or another. Everybody needs a second chance. If there's a person out there who has not fucked up royally and needed a second chance… well, that person hasn't lived yet.

And four years later, I do not regret one moment of all the effort it took to drag him out of his depression, his addiction, and his self-loathing, and hand him the opportunity of a lifetime.

Because no matter what JD is, he's smart. And he took that chance. He moved on. He made movies with me. He made money with me. Hell, he did more than move on. He moved up.

But that scar…

I saw his face last night when he lifted her hair. I saw him look up at me like that kid I found trying his hardest not to get his ass kicked in front of this very wall of concrete four years ago.

He expects answers this time.

And he expects me to help get them.

I get up and start walking back to the loft and then spy a drug store across the street. I cross and go inside to pick something up for Blue that she will surely be needing.

EIGHTEEN

BLUE

I FIND my dress in the trash. Not that I'd wear it again. It looks like it went through hell. But it would've been nice to be asked if I wanted to wash it, considering I have no other clothes.

I found something, though. Sweats and a t-shirt of JD's in his closet. But the pants have to be rolled over so many times, it makes the t-shirt bunch out over my belly. When I look in the mirror it makes me look pregnant and that just hurts like hell.

I unroll the sweats and hold them up as I make my way to the kitchen. There's still mess in there from last night, so I start cleaning up. I'm just closing the dishwasher after loading it up when the door opens and Ark walks in.

He throws his keys on a small table in the foyer and then hangs up his leather jacket. He's wearing a white button-down shirt with the cuffs casually rolled up. There's a tie around his collar as well, but it's loose.

I squint at him. Is that a fashion statement? Or was he really wearing a white shirt and tie for business reasons?

"What?" he asks, looking into the open kitchen.

I shake my head and start wiping down the counters. His shoes—dressy, I realize as I try to concentrate on the countertops—tap across the floor and stop just off to my right.

I lift my head a little to look up at him. "What?"

He throws a package down on the counter. "For you. I didn't see any birth control stuffed in your panties yesterday. And we both came inside you. So…"

I look at the package. "What is it?" When I look up at him, he's puzzled. "What?"

"It's the morning-after pill. You've never taken one?"

I open my mouth to speak, then close it immediately and go back to cleaning. I'm not even going there. "Thanks. I'll take it as soon as I'm done here." But he doesn't move. I wait a few more seconds before looking up again. "What?"

His dark eyes are squinting down at me. "You're not the maid."

"I know. I'm just…" I shrug. "I'm just trying to be helpful."

"We won't kick you out. Even if you don't help."

"OK," I say meekly.

"You should eat. And then go back to bed. You look…"

"Beaten?" I fill in the word he won't say.

"Like you need someone to be more careful with you."

When I look up this time, he's already walking away. "I'll be in my office if you need anything. Oh—" He stops and looks over his shoulder just outside the entrance to his office. "We're going out to dinner tonight."

"Who?" I ask, stupidly, since I can figure that one out. "What will I wear?" That's a better question.

"You. Me. JD. We're gonna get this all out in the open over a nice meal. Talk it through like civilized people. I have parcels coming. When they arrive, please have them delivered to my office."

He turns back to his office and walks through. "Ark," I call out. "What if JD doesn't come back?"

"I texted him. So he will. I told him I'm going to keep you for myself if he doesn't."

And then Ark goes inside his office and slides the doors closed.

NINETEEN

ARK

I SIT at my desk staring at her images for hours.

Hours.

The clock on the wall ticks away the seconds before I take this step, and I can't help but wonder if it's the right choice. I've been this man for four years. Can I be any other way? Can I imagine a life after this? Away from this work I'm so steeped in I don't even notice the things I do are wrong?

No one sets out to sell sex. It's not something to aspire to. It's something that happens. An opportunity, maybe. A stroke of luck for some. A way forward for others.

Do I take advantage of girls? Yes. I know this. We offer them money in exchange for a ten-minute video of them on their knees in public, licking JD's dick like it's candy.

But I've always rationalized it away. Perhaps our money pays for a babysitter for another week? Or fixes their car? Or feeds their family?

Perhaps I am helping to keep a girl away from more dangerous predators than myself?

Or not.

It's far more likely that giving them a taste of the money is the gateway drug that ruins their life. The ones who don't show up… those are the smart girls. Those are the ones who see what I am, and once they get a little fresh air and the smell of money is blown off them by the wind of reality, they come to their senses.

Selling sex is dirty.

Selling sex is filthy.

Selling sex is lucrative.

And I enjoy it.

No matter how much I hate myself, I enjoy it. I like the stalking JD does. I like watching him work the room from my seat at the bar, my camera trained on the approach. Sometimes, if we're lucky, that first meetup is gold. I add it to the movies. Those always get more hits online than the ones that just have some random girl sucking him off in an alley.

I like to see the girl from afar when she realizes the money is too good. The opportunity too fleeting. The repercussions too far away.

I love it. Because we are buying something they don't want to sell, but they can't turn us down.

I'm scum for this. I've come to terms with it. Hell, I've all but embraced it.

My name is Ark and I buy sex.

But one blue-eyed girl has turned my world upside down and I don't even know how it happened.

And now I couldn't be more disgusted, and yet so delighted, that I have these pictures on the screen. Whatever I sold to the Devil to get them, it was worth it. It was totally worth it.

I scroll through them again, choosing the best five to bring up in Photoshop. I crop our heads off first, so we're only shown from the waist down. No need to proclaim to the world that I am scum.

Plus, I don't want her to be seen online. Not her face, anyway. Her face belongs to me.

Her body, though... I will share her body. With JD here in the loft. With the world from the safety of anonymity. From the impersonal distance of a Tumblr blog.

Why would I do that? If I want her, why would I share her?

I can't say no to JD. It's not possible to deny him this. Not now. Not after he saw her scar. Not now that he has this desire to go looking again.

He needs to stay home. He needs to forget. He needs to let this girl take the place of the one he lost.

Because if he doesn't... if he slips up and starts down that path again...

I can't think about that right now. Not with these images of the three of us staring back at me.

Blue is sadly beautiful on the terrace, her body between us. Our hands between her legs.

JD is lost in his own want, still blissfully unaware of the scar on the back of her neck that will flip his entire world upside down.

And the rain. The streaked makeup running down Blue's face. The dress, the bare feet... all of it says *I need help*.

"I'll help you," I whisper to the lost people on the screen.

There's a knock at the door, so I reluctantly pull my eyes from my computer and redirect to the door. "Come in."

Blue appears, poking her head through the parting doors, like she's afraid I might bellow at her for interrupting. "I'm sorry—"

"Don't be." I smile, and she smiles back. "The delivery is here?"

She nods. "Yes, they're on their way up now. I'll tell them

to—"

"Come in, Blue. Have a seat on the couch and wait for me."
I get up and walk to the door. She stares at me like I might flip
out and strike her. I touch her arm and she lets out a breath. "Sit."
With a little urging, she does. She walks over to the couch and
takes a seat, folding her hands in her lap and trying her best not
to drop her head and look at the floor. "Wait," I command.

She nods, and then I leave and walk to the front door and
open it to the sound of the arriving elevator. "In my office, please,"
I tell the woman. "Other side of the living room and through the
sliding doors. Hang them on the suit rack."

The delivery woman smiles and moves forward to complete
her task like a professional, and then exits, accepting the twenty-
dollar bill I hand her with a slight nod as I close the door behind
her.

Blue is still sitting on the couch, just as she was instructed,
when I walk back in. "Your clothes for tonight," I say, waving a
hand at the garment bags hanging from the suit rack. "Go ahead,
take them out."

I sit on the edge of my desk as she walks over to the rack
and begins unzipping the first bag. She turns her back to me and
that's when I see the blood.

"Blue," I say, walking over to her and taking her by the arm.
"You're bleeding."

She swallows hard and looks at her feet. "I know. I'm sorry.
They're still fresh."

I lift up the t-shirt she's wearing and look at the welts down
her side. They aren't bloody, not really. But they are oozing a
clear liquid and that mixes with the little bit of blood to make
it seep through her shirt. "Why didn't I notice they were so bad
yesterday?"

"I was naked yesterday," she says, her eyes darting to mine,
then dropping again. "Today I'm wearing clothes. It rubs them

and makes them worse."

I lift the shirt over her head and she ducks out of it. "You can't go to dinner tonight. I won't make you uncomfortable just so I can take you out." I reach for my phone and dial JD. It rings through to voice mail so I end the call and text him instead. I was hoping this dinner would draw him out of whatever it is he's doing, but it looks like he's won.

"We'll eat at home," I tell her as I finish up the message. "We can look at the clothes when you're feeling better."

"I'm fine," she says, placing her small hand on my arm. "Really."

I squint my eyes at her. "Fine? Please don't, OK? Your skin is oozing from being beaten. You have bruises all over your ribs. I found you barefoot and wearing a sundress in the rain yesterday morning. You're not fine."

"I know what you guys want and I can't give it to you. I don't have the answers JD's looking for and even if I did, I wouldn't be able to tell him."

"Why?"

"Because they are bad, bad people, Ark. And I can take what they dish out, but I can't fight back."

TWENTY

BLUE

"**S**URE you can," he says in that businesslike tone he's had all day. Yesterday he seemed like a broody asshole who runs a porn website. Today he seems like a professional who runs a million-dollar corporation.

I don't get it.

"I get that you're afraid, but we're here."

I just shake my head. "You don't understand. I don't know enough to give you the information you need. I only know enough to allow you to alert them to dispose of the evidence before anything can be done."

"Evidence," he repeats. "That's an interesting word."

I cross my arms over my bare chest. Not out of modesty or embarrassment, but because I have a chill.

Is it sad that I'm more comfortable naked than clothed?

He grabs a blanket off the back of his office couch and drapes it over my shoulders. I wince when the soft fabric touches my welts. "Come here," he says, taking my arm. He brings me to the couch and sits down, patting his lap. "Lie across my lap, face down."

I do as I'm told, still hugging the blanket around me. Once I'm settled he gently lifts it off me and places it over my legs.

When his fingertips touch my side, I have to hold in a sob. Not because of my cuts, but because his fingertips are so light and gentle, it's almost more painful than if he was rough.

"Shhh," he says. "Try to enjoy it. Try to relax. Close your eyes."

I take a deep breath and when I let it out, I relax my shoulders and let the weight of my body settle into his lap.

He traces patterns on my skin. Little circles around each of the scars. The stars. And then a long, slow line down my spine that dips below the waistband of the sweats I'm wearing. That sends a chill down my whole body and suddenly, I'm craving more than he's giving me.

"Mmmm," I moan. "It feels so good." He says nothing, but his hand leaves that area and starts playing with my hair. My sex begins to throb as the craving for pleasure takes over. I hate that men can make me feel this way. I hate that even the most vile bastard can stimulate me and make me want more. But I don't hate that Ark can do this. I don't hate anything about him. I want more of him.

The front door opens and then closes and a few seconds later JD is standing on the office threshold. "What's going on in here?" he says, like he hasn't been missing all day. When I look up at him he smiles. It's warm and genuine from what I can tell. And then it falters as he notices my back.

"Hand me the camera, JD," Ark asks, calm as you please. JD takes the few steps over to the desk and unhooks the camera from the computer and brings it back. "Let's get this on film," Ark says, turning the camera on so that it makes a whirring sound.

"Why?" I whisper as JD lifts up my legs and takes a seat on the couch. Now I'm lying across both their laps. JD's fingers immediately wander between my legs, giving me the pleasure Ark denied me a few seconds earlier.

"I want them," is all Ark says in response.

But I'm gone. I've moved past the idea that the images of marks will be sold to sadistic assholes who get off on pain and sex.

People like me.

Because I get off on pain and sex. I crave it. I want it so bad.

JD's fingers slip inside me as Ark stands up and walks out. Weren't we going to have a conversation about this... *arrangement*?

JD's cock grows beneath my legs. I squirm down a little and place my mouth over his thickness, licking him through his jeans.

"You're a horny little thing, aren't you?"

"She's in trouble, JD," Ark says as he comes back into the room.

I am. Because I'm lost in the haze of lust. And when Ark kneels down on the floor and begins to clean my welts, the agony of his touch, mixed with JD's fingers teasing the bundle of nerves between my legs, send me straight into that place between pleasure and pain.

I stop feeling.

All the shame and fear falls away.

I give myself to these men as they tease me. One trying to elicit pleasure as the other unknowingly brings out the pain.

And when I come, I cry again. I lean on JD's chest and sob as Ark dabs ointment over the open wounds that feel like they will never have enough time to heal before the next one arrives.

TWENTY-ONE

ARK

"SHE'S asleep," I say, putting the ointment away. "And honestly, JD, I think she needs to go. We need to take her to the police—"

"What the fuck are you talking about?" JD looks down at me as I kneel on the floor trying to doctor up this girl. "We're not taking her to the police. If she wanted to go, that's where she'd be."

"We can't keep her like this. Someone's been abusing her. Raping her, JD. Holding her prisoner. She ran away."

"Yeah, and we found her. She's put her trust in us. We're not handing her over to the police."

"Her family—"

"Fuck her family. She's here, Ark. And as long as she wants to stay, she can." And then he stands up, cradling her in his arms, and walks towards the door.

"Where the fuck are you going?"

"I'm putting her back in my bed. Where she belongs. If you're not interested, fine with me. But I am."

I stand up and walk back over to my desk and take a seat. Why am I so reluctant with this girl?

Because it reminds you of who you are, my mind is screaming.

And she does. Everything about her reminds me of who I am. Why I'm doing all this. What I've spent the past four years building.

I go back to Photoshopping my images as I listen for sounds from JD's room down the hall. I hear nothing. He never comes back. So nothing is resolved. In fact, things are less resolved now than they were this morning when he left.

I have no idea who this girl is. I have no idea what I'm going to do about it. I don't know if I want to kick JD's ass and lock that girl up in my own bedroom, or kick them both out and pretend my whole world isn't about to flip upside down.

I sit there for a long time, just staring at the photos. I wait for JD to come back so we can work this out, but he never does. I wait for my feelings for this girl to manifest so I can come to terms, but they don't. So eventually I go into the kitchen and make a sandwich, then eat it sitting on the couch staring at the TV.

Finally I have to accept the obvious.

They don't need me to understand each other's anguish. They don't need me to fuck away the sadness. They don't need me to give them permission to abuse themselves with pain.

Because they have each other.

And I have no one.

Eventually I make my way into my bedroom, slip out of my clothes, and fall into bed alone.

But sleep eludes me. Questions run through my mind for hours. Questions and regrets. Anger at being discarded. Frustration at being confused.

I finally get up and make my way into the office to grab my camera, and then I walk down the hallway to JD's room. The door is unlocked and partly ajar. So unlike him before this girl came. The bedside light is still on, flooding them both in a hazy light. Blue is uncovered from the chest up and JD has kicked off all the covers. His leg is tossed over her thigh in a possessive gesture that makes me jealous. And her hand rests on his leg, just over his hip.

He's hard for her, even in his sleep.

I adjust the shutter time for the low light and begin shooting.

JD stirs with the clicking of the camera, and then his eyes open.

I wasn't sure how he'd react, but I was not counting on that grin. "About time you came to your senses, asshole." And then he turns over and hugs her close. Too close, because she whimpers in her sleep when he touches her wounds.

But then, like it's already second nature, he slips his hand under the covers and begins to play with her. The whimpers take on a new tone. One of pleasure.

"Put that fucking camera down and just get in bed, Ark. You know you want to."

He lifts the cover up, revealing the fact that he's got two fingers inside her.

There's no way I'm putting this camera down.

"You always like to watch," JD says, matter-of-factly. "Never want to participate. Just observe and record. But listen to me, brother." JD stops what he's doing to Blue and looks straight in my camera. "You're gonna lose her if you don't give in."

"Give in to what?"

"Us. The three of us, Ark. This is how it's meant to be. You knew it the minute we found her."

"I found her."

"We found her, asshole. A one-second headstart does not

give you the right to call her yours. Because she's ours, Ark. So you have two choices. Get in bed and be a part of it. Or take that camera and get the fuck out of our room."

"You'd choose her over me, just like that?"

"I'm inviting you in. If you say no, don't blame your loss on me."

"What if I don't want to share her? What if I want her all to myself?"

He shrugs. "Too late. She's ours. She wants to be ours. She wants you and me. Deal with it or don't. But it's not going to change."

"I don't want to sleep with you, JD."

"Yeah?" he laughs. "Well, since you're standing in my room naked, with a hard-on, and holding a camera taking dirty pictures of Blue and me, I'm gonna have to call you a liar."

"I want *her*, not you." I snap a picture of him as he kisses Blue on the head and she snuggles into his chest.

"Just get in the bed, asshole. I'm tired." And then he turns out the light.

I walk out the door and go back to my room. My dick is so fucking hard as I lie back down in my own bed.

Fuck that.

I'm not having a ménage relationship with my best friend and this girl.

Fuck. That.

TWENTY-TWO

BLUE

"**B**LUE," JD whispers in my ear.

"Hmmm," I say, relaxed, naked, and enjoying the way he twists my nipple as he kisses my neck. I reach for his dick and get a fistful of denim. "You're dressed already?" Is it even light outside? I open my eyes. It's not.

"I gotta go. I'll be back tonight." And then, before I can gather my senses, he's gone.

The coldness of being alone washes over me immediately. I swing my feet out of the bed just as the front door closes. And even though I run my fastest, my feet slapping on the hard concrete floor, when I open the door to see if he's waiting for the elevator, I get more emptiness.

I close it back up and stand there, my back pressed against the door, my thoughts wild.

Am I alone? I hate being alone. I can't tolerate it anymore. Not after constantly being in the company of others for the past year and a half.

Ark, my mind says. *Go find Ark.*

But I heard that conversation last night when they thought I was asleep. JD extended an invitation and Ark refused.

I try anyway. He said he wanted me, so maybe if JD isn't here, he will let me in his bed.

I tiptoe down the hallway opposite the one that leads to JD's room and stop at Ark's door. It's open a crack, which is the same invitation JD left him last night.

I accept it and walk in. My naked body is shivering from the cold already, my sex throbbing with the need for release.

Ark is naked and uncovered.

I walk around to the empty side of the bed and kneel down on the mattress, waiting to see if he wakes. But he's still. So I slip in next to him and close my eyes. Just this is enough to warm me back up. Just the fact that he's within inches of me is enough to put a damper on my sexual frustration and calm me down.

I can wait for him, I tell myself. I can wait for him to want me. My fingers slip down between my legs and glide past my slit where the wetness of my arousal is waiting.

"I'm awake, you know," Ark says next to me. "And if you think you can hop between us and get what you want each time, you're wrong." He turns over to look at me. "I'm a possessive asshole."

I look for the humor in that, but he's serious.

"So if you want to be fucked by me *and* him, you're gonna wait a long time."

"You already did it once," I remind him. "What's the big deal?"

"Number one, I don't want to share. And neither do you."

"I'm here."

"That's not what I meant."

I search his dark eyes for a moment until the realization hits me. "You want information about me."

"And you seem to be a sex addict."

"So…"

"So?"

"So you'll give in if I do?"

"What will you give me?" he asks.

I huff out a long breath of air. Why won't he just take what I'm already offering?

"I'll spell it out, then. I want to know where you came from. Who were you with the day you ran away?"

I bite my lip and weigh how much I can say.

"Let's play a game, Blue."

I look over at him, confused. What kind of man turns down a naked girl in his bed? And he's not gay, he made it pretty clear he was not interested in JD.

"Twenty Questions. Ever play that game?"

"Of course."

"Let's play now. Think of your first kiss. Picture it in your head. Picture where it was, who it was with, and how it felt. Now tell me about it."

"That's not how you play the game. I think of something and you guess by asking questions. You get twenty in all. That's why it's called Twenty Questions."

He's shaking his head the whole time I'm talking. "No, sorry. The game we're playing, also called Twenty Questions, is played by me asking you twenty questions and you giving truthful answers."

I laugh at him. "That's stupid. It's not a game, it's an interrogation."

He shrugs that off. "Maybe it is, but let's play anyway. Question one, what was your first kiss like?"

I open my mouth to protest, but his finger is suddenly there, tracing my lips. My heart beats faster at his touch. God, I need it. And then he slips it inside and my lips wrap around it automatically.

The throbbing between my legs is back and I'm just about to start masturbating when he withdraws his finger and drags it over my chin, down my neck, and then rides the crest of my breast until he stops on my nipple.

He squeezes it very hard and I arch my back a little.

"You talk, I'll get you off."

I look him in the eyes to see what this is about, but he's stoic. Why is he so closed up? "Why do you want to know that stuff?"

"Because we're going to start from the beginning, Blue. So long as you keep talking, I'll keep touching. And if your story rings true, if you tell me real things, I'll give you what you want."

I swallow hard again. "How do you know what I want?"

"I sell sex, Blue. I can recognize a masochist when I meet one."

"I'm not—"

"You are." He says it definitively, like he knows this to be true. "Maybe you're just realizing it. Maybe you've known it for a long time. But I'm stating the obvious. And I'm gonna go ahead and give you a little warning about JD. He's a lot better at dishing it out than you might expect."

"What's that supposed to mean?"

"It means he can get carried away."

"But not you, right?" I glare at him. "Not Ark, the man in control, right?"

"Not me. You described me perfectly. The man in control."

I let out a long breath and turn away from him. "I want more than a release. If I tell you true things about my past, then I want you to be invested."

"Invested?" He laughs. "You're in my house. You're on the run. You want me and my best friend to give you what you need." I start to protest, but his hand cups my mouth. "Shh," he commands. "You want more than sex, I get it. You want protection. You want a place to hide. You want a place to decompress and understand whatever happened to you. Maybe you want allies?" He stops to watch my face after that declaration. "And we're willing. JD might give it away, but I don't. JD doesn't know what's good for him. I do. So I'm going to take control of this situation and put things in order right the fuck now. You have no idea who he is. You have no idea what he's doing when he leaves here."

I slap Ark's hand from my mouth. "And neither do you, from the sound of it. You didn't know where JD was yesterday."

"You're right," Ark snaps back. "I didn't know where JD was. But I certainly know what he was doing."

The silence hangs there for a few moments.

"And you don't have any idea what you've walked into here with us, Blue. No idea at all."

"So tell me."

"Oh," he laughs. "Now you want answers *and* sex. Well, that's gonna cost you a little bit more than you have right now. So let's just stick to the sex."

I sit up, ready to bolt back to JD's room and get away from this asshole, but he grabs my tit and squeezes. I fall back against the pillow and moan.

And then, just to prove he's got what I need, he flips me over, drags the covers off my bare bottom, and smacks me hard, right across the bruises left over from a few days earlier.

I cry out at that one, but even though I'm ashamed to admit it, my clit is begging for more.

TWENTY-THREE

ARK

"**S**TART talking. Your first kiss happened when you were how old?"

She's in, I can tell. She might hate me right now, but she's in. She needs a release and for some reason, she wants it from me.

"Blue," I prod.

She turns those eyes up at me and blinks. "Seventeen."

My laugh surprises both of us. "What's that about? You were religious? Your teen years consisted of promise rings and youth group?"

"No," she snarls. "I was just *picky*."

"But now you're not?"

"Who says I'm not?'

"You're living with two strangers trying to negotiate with you, using sex as payment."

"JD doesn't want sex as payment. You do. And you have me all wrong anyway. I'm not only after sex."

"Then what else?"

She turns her body towards me slightly. Her hands are tucked under the pillow and it makes her look so innocent. If I didn't know better, I'd think she was just lost and confused. But I know my way around a lost girl. I know my way around an abused girl, too. We work with all kinds of girls, and let me tell you, none of them are in a good place. You don't suck cock for money if you're in a good place.

No. Blue is not like those girls. I can't put my finger on it, but something is very familiar about her.

"I'm not addicted to sex. And I don't enjoy pain. I just like it… a little bit rough."

"Is that how you got your ass beat?" It's a low blow, and her soft expression is immediately hard again. "Is that why your body is so battered right now, you can't even put on clothes?"

"I'm not talking about that. You asked about my first kiss."

"So talk. Where was it?"

"In the back seat of Jimmy Laslos' car."

"Were you coming home from youth group?" I don't smile, but she gets the sarcasm.

"No. I told you, that wasn't why I waited so long."

"Then why did you wait?"

"My best friend was… a bad example. The things she did scared me, so I was afraid to follow in her footsteps."

"Hmm," I say, looking at her closely to make sure she's not lying.

"But Jimmy L, he was very cute. And my dad liked him. And he wasn't a player, like most of the boys in my school. He was loyal. And sweet."

"So what did you see in him?"

She laughs at that. "You think I like the bad ones?"

"You like JD. He's as bad as they come."

"You're his best friend. So what's that say about you?"

"I'm so much worse than him, it's not even fair to compare us."

She huffs out a breath at that admission. "You're trying to scare me by talking bad about yourself."

"Was Jimmy L a good kisser?"

"Yes." She says this with a smile and I know it's true. She liked him.

"So why did you break up?"

"We didn't."

"What?"

Suddenly her demeanor changes and her smile falters. She turns her back to me. "I'm tired of playing."

"You didn't answer all twenty questions, so no playtime."

"I'm over it." And then she sits up like she's gonna get out of the bed.

"Hey," I say, grabbing her by the arm and pulling her back onto the mattress. "You're staying here and you're answering that question."

She closes her eyes and ignores me.

"I tell you what. I'll let you off with only seven if you tell me what happened to you and Jimmy."

"Why do you want to know that?" She turns her head to me, giving me a sideways glance. "So you can make fun of me? So you can use it to control me? Why?"

"So I can begin to figure you out."

"There's no mystery to solve, Ark. I'm just…" She lets out a long breath of air. "I'm just…"

She doesn't finish. And I'm not gonna push. I got a good enough start. "Come here," I say, slipping my hand under her waist and pulling her up to my chest. "You earned this at least. I'm not gonna smack you around to make you come, but I'll keep you warm." She's quiet and still in my arms. I count the seconds and as they tick off, I begin to regret prying into her past. "Good enough for you?"

"He died."

Fuck.

"That's what happened to us. He died of some weird blood disease. I'm not even sure what it was. Something exotic that could be fixed if they caught it in time. But they didn't. We were on spring break our senior year. We had this public service requirement for graduation, so we were in this small town in Arkansas with no hospital. And by the time they realized he needed a real emergency room, it was too late. He died in the ambulance on the way. I was holding his hand when it happened."

I wait for her tears, but they don't come. She's cried twice when JD's fucked her. But admitting that her first boyfriend died holding her hand gets me nothing.

Why? I need to know. I need to know what she's thinking.

She tries to get up but I hold her tight and she gives in, settling back against my chest. I count her breaths and they are even and deep.

Was it a lie?

I don't think so. No, that's not why she's calm. That's not why there are no tears. She's just turned it off. She's a good little liar, but it's not me she's lying to. It's herself.

"You can ask me a question," I whisper. "If you want."

She's silent for so long, I take that as disinterest. And I'm just about to close my eyes and try to fall back asleep when it finally comes.

"Who is the person you love most in this world?"

"That's easy," I tell her. "JD."

"Why?" She turns her body so she can look at me. "Why do you love him if he's a bad guy?"

I shrug. "Because you gotta love someone."

"And he was just there?"

"Yeah, he was just there."

"But now he's more than just there."

"Now he's the only person in this world I can trust. He's the only person in this world worth saving when the shit goes down. He's the only person in this world who won't fuck me over."

"How do you know that, though? How do you know he won't?"

"Because he loves me."

"But you're not gay?"

"Blue, please. It's not the same kind of love."

"Maybe so. But you could try."

"Try what?"

"Try loving us together."

"Why do you need two men?" I ask. "Why isn't he enough?"

"I told you. I don't feel safe unless I'm surrounded."

I give her a little squeeze. "My arms aren't enough for you to feel surrounded?"

She says nothing after that. And it's not so she can think up her answer, it's just because she's got no answer. She doesn't know why she needs us both. JD doesn't know why he wants me to share her. I don't know why I'm refusing.

Principle, I guess. She's mine, anyway. She was mine the moment I saw her.

"I know where JD went yesterday. Where he's going today, too."

She doesn't answer. Maybe she's asleep.

"And it's not good, Blue. I'll share you if that's what you want. But only because JD will never be able to give you what you need."

"How do you know what I need?"

"You already told me. You need Jimmy Laszlio."

"It's Laslos, not Laszlio. And he's dead. So if he's what I need, then I'm good and fucked."

"Not *the* Jimmy Laslos, Blue. But a guy like him."

She thinks about this for a moment. Serious, thoughtful consideration. "A guy who is the complete opposite of you and JD."

"Yup. We're just gonna fuck you up more if you stick around."

"Well, then I look forward to it. A person can never be fucked up enough in my book. My fucked-upness is the only thing I've got going for me at the moment."

I let that settle as the last word on the matter. What do I care, anyway? I've got her in my bed. Naked. I've got my arms around her. I got her to admit something personal. And when the sun comes up in a few hours, I'm going to take enough pictures of this girl to get me through a lifetime of loneliness and regret.

TWENTY-FOUR

BLUE

THE tub slowly fills with water and with each rising inch, the sorrow takes over. Maybe it's just a delayed reaction to the shock of the beating. Or maybe it's the realization that I got away. But I don't think so.

I think the sadness comes from losing hope. From giving up. From surrender. Sadness feeds on reality, that moment when you realize you can't win—not the war, not the battle, not even a street-corner fistfight.

Am I giving up?

Ark's footsteps are soft as he crosses the room. I can see him out of the corner of my eye as he enters the bathroom. "What are you doing?"

I'm taking a bath. But that's not what he means and I know it.

"Don't you think you should go look for him?" I look up at Ark. He stands tall and nude. His dick is long and semi-hard, hanging between his legs. His chest is muscular in a way that tells me he lifts. And his face…

Ark's face is the stuff you masturbate to. His two-day-old beard is hot in a movie-star way. His dark hair and dark eyes don't say dangerous, they say sexy.

He is one of the most handsome men I've ever seen. He is the opposite of JD. And that's not saying JD is ugly. Not at all. JD is charming. And cute. And hot. In all the ways that Ark is not.

They are like night and day. Dark and light. Maybe even good and evil.

"He'll come home on Thursday, for sure." Ark steps into the tub, pushing my body so I lean forward, and then he slips into the water behind me. "He won't miss work."

Who is this man?

How did I get from where I was to where I am?

Why do I constantly have to ask myself this question?

"Did you like school growing up, Blue?"

"You're out of questions. You owe me, I don't owe you."

His laugh makes his chest rumble beneath my back. "You're right. I do. But we've got all day, so let's just talk for now. High school. Yes or no?"

I let out a long breath and try to enjoy the intimacy he's offering. I don't get a lot of offers. "Yes, I liked school."

"Were you smart? Did you get good grades?"

"Yes."

"And what did you want to be when you grew up?"

And there it is. He's pretty good at this, I have to give him credit for that. He's asking questions about the distant past so he can draw conclusions about the present.

"It's not a hard question."

"What did you want to be?" I ask, not to be a bitch and throw it back in his face, but because I'm interested. "King of Public Porn was something you aspired to?"

"Believe it or not, I wanted to be a soldier. A Navy SEAL."

"Hmmm. Tough one. It's like me saying I wanted to be a

novelist." I look over my shoulder a little so I can get a peek at his face. But he surprises me by resting his scratchy chin on my shoulder, making the moment even more intimate than it was.

"Huh. I don't see the connection."

I roll my eyes even though he can't see them. "It's a dream people have. The reality of it is so much bullshit."

"Because it's hard to make it to the finish line?"

"Are you a Navy SEAL?"

"Are you a novelist?"

"No, that's my point. It's just a dream."

"Do you even write?" His hands slide up my front and cup my breasts. He squeezes them hard and the familiar throbbing begins between my legs. Goddamn, this guy is good. Always got his eye on the prize. And how the fuck did sex with him become a treat I desire instead of the other way around? How did he do that? Make me want him so thoroughly?

"Blue?"

I let out a long breath, hoping to calm the rising storm building inside me. But the heat of the water, and the heat of his body, and the heat of my own desire are all I can think about. So instead of evading, and because I want him to fuck me so badly, and at this point I realize he knew that denying me last night would make me even more susceptible this morning... I answer him with the truth. "I do."

"Mmm," he says, his hands rubbing down the inside of my thighs. They dip so low, I can feel the water swirl around my clit.

This makes me gasp a little, and for a fraction of a second, I'm embarrassed. But then the little swirls of water are back and that's all I can think about.

"Fuck me," I whisper.

"What do you write, Blue?" he asks like a man in control.

"Stories," I say, like a woman on the edge of sexual frustration madness.

"Where can I read one?"

"Fuck me."

"If I fuck you, will you let me read one?"

I turn around in the tub and look him in the eyes. They are knowing. Like they know I'm his. "Fuck me like you'd fuck your wife on her wedding night."

"And you'll give me a story?"

I nod. "I promise." It comes out as a whisper.

He leans down and kisses me. His hand cups the side of my face and I turn into him even more. My leg hits his erection and that makes him claim my mouth harder. His tongue pushes inside, searching. Like he's seeking the truth and it can only be found by twining ourselves together.

And then he stands up, his strong arms around me, taking me with him. And he lifts me out of the tub and walks me out of the bathroom. The entire time we're connected by our kiss. My knees hit the back of the bed and I stumble back.

But then his hands have me, and I finish my fall onto the bed in his arms. I pull him closer to me. I need to feel his skin against my skin, his chest against my breasts, our breathing building up to a wave of rising and falling as we stare into each other's eyes.

"Who are you?" I ask.

"I'll tell you when you tell me."

And that ends it. Because we both know we're not who we say we are. He can't be this man who takes advantage of women on the streets and puts their bodies up on the internet. He just can't.

And if he really believes I'm nothing more than a whore who likes to be beaten when she has sex, well, I'd be so disappointed.

"Like my wife on her wedding night?" he asks, changing the subject back.

"Mmm-hmm," I answer.

"Does my wife want it how I'd do it? Or how I think she'd

like it?"

"How you'd do it." I can't stop staring into his eyes. I want to know his secrets. I want him to know mine so bad.

"That's not lust, Blue. That's not sex. It's love."

I swallow hard, but I stay silent.

"Ask for it," he says, still in that sexy whisper. "Ask for it and I'll give it to you. But I want to hear the words."

"Make love to me," I say.

But he shakes his head. "That's not what you want. Tell me what you want."

I expect him to coax it out of me. Maybe tease my pussy or whisper dirty things in my ear. A little bit of coercion to take away the sting of want and longing.

But he doesn't. He goes quiet. His gaze is steady. And his hand, though resting over my mound, ready to proceed, is still.

"Love me," I say, giving him what he wants to hear and telling him what I want at the same time. "Love me."

His smile makes all the vulnerability worth it. And his kiss… he kisses me like he'd kiss his wife on her wedding night. His mouth is soft and hard. His lips are punishing, yet tender. He kisses me like I'm loved.

TWENTY-FIVE

ARK

STUDY her face when I stop kissing her. There's so much more to know. So many more little tidbits of information to ask for. So many more opportunities to claim her in ways that will last far longer than the heat of what we'll do here in my bedroom.

And then I reach under her ass and push her up to the middle of the bed. I open her legs and look down at her pussy. It's wet from the bath as well as her arousal. It's been professionally waxed very recently. I know this because when I sweep my tongue between her folds, it's smooth.

She bucks her back and I take my lips to her belly. It's flat. Too flat. It reminds me she needs to eat more, and that reminds me that we still have a dinner date waiting to be rescheduled.

She wants to be loved.

I want to take her to dinner.

She wants me to kiss her like I'd kiss my wife on her wedding night.

I want to dress her up and put her on my arm.

I crawl up her body, licking her soft skin that smells like my soap, and then stop at her nipple. I rest my mouth over it and she takes a little gasp of air. Like she needs it to tide her over until she can gulp it in. My tongue swirls around, stopping at her peak. And my dick, which is already hard, gets even harder as her nipple bunches together in my mouth.

I tip my head up to see if she's watching, but she's turned her cheek to the side. Her eyes are squeezed tightly closed, and she's biting her lip.

My wife would like it soft.

This girl wants it hard.

And as if she's reading my mind, Blue's fingertips weave through my hair and grab hold. "More," she whispers.

"More what?" I answer her back.

"More of everything."

I want more of everything too. More talking. More questions. More answers. More tension as we wonder what will happen next.

But I don't want it all at once.

And I don't want more *fucking*.

I don't want to take so much that there's nothing left. I don't want to use her up. I want to save her for later.

She arches her back so that her breasts press against my chest. "Please," she says, urging me to continue. "You promised me."

I crawl up her body further and place my hands on either side of her head as I stare down into her face. She turns so she's looking me straight on and she knows she's not going to get what she wants. She's going to get what she asked for.

"Please don't do this," she whispers.

I can see the lust in her eyes. "I'll love you, but you have to let me."

"Fuck me," she says with even more urgency. "I need it, Ark. I really do."

I lean down and kiss her mouth. Her hands are fisting my hair now, trying desperately to pull me closer. I put my knee between her legs and she opens them wider for me. Another small squeak escapes, and again, this makes her pause. She bites her lip and looks up at me. "Now," she says.

"Get yourself off," I tell her. "Put your fingers inside yourself and get yourself off."

"No," she whines. "You said you'd love me like your wife on her wedding night. I want that, Ark. Do it."

I don't even know how to answer her, but I don't have to. Because at that moment, we hear the front door opening.

JD is home.

I flop to the side of Blue and place my hand on her belly as we wait for him to find us. He calls her name a few times and for whatever reason, she doesn't answer.

But he does find us. He walks into the room and sees us on the bed, naked. My dick is hard and her fingers are between her legs. "What's this?" he asks, looking at me.

I shrug. "She wants to be fucked."

"Well." He puts on his charming smile he uses for all the whores on the street. "I can certainly accommodate." His hands go behind his neck and he lifts his shirt over his head in one fluid movement. His bare chest is well-muscled from the gym we frequent, and his biceps flex and contract as he unzips his pants and drops them to the floor. He crawls into the bed on the other side of Blue and swipes a stray piece of hair from her eyes. "What've you guys been doing?" he asks with a wink.

Blue's hand rests on top of mine and she squeezes. It's a request. A plea, maybe. To stay here with them. To be a part of... whatever it is.

"Just getting past the formalities," I tell him.

"Yeah?" he asks with a smile. "So everyone is satisfied? I'm too late for this party?"

"No," Blue says. "We haven't even started."

He leans down, both hands holding her face like he owns her, and kisses her on the lips. It's long. And lingering. And hot as hell. Blue draws up a leg and it hits my hard cock, draining the love I was feeling only moments ago and filling me back up with lust.

I know how bad she's aching. I know she's got a problem that JD will be very happy to accommodate once he figures it out. And I know there's no way in hell I'm gonna walk off and let him have her all to himself.

So I scoot back down to her pussy and take a swipe at it with my tongue. She moans immediately. JD squeezes her tits, which only stimulates her more.

"You want to fuck us both, don't you, Blue? You want to be our house slut?"

"Yes," she tells him back. "Fuck me, JD. Please. Fuck me."

JD gets up on his knees and then looks over at me. "Top or bottom, Ark?"

I get up and walk over to the dresser and pull out a video camera. When I turn back to JD and the little red light is on, he smiles. I take a seat on a chair with a good view and point my camera at them. "You first," I tell him. "Make it dirty."

I watch them fuck. I get it all on camera. JD rams his cock into her so hard she screams. He shoves his giant cock down her throat so far she chokes.

I fist my dick and pump it the whole time. And after he comes on her face, I stand up, hand the camera to JD, flip her over, shove her head into the mattress, and fuck her in the ass until she collapses underneath me.

If she wants it nasty, I can do nasty.

If she wants to be used like a slut, I'm happy to make her dreams come true.

I slap her on the ass. "Thanks, Blue."

And then I go back into my bathroom and get in the shower. Feeling more like a dirty whore than she probably does.

TWENTY-SIX

BLUE

JD is the antithesis of Ark. I knew this from the very first moment my eyes met theirs in the rain.

Ark. Serious. Brooding. Intense.

JD. Charming. Happy. Easy-going.

What am I missing? Because Ark and I have two very different takes on JD.

"You wanna go out for some food, Blue?" JD and I are kicking back on the couch and he's watching some football-related show with his feet up on the steel and glass coffee table. I'm wearing a pair of his boxers and a t-shirt. He's wearing a pair of boxers and nothing else. His chest is warm. I know this because my cheek is resting on it right now. He's clingy. Or maybe I'm clingy and he's accommodating.

Either way, I like it.

I look up at him and it takes him a second to pull his eyes from the TV. "Hmm?" he asks again.

"Not really. Can't we stay in?"

He watches a few more seconds of the program and then it goes to commercial. "You've been cooped up in here for days. Let's go somewhere. Tomorrow we gotta work. So I'll be gone every night until Monday. Let's go grab some beers or something."

I shake my head. "I really don't want to."

He plays with my hair, letting the long blonde strands slip through his fingers before he reaches the end and they fall back against my face. "What if I get Ark to come? Will you go then?"

I shake my head. I like having them both close, but that's not enough to get me to leave this house.

"I'll go grab something," Ark calls out from his office. He's been in there all day doing... whatever it is he does. Website building. Or editing porn. "I gotta go by Ray's anyway."

"Ray's?" JD asks. "Why?"

"He left me a message earlier. Probably about the party on Friday."

"What party?" I ask.

"Halloween, baby," JD says with a smile. "You gotta go out for that one. Ray has a huge thing. We've got our girl scheduled early that night, so you can either come with us, or we'll swing by and pick you up afterward." He turns his attention back to Ark. "Hey, I'll go grab food and talk to Ray. I'm sure it's about the girls we've got lined up this week." He lifts my head up off his chest and slips out from underneath me, jogging down the hallway to his room.

I stare at the empty hallway for a second, thinking about Halloween, when Ark speaks, surprising me. "You want to explain?"

"No, not really," I say with a smile. "You?"

"I'm not the one refusing to leave the apartment."

"I'm not the one encouraging intimacy and then slapping my ass and saying thanks, like I'm some whore you pay to pleasure you."

"We did pay you." He takes a seat in the chair just to the left of the couch and props his foot up on his knee, like he's getting comfortable.

JD appears wearing what I'm starting to think of as his uniform. T-shirt. Jeans, always well-worn and faded. Boots. And a flannel. He stops at the door and slips his black leather jacket on over the flannel and then turns back to us. "Be good, boys and girls. Back in like an hour."

The door opens. Closes. And then Ark and I are alone again.

"My turn. What was your college major?"

I shake my head. "It's not your turn and I'm done with the questions."

"Why?" He stands up and takes a step towards me.

I panic and stand up too, back away from him. "Don't."

He takes another step and I'm about to bolt back into JD's room, but he grips my upper arm firmly and yanks me towards him. I push him off but he squeezes my nipple under the t-shirt and I freeze.

"Why do you like it to hurt?"

"I don't."

He shakes his head at me, all but tsks his tongue in disagreement. "Are you ashamed of it?"

"You seem to be."

"I get the draw. I get the pleasure it can evoke. But what I don't get is why you ran away from it if you like so much." He stops, looking down at me with a very serious expression. "Did you run?" I slump back down on the couch and he lets go of my arm. "Did you?"

"I did."

"Why, then? If that's what you like? If that gets you off, then why run? It was too much? It was forced? It was rape? Or you agreed and got in over your head? Which of those is true?"

I fold my hands in my lap and it takes every ounce of control not to physically wring them together. "All of that."

"Did you agree to the branding?"

"Yes."

"Do you know who these people are?"

"Yes."

"Are you going to protect them?"

I look up at him, perplexed. "From who?"

"From us."

"What are you gonna do?"

"It's up to JD."

"I thought he was unstable? I thought he was unpredictable and violent? Isn't that what you want me to believe?"

"He is all those things, Blue. You need to accept that as truth. But he's not gonna let this go. He'll keep disappearing like this until he finds what he's looking for."

"He went out for food."

Ark shakes his head. "No. He's out now because he's compulsive. He needs to look for her. And she's dead, Blue. We found her grave about two years ago. So what's he looking for?"

I narrow my eyes at him. "Why are you asking me all this? Why do you care? What if my situation isn't what you think? What if I'm not involved in what you're looking for?"

"You are." Ark says it like it's a fact and not a guess. "What's he looking for?"

"Isn't that your department? You're the JD expert."

"He's looking for the people responsible for the death of that girl he knew. And he knows you came from them. Do you really think he's just playing house with you for the fun of it? He's using you to get information. And right now, you can bet your life he's not getting us food. Or on his way to talk to Ray. We might as well just start making our own dinner right now, because he's checked out for the night."

"Then why do you let him leave?"

"I'm not his fucking mother. I'm his roommate. I'm his business partner. I'm his best friend. But I can't tell him what to do."

"What do you want from me, Ark? Because I really have no idea what you're talking about."

"I don't know why we found you there the other morning, but none of this is good. For any of us."

"So pay me what you owe me and I'll leave."

Ark laughs. "You think JD's gonna let you get away? You're the only clue he's found in four years of searching. You're here. You're part of it now. And maybe you don't know what I'm talking about. But I'm guessing you do. So I'm telling you this as a favor."

"Is that right?" I snarl. "You're gonna do me a favor? Does that come before or after you break down my defenses and take advantage of me?"

"You walked right into it, Blue. I make a living off taking advantage of girls. We," Ark stresses, "make a living off taking advantage of girls. What makes you special?"

"You're serious?" I stand up but he pushes me back against the couch cushions.

"Sit the fuck down. Because on the off chance that JD *is* out getting food and shooting the shit with Ray about this week's whores, I'm gonna make sure we've got this straight before he gets back."

My heart starts beating like crazy and then my whole body breaks out in a sweat.

"Good," Ark says, noticing my reaction. "You're starting to understand me. Because I'm deadly serious, Blue. You've got two choices." He leans down into my face. "Right here. Right now. Stick it out with us and be part of the solution. Or get the fuck out of my house. Take your whore money, get on a bus tonight, and never come back."

I spit right in his face.

And I'm face down on the floor. He's got my arm twisted behind my back, and I'm screaming in pain.

"Don't fuck with me," he growls down in my ear. His body is pressed against mine, his knee between my legs, touching my pussy.

I moan.

"You like it like this. You want me to love you this way, Blue."

"Fuck you. How dare you talk all that shit to me earlier and then throw it back in my face."

"How dare you ask me to love you and then slip right into JD's arms."

"So you're jealous?"

"Why would I be jealous? I can take you right here on the floor and he'd never know. Because you'd like it and you'd never tell him. You're not gonna leave, are you? You want this fucked-upness, don't you?" My chest is rising and falling so fast, I begin to get dizzy. Ark pulls my hair. "Tell me," he demands. "Say it. Just admit you're in."

"I have no idea what you're talking about."

"You're in, Blue. You're gonna let us fuck you. You're gonna stay here and be our little fuck toy. And you're gonna tell us what we want to know." He pulls my hair again and this time I feel the wetness gush between my legs.

He pulls my boxers down and palms his hand over my ass. "Oh, God," I moan.

"Go ahead, fight it, Blue. Fight all you want." He slips his fingers between my legs. Not enough to penetrate me, even though my throbbing clit is begging for it. Just enough to check how turned on I am.

His zipper comes down and then his cock is pressed between my ass cheeks.

"Let's make a deal, Blue. I'll let you stay here, and we'll take turns feeding your addiction. And you'll answer my questions. You will not talk to JD about any of this. You will go on acting like everything is fine. But you will tell me the truth. Every answer you give needs to be the truth."

His tip pokes against my asshole and I bite my tongue to stop my urge to beg, that's how badly I need him inside me right now. "OK," I whisper. "OK."

"Good," he says, slipping his dick down my crack. "Then I'll repeat the next question. What was your college major?"

"Why does that matter?"

He withdraws and leaves me empty. "Answer me," he growls, pulling my hair so hard my whole body arches. I have to tip my head so far back, I find myself looking up at his face. "Answer. Me." And then his mouth crashes down on mine. He kisses me hard, bites my tongue, bites my lip, draws blood, and sticks his cock back between my ass cheeks in less time than it takes me to take a breath.

Or maybe I just forgot how to breathe.

"English," I whisper into his mouth as he continues to kiss me. "It was English."

He thrusts his hips and then sinks himself inside my pussy. All the way. I can feel his balls move against my clit. "Love me," I moan.

"I plan on it," he says.

But then he releases my hair, my head falls down to my chest, and he gets up off the floor, extending his hand for me to accept it.

I turn my body around so I can see his face. "What are you doing? Don't you dare leave me like this."

He holds his hand out for a few more seconds and when I don't accept, he withdraws it. "Oh, I'm leaving you like this, Blue. You want it rough, you get that from JD. You want me to love you?" He takes a deep breath, like he needs courage to get the words out. "Well, you come find me when you get to that place. I'm in for the love, but not for the abuse."

He turns and walks down the hallway that leads to his room. And a few seconds later, I hear the click of the lock.

Which, in my book, is nothing but a big fuck-off.

TWENTY-SEVEN

ARK

"LET'S make a deal, Ark." Ray is sitting at his bar and Silvie is getting him a drink. She passes him a Scotch and me a beer. Ray waits for me to pop the cap and take a long gulp. "You do understand I will buy you out eventually, right?" He takes a slow sip from his glass, the ice cubes clinking together.

"Maybe," I say, enjoying some time away from JD and Blue. JD came back last night. It was late. And he had no food. Just an excuse about getting hung up over here at Ray's. I had my ear to the bedroom door to hear that lie, because he'd never tell me that. Not when he knows I'll ask Ray straight out if he came by.

Which JD didn't. I asked Ray anyway, as soon as I got here.

"There's no maybe about it, son." I hate it when Ray calls me son. Not because he's a dick. I like Ray. He's a good guy. I think he'd have been a good father if he'd ever had kids. But because I'm not sure he means it. It makes me long for our relationship to be more than business. He treats me like family, sure. But am I family? Or am I just an opportunity? "You and I both know that as soon at Public Fuck is up and running, I'm gonna make an offer. So let's just do it up front."

I shake my head. "You'll shut it down. And I've worked too hard and too long to just shut it down."

"Twenty-five million," he says, calm as they come. "Sell it to me pre-launch and I'll give you twenty-five for it."

I swallow hard at that offer. I had no idea he was so interested. But I shake my head automatically. There is no way I can take an offer. Not after all the filth I've participated in to get this far in the game. This is all I've got left. My one and only chance at salvation is sticking it out until it's over. And even though I feel that we are close, it's not over yet. I couldn't bail even if I wanted to.

"Why?" he asks. "We both know you don't belong in this world. You're a photographer, Ark. Get out while you're still young. Go do something legitimate."

"This is legitimate, Ray. It might not be honorable, but it's definitely legitimate."

"You know what I mean. Porn? Really? You want to waste your life selling porn?"

"How is it a waste? It works well enough for you."

He takes another swig of his Scotch and looks over at Silvie, who is chatting with one of the bouncers. There's no one else down here in the entertaining area except us. But that's because it's not open yet. Wednesday night is Swingers. I know Silvie gets shared with no one, but Ray takes his pick of women on Swingers' Night.

And that makes me think of Blue. Why the fuck should I share her?

Because she likes JD better than you, Ark, my inner voice says.

Maybe she does. But that's because she really has no idea what's going on. If she knew...

"It's good enough for me, son, because I'm forty-eight years old and this is all I know. You're what? Twenty-seven? You've got time. You can sell this shit off, take the money, and go try your hand at something more... *honorable*, as you put it."

"But why would I want to, Ray? This business is a cash cow. It's easy fucking money."

Ray looks at me with sympathy. "You know why I never had kids?"

I shake my head no.

"Because this is no way to raise a family. If you choose this life, Ark, you're gonna end up alone. And you're the closest thing I have to a son. So I don't want that. Take the money. Get out of Denver. Go somewhere warm. And settle into a normal life. Come back for holidays and shit. Like kids do. But get out, man. I mean it."

"I can't," I say, looking away and taking a drink of my beer. "I'm in too deep. We're too far along."

"JD isn't gonna last, Ark. You know this. He's on a one-way trip to crazy. He's obsessed with that girl again—"

"Has he been here talking?" I wonder if he's mentioned Blue.

"No," Ray says in a low whisper. "But he's asking questions again, Ark. And I've already told you. People are getting suspicious. They don't want to talk about the shit he's bringing up. And since everyone knows you're partners, they shut up about it. But that doesn't mean they forget. And that doesn't mean they'll just let it go." Ray gives me one of those warning looks, with the single raised eyebrow and a sidelong glance.

"I'll talk to him."

"You better do more than talk to him."

I nod again, but I stare down at my drink, wondering just how far this will go. How fucked up this will get. How much I'm gonna lose.

"You coming for Halloween?" Ray asks, changing the subject.

"Nah," I say. Blue won't agree to a party. I know that for sure.

"Probably not."

"JD is. He said so last week."

"Well, things have changed since then. So if he doesn't show up…" I let my words trail off.

"Got it." And then Ray gets up and walks over to Silvie, planting a quick kiss on her cheek as he slips his arm around her waist. I know he loves her. He might fuck other women, but he always goes home to Silvie. And if it works for her, who am I to judge?

"Thanks for the beer, Ray." I get up and start towards the door. It's late now and I've been out all day, trying to avoid Blue. I want to fuck her brains out, but I refuse to give in to her. I refuse to play along with her and JD in this sick arrangement they're cooking up. No matter how much I want to, I just can't do it.

"You have girls lined up this week?" Ray calls out, just as I reach the door.

"Yeah," I call back, opening it and walking through. "We're good." And then I close the door behind me and take the stairs to the roof to my waiting Jeep. I have to go home sometime. And if I'm being honest, I want to see that girl so bad, I can't stay away any longer.

The drive back is too short and before I know it, I'm on my way up the elevator. It dings on the top floor and I get out and stand there. Staring at our door.

What did they do all day?

My jealousy is suddenly overwhelming as I picture the many, many ways in which Blue got fucked hard by JD. Why does she like it rough? Why? She responded to me when I was gentle. But if it's not enough, then why fight JD for her? Would it really be worth ruining what I have with him just to get exclusive rights to a girl who can't be satisfied with the way I want to love her?

Ray says to get out and start a life. But right now all I want is Blue. And she's not even remotely interested in giving up what she likes. So why should I waste four years of planning and hard work? Why give up my one chance at making a difference, just to get away and be alone again?

I push my key into the lock with this thought lingering in my mind. It's quiet inside and the lights are low. I toss my keys onto the little table in the foyer and that's when I see the video camera. "What is this doing here?"

"Start filming, cameraman."

I look into the dark living room, lit only by firelight flickering off to the left, and see JD sitting on the couch. The coffee table has been moved out of the way, and at his feet—naked and with her head resting on his thigh, staring straight at me—is Blue.

"What the fuck are you doing?" I ask them.

"Waiting for you. Now pick up the camera and start filming."

"Why?" I look down at Blue and she meets my gaze for a second, but then quickly closes her eyes and buries her face between JD's legs.

"We wanna make a sex tape." JD says this like he might say we're going out for dinner. "Blue's on board."

"She's got no identification, JD. We can't use her." The whole thought of putting her on Ray's site just repulses me.

"No, you dumb fuck," JD laughs. "A sex tape, asshole. For fun. We're not gonna sell her. We're gonna fuck her." And then he smirks up at me as I walk towards them. "On camera."

I just stare at them. "We?"

JD nods to the chair off to the left of the couch. "Turn the camera on, sit down, and enjoy the show." And then he pets Blue on the head and looks back to me. "Dude," he says, losing his patience. "I've been waiting for you all damn day. My dick is hard, her mouth is watering, and I want to come down her throat. So turn the fucking camera on."

And now *my* dick is hard.

I walk over to the chair and ease myself down, camera on,

and pointing at Blue's mouth as she licks her lips.

"Three, two, one… action," JD whispers.

Blue's tongue darts out and begins to lick him through his jeans. Her mouth opens wide, covering the thick bulge in his pants, and then she bites down a little, chomping playfully along his full length.

JD moans. Hell, I moan. My hand goes to my own bulge in my pants and I begin to rub. The camera shakes a little from my motions. JD notices me worrying about it, but then he nods his head to the fireplace mantel. I look over to my left and see the camera. Then across from me, on a wall shelf, I spy another one.

"I've got them all over." He presses a button on the remote in his hand and the lights come up, just enough to make an atmospheric movie.

They've certainly put a lot of thought into this little setup.

The sound of a zipper being pulled down yanks me back to my reality. Blue's got the little tab by her teeth and she's pulling it down to reveal a trail of hair leading to JD's cock. She licks the little bit of skin that is exposed by the open zipper, and then her small hand reaches in and pulls him out.

His cock is hard and long. I've seen hundreds of girls exclaim delight at the sight of JD's dick, and Blue is no different. She moans as her mouth covers his tip. I pan the camera up to JD and catch him closing his eyes to appreciate her attention.

I unbutton my jeans and reach inside to grab myself, but the slurping noise from Blue's blowjob directs my attention back to her. JD's hand clamps down on her head, forcing her to take him deep. She struggles for a moment, then her jaw opens wider and she breathes hard through her nose. "That's a girl," JD says, encouraging her to keep his cock in her throat. He bucks his hips a few times, essentially choking her, but she holds steady until he pulls her head back by her hair and the saliva spills out of her mouth in a long strand. I lean to the right in my chair to try to get her face on camera. She's looking up at JD with wide blue eyes. Waiting for a command, or a pat of reassurance. Or more likely, a slap for some made-up disobedience.

JD leans down and kisses her and then he snaps a leash onto a leather collar I just now notice she's wearing.

My jealousy rages again.

Not because I was wrong in all three of my predictions, but because I can see it now.

He's fucking falling for her, just like I am, and this action says he's claiming her for himself.

I'm just about to put the camera down and walk out when he looks me in the eye. "Blue," he says, staring at me. "Ark needs some attention too." He holds the end of the leash up to her mouth and she bites on it. "Crawl over there like a good girl and suck him off."

I don't get up. I don't put the camera down. I don't tell her, *No, this is degrading.*

I sit absolutely still. My camera remains focused only on her. And if I thought my dick was hard a second ago, I had no idea what hard really is. Because it feels like concrete right now.

"Yes, sir," Blue tells JD, through the leash, clenched between her teeth, as she looks up into his eyes.

And then she turns her face towards me. And the look I was trying to capture a second ago is right there.

Complete trust.

Insatiable lust.

And so many, many things that will need to be discussed, I cannot even begin to imagine how fucked up this is about to get.

Because I know what this is. A truce. An offering. And the beginning of a new way forward in our relationship.

A threesome taken to the extreme. A *ménage à trois* in the truest sense of the word. A household of three. A partnership and understanding that we are one.

But I can't think about any of that right now. Because Blue is on all fours, crawling across the hard floor, a black leather leash between her teeth, with her eyes trained on me. She maneuvers herself between my open legs and scoots up as close as she can get. Her breasts heave up and down with her breathing, and then she lifts her head and waits for instructions.

I just stare at her.

"Take the leash, Ark," JD prods.

I wait for her to say something, but she stays quiet. Moments pass. I can hear my heartbeat as I try to think of the consequences of going all in like this. But they are too far away at the moment. Right now all I see are her eyes. Her tits rubbing against my crotch. Her soft mouth curved around the leather.

She places her hands palm down on my thighs, their warmth radiating deep down into my own skin, and she tips her head up even higher. Urging me to take her leash and command her.

"I won't hurt you," I say. "I'm not going to play that game."

"That's what I'm for," JD says from the couch. When I look over at him, he's busy jerking off. His hand is wrapped tightly around his cock, and he's pumping at a good clip as he watches us. "Don't worry, Ark. She likes it both ways."

I am even more turned on by his words than I am by her nakedness. So I look down at JD's offering and take the leash from her mouth. "You're mine." She nods.

"She's ours," JD corrects. "*Ours.*"

I look at him. "OK."

JD gets up off the couch and walks the few paces over to us. He kneels down, one hand on his dick, the other on the back of Blue's neck. And he leans into her ear to say, "Take his cock in your mouth, darling." And then his hand wraps around my dick and he tugs on me. I'm so surprised, I don't react right away. My cock is so unused to the feeling of another man's hand on it. I moan.

I'm just about to rip into JD for touching me like that when Blue's mouth covers my head and begins to suck. JD pumps me as her tongue twirls around my tip. I lean back into the chair, extending my legs out more, pushing myself into Blue. And then JD lets go and begins to take off his clothes. I'm still trying to figure out what's going on when his shirt goes over his head, revealing his well-muscled chest and the shadows that play along the length of his stomach, outlining his six-pack.

I open my mouth to ask him what the fuck he's doing, but before I can, he fists Blue's hair and pushes her head down onto my cock. She takes me into her throat, just like she did JD a few moments ago.

And I lose my train of thought. The next thing I know, JD's dick is swinging up near Blue's cheek. She turns her head, grabs him with a greedy fist, and then shoves his head up to her mouth, letting me fall out a little bit. She pumps us both, her mouth eager to try to fit every bit of cock she can inside it. JD moves close. He's standing over me, my thigh between his legs, his balls bouncing against the sensitive skin near my cock. "Climb on him, Blue," he says in a deep throaty voice I've never heard before. "Sit on his dick, baby."

Blue looks at me as she rises. Her leg comes over mine and her knee settles on the chair, next to my hip.

"Keep filming," JD says, pointing a camera down at me.

I'd totally forgotten about the camera in my hand, but now that I remember, I need every moment of this on film. I need to be able to watch this over and over and over again once we're done.

Blue drapes another leg over me, positioning the entrance of her pussy over my tip. I reach up and knead my fingers through her long blonde hair and pull her face close to mine until we bump our heads. "You sure about this, Blue?"

She looks down at me, meeting my gaze. And then she nods.

THREE TWO ONE

"I am," she says in a soft whisper. "I've never been so sure of something in all my life. I want you both. I'll do anything to have you."

TWENTY-EIGHT

BLUE

CAN feel a sigh escape from Ark. His chest falls with it and so do his eyes. He's thinking, *Should I do this*? He's asking himself what the consequences will be.

JD and I have discussed it all day. And we both knew Ark would not automatically be on board. Even sitting here, my pussy positioned over the tip of his cock, he's not ready to say yes.

"I want you, Ark," I tell him softly. "I want you and I don't want you to change for me. I want what you're offering."

His eyes dart up and seek me out. That is what he wants to hear. Needs to hear. That his desires are legitimate. That maybe love can grow out of the sex, if we all get what we need. JD wants to make me submit. I want to feel the pain of pleasure. Ark wants to control.

It works. It will work, I know it.

"Please, Ark," I beg. "Take me the way you want me."

He looks up at JD now, this time taking a deep inhale. "I

don't know, dude."

JD places his warm hands on my chilled shoulders and squeezes. "What's to object to? I like it my way. You like it your way. She likes it both ways. We got sex, and lust, and maybe even love. What's confusing about it?"

Ark squints his eyes with disapproval at JD's words. "You're my best friend. You're my business partner. You're my roommate. And now you want to be my lover?"

JD shrugs. "So?"

Ark pushes me off him, sending me into JD's arms, and then he pulls up his pants and walks towards his bedroom.

"Hey, asshole!" JD jogs after him, catching him by the shirt. Ark pushes him off, and they stand there, chest to chest, like men do when they feel the need to flex their testosterone.

"Don't touch me. You think you can just start shit like this and say fuck the consequences? You think you can just play with everyone's emotions? How far has that gotten you in the past, JD?"

"Fuck you," JD says, giving Ark a push to the chest that sends him back a step. "Don't throw the past up in my face. That's just your chickenshit way of avoiding the real issue here."

"Which is what?" Ark growls, giving JD a push back.

"You just don't want to be invested. You don't want to get your feelings hurt. You don't want to have to compete with me. Hell, that's probably the reason you never fuck on camera—"

"I got my dick sucked off on camera this week, didn't I? I was the one who got our quota in on time this this week, wasn't I?"

"Congratulations. You used some ex-whore girlfriend to meet the contact. So what? I don't know who that bitch is. After four years, I still don't know who that bitch is. Why is that?"

"What's this got to do with now? Today? Blue? Me? You?"

JD takes a step forward, but his shoulders drop a little and his head turns a little, giving him the appearance of backing down as he gets closer. "You hide, Ark. You're hiding. Whatever it was that made you leave Florida and come to Colorado, it's still chasing you. And you're hiding. You're hiding behind a camera. Behind a computer. You're hiding behind me, Ark. And you want Blue, just as much as I want Blue. And yet you're gonna use me to push her away. You don't like the kinky stuff, Ark? Is that what you want her to believe?"

"That's not what I told her," Ark snaps.

All this is news to me, so I get to my feet. Ark has secrets. And I'm very interested in knowing about them.

"I told her I'm not into abuse. She likes the pain. You like inflicting it. I'm not on board with that and I won't look the other way."

I place my hand on Ark's bicep. He's hot with anger, or desire, or maybe even frustration. Because he's conflicted. I need to know what's conflicting him.

"You want to control her, just like you want to control me."

Ark clenches his jaw and rage fills his eyes.

"You want to tell her how to dress and how to fuck. You want to give her rules and limits and parameters."

"To keep her safe. You want to slap her around and make her cry."

"To keep her happy," JD retorts back.

They stare at each other, JD naked, Ark clothed. Both men are still very hard. This is definitely turning them on. So I reach down and grab them both by the cocks. They look at me, surprised. Like they forgot I was here. "Don't you want to know what I want?"

They just stare.

I look at JD first. "I don't know why I need it, JD. I don't know why the rough stuff turns me on. All I know is that I can't help myself when it starts. That stuff... it's exciting." I look at Ark next. "Not always in a good way. I know it's something I've been conditioned to because of…" I choose my words carefully. "Because of the arrangement I just came out of. But I can't help that, Ark."

"Blue," he says, placing his palm over my cheek. "You just need to experience love without violence, that's all."

"I know," I admit. "I want to do that with you."

"But you won't give up the pain?" His look of disappointment almost crushes me. I really do think he cares. I really do think he wants to offer me a way forward.

"JD is a good guy. You know this. You love him. He's your friend. He's a huge part of your life. And you trust him. Trust him with me."

"Why the fuck should I share?"

"Because," JD says calmly. "Because you, of all people, understand the idea of short-term sacrifices for long-term results."

I begin to pump them slowly. Both men look at me, then each other. "Just join us, Ark," JD says. "Just stop trying to control things and let it happen. One time, man. That's it. One time, right now."

"I'm not gay, JD. I'm not interested in fucking you in the ass."

JD chuckles. "I'm not either, asshole. But I'm open to"—he looks down at me, then back up at Ark—"experimenting."

"I'm not open to experimenting, either."

I get in my knees and take Ark in my mouth, still pumping JD's cock. Ark watches me for a few seconds as I twirl my tongue around his tip, thrusting it into the small opening. This makes him inhale sharply and then JD pushes on my head and guides me to take him deeper.

"You like that, though?" JD asks him. "You like when I tell her to suck you off? When I push her to give you a little more. When I"—he drags a fingertip down my cheek and cups my chin. Then, a moment later, he's cupping Ark's balls—"when I help you along a little, right? Make it feel a little bit better. Make you come a little bit harder." JD crouches down and pulls my face aside, his lips claiming me. But gently. So very, very gently. He kisses me like we're in love, his tongue twisting against mine, his breath soft and even, one hand in my hair, one hand still cupping Ark's balls. And then he bites my lip and slides his mouth over. Just enough to brush his cheek against Ark's hard length.

"Fuck," Ark moans. "Dude, don't—"

But it's too late. JD turns his head and opens his mouth and there's no way his tongue isn't going to lick.

Ark's tip disappears inside JD's mouth, and then reappears just as fast. JD stands up and guides my head back to work. I suck on Ark like none of that happened. But I know the men are staring each other down right now.

"You liked it. You know you did." JD is confident. As am I. Because we both know that was hot as fuck.

Ark answers with a long exhale and it says a million things. It says he's turned on. It says he wants more. It says he's unsure of what just happened, but he is sure he likes it.

It says yes.

I let his dick slide out of my mouth and then I stand. I take each of them by the hand and start walking to Ark's bedroom. They both follow in silence.

When we get there JD flicks on the small bedside table lamp, climbs on the bed, lies down, and starts masturbating. Ark squeezes my hand as we both watch him. "Come on, cameraman." JD nods to the dresser where he's set up a camera that faces the bed. Then another one on the bedside table. "I'm ready for my closeup."

Ark and I both burst out laughing, and JD gives us one of those crooked smirks he uses when he knows he's being appreciated for what he does best. Charming people.

"I'm serious, asshole," he continues. "I want lust, Ark. I want sex. I want it all ways. I want it on film so I can watch it tomorrow. I want passion, and sweat—"

"And love," I say, cutting him off and looking up at Ark. "I want love. I want it all ways too. I want the pain and the pleasure. I want the good and the bad. I want the light and the dark."

JD and I wait Ark out as he looks between the two of us. "It's never going to work," he finally says.

"Why?" JD prods. "What's so complicated about this? Two best friends who can always find mutual ground. One pretty girl who wants us both. It's the trifecta, Ark. We just went to the races, made a one-dollar bet, and came home ten thousand dollars richer. We won the fucking lottery, man. Why would you ever turn this down?"

"Because, JD. Not everything should come in threes. It's never going to work."

"What needs to work? We have sex together, end of story."

Ark still wavers. I know he's in. I know he won't walk away. Not after all this. He might walk away tomorrow, or next week, or next month… but he's not walking away today.

It's just, he needs to rationalize this in his mind before he gives up control. And from what JD says, control is his thing.

"Where does she sleep?"

"We'll sleep in here."

"We?"

"The three of us," JD explains. "If we're in, we're in. We're together. We're a… a… trio. Not one, not two, but three. We can sleep in here. Or we can sleep in my room. Who cares? We'll be having mind-blowing sex and then we'll fall asleep. Just like everyone else. And it's getting pretty fucking late, asshole. So take his clothes off, Blue. And get your asses in here so we can fuck."

Ark is smiling when I look up at him and I know we've won. That was it. That's all he needed. Just some straight talk between them to set the ground rules.

JD wants fun.

Ark wants commitment.

And I want both.

I reach for the bottom button on Ark's white dress shirt. It's not tucked in. It never is, from what I've seen. I unbutton him from the bottom up and when I get to his blue tie hanging loosely around his neck in that unkempt bad-boy businessman kind of way, I lift it off and toss it on the ground. He peels back his shirt, revealing a chest that is muscled to perfection. The ridges and dips that make up the landscape of his abs are shadowed perfectly to show off his impressive physique.

I expect to have to lead him over to JD, but he surprises me by swinging me up into his arms and walking me across the room to the bed. He places me gently down next to his best friend, and then kneels in front of me, opening my legs and positioning himself between them.

"You're sure?" he asks.

"I am," I say.

And then his eyes dart to JD and he nods. "OK. But we keep it open and we keep it respectful."

JD gets on his knees too, but he lifts my back up a little and positions himself behind me, grabbing my tits a little rougher than he should, just to show Ark he's got his own ideas about respect.

But Ark is staring at my pussy now. It's so fucking wet. I've wanted this all day. JD didn't touch me as we made our preparations to seduce Ark. He left me wanting and I am nothing but a sloppy wet vessel of want right now.

"Hold her open for me, JD," Ark says.

I almost come right there.

JD's hands leave my breasts and grab me under my knees, hiking my legs up so my ass is lifted a little off the bed.

And then Ark dives in. He buries his face in my folds. His

tongue licks me from seam to seam. His fingers push inside, stretching me—slipping around inside as he searches for my pleasure spot.

He finds it and I arch my back, pulling away from JD's hold. I get a sharp bite on the shoulder for that. "Be still, Blue," JD growls in my ear. "You're gonna come hard tonight. And you're gonna do it more than once."

His dirty talk, combined with Ark's talented tongue and fingers, has me writhing even more. "Fuck me," I whisper. "Just fuck me now and we can play afterward."

JD reaches under my ass and lifts me up so he can slide all the way underneath me. His hard cock presses between my ass cheeks, seeking me out. Ark backs off a little, his eyes never leaving the action happening down below, as JD positions his dick at my puckered asshole.

"Get her wet for me," JD asks him quietly.

Ark responds by pumping his fingers in my pussy a few times and then dragging my slick juices down to my ass. He inserts his finger, parting the muscles and making me cry out.

But I love it. The pain is gone too soon, and the channel is wet and ready when JD positions his cock and thrusts himself inside me.

"Oh, yes," I moan. It's pain, but it feels so good. He stretches my ass and then he's in far enough to get past the constricting muscles and make them relax.

Ark scoots in closer, pumping his cock.

"Camera," I say. "Get the camera."

"Fuck the camera," Ark says. And then he slaps my clit with his dick, making me squeal. A moment later and he's inside me too. They fill me up. JD pumps slowly from below. Ark thrusts in from above. His chest comes down on top of mine, and then he leans into my ear and whispers so low I can barely hear him over the panting of lust, "I want you."

I don't have time to tell him back, or say he's got me, or anything because JD's fingers reach around and find my clit. And that's all it takes. I clench down, making both men grunt and moan from the pressure, and the three of us come together.

One long, simultaneous outpouring of release that hits me so hard, my head spins.

After a few moments of heavy panting JD grabs my tit and squeezes, just as Ark collapses on top of us.

"Get off! You dick!" JD says next to my ear.

Ark rolls over and collapses against the pillow as JD shifts me to the side and hooks his leg over mine, pulling me into his arms. "Don't move, darling," he says, still out of breath. "Just stay right there."

I look over at Ark and I know he's annoyed with JD's claiming leg move. He rolls his eyes and starts to turn his back to us. But I reach out and grab his hand and bring it to my lips. "Come closer," I say, kissing his fingers. I slide my lips around them and suck for a moment.

His eyes light up with his smile. "You're a dirty girl, Blue."

I remove his fingers from my mouth. "They taste like me."

He withdraws his hand, but scoots over just enough to let me cuddle up to his bicep.

And that's an offer I can't refuse. It's a monumental step forward on his part. Letting the three of us sleep together—in his bed—well, it's more than JD and I ever hoped for when we set this all up before Ark got home.

TWENTY-NINE

ARK

WAKE up smelling like sex.

Blue's warm body against mine feels so right, I wrap my arms around her and pull her close. "Where's JD?"

"Shower," she mumbles into my chest.

I open my eyes and check the clock. Eight AM. "Where the fuck is he going?"

"To get breakfast, he said."

Fucking JD. "Move over, Blue. I gotta go see what he's doing."

I swing my legs over the side of the bed and put my face in my hands and try to come to terms with how my life might be changing before my eyes. I'm still naked and I had a threesome with my best friend and a girl I want so bad, it's making me crazy.

In all four years I've been here in Denver, never before have I put my goals at risk. Until now. I've always had one eye on the prize. I might've taken my time about it but I never walked away from my original goal.

Is this walking away? Will I risk everything just to have this relationship on terms we can all agree to?

Is she worth it?

I look over my shoulder and find her sleeping again. Her mouth is open slightly and her chest is rising and falling in a slow, even rhythm.

She's worth it.

I don't know why, I just know this girl is the one. And if I have to play house with JD for a little while to keep her, I will.

I stand up and walk over to my clothes on the floor, drag my jeans on, and go looking for JD. I didn't see him getting up at sunrise, that's for sure.

I knock on his door and it opens a crack. "Come in," he calls.

"Where the fuck are you going?" I ask, annoyed.

"Get some chow. You got a request?" He pulls a t-shirt over his head and then pulls a clean flannel off the hanger in his closet.

"We can all go together."

He shakes his head. "Nope. Blue said she's not leaving the apartment."

"What? Like today?"

"No, like ever. She says she has some phobia about going outside."

"What? This has gone on long enough. That's bullshit—"

"Hey," he says, putting his hands up. "I'm just telling you what she told me. So I'm gonna go out and grab some food and I'll be back in half an hour."

"Let's make food."

He stops, his foot halfway inside his boot, and shoots me a wink. "You mean like a family?"

"Fuck off."

JD resumes putting his boots on and then works on buckling his belt before looking back to me. "I'm fine, OK?"

"I don't believe you."

"Well"—he tucks his wallet into his back pocket—"who cares? I don't need your permission to go out and get breakfast. I don't need your permission to go out and do shit you think I'm doing when I'm not." He stops again, looking me in the eyes. "I'm not doing that. So if that's what you think, fuck you."

And then he walks out of the bedroom and I listen to his boots clunk along on the floor until he opens the front door and slams it closed behind him.

I walk back to my room and get back in bed with Blue.

"What was that about?"

"Nothing," I say, pulling her close to me again. I like the way she smells right now. It's a mixture of the three of us. "I need to take you to the clinic today. Get some pills."

"No," she says, very firmly.

"What do you mean no? I came inside you. You're not on any birth control. We need to be more careful, so that involves a trip to the clinic."

"I'm not leaving."

Hmmm. So it is true. She's confining herself inside. "Why not?"

She turns in bed so she's facing me. "I panic when I have to go outside. That's why when you found me, I was all shaky and out of breath. I was trying to hide under that awning, to make the space close in on me. I need closed spaces."

Well, that's interesting. "How am I supposed to take you out to dinner?"

She laughs. "What?"

"Dinner. I have those clothes for you, remember? We were gonna go to dinner the other night and we got sidetracked. So if you don't leave the house, I can't take you out."

She studies my face intently. Like she's trying to decide if I'm serious.

I am. So she's convinced. "I can cook."

OK, that's all I needed. She's not unreasonable. She's scared of something. I highly doubt she has agoraphobia, but I do believe she has a good reason for wanting to stay in.

She doesn't have a fear of leaving the house. She has a fear of getting caught. It's just, I can't figure out what she's afraid of getting caught for. Was she raped? It seems possible with all the marks on her. They are beginning to fade now, which tells me they probably happened that morning we found her.

But she's alluded to being a willing participant in some sexually deviant thing on several occasions. So who is looking for her?

"I can see your mind spinning, you know."

"Is that right?" I ask. "What am I thinking?"

"You want answers. And I'm not going to offer them up. Not yet. If I leave this loft, I'm not coming back."

"What?" I sit up for this part. "Explain."

She shrugs and turns over, showing me her marred back in the bright morning sun. I lift up her hair and study the brand. "It's a circle, so that means forever."

"Yes," she says in a low voice.

"But there's no legally binding contract on forever, Blue."

"I'm aware."

"So what are you afraid of? That someone will see you and take you back?"

"Something like that."

"Kill you?"

Silence.

I take a deep breath and lie back down, my arm pushing under her hip so I can circle her waist. "We can stay in. It's no big deal. We'll have dinners together."

She turns her head a little, looking over her shoulder at me. "We can? All three of us?"

I shrug. "I don't control JD, but yeah. I'll eat your food."

She turns all the way over this time and stares at me. "What's this about? You're Mr. Agreeable now?"

"I'm never Mr. Disagreeable."

"Whatever," she laughs. "You're nosy and bossy. You want to call all the shots and you hate it when you can't. I barely know you, and these things are so true, I figured them out on day one."

"Day one? You were out of it on day one."

"And still I had you pegged."

I stare at her for a few seconds. She needs to eat more, that's for sure. She's not sick-looking, like the first day she got here. But she's still too thin and she looks weak. Her complexion is far too pale and her hair isn't shiny and bright. But her eyes are getting there. And this gives me hope. Enough hope to allow her some leeway in finding her way forward. "I just want what's good for you, that's all. Staying in or going out isn't a fight I'm interested in fighting just yet."

She reaches up and touches my face. "Why are you interested at all?"

I take her finger and pull it to my lips to give it a kiss. "I think you need help. And I want to be the one to give it to you."

"You're a good Samaritan?"

"Something like that."

She chuckles at the way I mimic her answer a few seconds ago. "OK, then. I'll make you guys food and you will eat with me and not pressure me to leave here."

"Deal," I tell her. "Now let's go back to sleep. With any luck, JD will get lost on his way to the breakfast place and leave us alone for a little while."

She turns back around, her back pressed against my chest. "I know you worry about it. But I don't understand why. He seems fine to me."

"Well, Blue, if you ever get a desire to leave the loft, maybe one day you can follow him. Then you'll know what he's up to.

Then you'll know why I worry."

"Is it bad?" Her voice betrays her worry.

"It can be. But it's not bad now. So just let me take care of it. And the birth control. I'll set up a time for the doctor to come here and see you."

"What doctor? You have a doctor in mind?"

"The one we send the girls to."

"Your whore doctor?" She pushes off me, but I wrap my arms tighter and lean into her ear.

"Stop. I'll find a good one, then. I wasn't trying to insult you. It's just something we need to take care of and it's non-negotiable." She huffs out a breath and relaxes. "But it would be a lot easier if you just agreed to leave the loft."

"I don't have my ID. I don't have a health card. And I don't want to give my real name."

I don't know why, but hearing her admit that Blue is not her name stops me cold. I mean, I gave her the name. I know it's not real. But somehow it slipped my mind. "What is your real name?"

"Blue," she says, huffing out some air so that it blows her hair up above her eyes. "I like being Blue, so that's my real name. What's your real name?"

"Ark," I tell her back. "I'm just Ark."

"Ark is a weird name. What's JD's name?"

"He never said," I lie, thinking about the day I met him outside the bus station. "So it's never been anything but JD since I've met him."

"I don't need birth control, Ark."

I close my eyes, immediately understanding, but not wanting it to be true.

"I don't need birth control because I can't get pregnant. So don't worry about it."

With most girls, I'd call that bluff. But I know it's not a bluff.

We lie there in silence for a little while. Thinking about babies that will never be conceived. And fake names. About finding people when you're not looking. About escaping the past and pretending there's no such thing as a future. We live in the present for a few moments and then the contemplative mood breaks when the front door opens and closes.

"I'm back, asshole. And I got breakfast," JD yells from the living room. Neither Blue nor I move as he walks into the bedroom. But JD can read us immediately. "What's the matter?"

I unwrap myself from Blue and sit up. "Nothing."

"What's your real name?" Blue asks him.

"Huh?" JD smiles at her in that way he does. God, sometimes I wish could be him. Sometimes I wish I could let all this baggage go, and be JD. Cool. Fun. Charming. Beautiful.

Because JD has everything going for him. I've watched him sweet-talk girls enough to know. He's exactly what they want. Add in the fact that he's worth almost fourteen million dollars, and that seals the deal.

"James David," he says, bouncing on the bed, making Blue and I bounce with him. He settles next to her and leans down for a kiss. She obliges him without even missing a beat. Their eyes meet before she closes hers, their lips touching as he sweeps his tongue inside. I should feel jealous, but oddly, I don't. It makes me feel... content. "But I hate that name. My parents never called me that. It was always JD."

And then he looks at me to see if I have anything to add. But fuck that shit. I'm not touching it. "What'd you get for breakfast?" I ask him instead.

"Bagels. Lots and lots of bagels. And coffee too. So we don't have to drink that shit Ark calls joe." And then he rips the covers off us in a whoosh and scoops Blue up in his arms. "Eat, shower, fuck. Those are my plans for today."

Blue laughs as he carries her out the bedroom door. I follow along a few seconds later and find her sitting naked on top of the breakfast bar. "Brrrr," she says, rubbing her arms.

"You need clothes," I say, taking a coffee from JD and handing it to her. "How will you get clothes if you refuse to leave the loft?"

"I'll shop for her," JD offers. "I have excellent taste. I'll go after we fuck."

Blue laughs and shakes her head. But all I can think about is what he might do while he's shopping. "I'll go," I offer up, taking a bagel and grabbing the cream cheese. "You can stay with Blue."

JD scowls at me. "I said I'll go."

I hold my hands up, surrendering. "Fine. I'm gonna make Blue stay naked all day until you get back." When I look over her, she's chewing slowly, watching us interact.

"You do that. But tonight when we come home from work, and I'm ready for bed, while you have to stay up all night editing, she sleeps in my room."

And then he winks at her. Knowing full well he just outlined a parameter of our budding relationship.

On nights we work, she belongs to him.

And we work more nights than we don't.

So yeah.

He wins.

"What exactly do you guys do at… work?" Blue asks.

"Nothing you need to worry about," I say quickly.

"What the fuck?" JD asks.

"What?" I ask back. "I don't want her thinking about what we do."

"Why?" Blue interrupts.

"Yeah," JD says, all pissed off. "She already knows. That's something I never understood about you, Ark. Why the fuck do you care what people think of our business?"

"It's porn," I say. Like, hello?

"So? Ray is the King of Porn here. And he never has a problem telling people what he does. We're opening up our own site in a few weeks. There's no way you're gonna be able to rationalize it then."

"I'm not worried about rationalizing it."

"Bullshit. You hate the fact that we make porn. You'd rather do anything else, but you can't because condos, and sports cars, and whatever you spend your money on, aren't free. You're only in this for the money."

"And your point?" I roll my eyes in Blue's direction, but she's got a serious look on her face that makes me stop and reassess. "Do you want to know what he's gonna do tonight? I mean, really? You want me to tell you how we've got a girl lined up to suck his dick in a crowded club right there on the dance floor?"

She ducks her head and chews on her bagel. "It's none of my business what you guys do."

"Jesus fuck. What's wrong with the two of you? Don't you have any feelings, Blue? It doesn't bother you that JD will have another woman on her knees tonight?"

"You're an asshole," JD says to me.

"Why? You wanted to talk about work."

"Because you want to hide it. We're not doing anything wrong."

"Last week we weren't doing anything wrong, this week we are."

"Why's that?" he snarls. "This week you're too good for porn?"

"No, asshole. Because this week we're in a relationship."

THIRTY

BLUE

RELATIONSHIP.

Wow. For a guy who was resistant up to the last second, once he's in, he's all in.

JD laughs. "We're fucking her, Ark. We're not marrying her."

I slip down off the counter. "I'm gonna take a bath, if that's OK." They both stare at me as I walk between them and head towards the hallway. Their arguing continues after I'm gone. I can still hear them in the bedroom.

How are these two guys even friends? I don't get it. They could not be more different.

I close the door so I don't have to hear the argument. It's stupid, anyway. They make porn. They are scum. Not talking about it won't change that fact.

I walk into Ark's bathroom and start the water for the tub. I spot the morning-after pill package in the trash and it makes me even more confused. He's so strait-laced. He's so put-together on the inside. If it wasn't so disconcerting, I'd laugh about it. Because I don't get how a guy this practical and logical carves out a kingdom making and selling porn.

He does not add up. Not one bit. The half-ass dress suits? I mean, I love the look. He's rough in a very neat way. The untucked white shirt. The loose tie. Why wear a tie like that? Why bother with a tie that's not neat? Always jeans and boots and that tattoo they have, dragons fighting over some blue pearl. Where the hell did he come from? It's like Ark can't decide if he's a biker or a businessman.

And JD… Jesus. I have no idea what to think about him. The way Ark talks, he's insane or something. He's unstable. He's got 'issues'. What kind of issues? So he takes off every now and then. If I could leave this loft, I'd be gone too. But just like the things with Ark, there's something there with JD too.

Relationship?

Is that what this is?

I look up and find my face staring back at me from the mirror. "What are you doing?" But the girl on the other side doesn't answer. Instead there's a knock at the door. "Come in," I say.

Ark pushes it open and stands at the threshold holding his camera. JD is behind him. Neither of them say anything and I'm immediately ticked off at this. "What?"

Ark opens his mouth, but JD is the one who answers. "Never mind our bitching, Blue. We do this all the time."

But I know somehow, deep inside me, that isn't true. I think that before I came, nothing upset these two. I think before I came, they hadn't had an argument in months. Maybe years.

But fuck it. If they want to lie, I've got enough lies of my own I need to keep telling. So whatever. "Wanna join me in the tub?" I say instead. "It's huge. We can probably all three fit." Ark walks past me and peers inside the tub. He looks back at me and JD, then the tub again. Like he's calculating the volume or something. "My God, do you always overthink things?"

"Pfffft," he says, placing the camera on the counter facing the tub, and then unbuttoning his jeans. "I never overthink anything."

I look over at JD, who's watching us with a bemused smirk on his face. He pulls his shirt over his head and kicks off his boots. "Let's fuck in the tub then."

"No," I say, exasperated. "I don't want to fuck in the tub. I just want to relax in the tub. If you two want to relax with me, then OK. Otherwise—" I stop. Because they are looking at me with frowns and scrunched-up eyebrows. I'm being bitchy. "Otherwise"—I soften my tone—"just let me wash and I'll be right out."

"We'll relax with you," Ark says in his no-nonsense manner. And then he takes off his jeans and walks towards me and extends his hand. "I'll hold your hand while you step in."

I take a deep breath and smile at the gesture. And then I take his hand and step over the rim of the tub. The hot water presses against my legs and when I lower my butt down, I look up and hiss from the sting.

Ark lets go of my hand and then JD dumps some shampoo in the water to make bubbles. "Scoot over," Ark says, stepping in on one side of me. JD steps in on the other, and then they simultaneously lean back, stretching their legs out as much as they can on either side of my body.

"We don't really fit, do we?" I laugh.

"We'll make do," JD says, grabbing my shoulders and turning me around so my back is resting against his chest. When I look up at Ark, he's amused. Which is nice, since he seems to be the jealous type. "You know how long it's been since I sat in a bathtub before you came, Blue?" JD asks.

Ark's smile creeps up as he thinks about this.

"I must've been like ten years old," JD continues. "We had an old ugly claw-foot in our house. Not something vintage and cool, but rusted and shit. I hated that thing. It took forever to fill."

"Did you grow up in Denver, JD?" I ask.

"Yup. Born and raised."

"How about you, Ark?"

Ark shakes his head at me, but doesn't offer up a place.

"Ark grew up in Iowa or some shit."

"City or farm?" I keep it going.

Ark just stares at me with that smile. His arms are draped across the rim of the tub on either side of him and his knees are drawn up because JD is taking up most of the room with his legs.

My toes wiggle and I can feel Ark's hard cock press against them. He gives me another smirk.

God, I'd love for him to fuck me. Not with JD, but alone.

"If you're from Montreal," Ark says, putting me on high alert, "why don't you have a French accent?"

"I went to school in the States." And I did. That's not even a lie.

"Where?" JD asks. And now I feel like they are tag-teaming me for info.

"The East Coast. And that's all I'm gonna say about it, if that's OK." I wait for an objection, but JD is silent and Ark just shrugs. "What about you guys?"

I'm looking at Ark, of course, since I'm facing him, but JD is the one who answers. "I went to North. But I dropped out in eleventh grade."

"Really?" I turn my head to look at him. "I'd never have guessed."

"Really," he affirms with a smile. "It's pretty cool to say that, and know it never made a difference. I'm a millionaire high-school dropout. But, if I could do it over, I'd have stuck it out. Maybe gone to college instead."

"How come?"

"Because all I do is act. And really, you can't call what I do *acting*. I stand there and let girls suck me off."

"JD," Arks says, annoyed with the talk of work.

JD shrugs behind me. "It's true."

"It's not true," Ark says. "He's a natural salesman. Not many people could charm strange girls into doing what we need them to do."

"What will you do tonight?" I ask.

Ark takes in a breath, holds it for a second, and then lets it out. "Meet the girl at the club. Wait for the show to get going. Let people get nice and drunk. Rowdy. Then take her on the floor, put her on her knees, and say *action*."

"Don't people say anything? Like try to stop you?"

"We have verbal contracts with the club owners. Management, security, the bands—they're all in on it."

"So you pay them to let you film there?"

"Yup. Every palm gets greased."

JD grabs the soap and starts rubbing it up and down my arm. I look back and him and smile. "That feels good."

"It's supposed to," he says.

"So, if you won't talk about school growing up, let's talk about college," Ark says.

I squint my eyes at him. "OK. You first. Where'd you go?"

"I didn't. How about you?"

"Me either." I'm lying, but so is he. So fuck it.

JD's chest rumbles with a laugh behind me. "You two are something else. Why waste so much energy being hostile?"

"We're not hostile," I say, feeling very hostile.

"Whatever."

"OK, then," Ark continues. "I'm a Gator. University of Florida. Your turn."

And this rings true for some reason. He does have a slight

southern accent to his speech. "Columbia," I say.

"Columbia?" JD says. "Dayum, girl. You grew up rich and smart. How the fuck did you end up here?"

"It's a long story." My eyes never leave Ark's face.

"We have time," Ark says, staring back. "Give it a go, Blue. You're gonna have to tell us eventually."

How did I end up here? It's been so long since I thought about it, I have to trace back my steps. "My best friend from when I was a kid—"

"School?" Ark interrupts. "Or home?"

"Home," I answer, acutely aware that he's fishing for details. "She moved to Denver and so I followed her here."

"How old are you?"

"Jesus, Ark," JD says. "It's not an interrogation. Calm down."

"Twenty-four," I answer. And it is an interrogation. I'm just having a hard time piecing together why this guy feels the need to interrogate me. He's protective, I get that. He's controlling, and that too makes sense. But why me? I'm not that pretty. I'm at least fifteen pounds underweight, my hair is brittle, and my skin is pale. I look weary, even after a few days of rest. I look downtrodden. So why is he so interested? Why are either of them so interested? "How about you?"

"Twenty-seven."

"Twenty-five," JD adds.

"So, your friend came to Denver and…"

I lift my knees up and wrap my arms around my legs, hugging them to my chest. "She came to Denver and worked as a waitress at first. But then…" I have to stop and make this part up. "But then she called me and said she was pregnant and could I come spend the summer with her and babysit."

Ark narrows his eyes at me. "Why would she assume you'd drop your life and go help her?"

"We were BFF's, ya know? And I wasn't working."

"So you came to Denver last summer?"

I shake my head.

"Summer before last?"

I nod.

"Well, fuck, Blue. That's a long time to be in town. What the hell have you been doing here?" JD is starting to put things together. Ark has always known. It's like he took one look at me out in the rain that morning and he could read my mind. But JD was just along for the ride. "Blue?" he prods, poking me to keep it fun.

But the fun is gone. I have to make a decision and I have to make it right now. Trust them or not. And if I do, then yeah, that's a big move. And if I lie, they will know. I won't be able to stay here much longer. A day or two at the most.

And then where would I go? I can't call my father. That would be a huge deal. I can't just go back out on the streets. There's no way they won't still be looking for me. They know I have no ID, no clothes, no passport. I can't leave the country. I can't go to the local charities, they'd find me first thing. I can't even go to the police. Who knows how many officers they have on the payroll? And who knows how high up they go?

"You gotta trust someone," Ark says, calm as can be. He's used to this. Something about his detached professionalism is very familiar to me. And he's right, I do need to trust someone. But two guys who make porn for a living? Really? "Start with the brand."

JD's whole body stiffens behind me when Ark says the word brand. I shake my head automatically at that one. "That's an ending, not a beginning."

"Fair enough. What happened when you got here?"

"We had lunch at a place down on Colorado Boulevard."

"What city did you come from?"

"Montreal. I was home for the summer when she called.

That's the only way she knew to get a hold of me."

"And you just took off for Denver."

I know what he's implying. And fine. Whatever. Who cares if he figures out I come from privilege? "I told you, I wasn't working. I couldn't find a job. I had nothing preventing me from going."

"What kind of job do you do, Blue?"

I don't know why when JD asks that question it sounds so… genuine. But when Ark asks it, he makes me want to lie. JD makes me want to tell him all my secrets. I can hear the sympathy in his voice. "I'm a reporter."

Ark's eyes meet JD's for several seconds like they are having some secret communication. His jaw clenches. "So you came to Denver to find a job? Or to help your friend?"

"Both."

"Did you get a job, Blue?" JD this time.

"No. I got…" I have to take a deep breath, so I stop. And once I stop, I can't find a way to continue.

"Just say it, baby." JD leans into my neck and kisses me. "Just tell us what's going on. We won't judge you. I mean, look at us. We make porn."

"I thought if I could just help her, I could maybe write about it. And then publish it online. And maybe that would get me a real job. I mean, they wanted me to be a blogger, you guys."

"What?" Ark asks. "Who?"

"After school. I applied to hundreds of publications. And I got one offer to blog. Blog," I repeat. "And I know some people have huge careers as bloggers, but that's not what this was. It was blogging statistics. It wasn't even writing. Just copying and pasting."

"OK," Ark says, a little bit annoyed. "I don't get what that has to do with any of what's going on. How is your friend connected? Where did you get that brand? Who the fuck are you hiding from?"

"When Janine came to me and asked for help, it was a huge favor, OK? She was pregnant and she told me that they were gonna take her baby and give it to another couple to adopt."

"Who?" Ark demands, making me jump.

JD's arms wrap round me, trying to calm me down.

"And I thought that was the perfect opportunity, you know? I could help her, right? I could stop those people from taking her baby. And I could write an expose on what they were doing and maybe get a job out of it."

Ark leans his face into his palm. He takes a deep breath. "Please tell me you did not infiltrate this group to write a story."

I swallow hard. "I did."

He stands up, gets out of the tub, looks at the camera like he forgot it was there, then grabs it and walks out, trailing a puddle of water on the floor behind him.

"Damn, Blue," JD says. "That was a pretty stupid idea."

"I realize that now. I mean I realized that back then, too. It took me about five minutes to understand I fucked up in a major way."

"So where did the brand come from?"

"I… I… I joined up."

"You joined?" Ark peeks his head into the bathroom as he buttons up one of those white dress shirts. He's already got jeans on. Like he's going somewhere. "Now why the fuck would you do that?"

I shrug my shoulders and look up at him. He's so angry. Why is he so angry? And then he disappears and then reappears pulling on his boots.

"I don't know, you guys. It was like they brainwashed me or something. I became… Are you going somewhere?" I ask Ark. Because he's got his boots on and there's a leather jacket in his hand.

"Yeah, we're going somewhere. You're gonna show me where the fuck it was they had you."

"I don't know that."

"You *do* know, Blue." He snarls this at me. "You do know. And I'm not playing here, I want you to show us."

"I don't know! They blindfolded me and kept me in a basement or something. The other day, when you found me, I was at some special party that night. They drugged me before they took me out of the basement. So when I escaped, I didn't understand where I was. I have no idea where they are. I have no idea who they are. The only face I ever saw was my husband's."

"Your husband?" They say this at the same time.

"It was never legal. I had a fake name. So he's not my real—"

"What the fuck is wrong with you?"

I jump at Ark's shout again.

"Shhh," JD says behind me. "He's not gonna hurt you, Blue. He's just pissed off that you didn't say something earlier."

"Why would I tell you guys? You're porn scum! Why is this my fault all of a sudden? Why do you care so much?"

Ark stomps into the bathroom and looms over me, making me tip my head up to look him in the eye. I feel more vulnerable here, sitting in this tub with JD's arms around me and Ark's disapproval, than I have ever felt in my life. Even after all the shit I've been through in the past year. "Listen to me, Blue. These are the people who killed JD's girl. That brand was their brand. They killed his girl and stole his kid. That's why we're so fucking interested. OK? So you're gonna get your ass up and—"

"No," JD says. He stands up, bringing me with him, and looks Ark in the face. "Just stop, OK? Fuck this shit. I don't want to hear any of it. I can't do it again. I can't let this shit take over my life again. I can't." And then his embrace evaporates and he steps out of the tub and walks out.

Ark and I stand there. Staring each other in the eyes.

I'm naked.

I'm bared to him.

I've been stripped down to nothing.

"How long?"

"Huh?" I feign ignorance.

"Don't," he says in a low voice. "Just stop pretending you're ignorant, or stupid, or whatever it is you're trying to make us think. Because it won't work. How. Fucking. Long?"

"Fifteen months."

"You've been missing for fifteen months?"

I nod.

"And no one missed you?"

"Oh, they missed me all right. My father was a Canadian premier for ten years and he's been the ambassador in DC for four."

Ark reaches out, grabs my shoulders, and stares into my eyes. "Oh my God. You're Zoey Marshall. I knew I recognized you from somewhere."

The tears spring to life and before I can stop them, they are streaming down my face. It's been so long since someone called me by my real name. Way too long.

"I'm sorry," he says, taking my hand and urging me to step out of the tub. I stand there on the bath rug and then he wraps a towel around me, pulling me into his chest in a protective embrace. "I'm so fucking sorry."

THIRTY-ONE

ARK

BLUE and I stare at each other for a few seconds. She looks like her world just fell apart. But then the front door slams so hard the artwork in the foyer shakes on the walls.

I walk to the bathroom entrance and stare at my bedroom doorway.

"Are you gonna go after him?"

I look back at Blue. "No. I can't do this again either. I spent the better part of two years making sure he didn't do anything stupid. And you know what? I love him like a brother. I do. But I can't fight this battle for him. If he wants to go off looking for those people alone, there's nothing I can do."

And it's true. You can't save people from themselves.

Blue pushes past me and runs down the hallway. I follow her. When I get to the foyer, she's standing there in her towel, soaking wet, holding the door open.

"He's gone," she says, the sadness in her voice clear. "If

anything bad happens it will be my fault."

"Don't be stupid. He's a grown man, for fuck's sake. He can—"

"You say you care?" she yells. "Then go after him!"

"You go after him. He likes you. He'll listen to you just as much as he will me."

She looks out at the hallway again. Will she go? I mean, she needs clothes, obviously. But she's been making do with JD's sweats and t-shirts all week.

But no. She closes the door with a sigh. "I can't."

"Can't?" I sneer. "More like you won't. I'm not buying this whole afraid-to-leave-the-apartment bullshit."

She walks off towards JD's room. I follow again, and when I get there she's searching for something to wear. She pulls on a pair of JD's boxers and a summer t-shirt.

"So obviously you're not going after him."

"I can't leave. If they see me—"

"If who sees you?"

"They," she whispers, looking up at me with bleary eyes. "They know who I am, Ark. And they don't care. They know my father would have the power of two governments on his side if I made one phone call."

"Then make it."

"I can't. I can't go home. I can't leave here. I can't do anything. They..."

She stops. And it doesn't take a mind reader to understand why. "They have shit on you, don't they?"

She tips her head up and takes a deep breath. "It seems you have a lot in common with them."

I narrow my eyes at her. "How do you figure?"

"Because they have an affinity for filming girls as well. Only they set us up. They filmed me doing drugs. Having sex. And..."

"Just fucking say it, Blue." I want to pull her hair out right now.

"And babysitting." Her words are so soft, I almost miss them. My heart actually skips a beat. Maybe two. "Only it's not babysitting, Ark. That's just the code word."

I'm reaching for her throat to throttle her, but she misunderstands and sinks into my chest, wrapping her arms around me. Holy fuck. *Just keep cool,* I tell myself. *Just keep cool.* "What's babysitting, Blue? Come on now, just tell me. You've said this much, might as well get it all out."

"We weren't sex slaves, Ark. We weren't whores, or strippers, or mistresses. They kept us for babies."

The blood is pounding so hard in my head.

"And when a girl had a baby, they took it and gave it to someone else. They sold them, Ark. And the girl was paid to give the baby up."

Disgust runs through my veins. Bile rises in my throat. "Did you sell a baby, Blue?"

"No. I never got pregnant." And then she drops her head and cries. She falls to the floor on her knees. Her hands cover her face and then she lowers her forehead to the ground and wails.

I just watch her for a few seconds, and then I snap out of it. "Come here," I say, picking up her too-thin body and carrying her back to my bedroom. I lay her down on the bed and climb in next to her as the sadness pours out of her in heaving sobs and rivers of tears.

"Shhh," I tell her, putting my arm underneath her so I can keep her close. "Calm down, OK?" I drag my fingers up and down her arm to try to soothe her, but she's lost control.

This is the girl we found out in the rain. This is how she should've reacted that day. This is the reaction that never came. Because she never admitted to what happened to her. She couldn't.

No one knows when Zoey Marshall went missing, but all of

North America heard about it the minute they realized. It was on every nightly news report last year. And from what Blue says, that was months after she was actually gone. There were rewards and heartfelt pleas for her safe return on the news by her family. Vigils were held outside the ambassador's home in DC and her family's home in Canada.

It was a multi-national affair and lasted about three months. And then no one ever talked about the missing college grad again because she made a YouTube video telling people she was on a writing sabbatical in some rainforest. There was some buzz, but then it all died away. People forgot all about Zoey Marshall. She simply disappeared.

I stroke her hair as she begins to calm down. "We should call them, Blue."

"No," she says, hiccupping. "I will not disgrace my father like that. I will not let them read that contract."

"What contract?" Jesus Christ.

"We all signed one. It was a big production. It was videotaped. And they had me stand up and recite it out loud. Pledging to sell my baby to a man who was present in the room, but wearing a mask to protect *his* identity. There's no way I will disgrace my father like that."

"Why did you do it, though? I don't understand." How? How could this girl sell an unborn child?

"I was looking for my best friend, Janine. Remember?" She tips her head to look up at me. "It was fake, Ark. I knew she was pregnant, but then she disappeared. I figured the only way I could have any chance of finding her was to get with the program. They didn't know who I was back then, I had the fake ID. But week after week of doctor visits and not getting pregnant—"

"Wait." I stop her here. Because I need to know. "How were they trying to get you pregnant?"

"He fucked me. Every night while I was ovulating. It was like a perk of the contract, I think. He was the leader."

I have to close my eyes for a moment to process this. I take a deep breath. "The leader of what?"

"The baby-selling ring."

"And he needed a baby from you?"

"That's what he said. I didn't know who he was at my contract party, everyone was wearing masks. It was like a masquerade ball. Everyone but me was dressed up."

"So when did he find out who you really were?"

"When they discovered I had gotten a Depo shot the day before I was contracted, I thought for sure I'd be in and out in a week or two. The shot lasts for about three months, and there's no way to stop the effects once it's given. I thought… I thought I was so smart, Ark. I really did."

I continue to stroke her arm. She's calming down, but my heart rate is speeding up. "But they know the tricks, I'm sure."

"Yeah. It only took them a few days to figure it out with a blood test after they got suspicious."

"And then what happened?"

"They locked me up. Took my fingerprints. And they said they ran my face through some facial recognition program. But that might've been bullshit."

"So they knew you were Zoey."

"Yeah. And then the leader kept me as his… personal…"

"I get it. You don't have to say it."

"And when my three months was up, he tried getting me pregnant. But it took me months to get pregnant, and then when I was, I miscarried every time."

"Holy fuck." I pinch the bridge of my nose with my fingers. "Did you find your friend?"

"No. But one girl remembered her. And can you believe this, Ark? Those contacts?" Blue laughs, but it's not a happy laugh. It's a laugh that says there's more crying ahead. "Those contracts aren't even honored. Imagine that. A girl sells her baby and she never gets paid. And you know why, Ark? Do you know why she never gets paid?"

I do know, but I can't make myself stop her from telling me.

"Because they kill them. They rape us, they steal our children, and then our reward is death."

"Were they all kidnapped? Or were they there to sell their babies?"

"I was the only one they locked up in the basement, so I can only assume the other girls were there for the money. They kept me company sometimes."

"And no one tried to help?"

She shakes her head no. "They needed money—"

"Fuck the money. No one needs money that bad." My shout scares her, making her shrink inward. "Sorry," I whisper. "Sorry. It's just, you can't put yourself in that category, Blue. Don't identify with them. You're not like them. You were a prisoner. They were selling their children. It's not the same thing."

"I know," she says in a soft whisper.

But I don't think she does and I need to hammer it home. "You were a prisoner."

"I still am."

"No," I say, leaning down to kiss her neck. "No, you're free now, Blue."

"I'm not though. They have me with that video. No one will believe my story. Not after I lied about where I was."

"Did they force you to make that YouTube video?"

"What do you think?" she snaps.

Right.

We lie there in silence for a long time. Her breathing slows and she begins to relax. But I'm so amped up I feel like my brain might shatter. It starts to rain outside, making the atmosphere in here even more gloomy. There's a clock on the wall that ticks off the seconds, and my mind is spinning with options.

But none of them feel right. None of them feel like they will make a difference.

Finally, after hours of lying there, I find myself able to talk. "What do you want to do about this, Blue?" I ask. She's been so still, I almost thought she was asleep. But no one sleeps with this conversation hanging over them.

"I want to forget it ever happened."

"What about your parents? Don't you want to go home?"

She tucks her head into my chest and sighs. "I am home."

THIRTY-TWO

ARK

AFTER Blue falls asleep, I sneak out to my office and chain-smoke as I watch the clock. JD has been gone for hours now. And there's no telling what he's up to or what he might do. Fuck, if he'll even show up for work tonight.

Finally, at eight forty-seven, he comes through the loft door. I'm sitting on the couch, my hand poised over the ashtray, ready to flick, when he appears.

"Since when do you smoke in the house?" he asks, closing the doors behind him.

"You had me worried, dude."

"Since when do I miss work?" he says, grabbing a smoke from my pack on the side table and lighting up.

"You know that's not what I meant. Please don't insult me by pretending I was worried about the fucking *job*. You wanna tell me what's going through your head right now?"

He takes a seat in the chair off to my left, inhaling a long drag of nicotine, before blowing it out in rings. "I can't do it, man. I just can't do it. Looking for them will suck me down a black hole I might never crawl out of. If you hadn't come along when you did, I'd be dead right now."

He's said it before, but tonight it seems real. More real than ever. Because we're all standing at the edge of something. Something that will change us forever. "Well, she told me a lot, JD. And I think you need to know what her story is before you make any decisions."

He rolls his cigarette back and forth between his finger and thumb. "I'm not sure it will matter." And then he looks up at me and his eyes are red. His face is pale. And I know where he's been.

The cemetery.

"She's dead. The baby is gone. Maybe dead too. And you know what, Ark? I'm tired of thinking about it. I'm tired of feeling this way about something I can't change. And all these years you've given me the same piece of advice. *Let it go*. So that's what I'm gonna do. I'm gonna let it go. Blue is here and maybe she's not the love of my life, but she's here. And I like her. I want to spend time with her. And you. We've got something good right now. We're rich. We're about to fulfill our deal with Ray and start our own site. We've got it all. Why fuck it up? Ya know? Why fuck it all up over something that can't be changed?"

I do know. But I also know what he really wants to hear. That we'll get those fuckers. That we'll make them pay. That we will take every last one of them down. He wants to hear that because that's what I'd want to hear if it was my girl who was killed and my baby who was missing.

"I hear ya," I say instead. I'm not a hero. I'm the Prince of Porn. I sell come down a girl's throat. I sell face fucks in public places. I sell filthy videos that degrade women and use my friend's cock to make money.

I'm not the hero he's looking for. I am scum.

"Still wanna work tonight?" I ask him after a few moments of silence, puffing out smoke rings.

"Why the fuck not," he says, getting up to stub out his cigarette in the ashtray next to me. "Why the fuck not."

"OK." I nod. "Grab my gear bag. I'm just gonna go let Blue know we're leaving and what time you'll be back."

"How's she doing?" he asks, looking down the hallway to my room.

"I'm not sure, actually." I open my mouth to tell him who she is and what she really did, but he turns away before the words can come out. And then I lose my nerve.

Maybe it's better he doesn't know. If he knew who she was, he might do something stupid.

It's a risk I can't take.

I leave him to gather our gear and walk down the hallway, trying not to make my boots thud too hard on the floors. I don't turn the light on, I just walk over to the bed and sit down next to her.

"Is he OK?" she asks.

"I think so," I tell her back. "We're gonna go to work tonight. I go to Ray's to edit after each shoot, so I won't be home until tomorrow morning. But JD should be back a little after two. You gonna be OK?"

"Yeah," she says.

"Don't say anything to him when he comes back tonight. About who you are. Where you were. That kind of thing."

She turns her whole body so she can look at me. "Do you really think that's a good idea? Considering how... connected we are?"

"I do, Blue. I wouldn't ask you to keep secrets if I didn't think it was absolutely necessary. But it is. Please trust me. It is."

She nods her head at me and then her tired eyes win the battle she's having with fatigue.

"We gotta get you a phone tomorrow," I say, leaning in to kiss her. "And clothes. And shoes. Shit, we have a lot to do tomorrow. So try to sleep." I place my palm against her cheek and feel wetness. She's still crying.

"I'm sorry," she says, the tears coming out freely now. "I'm so sorry."

"Why are you sorry, Blue?"

"For being a part of that. For being part of the thing that tore his life apart."

"It's not your fault. You were trying to save your friend and you got in over your head."

"I was stupid. And naive."

"It's over now. JD wants to move on. He wants to move on with you. And me. Give this shit a go. See where it takes us. And I'm all for that too. Sometimes you just gotta drop that baggage you've been carrying around and leave it behind."

"I feel like my baggage is inside me, Ark. It fills me up and overflows."

"I know, baby. I know. But every day that goes by, a little bit of it will evaporate. And one day you'll wake up and realize you're OK. It's over. And they can't get you ever again."

"But they can get me. They're not far away. Maybe right down the street. Sometimes I hear the bells—"

"Shhh," I say, leaning down to kiss her wet cheeks. "Don't do that, Blue. You'll stay inside for now. They don't know you're here. No one saw us take you home. No one's seen you in the building. We're going out alone tonight and they're not gonna know. We'll find a way to get you a new ID and then we'll go from there."

She relaxes and I sit with her another few seconds before leaning down and kissing her on the lips. "I'll see you tomorrow. JD will be back in a few hours. Just get some rest."

She nods to me in the darkness and then I get up and walk

out, closing the door behind me.

JD is standing in the hallway, a few paces off. I hold my breath and wait to see if he heard me tell her to lie to him.

"She's OK?" he asks.

I exhale my relief. "She will be. Just sleep with her when you come home, eh? Take her into your room. Don't let her spend the whole night alone."

He nods at me and then hands over my bag of camera equipment. "It's still raining so I put it in the waterproof bag."

"Thanks, man."

"Yeah," he says. "No problem."

And then we leave the condo together. Going out to do what we do. And I don't know about him, but I'm feeling pretty damn ashamed of how I make money right about now. The whole walk over there I talk myself up.

It's just temporary.

You're gonna make a difference.

Things are moving fast now.

Don't give up what you've worked so hard to get.

Be strong and finish what you started.

And by the time we walk up to Aldo, the big German bouncer manning the door to The Sanctuary Club, I believe it.

"Hey," Aldo says, sticking out his hand. I shake and he thumps me on the back a few times before moving on and doing the same thing to JD. "What time will you need us?" he asks in his thick accent.

I look at JD and shrug. "We probably need to throw back at least half a dozen shots before we get this party started. Let's say twelve thirty." I pull out an envelope with his take in it from the bag JD packed. "Here you go, man." I study the line outside—which wraps around the building—and the level of noise from inside—which is pounding—and make a decision. "All six guys watching tonight, Aldo. They seem a little rowdy."

"They do," Aldo laughs. "There's a party of bigwigs here tonight. Been here all week. Everyone feels it. Like something is happening."

JD claps him on the back as we pass into the club. "Thanks for the heads up."

We make our way down the long hallway that leads to the main dance floor. This place is an old Catholic church that went up for sale during the recession a few years back. It got snatched up, remodeled, and turned into party central for the city's goth crowd.

It's creepy as all fuck, especially this week, since Halloween is tomorrow. It's decked out like Satan's lair.

We make our way to the VIP section and the guy at that checkpoint, Sinclair, just unhooks the red velvet rope as we approach and lets us pass. Now we make our way upstairs, where the choir used to belt out hymns.

It's filled with topless women serving drinks, men in suits fondling them, and a lot of security. "What's up with them?" JD yells, leaning in so I can hear him over the thumping bass. He points at the bouncers standing in front of one of the private rooms.

"No clue. But we've got enough mystery on our hands. So let's stay out of it, no matter what."

"Fine by me," he shouts back in my ear. "I'm gonna go down and find our contract. You gonna stay here?"

I gesture to my clothes. JD's wearing jeans, a white t-shirt, and a black leather jacket with the Public Fuck logo on it that glows under the UV light. "I'll watch from above. Get her down below and I'll shoot with a zoom from above."

This is how we set the mood of the shot. This cybergoth shit on Thursday nights isn't always our thing, but when it is, we make the whole thing seem sinister. It's easy enough. The stained-glass windows, upside-down cross on the 'altar' directly across from the VIP boxes, and the tolling bells give it enough atmosphere for a horror movie. Add in all the fluorescent dreadlocks, platform boots, and glowing outfits, and you've got *Dracula Goes to a Space Rave.*

JD makes his way through the crowd, looking for our girl. It's early still, but she was told what time to be here, so I help him scan from above. Tonight's contract is a girl who's been watching us do this for a few weeks. Somehow she got a hold of our schedule, because she turned up at every gig for a while there. Just hanging back, watching. JD saw her the very first night, but back then, we weren't having problems getting the girls to show up. So he left her alone for a while.

Now we are. So he approached her a few weeks ago and gave her the speech. Testing, contract, ID, waiver of liability, and, if they are one of the girls we will use for the upcoming Public Fuck website, a non-disclosure agreement.

But this one isn't for Public Fuck. She's fetish shit. That's why she's dressed up in a pink tutu with white lace stockings, ripped in all the right places. Her cyberlocks are in a variety of glow-in-the-dark colors, and she's got on a tight pink corset. I can't tell from here without the zoom lens, but she's probably got something painted on her face too. I take my phone out and text JD, letting him know she's over by the east bar.

He checks his phone, shoots me a thumbs up, and then makes his way over.

"Your next victim?" A man leans down in my ear.

I turn. The man is wearing a black suit and a collar like a priest. So he must be some kind of manager here. I give him the once-over. He looks familiar, but no one I recognize.

"Contract," I correct him. "We don't deal in victims, only willing participants."

"Ah," the man chuckles, again close to my ear, so I can hear over the thumping music. "Us as well." He shoots me a smile when I look at him funny. But then he extends a hand and when I accept his offer, he leans in and says, "Father Gabriel." And then he pans a hand down to the dancing crowd below. "My flock."

"Nice," I say back. Father Freak is more like it. What do I expect though? He deals in fantasy, same as me. We're all freaks in here.

"How often do you film here, Ark?" he says, this time in a much lower voice, and much closer to my ear.

I recoil a little, because I never gave him my name. It's not hard to figure out who I am if you're paying close attention. And it's his club, so I guess he is. But to come right out and use that knowledge to unseat me is fucking rude.

"Let's talk," he says, turning to walk away. He gives me one last smile over his shoulder and beckons me with a finger.

"Fuck." Now I know he's management and he probably wants to ask me for more money. Ray warned me that once we took over our own business, the leeches would come out of the woodwork.

I follow Gabriel to the back of the lounge and wait as he keys in a code to open a door. Inside is a stairwell. "Please," he says, waving me forward. "My private area is above."

I do an internal shrug and start climbing the stairs. "I feel like we've met, but I'm pretty sure I'd remember you." We enter the private box and I walk over to the far wall. It's floor-to-ceiling glass that overlooks the entire lower level of the club. The music is only detectable by the thumping of the glass, so it's essentially soundproof. "Huh. We're up in the ceiling beams. I never realized this was here."

"Yes," Gabriel says as he walks up behind me. "This is where I watch. And we have met, just under different circumstances."

I turn to him and he beckons me to a seating area. Just two chairs with a table barely the size of a dinner plate between us. There are two drinks waiting, but neither of us takes one. "What circumstances?"

He smiles but something about this is off, so I don't smile back. "Last weekend I was at Ray's. I saw you from a distance. I was there trying to get your attention."

I squint, trying to think back.

"The offer. To fuck my wife while I watched."

I can't help myself, I belt out a laugh. "Jesus Christ. You are very blunt. And I guess I can stop thinking of you as a priest, since you're clearly playing dress-up tonight."

He lifts his hands and shrugs, like I caught him in the act. "I'm not a Catholic priest. This was once a Catholic church, and the icons are deliciously sacrilegious in this club environment, so I couldn't resist. However"—he pauses to shoot me another creepy smile—"I am a leader of a small religious sect."

Cult, is the word I hear in my head.

"And since you and I work in the same business, I thought you'd understand." Another pause so he can steeple his index fingers and press them to his lips. The gesture reminds me a little of Ray, but not in a way that sets me at ease. Father Creepy here studies people, picks up on their mannerisms, and uses them to influence. It's an instinct more than anything. But I didn't make it this far into the job by not listening to my instincts. "Perhaps even find a common ground."

"What does any of that have to do with fucking your wife?" If he wants to be blunt, I can be blunt.

The creepy smile and stare continues for a few more seconds, just to make sure I get it. "I need a third person in my relationships and they seem to find you desirable."

"They?"

"I have just one wife. But we are a flock. The others are just as much a part of the inner circle as my first."

My mouth does not gape open like an idiot's, but he's stunned me. Me. The Prince of Public Porn has been stunned by a middle-aged man pretending to be a priest.

I don't react at all. I don't flinch or lean back in my chair to show my revulsion. I don't even smile and shake my head and play this one off as I plot a quick escape. I just sit there and take it all in.

Because something is very wrong with this man. Something I really do not want any part of.

"Mr. Ark?"

"Father Gabriel," I say back, buying myself another moment to collect my thoughts.

"Are you interested?"

I stare at him. His eyes are light brown. His hair is thin and mostly gray. His body is lean, his face long, his arms spindly. If there was a picture in the Urban Dictionary for 'dirty old man,' then Father Gabriel is the spitting image.

I shudder. "My answer is no, Gabriel. Like I told Ray, I'm not interested. I don't need the money. I don't need the beautiful girl. I don't need anything, to be honest. And I'm sorry to cut this short, but I need to get back to my partner."

I stand up and give him a nod, and then turn my back and walk to the stairwell we came up.

"Mr. Ark," he calls out.

I stop but don't turn.

"I can understand how you'd think you have it all. And I can understand how you'd think there's nothing I can offer you that would make you change your mind. But I actually do have things you require. I have information you might be interested in."

I look at him over my shoulder. I get a feeling in my gut. A feeling that says keep going. Just walk the fuck out of here. But I know what he's going to say. Somehow, some way, I know what he's going to say.

And I need to hear it.

"Not specifically pertaining to you, of course. Since you're an enigma. You're the man who has no past. You're the guy who steps off a bus, finds a business partner, and starts a porn empire under the protection of the reigning king, all in the span of a few months. You're the untouchable one. So you're right. I don't have anything *you* need."

I turn to face him now.

"But JD is an entirely different story."

My jaw clenches and my hands are making fists before I can stop the reaction.

Father Sister-wives belts out a smug laugh. "He's your Achilles' heel, do you realize that? He's the only one who can bring it all crashing down. And not because he has dirt on you. I really don't think he does. No. He has this power over you because you give it to him. Because you love him, don't you, Ark?"

"Say what you've got to say."

"Your business partner"—Gabriel chuckles, like that's funny—"has a big mouth. He's been around asking lots of questions. Questions he shouldn't even know to ask."

My mind races with the questions. Blue? Did he mention Blue?

"We both know it's better that he keep silent."

Not Blue. "He lost someone and he wants her back."

"He can't undo the past."

"He just wants to set it right."

Gabriel laughs. "I think that's a tall order. But perhaps..." His smile lingers, then falls. "Perhaps we could help each other out? Hmmm? Perhaps we could do a trade?"

My eyes squint down at him.

"I know where JD's daughter is."

I don't know what to say.

Creepy smile all over again. "And I can deliver her. I can fix his heart. I can make him a new man. I can erase that year and make it all better."

"It was two years, asshole. Two years of hell for him. Two

years of drug addiction and—" I stop before I let that last secret out. This guy doesn't deserve to know JD's shame. "It doesn't matter," I say, recovering. "Your offer makes no sense."

"It makes perfect sense, Mr. Ark. Because so many couples have asked for you now, I can no longer refuse them."

"What the fuck are you talking about?"

"Children, Ark." He says it like I'm one of them. "I'm a matchmaker for families who want to have a child, but are not able to conceive." He waves both hands down his front as if the fake clerical clothing and white collar legitimize his role as cult leader, polygamist, and baby-seller.

"You want me to get your sister-wives pregnant?" I'm stunned. So stunned I laugh. "And in exchange you'll tell me which family you sold my best friend's kid to four years ago?" I cross the room and grab him by the throat, pushing him back and slamming him up against the thick glass that separates us from the club below.

His hands claw at his neck as I choke the breath out of him. The thumping of the bass against the window is the same as my thumping heart. "I'm gonna forget you just said that. I'm gonna forget you just asked me to fuck your whores so you can sell my children. I'm gonna forget that you exist, you piece-of-shit pervert. And I suggest you do the same. Stay out of my business. Stay away from JD. And stay away from me. Because the next time I see your face, I'm gonna blow it off your goddamned head."

I squeeze his pulsing jugular until his eyes bulge and he goes unconscious. And then I let him slump to the floor.

"Fuck you," I say. And then I spit on him, turn, and walk back down the stairs. No one pays any attention to me as I make my way back down to the dance floor. It takes me a few minutes to find JD, and that's long enough for Gabriel to wake up from his very non-erotic asphyxiation, but no warning alarms go off. The music still bumps, the dancers continue their routines, the drinks never stop flowing.

"JD," I call out at the top of my voice. But it's so loud he doesn't hear me until I'm practically right on top of him. "Dude, we're out of here. If cyber girl here wants to play, we're gonna do it outside."

I roll the conversation upstairs in my head as JD explains the turn of events to whats-her-face. Do I tell JD? Do I tell JD that this freak said his kid might be alive and all I have to do is get some girls pregnant and he can have that information?

Why the fuck would I do that? Seriously. So we can trade places? So I can spend the rest of my life searching for the children who were stolen from me?

And what are the chances this guy is even telling the truth?

No. It's far more likely that Father Freak is full of shit. Everyone knows JD's kid is gone. He talked about it for years. This asshole wandered in to something, put two and two together, and then made his move to get me involved in his procreation fetish.

I'm not buying it. He yanked my chain pretty hard upstairs, but the longer I think about it, the less likely it seems.

It's bullshit, Ark, my inner voice says. *Stay the course.*

I came to Denver for a reason, and this asshole is not going to derail me now.

THIRTY-THREE

BLUE

I CAN'T believe they'd leave me alone in here. If it wasn't so stupid, it might be cute. I mean, I just confessed to Ark that I'm a reporter and everything about that guy says newsworthy secrets.

After waiting thirty minutes—just enough time to be sure they won't come back and check up on me—I head straight to his unlocked office. The first thing I see is the garment bag, still hanging on his suit rack. Zipped and unused. God, it feels like a lifetime ago that he bought me that outfit with the intention of taking me on a date.

I walk over to it and feel the bag. It's not some cheap plastic, it's more like the kind of bag you'd use over and over again. It's got some boutique store name on it that I've never heard of, so it must be local.

He's got a suit coat hanging behind the garment bag and a few of those blue ties dangling down as well. I've never seen him wear a proper suit, so I stop and picture it for a second.

Ark is fucking hot.

JD is hot too, but in a dangerous way, like he used to be the all-American hero, but then life shit on him and now he's irreversibly damaged. The hot you feel between your legs when those blue eyes stare at you and you can't look away. The hot that sends a chill up your spine when he takes off his shirt and those muscles ripple and stretch because they say, *I'll leave bruises before I'm done, so make sure you know what you're getting into.* The hot you desire, because he's so full of testosterone, everything about him screams lust.

Ark is hot in a very different way. Like he's got all these compartments and he only lets you open one of them at a time. But you know, if you could just open two or three at once, you'd find something amazing. He's the kind of hot that only comes in movies filmed in the dead of winter when everything is cold. Where the government is corrupt, the city is dirty, the characters shady, and the sex is nothing but a way to forget the fucked-upness of life.

Both of them come with warning signs, and if I was smart, I'd get the hell away from them before the shit gets complicated.

But I can't. For so many reasons, I can't.

I owe Janine. If she's dead like Ark says JD's girl is, then I need to know. Her story needs to be told. And if her baby is alive, then that baby needs to come home. That baby deserves to know who her family is. Needs to know that once upon a time her mother was so much more than what she ended up being.

I owe her.

I sit down at Ark's desk and shake the mouse so the monitor comes on. And nope. Not locked. Which, if I was a suspicious bitch, I'd take as a signal that he knows I'm going to snoop tonight and there won't be a single file on here with anything useful.

When the desktop comes up, there are only three file folders to choose from. One is called *In progress*. One is called *Completed*.

And one is called *Blue*.

The satisfaction that I get from having him figured out evaporates when I double-click the file and images come up in a cascade of windows.

What the fuck is this?

I really expected a note. *Hey, Blue, I got your number, you snoopy bitch. I'm normal, JD is normal. Now be a good girl and open your legs and wait for us on the bed.*

That note is not a bad way to go. I'm just saying.

But that's not what this is at all. These are the photos he was looking at the other day when I was in here. Beautiful, retouched photos. Black and white artsy photos that have the lights and shadows manipulated in such a way that you only see what he wants you to see.

And they are not just of me, but all three of us. Dozens and dozens of them in the tub. Ark on one side, JD, with me in his arms on the other. The steam from the hot water obscuring our faces, but not the intentions of the people.

Most of them are blurry, because he was using a long exposure time to capture the light bouncing off the mist in the air, and we were moving around. But there are enough in focus to fall in love with this newly discovered artist side of the strait-laced wannabe.

"Goddamn," I whisper. "Could you be any more perfect?"

There are also several videos of that scene out on the terrace where they both had their fingers inside of me.

Those make me wet. No. Those make me throb.

I wonder how far Ark wants to take this threesome stuff. He doesn't act bisexual at all. JD I can see. He seems more open.

Maybe because he's a porn star, stupid.

Right.

I close all the windows and open up the other folder called *In progress*. This one has two movies with last Sunday's date. The day JD brought me home. The day he made these movies with us in the tub.

My jealousy kicks in because these movies are of a girl sucking off Ark, not JD.

Asshole.

Why this ticks me off, I'm not sure. But it does. I open the attached documents to see if I can find out who she is, and there is one contract and the sum she was paid. Ten thousand dollars.

Jesus Christ. If I had an ID I could make one movie and go home.

No, my mind interrupts. *I can't go home until I find Janine and write this story.*

The girl's name is Lanie Porter. She's thirty-two, redhead, blue eyes, and she looks like a hooker. Gross.

OK, I'm done with the desktop folders. It's all on the up and up. He's got contracts, STD tests, and photocopies of their driver's licenses. It's obvious to me that Ark's real business is not this public fuck porn. Because that's all legitimate and I just know that deep down, he's as illegitimate as they come.

I check the hard drive for more folders, but there are none. Which means he uses this computer for personal stuff and maybe the initial steps in the digital record chain, and then all the files get transferred somewhere else.

I look over at the three tall filing cabinets that look like expensive pieces of modern art made of steel, wire, and glass.

No. That's too easy. He wouldn't keep paper records. Would he?

Obviously if one has filing cabinets—custom-made filing cabinets, no less—one keeps files in them. I pull on the latch on the stainless steel box but it's locked.

I try each one, but nope. They are all locked.

If this was a nineteen-twenties gumshoe movie where the reporter was the heroine, I'd find the key in the oversized desk drawer. But the desk has no drawer and even if it did, I'd never find the key in there. Because the lock on those filing cabinets requires a fingerprint and a code.

"OK, then," I say to myself as I walk out of his office and slide the doors closed behind me. "Operation Ambush Ark is over." I've got nothing but an unsettled feeling about those pictures of us. It was like... it was like... he was creating something from it. But I'm not sure what.

I shake it off. Because that stuff was personal and if I want to know personal stuff, I'll have to ask him myself. So I walk down the hallway to JD's bedroom and then flick the lights on before entering.

JD's room has the same custom furniture as Ark's office, and the rest of the house, for that matter. Steel boxes instead of cabinets. Cables and wires to add to the industrial effect. And glass. But there are some subtle differences between the two rooms.

One, JD is not neat like Ark. His shit is all over the place. And two, he's not nearly as worried about security. Because he's got porn everywhere. Most of it is him getting his dick sucked by these random girls. Girls who look a lot more enthusiastic than that one blowing Ark, that's for sure. And JD is animated and talkative in his starring roles. He pulls their hair and slaps their faces. He always makes them come, too. It's just fingering, but hey, it counts.

Ark never acted like that with the woman in his movies. And that makes me feel better for some reason.

JD, for being the guy who does all the acting, has plenty of cameras in his possession. Big expensive ones with zoom lenses. Small pocket-sized ones. Video cameras, everything from a professional one that goes on your shoulder, to a little hand-held hiding in the back of a knocked-over stack of video games.

The cameras all have photos of him and girls on them. Some

sexual, some not. Just random conversations with people.

But this little hand-held video camera has more than forty hours of video on it. All of it is of JD, and none of it has girls. Because it's a video diary. The last entry was five days ago. The day he met me.

I press the button that will take me to the beginning and then press play.

The first was four years ago.

I look around, suddenly ashamed of my snooping. Do I watch it? It's wrong. I know it's wrong. But then the little screen in front of me comes to life and there's a face.

I almost don't recognize him, that's how different he looks. He's skinny, for one. Gaunt. And his face is black and blue. The kind of black and blue you see in police photos after a mugging.

Someone beat the ever-living fuck out of him. And that seals the deal.

I need to know how he got so broken and all I have to do is not turn it off.

"Hey," JD says from the camera. He stops. Just one word is enough to shut him down. His eyes begin to water and for a moment I think it's because it's painful to talk. From the beating.

But then he swallows hard and wipes his eyes. He clears his throat. "Hey," he repeats. "I just want you to know, I miss you." Another pause. Tears well up in his eyes. "I got this camera from a guy I met today, baby. And he said I could use it. I know what you're thinking. Don't trust anyone bearing gifts. I know. I shouldn't trust him. But I got no one, Marie. I've got no one else."

JD lies down on something, and from this close-up angle I can't tell if it's a bed or the floor. But I suspect it's the floor because he looks homeless. He looks nothing like the healthy, charming JD I know.

"So I'm gonna take a chance and help him out. He'll help me if I help him. That's what he said. He'll help me look for you. And when I find you, I want you to know that I never gave up. I never stopped looking. So I'm gonna record it all on this camera." JD stops and his eyes dart back and forth. Like the lens is a pair of eyes. "I love you. I love you, and I love our baby. I'm so sorry and I will never stop looking."

There's silence after that. Well, not quite. There's no more talking, but the film goes on for three more minutes of sadness. Of JD looking into the camera, desperate for his Marie to see him. To see his grief. To believe that he's gonna save her.

I stop the recording because an overwhelming despair washes over me. He didn't save her. He lost her. She was killed, or died on her own, or whatever. Ark said so the other day. And there's no baby here, so obviously there was no happy ending with that either.

I watch the next entry. He's still a mess. And the next and the next and the next. All of him a mess. There's plenty of mentions of Ark, but no one else ever appears in the videos. Just JD and his depression. JD and his sadness. JD and his overwhelming problems.

He talks about killing himself at least once a week. Sometimes every entry has a mention. And month by month, he appears to be getting worse instead of better.

But then he explains the business they're starting and something changes inside him. It's small on the first day. A pause. It's a short pause, only a few moments. But in every other video, the pause is so he can cry.

After this pause, he does something different.

He smiles.

All because of Public Fuck America. Ark's brainchild to a life of luxury.

JD buys into it. Every bit of it. Because after that one smile, there are more smiles. Not every day, but every week. I find myself fast-forwarding the recording until I see the smile before stopping to hear what he has to say. And then… he laughs. Exactly four months after meeting Ark, when he was at his lowest point in life, JD laughs.

From there, his diary is all about business. His acting. The girls. The money. The loft. That Ray guy. Holidays are happy and the entries become less and less frequent. Once a day turns into once a week turns into once every two weeks and on and on. Until there's a six-month gap in the dates.

And that movie isn't of JD lying down, like all the others are. A bedtime ritual that cleared his head and set him up for the next good day.

No, the next one is outside and JD never even makes an appearance. Because it's nothing but one long shot of a headstone. Not the nice kind that stand up, but the flat ones. A marker, really. Just a marker of a girl he used to love. Marie Lagucci. Dead at age twenty-two.

He never talks, but the crying is audible, even over the roar of traffic.

This is the first time Ark ever appears in the diary. He picks JD up and takes him to a waiting car. The whole time the camera is recording. Ark is patient and sympathetic.

JD is a mess.

Ark must figure out the camera in JD's hand is still recording in the car, because that's when the footage ends.

There are no other entries for a year.

My mind fills in those dark days after her grave was found. JD is a guy who feels. Not like Ark, who seems to be a guy who watches. JD is a guy who is invested. When he's in, he's all in. Heart, soul, mind.

I don't bother watching the rest of the video. Instead, I fast-forward to the end. And even though it's more of a breach of privacy to listen to him talk about me, I do anyway.

And I feel like total shit once I'm done. Because he tells Marie

I'm good. And pretty. And deserving of a nice life. Like the one Ark gave him. He tells Marie they can save me from whoever—whatever—the problem is.

But the problem is me.

So can he really save me from myself?

THIRTY-FOUR

ARK

JD pays the girl in the alley afterward, while I pack up my lenses and put them in my bag. There's a small crowd gathered, and since this is not how her contract was written, I'm gonna take the girl home in a cab before heading over to Ray's.

"You ready?" I ask, nodding at the waiting cab.

The girl won't meet my eyes, but she nods back.

"See you tomorrow, JD."

"OK," he says, walking off and lighting up a cigarette at the same time.

The girl is already climbing into the cab, so fuck it. He doesn't know about that asshole Gabriel tonight, and I'm not about to tell him until I have a chat with Ray about it. So I let him walk off while I join the girl.

"Where do you live, darling?" I ask her, the cabbie looking over his shoulder at us.

"My boyfriend is waiting over at Skates Pub."

"Your boyfriend?" Do boyfriends let their girls do this shit? I swipe my credit card and key in the address so we can get going. I have a lot of editing to do.

"Yeah," she says, looking out the window so she doesn't have to meet my eyes. "We're having some trouble paying the bills." And then she does look at me. "He lost his job a few months ago. I have to feed my kids."

I nod at her, shoot a smile to let her know I don't judge. But internally I judge. Not her. Him. What kind of asshole lets his girl do porn to feed their kids?

"My girlfriend worked for you guys a while back. Four or five times. She does real movies now."

"Oh." Real movies my ass.

"Her husband told my boyfriend about it. So we went looking for you guys. And that's how I met JD. He's real nice."

I guess. I ignore her for the rest of the ride because honestly, I can't understand how a man could let his girlfriend suck another man's cock for food money.

"This is good," the girl says, knocking on the glass that separates us from the driver. "That's my boyfriend."

The cabbie pulls over and I smile at the girl when she says thank you. Her boyfriend waits a ways off, letting her come to him.

"Where you going, mister?" the cabbie asks me, jolting my attention away from the scene playing out in front of me.

"Back to 16th and California," I say, swiping my card again.

I think about Gabriel the whole five minutes it takes me to get back home, and then I go down to our parking garage and grab my Jeep. I wonder if JD is upstairs with Blue yet? I'm tempted to go check, but I can't see him alone yet. Not until I talk to Ray. Because all that bullshit will come pouring out, and I'm not sure that's good for anybody.

Not because I'm selfish. Not because I want JD to forget the past and concentrate on the future. I do, but that's not why I don't go up there and tell him his kid might be alive.

I don't tell him because the last time he got wind of this, he was obsessed for months and it ended with a trip to the emergency room to pump his stomach from an intentional overdose.

This is a no-win right here. Don't tell him shit and lose our friendship if he ever finds out. Tell him, and he gets obsessed, never gets any closer—because I'm not fucking a pack of sister-wives to get that info—and he tries to kill himself again.

I need advice. I need Ray's advice. JD and I don't see him together that often. Holidays mostly. But I know Ray takes care of JD like I do. He watches out for JD as best he can. And he lets me know when I need to step in. Ray will know what to do.

I get in the Jeep, start her up and then pull out of the garage and head north.

A few minutes later I pull into the garage and park on the top level. Cut the engine... and sit. I have no clue what I'm doing. Why the fuck did I let this shit get so far along without having an exit strategy? What if Gabriel is lying?

And then a thought pops into my head.

A traitorous thought that derails my whole night.

What if Ray is somehow involved?

THIRTY-FIVE

BLUE

'M waiting on the couch, wide awake, when JD comes through the door at ten minutes to two. He immediately smiles at me.

"Whatcha doing?" he asks, plopping down next to me. His smile is contagious, but in my head, all I see is the destroyed man in the first entry of the video diary.

I manage to give him a weak smile back. "Waiting up for you. I didn't want to miss you. And I didn't know where you wanted me to sleep."

JD shrugs. "We can sleep in my room. But Ark won't come in and join us. So we might as well hit the sack in his room. That way he can't avoid us."

"Why would he want to?" I'm genuinely interested. Plus, this is a whole lot better than talking about JD's dead girlfriend.

"Ark's not into this shit, ya know?"

"What shit? Sharing?"

"No," JD laughs. "He's down with sharing, obviously. But

sharing isn't a real relationship. If we want him to be in a real relationship, we gotta talk him into it."

He's serious.

I lean in and hug him, but he pushes me back. "I need to shower first. Get the smell of that whore off me."

"Oh," I snort. "Mood-killer."

"Yeah, well, three more nights and we are done. I'm retiring from acting and going strictly into acquisitions." And then he pats my leg and gets up. "I'll meet you in there in ten minutes. Go get naked."

I watch his sexy ass as he walks off to his side of the loft. My heart has this little ache in it. Not for myself—for once— and not for the best friend I probably lost. Or the sadness that comes when I think of my parents and what they must be going through.

But for him.

And for us.

Because I want more than anything for this to be real. And it can't be real. How can it be real when all three of us are lying? I don't know what Ark's lie is yet, but clearly JD is not over what happened to his girlfriend and baby. He never mentions the baby in the video diary other than that one promise to find out what happened. And the only conclusion I can draw from that is it hurts too much. It just hurts too damn much to speak the words.

How can I fix this? How can I make these men mine when they have this shared sad past?

Find me, the voice in my head says. *Find me and you'll find out what really happened to Marie.*

I want to believe her. That girl in my head who sounds an awful lot like Janine. I really do. But I'm not sure JD can handle the truth.

My fingertips go to the raised scar on the back of my neck. If Marie had this brand, I know what happened to her. I know what happened to her baby, too. The same thing that would have happened to mine.

Of course, mine would've been folded into the flock because I was one of Gabriel's wives. But Janine... her baby didn't have the pedigree to be kept. I was only granted this privilege after they found out who I was and Gabriel claimed me as his. For every one of us on the inside, there were dozens of girls on the outside, who just ended up dead and their babies sold to a long list of couples eager to buy, regardless of how the child came on the market.

That word in my mind makes me gag.

You were part of a baby-selling ring, Blue.

No. I shake the thought out of my head. I was a prisoner, like Ark said. They locked me in a cage for four months when they first found out. That's how they kept me in the months after it was determined I couldn't conceive. Every night they came and took me to the lounge. And every night I had a flock member to please in any way they wanted.

I was *not* one of them.

But I'd be lying if I said I believed that. Just like JD is lying if he thinks he wants to put this behind him. Because when Gabriel came to me and offered me a deal, I took it. I made that YouTube video and lied to the world. I signed the contract. I let them brand me.

"Blue?"

JD's voice startles me so bad, I let out a whimper.

"Blue?" He comes over to me, still sitting on the couch, in the exact same position as when he left. "What's wrong?"

I can't lie to him. I can't. Not after all those hours I spent watching him bare his soul to a camera called Marie. But I can't tell him the truth either. At least not that truth. "I miss my parents," I say instead. "I miss them so bad."

"Where are they?" he asks, sitting down. He's naked, just a

wet towel wrapped around his waist.

He smells like soap and shaving cream. He smells like a fresh start.

And then I realize he doesn't even know who I am. Ark never told him. I figured they'd be talking about me all night, but clearly not. "Canada," I say, unable to tell that story again.

He just leans over and puts his arm protectively around me. And that small gesture is what seals the deal. I hug him hard because it feels so good to have something in common. I'm running from my past. He's running from his. And the two of us are clinging to each other. Sharing our regrets and shame.

"Wanna go to bed now?"

It's a change of subject. No, it's more than a change of subject. It's denial and escape and salvation all rolled into one five-word sentence. "Sure," I say with a smile. "What good does it do to dwell on what you can't change?"

He stands, scoops me into his arms, and carries me towards Ark's bedroom. "Darling, no truer words have ever been said."

He lays me down on the bed. Gently, like he might do for Marie. And then the tears are there and I roll over and bury my face in the pillow.

"Shhh," he says, sliding in next to me. "Let's not do this, Blue." He whispers the words. They are soft and calming. His fingers lift my shirt up, and I let him take it off. I push down my borrowed boxers without being encouraged.

"Make me forget, JD. Make me forget what they did." I turn on my side so I can see him, and I cup his face in my hands. His face is smooth now that he's shaved, and it feels so good. It feels like strength. It feels like protection. It feels like forgiveness. For all of my sins. "Make me forget and I'll make you forget too."

He smiles, a genuine JD smile, and I melt. He wraps me up in his arms and pulls me close, so we are face to face. And then he touches his lips to mine and shakes his head as he pulls back. "I can't forget, Blue. That's my problem. If you know how to make that happen, tell me." His blue eyes search mine. "Tell me how you forget, because I've never learned that skill. I never stop thinking about her. Never. I see her face in everyone. Even you. That's why I took you home, Blue. Every girl who sucks my dick on camera, in my mind they are all my girl. The one I lost. That's why I do it. That's the only reason I do it. I haven't had a girlfriend in four years. I haven't asked a girl out on a date in four years. All I have left are the ghosts of her. I live my life every day with the hope that I can get a glimpse of her in a girl on her knees in front of me. I'm sick, man. I want to be the one who can take away whatever it is you're feeling, but the truth is, I'm a mess."

I stare at him for a moment. I want to choose the right words. I want to make him better. I want to save him the way he saved me. "I'm very new at this coping stuff, JD. I'm just a baby at it. But you take it away for me just by being here. And Ark does the same thing. And that's why I want you. That's why I need you. So maybe—when you look at me tonight—you can see me instead of her? Maybe that will help?"

He presses my palm into his cheek. The freshness of his skin grounds me again. "You're so beautiful. Your eyes are like the water you see in those pictures of paradise. A color that can't be described because a word for it can't do it justice. And your hair is gold, like the sun. You're my paradise, Blue. You and Ark are all I have left."

"I'm yours, JD. If you want me, I'm yours."

"No, Blue," he whispers back. "You're *ours*."

And then he pushes me back onto the bed and gets up on his knees. He grips my thighs and opens them up so he can position himself between my legs. His cock is so hard it stands up, like it's reaching for his belly. The tip is glistening and my pussy throbs with anticipation. As soon as he enters me, he places his hand on my throat, lightly squeezing. His thumb is on my pulsing artery, his fingers along the other side of my jaw.

He thrusts inside me, pressing against the aching throb in my neck, filling me up and making me cry out with my last breath.

I see stars. I see heaven. I see every good thing I ever forgot. I feel the pain mixed with the pleasure. And his hard body—muscled and sweaty from confessions, and lust, and need—weighs me down. My throat stops drawing in air and my chest stops rising. And in that same moment the darkness takes over.

In that same moment… we come.

THIRTY-SIX

ARK

RAY is nowhere to be found when I get to his private quarters where my editing office is, so I spend the next four hours wondering. And I have no shortage of things to wonder about.

JD. How strong is he these days? Strong enough to hear what Gabriel told me without killing someone if it turns out to be true? Killing himself if it adds up to nothing? Do I want to risk either of those things by telling him? Do I want to risk our friendship, and whatever may be developing with the addition of Blue, by not telling him?

How am I competent to make this decision alone? Why am I in this position in the first place? Why do people trust me? Why in the ever-loving fuck do people put their trust in *me*?

I admit, that has been on my mind a lot over the past year.

When I got off the bus and found JD, that was a stroke of luck. I thought for sure my life was on track.

But it wasn't. It's not on track. It's so far off-track, I don't even know who I am anymore. No matter how much money I make, it's not enough to erase the reason I came to Denver in the first place. No matter how successful I appear, the last four years add up to nothing but failure. After all the girls I've come across on the streets, why does Blue have to be the one who makes a difference? Why now?

Because you got comfortable, Ark, my inner voice says. *You got used to this life. Started to enjoy it.*

And that's true. It's not a bad life. And it's about to get even better. We are a few weeks away from Public Fuck America going live.

Why now?

I stopped questioning the whole idea that doing bad things can lead to good. I stopped feeling guilty. Stopped keeping myself awake at night wondering what I'm doing. Why I'm doing it.

Blue was wrong when she said I wasn't invested. I am invested. Just not in the way she thinks.

The software I'm running completes the rendering of the movie, and I save it to the weekly outgoing folder so I can upload it on Sunday when we complete our last week of contract work for Ray.

This is it. I'm about to go big time. And all those doors that have been closed to me for the last four years will open. But if men like Gabriel are behind those doors, what then? Does the end really justify the means? Am I a sick piece of shit for participating in this business, even if my intentions are good?

I can't answer that. I'm not capable of self-judgment. The money blinds me. The partnership with JD blinds me. Hell, even Blue blinds me.

I shut down my computer and push away from my desk feeling more lost than I have in years. Seeing Lanie last weekend isn't helping things much, either. In fact, I think she's the whole reason I'm having this reawakening in the first place.

I came into Ray's place thinking he might be part of the problem. But he's not the problem. I am. He's not the one hoarding secrets. I am. He's not the one selling his soul. He never wrestled with the line between good and evil. Ray is just a guy who saw an opportunity and took it.

And I could be just like him.

Or I *could've* been just like him.

But now that Blue is here I'm questioning the road forward.

Public Fuck with JD and Blue?

Or cash out and go home?

I nod to the guards standing outside Ray's private floor and head back up the stairs to my waiting Jeep. The ground is covered in a few inches of fresh snow and I have to warm the old girl up for a few minutes before heading home in the pre-dawn light. By the time I make it back to my own parking garage, the snow is falling in large, round flakes.

Inside the apartment it's cold, our winter heating settings not yet ready to kick in, so I adjust the thermostat and walk outside onto the terrace to take in the city before it wakes up.

Is this my city now? Denver? Will I stay here forever? Take Ray's place once he retires?

Or will I move on? Get out as soon as I can?

I look over my shoulder, past the terrace doors. Into the condo. Will I leave JD behind if I go? I try to imagine a life without JD and find that I can't. And it's not because I want to marry the guy. I don't. I want a wife and kid. I want what most men want.

But I want JD to be there too. It hurts to think of leaving him behind if this ends. What will happen to him? Will he be able to go on without me? And aren't I full of myself? To think that he needs me as much as I need him.

Gabriel is right about one thing. I love JD. And I'll do anything for the guy.

I turn around and go back inside, the snowflakes sticking to my hair, the cold sticking to my body, making me need to warm up in the shower. I head to my room and stop short when I see them both in my bed.

Fuck. My eyes linger on JD's hand on Blue's bare breast, JD's long, muscled leg wrapping over her in a protective embrace. And there's empty space where I'd fit in perfectly, if I just gave in to my feelings.

I turn away and get into the shower, letting the hot water wash away the filth I deal in four nights a week.

If I give in… we'd have a life of porn-selling. And as long as we ran the business by the book, it'd be a very nice one. Filled with whatever we wanted. Vacations together. Christmases. Birthdays. Hell, kids. We could have kids like any other partnership. I picture this place filled with a family we make together.

Is that stupid?

Is Blue even invested? She's a girl missing from a very prominent family. How long can we keep up the charade? How long before she misses her family so much, she risks contact? And once there's contact, this life evaporates. There's no way she'd stay with JD and me. No fucking way.

The only possibility of making something real out of this is to take care of all the outside threats. And if I do that, can I continue to be this person? Can I continue to contribute to the demise of hundreds—hell, thousands—of girls involved in the industry each year?

How the fuck do I justify that?

It's a no-win. There is no way to win this game without tearing my whole life down in the process.

I turn the water off and grab a towel, wrapping it around my waist. When I open the door, the steam from the bathroom pours out into the bedroom, covering the two people in my bed with mist. Making them look like apparitions. Like they can disappear at any moment.

I drop the towel and walk over to the bed. JD is facing me, hugging Blue to his chest. He opens one tired eye and smiles. "Just get in bed, Ark."

His voice is soft, but Blue stirs, twisting her body so her shoulders are flat on the mattress, her breasts exposed to me. Her breathing is still deep, telling me she's asleep.

I pull the covers back and slide in next to her and when she turns into me, her cool body hits my overheated one from the shower. She moans and snuggles in closer, making me chance a look over at JD to see what he's thinking about this.

He closes his eyes and places a hand on her hip, then slides it down her belly so that it rubs me as well. My dick is already hard, but that adds to my growing desire. I want to touch him. I want him to touch me. And I want to share more than Blue.

His hand spends a few moments caressing Blue's pussy, and she moans again, but this time her eyes flutter for a few seconds. When she finally opens them, the desire in there seals the deal.

I want them both.

They both want me.

We want each other.

Her hand comes up, her palm sliding along the rough stubble of my cheek. And then JD's hand is on top of hers and we lie there, enjoying the moments. Enjoying the beginning of something new.

Not sex.

Not lust.

Love. It's the official beginning of our shared love.

And then we pass the start line.

"Blue, baby," JD says in that low throaty growl he likes to use on the whores. But this time, it opens up a level of desire in me like it never has before. And when he grabs Blue's hand and slides it down my chest, both their fingertips caressing my skin the whole way down to my cock, I reach up and grip his hair in a tight fist.

Blue's little palm circles my dick, and JD's big one circles hers. Together they pump me in a slow, easy rhythm. My eyes dart between them. And then JD's hand lifts off of Blue's and he brings it up, pressing down on her head. "Suck him off, Blue."

She smiles at me and lets JD's pressure guide her head down my stomach. She kisses me as she goes, her tongue licking my abs, then my groin, then her hand cups my balls as her lips find my head.

"Fuck," I moan out, my eyes closing. Her mouth moves up and down my shaft, licking me, then sucking my tip, her hand still kneading my balls.

"Take him deep, baby. Like you did me earlier."

I should feel rage at Blue sucking another man. But I don't. I don't even come close. Those words turn me on so bad, I yank on JD's hair, pulling his face to mine. And when our faces are only inches apart, I do something I never thought I'd do.

I lean in and kiss him on the lips.

His mouth opens in response, his tongue twisting us together. I pull his hair again and he groans, grinding his hips against the back of Blue's head as she continues to suck me.

He tastes like pussy, and my tongue can't get enough of it. My hand falls from his hair, pressing against his throat, squeezing him the way I've seen him squeeze hundreds of girls as they sucked his dick in public.

"Fuck, Ark," he says, pulling out of the kiss.

"Fuck, no?" I ask. "Or fuck, yes?"

He stares at me. It's the most intimate moment I've ever had with him. Maybe with anyone. "It's a definite fuck, yes."

And then he smacks Blue on the ass. "Baby, climb on Ark." He guides her up to her knees, then turns her around so she's facing me and has her straddle my hips. I watch the whole process, my dick swelling, so fucking ready for this it almost hurts. She hovers over my tip, her pussy so wet it's practically dripping. And then JD's hand is there, his finger pushing up against her opening, making her moan in the most delicious way. My hand goes to JD's shoulder and then drops down, caressing his muscular back.

And he shoots me a smile.

I laugh at that smile, and any leftover inhibitions evaporate. That's a smile I've waited four long years for. A smile that says, *You make me happy.* A smile that says, *This is right.*

And in that moment Blue lowers herself down onto my waiting cock. I fill her up the way JD's smile did me. I stretch her pussy out with my thick shaft, and she bends down, her face to mine, pressing our foreheads together.

And I kiss her too. I cup her face and kiss her hard. I kiss her good and long. My tongue can't get enough of her. I thread my fingers through her hair, pulling it in fistfuls, just like I did JD's.

I feel pressure down between my legs and realize JD's hand is still between Blue's legs. She moans hard, like she's in pain, and I know he's fingering her asshole. The thought of us both fucking her drives me wild, and I begin to thrust inside her, my hips bouncing on the bed, skin slapping skin, my balls smacking against us both.

And then JD kneels behind her, pumping her ass for a second, before lowering his head to lick. His chin skims against the lower portion of my shaft. He strokes me as he gets her ready for him, and this feels so fucking good, I have to close my eyes and concentrate on holding onto my load.

JD rises up, positioning his dick over Blue's back entrance, and then there's a tightening of her pussy as she clamps down on me. JD's cock pushes inside and Blue sits up, her back arching. But JD slams her back down onto my chest and leans over so his face is pressed into her neck. "Be still, baby. Be still."

She whimpers, and I wrap my arms around her, holding her

tightly against me, kissing her everywhere my lips can reach. "Relax," I say. "Let us love you," I tell her.

And she does relax. JD thrusts once, hard. And then we are both fully inside her. Him on top of her. Her on top of me. Our arms and legs tangle together, our faces seeking each other out, our lips touching, tongues searching, breath mingling.

It's the most beautiful moment I've had in my entire life.

She is not one lost girl.

We are not two best friends.

We are one trinity of perfection.

THIRTY-SEVEN

BLUE

WE come together. All three of us. I scream so loud from
the release, Ark laughs and JD slaps me on the ass, telling
me I'm gonna wake up the neighbors below.

So I lie still, whimpering as wave after wave of pleasure rolls
over me. JD collapses on top of us and Ark pushes him off with
a grunt. And then he holds me tight and rolls us over so I'm
sandwiched between them.

This. I have no words to describe it, but I need this for the rest
of my life. These two men on either side. I have found Heaven,
and I'm still alive. I have cheated death.

We fall asleep like that. We sleep all damn day. And we only
get up for a shower and food when it's well past four PM.

I sit on the black stone island that separates the kitchen from
the living area, watching JD cook. He's making pancakes and
eggs. Ark is on his laptop, sitting in a stool across the island from
me. Working, I guess.

It feels like we've been living this life forever.

This is what love feels like. Complete, one hundred percent contentment. I can think of no other place I'd rather be. I can think of no other girl on the entire planet who has a life as full and rich and perfect as mine.

"How many?" JD asks me, pointing to the pancakes and eggs.

I can only smile at him and shrug. "I don't care. If you feed me crumbs, I'm happy. If you stuff me until I'm full, I'm happy."

Ark peeks over his laptop and laughs. "I'm famished. I'll eat all of it, if you let me. But some business first, JD."

I make a face. I don't want to talk about their business. I don't even want to think about what they'll be doing tonight.

"It's Halloween and Ray thinks you're going to the party."

"Well," JD says, looking at me before taking his attention to Ark, "the girl I have lined up is a waitress tonight. So I guess we're both going." He looks back at me. "You wanna go, Blue? We can dress you up. No one will know it's you."

I shake my head. "No, thanks," I say quietly, not able to meet his gaze.

He walks over to me and lifts my chin up, making me acknowledge him. "You want us to stay home?"

I glance over at Ark, expecting him to object. He's a businessman, after all. And this is business. Something I have no say in.

But Ark just shrugs. "We owe Ray two more videos. But we have more than two hundred squirreled away for the Public Fuck release coming up. We can afford to give up two of those to finish up our contract."

"You'd do that?" I ask.

"If it makes you happy, sure. Why not?" He looks over at JD. "I'll call Ray and tell him we're staying home and I'll be around on Sunday to upload the final videos. After that, we'll celebrate." And then he smiles at me and returns his concentration to his computer.

JD turns my head back to him and gives me a kiss that makes me wet between my legs. "Works for me," he says. "I got what I need right here."

His attention makes my whole body warm, and it takes me a second to realize I'm blushing. When I look over at Ark, he's laughing as he gets up from his computer and takes a seat at the breakfast table. "Don't be embarrassed. Just enjoy it."

"I am," I tell Ark back, jumping down off the island and walking over to him, my hand lingering on his shoulder for a moment as I take the chair on the other side of him. The table is small and round, so it's got an intimate feel to it. "I don't know how I got here." I look at both of them, one at a time. JD puts a plate of pancakes down and pauses. But all I can do is shrug. "I don't know. But I feel... lucky."

"Maybe it was just meant to be?" JD walks back to grab the eggs. "I believe in fate instead of luck," he continues, setting the eggs down and taking his chair. The table used to only have two chairs, but Ark brought out a chair from his office that he's sitting on. "I mean, look. I've been living with this control freak for four years now. And I will tell you, I've never thought about kissing him before this morning."

Ark grins, shaking his head. If he feels uncomfortable about how things have changed overnight, he hides it well. Because he doesn't seem to be shy. In fact, JD is right. He is a control freak. And he's still in control now.

"Well, I did," he says with a straight face.

"Bullshit," JD says back, stuffing a pancake into his mouth. "You never did. And you wouldn't be here now if we hadn't ambushed you with the leash."

"Oh, God." I shake my head and grab a pancake and some eggs.

"You don't like the leash?"

It's Ark asking, not JD. And that stops me for a moment.

"Did you?"

"It was hot as fuck," Ark says.

"I thought you hated the kink?" I look over at JD and he winks at me.

"Not true. I just don't like to cross any lines."

"But collars and leashes are acceptable kink?"

"I think she should wear the collar all the time, Ark," JD says, bypassing my question.

And even though I hate the fact that it affects me this way, the wetness begins to build between my legs again.

How does he do that with words?

Ark just stares at me, like he can read my thoughts. And then his hand is on my leg, rubbing. I watch his face as he does this. He remains stoic, no smile, his mouth just a flat line. And then his hand travels up to the v between my legs, slips inside the boxers I'm wearing, and fingers my pussy.

I swallow hard and close my eyes.

"Go get the collar, JD," he says in a commanding tone.

I suck in a breath and bite my lip, trying to calm down. JD's chair scrapes against the polished concrete floor as he gets up to go find the strip of leather.

"You want it, don't you, Blue?"

I nod my head, but keep my eyes closed. "I can't help it." I don't know how much they want to know about my captivity, so I remain silent. JD returns a few mounts later and hands the collar to Ark. His chair scrapes as he pushes back too, and suddenly I'm trembling.

"Shhh," he says, placing a hand on my shoulder. "I'm not going to hurt you, you know that."

"I know," I say. Because I do know. Ark is not into the pain. "But the problem is—" I look up at him and take a deep breath. "The problem is, I like to be hurt." It's a soft whisper, but everyone hears it. When I look over at JD, he's grinning big. When I tilt my head up to see Ark's reaction, he strokes a finger down my cheek.

"Hold your hair up," Ark orders.

I do as I'm told and he slips the collar around my neck, fastening it so that it's only loose enough to allow his fingers to slip between it and my skin.

I take a deep breath.

"You're ours now. And that means you're honest if we ask you a question. So my first question is, how hard do you like it?"

I let out a long gush of air and fold my hands in my lap.

"Be truthful, baby," JD says. "We're not going to judge."

I nod, and then look up at his charming face. I believe him. With all my heart. I believe that I'm accepted here. That we all have a dark part to our souls. And even though it would be better if that darkness was never there in the first place, the next best thing is to have the people we love accept that we are imperfect.

And that's what we have here.

"Can I tell you how it happened? Before I tell you what I like?"

"Of course," Ark answers. He takes my hand and pulls me over to his lap. I climb on, grateful for his tenderness. One arm wraps around my waist and the other strokes my knee. "Take your time."

I know he didn't tell JD who I really am, so I avoid any talk of that. "The first time I was taken, it was mutual. In fact..." I swallow down the shame and continue. "In fact, they all were. Up until last Saturday night. He was never tender, but that excited me. The rough play was thrilling. Something I'd never experienced before. I responded... Oh, God, this is so embarrassing."

I look up at Ark, but he's not gonna let me out of it now that I started. So I look over at JD. He's got his eyebrows up. "You responded to the orders? Or the humiliation? Or the violence?"

"All of it," I say, so ashamed of myself. "I responded to all of it. Even though I didn't want to."

"I'm not going to humiliate you, Blue. I put the collar on you because you want it." I look up at Ark and see the truth in his eyes.

"I know. But I hate that part of myself."

"Why?" JD says, getting up from his chair and coming over to us. "If we agree it gives us pleasure, then why are you ashamed?"

"Do you feel shame?" I ask him. "For wanting to be… rough with girls?"

JD shakes his head slowly. "No. I only do it with girls like you."

"What about you?"

Ark shakes his head too. "I don't do much of it. Not enough to cross any lines. But I'm happy to slap your ass and pull your hair." And then he smiles and a small laugh comes out before he can control himself. His hand dips between my legs, pushing inside my pussy. "You are so fucking wet just from talking about it. And now that we know you like it, we can push some limits if that's what you want."

"Do you want that, Blue?"

I nod at JD. "I don't want marks on my back, like the ones they left last weekend. And I don't want jealousy. We need to be clear on that. I can't do the jealousy. If another man or woman tries to come between us, then yeah, I expect those feelings. But not between us. Because he told me to…" I have to take another deep breath. "He told me to do things and then he beat me afterward. But I had no choice. He made me pleasure other people. And then he accused me of liking it. And I did like it. I was conditioned to like it. So I don't want to be punished for loving both of you."

Ark holds me tighter. "Done."

I look at JD and he grins. "Ark makes me hard, Blue. Watching you suck his cock makes me hotter. And tonight I plan on sucking it with you. So I'm fine, babe." He winks at Ark, who gets hard underneath me as a response.

"Anything else you need us to know, Blue?" Ark asks, trying to take the subject off him.

"I need aftercare. I didn't get much aftercare, but when I did, it made all the difference in the world."

"We can do that, baby," JD says, leaning in to kiss me. His teeth catch my lip and bite, hard enough to make me whimper and release another gush of wetness, but not enough to draw blood. "I know what I'm doing. I'll fuck you hard and make you love it. And when we're done, I'll soothe away any shame. You will never feel shame with us, Blue."

I want to cry, that's how much his words mean to me. But I just take a deep breath and snuggle up against Ark's chest while JD goes back to his seat and resumes his eating.

When I try to get up and go back to my chair a few minutes later, Ark restrains me. He brings a forkful of eggs to my mouth and I open. Letting him feed me. Letting him take care of me.

When breakfast is over, we leave the dishes and lounge on the couch and watch a movie. JD is lying down on his back on the long end, his arms propping up his head, while Ark sits up on the lounger. I drape my body over both of them, my head in Ark's lap.

I daydream about this life. What it might look like in the weeks and months to come. What I'm giving up to be here. I miss my family, but I can't go home. Not until I get what I came for. Not until I get back what they took from me. Not until I get a hold of that contract and that footage of me signing away my future children.

And now I have two allies.

They might not know it yet, but I've just recruited them in my war.

I will get justice for Janine.

And maybe JD will get justice for Marie too.

THIRTY-EIGHT

ARK

SOMEHOW we spend the whole day just being... normal. My dick is in a state of semi-hardness the entire time. And every time JD gets up to do something, his bulge is there as well. I wonder if he's jacking off every time he goes to the bathroom.

Will it always feel this good to be around them? Will I constantly be aroused just looking at them? Will the thought of JD's lips on my cock ever disgust me?

I don't know the answer to any of these questions. So when Blue gets tired and announces she's going to bed, JD joins her. But I go into my office and start dicking around with my cameras.

About an hour later, a naked JD steps into my doorway and knocks on the wall. "What are you doing? Come to bed."

"I will," I tell him as I clean a lens.

"When? I'm horny, man. And every time I touch her, she wants to come. But I don't want to start this shit alone. You need to be there."

I finish up the lens and then pack it away.

"You're nervous?" he asks, coming into the room. I glance down at his dick, which is so hard, it's practically pointing at me. "You afraid of this part, Ark? Of crossing that line?" He reaches out and grabs the long bulge beneath my jeans. He takes my inaction as a sign to proceed, and then his hand drifts upward to the button on my jeans. "Should we have a practice run in here? Get it over with?"

And then he leans in, his bare chest pressing against mine, the heat between us drawing our bodies together. His hand slips down my pants and grabs me... hard. I grit my teeth and suck in a breath. "Tell me what to do," he says. "Tell me what you want. Because Blue is waiting, man. And I don't mind sucking your dick to put you at ease, but I want to fuck that girl tonight. And I want you to be there."

I look at him, meeting his blue eye with my dark ones. "That's not what I what I'm holding out for, JD. I'm not nervous about you sucking my dick. I just need you to know I'm probably not going to fuck you. Maybe ever. And I'm probably not going to let you fuck me, either."

"So, we have limits with each other, but not with Blue? Is that what you want me to know?"

"Yeah, basically."

"Are you gonna suck my dick?"

"I don't know."

"So what do you want to do with me?" He pulls his hand out of my pants and takes a step back.

But I catch him by the shoulder and grip him tight. "This, for starters." And then I pull him in, my hand wrapping around his neck, my fingers threading through his hair. I touch my lips to his and the kiss takes me by surprise once again. How soft his lips are, but how hard and masculine his response. He grips my head the same way, pushing himself into me. Our bodies press against each other as I slip my tongue inside his hot mouth and then when he responds, I withdraw and bite his lip. Hard. Hard enough to make him pull back. But I stop him, keeping him in contact with me. I look him in the eyes and we both taste the blood. I let go with my mouth, but hold him captive with my gaze. "I won't do this to Blue. I can't. But I can do it to you."

He stares at me.

"If you want."

He grins and then he laughs, pushing my chest hard enough to make me step backwards. I grip his neck harder, pressing my thumb against his jugular, just like I did that Gabriel fuck last night. But this time, it's not out of hate or anger. It's desire.

"I want to stick my dick so far down your throat, you'll choke on my cock."

His grin grows wider. "You want me to submit to you?"

"You can dish it out but you can't take it?"

"Is that the deal then? She submits to me and I submit to you?"

"You both submit to me, JD. I want to collar you too."

"Fuck you," he says, stepping back with a laugh.

"Not literally, asshole. But we need to have an understanding. And the understanding is, I'm in control. At all times."

"What if you're not there?"

I shrug. "You want to fuck her alone? Because I'm in it for you, just as much as I am for her."

"Well, yeah. I figure I can fuck her anytime I want. She's mine too."

I turn around and walk back to my desk, getting a fresh battery for my favorite camera. "If you fuck her alone, I want it on camera. So I can watch it later."

"You kinky motherfucker. I never suspected, Ark."

"Yes, then?"

He rolls his neck and shoulders, like he's trying to release some tension. "Sure, OK. Like I care if we're filmed. There's more than five hundred videos of me on camera already. What's a few more?"

"And I want you to pose with her. And me. Around the loft. Fucking. Doing normal shit. Whenever. I want pictures. I want memories."

He shakes his head at me. "Why would I object to that? You want to make sex tapes instead of porn? Fine."

"And this shit never leaves the apartment."

"Dude—"

"I mean it, JD. You never let anyone else see her. Or us. Ever."

"Why would I show her off? She's on the run from some asshole who would probably like her back."

I let out a long breath, relief flooding through me. "OK."

He stares at me for a long moment, and then he laughs the way he does. The way that charms pretty much anyone who has the pleasure of watching him turn it on. "Can we fuck now?"

I reach down and grab his dick, which has softened a little from the conversation.

"Oh, fuck, yeah," he moans. I pump him a few times and then pull on his cock, making him take a step forward. "You're killing me, man. Let's go."

I lean in and kiss him again, but this time I don't bite. His mouth melds with mine, our tongues seeking each other out. And his dick thickens in my palm, so I pull back and grab the camera from my desk. "I want this, JD. Do you understand?"

"I get it," he says in a whisper. "I want this too."

"We are not a couple. You and her aren't a couple. We're in this together, no matter what." I don't wait for his answer, I just tug on his hard cock until he follows me out of my office and down the hallway to my bedroom. When we reach the door, I let go and push him into the room.

I expect a little look of anger from pushing him so hard, so fast. But he handles it like a champ. He walks forward to the bed and I turn the light on as I follow. He gets in on one side, I get in on the other.

And Blue lies between us, her eyes barely detectable in the light that filters through the open blinds of the window. They are filled with questions. And I am nothing but answers.

I pull the covers down, exposing her to the chilled night air. "Spread your legs open for JD, Blue."

She does it without hesitation, and that makes my cock so fucking hard.

"Lick her until she comes all over your face, JD. And then kiss me, motherfucker. And I better taste that come, or I'll stand you in the corner and make you watch me fuck her blind from behind."

Blue whimpers. This is what she wants. What her body craves. Humiliation is something she's on board with. I said I'd never humiliate her, and I won't. But I never said I'd spare JD the same fate.

He does as he's told. He sucks her clit while I film. And when she releases, he kisses me, her come still pooled up in his mouth.

After that it's a blur of cocks and pussy. Him on top, me on the bottom. Me on top, him on the bottom. His mouth over my dick, me thrusting it down his throat while Blue fingers herself.

By the time they fall asleep, the dawn is upon us. And even though I'm worn out, I'm too amped up with adrenaline to sleep. So I leave them, exhausted, all wrapped up in each other, and take my camera back to my office, so I can turn our fucking into art.

THIRTY-NINE

BLUE

"NO," I tell him, burying my face in the pillow.

"Why?"

"You know why." I look up at Ark and sigh. He's so fucking beautiful, I swear. He's not wearing that pseudo suit today. He's in jeans. And he's shirtless. God, they both drive me wild when they have no shirts on. And those tattoos...

All we've done for three days is fuck. And I get it, he's feeling cooped up and wants to get out of the house. But I'm not. I'm feeling safe and comfortable. I'm not going anywhere.

"Blue. You have to leave the house at some point."

"Not today."

"Don't you want to go shopping? Get real clothes? Stop wearing JD's t-shirts and boxers?"

"No," I say in a defiant, child voice. "I like these clothes. They smell like him. I'd rather go naked than leave."

Ark laughs and drags his fingertips up and down my spine.

"I want to take you out to dinner. Today is the last day we work for Ray. It's a big deal."

I let out a long sigh. I don't want to tell him no. I want to go to dinner with him. See him in a proper suit for once, with a jacket and trousers. I bet he's hot as fuck in a real suit. My clothes are still hanging in his office, unused. Hell, unopened. I never even peeked to see what they look like. I know they are fancy, so not appropriate for wearing around the house.

"I want to make you happy, Ark. I do. But I get a sick feeling in my stomach whenever I think about going out. I won't be any fun at all. I won't. And I'll be sick the whole time." I lift up from his chest and look him in the eyes. "I'll be too sick to enjoy it."

He groans. Long and hard. "Fine." And then he lifts me off his chest and gets out of bed. JD is already up, eating or making breakfast or something. He gets up early. In fact, JD gets up at very strange times. Three AM one morning, five the next. Sometimes he sleeps until noon. "But I gotta get out of here. I'm not used to staying home so much." Ark walks over to his dresser and pulls out a black t-shirt and a pair of socks.

"I'm sorry." I use a pouty voice for that.

"You've got nothing to be sorry for, Blue. I get it." Ark says it with his back to me, so I can't see his face. I just stare at those fighting dragons on his back and wonder why they'd get matching tattoos that pitted them against each other. It looks to me like they are fighting over that round thing between them. It's blue, so it might be the world. Or maybe they are conquering the world? The dragon bodies wrap around it like they own that little blue ball.

"Besides," he continues, pulling his shirt over his head and obstructing my view of his back art, "we can celebrate at home just fine." He turns to face me and now he's smiling. God, I love when Ark smiles. He doesn't do it that often. JD is a compulsive smiler. Ark is always deep in thought. Making secret decisions in his head. He's definitely not impulsive. "I'll bring home a bottle of something special."

"I can make us dinner," I offer. "If JD goes shopping for me."

Ark pulls his boots on standing up, hopping from one foot to the next. And then he walks back over, leans down, and gives me a kiss. "I'll see you tonight, OK?"

I just stare at him. His beautiful face. I didn't think it was kind when I first met him, but I was so wrong. Everything about Ark is kind. He does everything with purpose. And I can't ever picture him hurting someone.

"What?" he asks, with a laugh.

"I want to love you."

That smile again. I die.

"I think I could marry you and live happily ever after."

He chuckles and leans down for one more kiss. We linger this time, our tongues twisting together, smiles on our faces, laughs in our breath. "I'd marry you right now if JD wasn't here. But it's kinda hard to marry two people at once."

"I want to love him too," I say when Ark pulls away.

Ark is walking out the bedroom door when he looks back over his shoulder and calls out, "Ditto." A few moments later I hear him talking to JD and then the front door opens and closes.

And I think Ark really does love him, too. I'm not sure it's the kind that most people imagine when they think of two men being together. But it's definitely love. Why else would he be so protective of JD?

That's something I'd really like to talk about, but any time I bring up JD when Ark and I are alone, he changes the subject. I don't get it.

"Hey," the devil is calling from the living area. "Baby Blue?"

"What?" I call back.

"Get your mopey ass out of bed." JD peeks his head into the bedroom. Shirtless.

I grin at that. "Why should I?"

His grin goes flat and his eyes narrow. "Because you've got our collar on, bitch. And I said so." He points to the ground in front of him.

I knew this was coming. The domination stuff. He's mentioned what we might do together once Ark leaves the house. Not because we're hiding it from Ark, we have to film it all. But because Ark isn't into that stuff so much.

"You better move, slut."

I slide out of bed and get on my hands and knees, crawling over to JD and stopping at his feet. I sit back and look up, opening my legs so he can see my pussy.

"Goddammit," he whispers as he crouches down to take my face in his hands. "You like this shit? For real?"

I nod, blushing from embarrassment.

"Hey," he says, kissing me on the lips. "Don't be ashamed. OK?"

"It's weird, isn't it? I don't understand it."

He studies my face for a moment. "It's not weird, Blue. It's just a fantasy."

"But I like it…" I can't even say it.

"How?" he asks. "Tell me, so I can give you what you want."

"I like to feel…" I look up, then down quickly. Jesus Christ. I can't believe I'm going to admit this out loud. "Forced."

He kisses me, his lips gentle and his mouth soft. "Lots of girls want to feel like that, Blue. I've done a lot of porn, and some of them like it so rough, it scares me."

"They do? What do they want you to do to them?"

"Slap them. They all like to be slapped. Twist their nipples so hard, they cry. Spank their pussies. Spank their asses. Come on their faces. One girl, I shit you not, wanted me to piss all over her."

I recoil. "What?"

"Now that is a weird fetish, right? Or the ones who play with shit. Or the men who wear diapers and act like babies."

"Oh my God."

He laughs with me and pulls me to my feet as he stands. "What you like, Blue, we call that ravishment."

"Ravishment?"

"It's a rape fantasy. And you'd be surprised how many women get off on that. Hell, men even. It's so common, it's not even considered fringe." He shoots me a devious look. "Well, at least in the world I live in."

"Ravishment," I say again, bewildered that it has a name I don't mind saying aloud, and turned on by the fact that JD and I are talking about it.

"I can ravish you, Blue. I can rip your clothes off, slap your face, tie you up, and stick my cock down your throat. I can call you names and pull your hair. I can fuck you from behind so hard you come in waves. One after the other, constantly crashing you into the shore of ecstasy." His hand sweeps down my hip and then slips between my legs to check me for arousal.

I'm so fucking turned on right now.

"Would you like to be ravished?"

I pause.

"Be sure, Blue. Because what you desire can't be achieved unless we cross some lines. Do you want to cross lines with me?"

I take a deep breath and look him in the eyes. "Yes, please."

He slaps my face so hard, I fall to the ground. My knees hit the hard wood floor, making me scream out. He grabs my hair and pulls me back to my feet, and then drags me over to the bed and throws me down face-first.

My heart beats fast, but it's a weird mixture of fear—which I'm familiar with from my captivity—and desire for the actual man who wants to ravish me. Which is brand new.

"You're my whore, you understand?" He yanks my hair,

forcing my head back so far I have to look him in the face as he looms over me from behind. "Say yes, bitch."

"Yes," I say, panting for more. He twists my nipple hard, giving me what I secretly crave. And then he flips me over, whips off his belt, and wraps it around my face, right across my mouth. He cinches it up so it's tight, the leather burning the corners of my mouth from the tension. And then he takes his cock out of his pants and lifts my legs up.

I squirm, and he slaps me again, making my pussy flood and throb. But I fight him off, punching him in the face. He slaps me again for that, and then grabs my kicking legs and flips me over onto my stomach.

"Yes," I whisper softly into the hard concrete floor.

"You get it in the ass for that little move, cunt."

"Yes," I say again. But his dick is pushing against my ass so hard, I cry out from the very real pain.

He fucks me in the ass so hard, I cry. But when he comes, I come with him. Because this is what I've wanted.

I want to be ravished.

And I have never been so fucking turned on in all my life.

When we're done he takes the belt off and kisses my lips. "Wait here," he says in a whisper. And then he goes into Ark's bathroom and returns with some sweet-smelling balm. He rubs it into the little cracks the belt made in the corners of my mouth. "Ark will kill me if he knows, Blue." JD puts the little stick of lip balm on the nightstand and climbs into bed with me, wrapping me up in his arms. "He doesn't get it. He won't like it. And he'll put a stop to it. So if you want to keep doing it, we need to keep it a secret."

I watch JD's face as he says all this. Another secret.

Ark wants me to keep quiet about who I am and the people who had me.

JD wants me to keep quiet about how rough we like it.

It's not a good start to a relationship.

"Blue?" JD asks after a few moments. "You can tell him if you want, but he'll make us stop. He won't understand it, Blue. So if you want me to fuck you like this again, you can't tell him."

He waits in silence as I consider my answer. My body is sore. My face is still stinging from all the slaps.

But my God, I've never felt so... alive.

I don't want to keep secrets from Ark, but I really do want to have this special sidebar sex with JD.

"OK," I say, knowing everything about what we're doing is wrong. "I will. I mean, I won't tell him. But the cameras. We should record them, so he won't be mad if he finds out."

JD kisses me on the lips, taking a moment to lick the little sore spots. "I love you. We'll film them, like he asked. We just won't give them to him. Fair?"

"Fair," I say.

We spend the rest of the day doing normal stuff. We even fuck for the camera once. Not a ravishment. Just a hot fuck for Ark's eyes only.

I almost feel like a performer when I'm with JD. Like we're actors in our own movie, only our movie is real life.

But is this real life?

It blurs the lines, if you ask me.

Ark comes home and we eat a dinner that JD shopped for and I made. Life is so weird. A week and a day ago I was a captive, being forced to comply with a sick man's wishes. One week ago I was in a strange loft with two strangers, getting paid to suck them off. And tonight... Ark brings home special champagne, and we toast to our new arrangement.

One girl.

Two friends.

Three soulmates.

Does it get any better than this?

FORTY

ARK

JUST go buy her a Christmas tree, for fuck's sake."

"I can't, JD. I already told her she has to come with me if she wants a tree." It's been six weeks since Blue came to live with us. Six weeks of pure fun. I only have to think of her in some small way—like the way she taps her finger on the counter when she's deciding what she wants to eat, or the way she tiptoes across the polished concrete floors, squealing about how cold they are. Everything about her makes me happy. Even JD is happy.

But after six weeks of confinement in the loft, I'm going crazy. Not that I've been confined. I've been on four business trips in that time. But Blue refuses to leave the house.

"I've had it," I tell JD. "There's no way those people are still looking for her. The shit is over."

"You don't know," JD says. He's watching football, which means he's ignoring the rest of us. "Maybe she's right. Maybe she needs to stay inside for the rest of her life." He drags his attention away from the flat screen and looks up at me. "I like knowing she's always home. I like her being here all the time. I'd probably go crazy if I had to worry about where she was and who she was with."

I sit down on the chair to his left. "That's insane, JD. The girl needs friends. We've got nothing to hide. Or be ashamed of. Maybe she needs a job?"

"Why the fuck would she need a job? We have enough money to buy her anything she wants."

"To give her life purpose, dumbass. She needs goals and shit."

"Fuck goals. She needs to stay here and hang out with me."

"You need goals too."

"I have goals." He gives me one of those famous JD winks. "And they all involve you and her at the moment. The outside world can fuck off."

I look out the window where Blue is standing on the terrace, gazing down at the snow-covered streets below. Large round flakes swirl around her face and settle on her hair. Her knee-length tan coat is stylish, with fur trim on the cuffs, the hood, and the collar. She looks like she's ready to go out somewhere. She does this all the time. Dresses up and then sits around the house. It's not good.

"Just get the girl a tree."

But I shake my head. "I want her to come with me."

"Well, I don't want to go. I'm watching football."

JD is obviously not going to help, so I get up and grab my coat off the hook near the front door, then put it on and join her outside. The air is cold, but not too bad. "You ready?" I ask. "You look ready." I join her standing at the edge of the terrace, and look down onto the congestion of California Street. There's a little Christmas tree lot about half a block up. And it's busy today, because Christmas is next week.

"Look how close it is," she says. Her warm breath puffs out of her mouth as steam.

"I know. It's steps from here. So let's go."

She turns to look at me. Her face is so pretty now that she's put on weight. Those dark circles under her eyes have faded. Her complexion now is one of well-fed health. She's gained at least fifteen pounds and she could use five more, if you ask me. But she's self-conscious about it. Complaining about her clothing sizes. We started ordering her clothes online the day after we closed our contract with Ray and she's been shopping ever since. "I'll watch you the whole time, Ark. And if anything happens, I'll scream for JD to go rescue you."

"Haha," I deadpan back, pulling her in for a side hug. "You have to go outside sometime, Blue. Today is your day."

She shakes her head against my chest and then takes a deep breath. "I'm sorry. I know I disappoint you. But I can't go. And it's not even for the reasons you think."

"What? You're not afraid?"

"I am," she says softly. "But that's not the reason I don't want to leave the loft." She takes a step back, forcing me to release her from my tight embrace. And then she just stares at me.

"Tell me," I say.

She opens her mouth, then closes it just as quickly. When the words finally come out, she has to look away. "I'm afraid if I go out there again, I'll remember what he took from me. All these feelings of captivity will finally disappear and I will realize I'm free. And I'll be like a bird whose cage door is left open. They don't understand that they're free. So they sit there, inside the cage, and refuse to fly away."

"Blue, you're not a prisoner—"

She places a hand on my chest to stop me. "I know that. I'm just telling you how I feel, Ark. I know I'm free. The little bird can see the opening door and the way out. But it won't leave out of fear. And I don't know what little captive birds fear. But I fear that once I walk out that door, I'll never find my way back. I'll call my parents and get them mixed up in this, and then someone will swoop in and take me away. And that's not a bad thing, Ark. But you and JD..." Her words trail off as she peeks around me to watch him inside. I can feel her love in this moment. I've had doubts over the past few weeks, wondering if what we have is love, or maybe just an unusually strong case of lust. Or maybe all we are here for is the sex? I just don't know sometimes.

But this pause… this pause is all I need to know. What we have is real. No matter what you call it, it's real.

She finally looks back up to me. "I can't lose you. I know nothing lasts forever, but I'm not ready, Ark. I'd rather stay in my cage and watch the world from my high perch than risk flying out that door and never finding my way back."

I take a deep breath and nod. "I'll go get us a tree."

The snow crunches under my feet as I walk back to the terrace door.

JD never looks up from his wild cheering as some big play happens on the TV in front of him. I walk straight to the front door and let myself out.

Once there, I place my palms against the wall and lean forward until my forehead hits the brick.

I'm not sure which part of that conversation hurts the most. The fact that she doesn't trust herself to stay if she leaves. The fact that she thinks of herself as a bird in a cage. Or the fact that this is temporary, and we both know it.

Love happens in twos.

There is no holy trinity of love.

Would I still love JD without Blue?

I shake my head and push away from the wall. I head to the stairs, needing the physical activity to clear my thoughts. But all the way down, with each thumping step of my shoes on the steel, I can only hear one word in my mind.

No.

I would not want a relationship with JD without Blue. I love him as a friend. I love him as part of this arrangement. I love him in many different ways. But I don't love him as a man.

I push through the stairwell door and end up in our lobby. I can see the Christmas tree lot down the street from here, so I go outside and start weaving my way through the slow-moving stream of cars when my phone buzzes.

I reach into my pocket and read the message from Blue.

Will you buy ornaments and lights tonight too? So we can decorate it?

I'll do that first, I text back.

She sends me a little picture of a Christmas tree and then a heart.

No, I don't love JD as just a man.

But I do love Blue as just a woman.

I would definitely be happy with her all by herself.

The tree lot is full of people as I pass, and I notice they are low in inventory, so I step into the roped-off area and figure I might as well pick a tree first. Then I can drop it off at home and go back out for the other stuff.

There's not a lot to choose from, so I grab the tallest one they have left and wait patiently as my tree goes into the checkout line where they will wrap it in a net and take my money. Fifteen minutes later, I'm walking back across the street with my first Christmas tree purchased as an adult.

Before I came to Denver, I lived in Miami. And Miami just wasn't the same at Christmas. I never had time for a serious relationship back then, so I never bothered to get a tree. But this is meaningful for partners. Celebrating holidays is part of strengthening the bonds of love.

JD and I never got a tree either. The holidays were always a busy season for us. Lots of girls need money at Christmas. We never had a shortage of willing participants.

I drag the tree inside the building and then inside the elevator, picturing how nice the loft will look once it's decorated.

The car dings and the doors open, so I drag my tree out and head to the door.

I expect squealing when I enter the loft. And I do hear that. But it's not for the tree I dump in the foyer.

It's Blue, screaming like she's getting a beating.

I run down the hallway to JD's room and fling the door open. It takes me whole seconds of silence to come to terms with what I'm seeing.

Blue is face down on the floor, her cheek pressed so hard against the polished concrete I can't even see her left eye. The right eye is wide open, looking up at me. Makeup runs down her cheek from the tears. Her face is red, like she was just slapped. Her breathing hitches, letting me know she's really crying.

JD's dick is in her ass, her dress ripped open up the back to give him access. And her panties are still on, but skewed off to the side. One hand is wrapped around her throat, his thumb pressed over her artery. The other is pulling her hair.

"It's not what you think," JD growls. Almost like he's pissed off I'm interrupting his fuck.

I walk over and punch him in the face, and he goes reeling across the floor.

"I told you," he yells. "It's not what you think!"

I pull Blue up from the floor and pull her close. "Are you OK?"

She can't or won't meet my gaze. But she nods.

"Ark—"

"Shut the fuck up, JD!" I yell it. My voice booms up to the very top of his high ceilings, making Blue jump in my arms.

He's up off the floor now, his dick still hard, his eyes raging with anger. "We had an arrangement."

"Yeah, our arrangement was that you'd treat her nice."

"Not me and you, Ark. Me and her."

His words stop me cold.

"She likes it rough, man. She does. Just ask her. She loves to be ravished—"

"Raped!"

"I'm not raping her, asshole. It's fantasy."

"It's sick!"

As soon as it comes out, I regret it. Because Blue wriggles in my arms, manages to escape, and then runs to JD's bathroom and slams the door.

"Good one, dickface," JD says as he follows her. He twists the handle, but it clicks from side to side. "I'll break the door down, Blue. You know I will. So unlock it."

She does not unlock it.

And that's when I notice the cameras. "You've been filming all this?"

"You told me to," he says, still twisting the handle. "Blue?" He pounds on it a few times. "Open the fucking door."

Silence.

I sit down on the bed and hold my hands in my head. "What the fuck is going on?"

JD is staring at me when I look back up. "We give you the vanilla tapes. I keep the ravish—"

"Stop using that stupid word!"

"Whatever. I keep the rough ones. But I taped them, just like you wanted. She's happy with this, Ark. She is. All you have to do is watch them and you'll see. You just told her she was sick for liking it, so she's gonna have a hard time admitting that to you, but this is fact. The girl wants to be choked. And spanked. And I'm not talking little swats to the ass. She likes it hard, dude. She wants my dick down her throat, the tears streaming down her face, on her knees—"

"Enough!" I bellow. "Jesus fucking Christ. How the fuck can you be so stupid? So blind? Did it ever occur to you that she likes it because she can't stop thinking of herself as a goddamned prisoner?"

"She likes it because it feels good. You just refuse to admit that."

"She told me tonight she feels like a bird in a cage with the door open, you idiot. In her mind, she never stopped being a fucking captive! And you're making it worse!"

"Fuck you. You're just jealous—"

I cross the room so fast, I even surprise myself. The next moment, JD is sprawled out on the floor and my hand is wrapped around his neck. I'm bigger than him by twenty pounds and three inches at least. And I'm stronger than him. I work out five days a week in the gym downstairs. So he never has a chance.

I lean down into his face as it turns red. "I'm only gonna say this one time, my friend. If you ever fuck her like she's a whore on the street again, I will kill you."

FORTY-ONE

BLUE

I LISTEN as they fight. When JD pounds on the door, I stumble backwards and fall on my ass, and then I crab-walk myself into the corner near the shower and pull my legs up to my chest as they continue to argue outside.

Ark is bigger than JD. Not by much, but in all the ways that count. Longer arms. Taller. Heavier. More muscular. He's built like a Navy SEAL, even if he never became one. And that's how I know he's the one doing the choking and JD is the one making those noises on the other side of the door.

I want to go out there and tell Ark JD is right. I do like it. Every time JD slaps my face I only want him to fuck me harder. Every time he calls me a whore or a slut, I only want him to hold me tighter.

But I don't like it. I need it. And I'm not sure that's the same thing.

A wail echoes through the bathroom and it takes me a

moment to realize it's coming from me. And then the sobs start. I'm out of control as the images flash through my mind. The beatings while I was being held against my will. The rapes I was subjected to. The way they used my body to betray my mind. Made me come after reducing me to nothing but a thing.

JD and Ark are yelling and fighting again on the other side of the door. Things break. They crash into the bathroom door, and I'm immediately grateful that the doors in this place are thick, hard wood. Because it doesn't burst open.

I can't move. I can't think straight. I can't do anything but huddle in the corner and shake.

What will happen to me now? Who will ever love me like this? Why am I so fucked up?

A door slams and vibrates the wall I'm leaning against.

The front door.

But which one of them left?

Another sob escapes as the fear grows. Will he beat me? Will he rape me?

"Blue?" Ark asks.

I let out a cry and then I just break down, throwing myself forward on to the rug. My fear is replaced with relief and that's almost as bad.

Because maybe Ark is right.

Maybe I was letting JD keep me prisoner. Sexually. Mentally. And emotionally.

FORTY-TWO

ARK

"**B**LUE?" I can hear her crying on the other side of the door. My heart is beating so fast I have to lean against the hard wood to calm down. "Blue, baby? You OK?"

She's sobbing now, but it's muffled. Like she doesn't want me to hear.

"Blue? He's gone, OK? He left. You can come out now." For a moment I wonder if I'm the one she's afraid of. *Please, God*, I pray silently. *Please don't let her be afraid of me.* "Blue, I'm not gonna hurt you, you know that, right?" Silence. "Blue, just unlock the door and you can do whatever you want. You can call someone. Or leave."

More crying.

"Or stay. You can stay, Blue. You know I love you, right? I love you and it's not dependent on this relationship, or JD, or the sex. OK? None of that matters. I just love you."

She's sniffling and I can picture her on the other side of the door, lying on the rug.

"Blue, if you open the door, we'll just go to bed. Just rest and not talk about it. Sleep together. Just hold each other. OK? No talking. No sex. No calling anyone. Just…" Fuck. *Just open the door,* is all I want to say. "Just be together. That's what couples do, right?"

Goddamn it. I should have known better than to leave her alone with JD.

"It's not your fault, Blue. It's mine. JD… he's…"

Fuck.

I take a deep breath and slide down the door until I'm sitting on the floor with my back against it, letting out the long sigh of air as I settle.

"He's what?" she says from the other side.

I rub my hand down my face and pull my legs up so I can rest my elbows on my knees.

"He's what?" she asks, more mad than sad now. "Just tell me what the hell is going on here!"

"Just open the door," I whisper. "You have to open the door because no matter what he's done, I still love the guy, OK? And I'm not going to tell this story unless I can tell it to your face."

Silence. For several long moments.

She unlocks the door with a click, and I scramble to my feet so I can see her face when she pulls it open. Her eyes are red and her face is pale. Like she's sick. Or scared.

"Blue," I say, reaching for her. But she pulls back, just out of reach, and wraps her arms around herself in a tight hug.

"Just tell me," she begs, her anger gone. "Because I love him too." Her eyes get glassy and then tears spill down her cheeks like rivers. "I love him too. I didn't know," she says, starting to sob again. "I responded to everything—"

I reach out and pull her into a hug. "Shhh. No more of that. Stop thinking about that. I should never have let you stay here, but I wanted you, Blue. I wanted you like nothing I've ever wanted before in my life. And maybe it's just because I was lonely. And tired of this job. Tired of the lies and the girls, and the dirty sex. I needed something good. Something that could wipe away all that stuff and make me feel human again. And I knew the whole time you needed help. Just like I knew the whole time JD needed help."

She crumbles. Her body goes limp as her knees buckle. She almost falls to the ground before I scoop her up and carry her out of JD's room, down the hallway, past the living room, and back to our bedroom.

I set her down on the bed, and then climb in next to her. She's naked and I still have my coat and boots on. But who fucking cares.

We just get in bed like that and I pull her on top of me so her face is tucked up under my chin. Her tears drop onto my skin, round the curve of my neck, and then slide down my back until they met the sheets beneath me.

I take a deep breath.

"The first time I saw JD, I was coming out of the bus station and he was across the street, fighting his way out of a four-on-one fight, and even though JD is pretty badass, he's not that good. But he was yelling like a motherfucker. *You took my kid*, he said, over and over. And each time he said it, he landed a punch or a kick or some other attack. Like those words were his mantra. The only thing keeping him going.

"By the time I got across the street, they pretty much had him. So I intervened. First with a threat of the police, which got nothing. And then a gun."

Blue is silent on top of me.

"They backed off with lots of threats for JD. They'd be back. He was dead. Blah, blah, blah. And since I had nowhere to stay, and I just saved his ass, he let me stay with him for a little while."

"They took his baby? Sold it?"

I nod. "She was given to some family. He knew that, but he didn't know which family and, of course, they never told him. His girlfriend was dead by then. We didn't know that though. So I bounced into town with a bunch of money and a plan. But my whole life, everything I thought I was doing, got sidetracked that night when I met JD. He had this immediate problem, ya know? Something I could grab onto and maybe even fix. Right? And that's how all this started."

"So what's wrong with him? I can feel it, Ark. When we're alone together, I get glimpses. Like there's something dark behind that charming smile. Behind those amazing eyes. Something he hides away. But when we were having sex—"

"Fuck," I say, taking a deep breath. "Fuck, fuck, fuck."

"—he'd look at me when he put his hand on my throat. There was always a moment when I was terrified. Just before things went black and the stars took over. But when I came to again, he was always telling me sweet things. He loved me. He'd never hurt me. This was only in fun. And I believed him—"

"He means it, Blue. He does. But he's fucked up over what happened the night before I came to town. The night we think his girlfriend died and he lost his baby girl. He never got over it."

"How did she die?"

"I have no idea. We never did figure that out. It took us two years to find her grave. Just a little marker in the ground."

"Why does he like to be so rough?"

I close my eyes. So tired of this. So tired of thinking about JD and his violence.

"You know why don't you?"

I shake my head, like I always do. "I don't know why, Blue. But he's always been like that since I've known him. He's rough with the Public Fuck girls too. Too rough. But that shit sells."

A wave of shame floods over me.

Blue isn't dumb. She's gonna figure all this out sooner or later. And then she's gonna leave me. She's never gonna talk to me again. She's going to turn around, walk out, call her family, and never look back.

Because we are a couple of sick motherfuckers.

"Do you know why?" She asks it as a question this time.

"I don't. But I have a few guesses that I'm not going into tonight. I just want to say I'm sorry, Blue. And if you want to leave—"

"You want me to leave?" She tries to sit up so she can look me in the face, but I can't do that now. I can't.

So I hold her close. "I don't want you to ever leave. It's wrong to keep you here, I understand that. But I don't want you to leave, Blue. I've never desired someone so much in my life."

"Don't leave me, Ark. Please. I know I need help. I do. I know that liking what he does to me is wrong—"

"That's not what's wrong, Blue." I sit up a little so I can see her for this part. She needs to understand the difference. "Liking it for the right reasons is fine. It's OK to like a little pain with the pleasure. But what's not OK is JD taking advantage of that after you were held captive by people who forced you to feel that way through psychological conditioning."

She just stares at me, like her whole life depends on the words I tell her now.

"Did you like it rough before you became a prisoner?"

She shakes her head. "But I never thought about that stuff."

"You just need some distance, Blue. To figure it out. You need to talk to someone. JD never talked to anyone and that was a mistake. He's just—"

She watches me struggle for the words. "Say it," she whispers. "Please, just tell me."

"He's just fucked up. He's just so fucked up."

And this is the do-or-die moment. The moment where I lose

her trust or gain it. The moment when I let as much out as I can without giving away his final secrets. Secrets I swore on my life, on the death of the one person who haunts me, just as his dead girlfriend haunts him, that I'd never betray.

"He likes to hurt people. And this"—I wave my hand at the bedroom—"this is over now, baby. I'm sorry. But he can't come back. He can't."

She stares me in the eyes for a few seconds. "So we're just two now?"

"Do you want to be two with me?"

She nods her head. "Yes, please." And then she cups her hands around my face and kisses me on the lips. "Please. Don't leave me. Don't make me go. I'm not ready to face the world, Ark. I'm not. I can't tell my father what happened to me. I can't answer those questions. I can't admit that I fell into their trap. That I got that Stockholm thing and started to like those people. That I told that man I'd marry him. Be his wife. Let him fuck me. Sell him my children. I can't do that. I need this world a little longer. And if you let me stay, I promise I will work harder at getting better. I will go out with you. I'll try harder. I'll do better, I swear."

FORTY-THREE

BLUE

ARK never sleeps with me the way JD does. He's never wanted secret sex like JD did. Ark never wanted to share me. He's always wanted me for himself.

But JD walking out scares me. Because JD was the glue. JD was the one who joked around and put us at ease. JD was the one who loved freely and openly.

Ark has always been closed off. Secretive. Working out of town. Only a few days at a time, but that time was enough to let JD and me take our game a little farther.

"Let me see you," Ark says, turning on the bedside lamp so it lights us up.

I cover myself with my arms and look down as he touches me, his fingertips tracing my ribs, my hip bone. He crouches down and feels my leg, first the one and then the other.

My ass is stinging, so I know it's red, and he gently turns me over and caresses it for a lingering moment.

"Has he hurt you?" I'm silent for a moment. "Tell me the

truth, Blue. Has he hurt you?"

I nod my head. "But that was the point."

Ark drops his hands and sits up in bed with a sigh. And then, like it's just too much, he drops his face into his palms.

I scoot over next to him, my hand on his leg. "I'm sorry." I know this is the end. I can feel it. Six weeks was way longer than it should've lasted. Six weeks was so much more than I ever dreamed of. Six perfect weeks where I felt safe. "I'm sorry," I say again.

He looks up, but doesn't turn his head. He just stares at the wall across the room. "Tell me something, Blue. What exactly are you sorry for?"

"Being…" Being what? Unfaithful? I wasn't. I know that's not what he's thinking. But my mind can't seem to go anywhere else.

"Why do you feel guilty, Blue?" Ark prods.

"Because it was a secret," I whisper. "JD told me to keep it secret and I did."

Ark nods, but still refuses to look at me. "Secrets are bad." He finally turns and meets my gaze. "Secrets between people who love each other are bad. I can't do this anymore. I can't keep this lie up. I'm calling your father, I'm taking you home, I'm putting an end to it before the shit gets out of hand. I can't do it anymore. And I certainly can't do it if you're here, right in the middle of all the shit that's happening."

"What?" Do what? He's not making sense.

But he ignores me. "I mean, I've not had a lot of heroic moments over the past four years, I get that. I'm no different than Ray or anyone else using women for financial gain. No matter what the reason is, there's no excuse for letting it get this far. None." He looks me in the eyes again. "Greed was what drove it, I think. The money just started coming. The girls were there. We had contracts, and blood tests, and scanned copies of legitimate driver's licenses. Up and up, I always said. Up and fucking up.

But it's all bullshit, Blue. I'm one hundred percent bullshit. If I say I live by a moral code, but I can't walk the talk, then there is no difference between them and me."

I don't know what he's talking about. The only thing I do know is that he's dead serious. My mind races for something to hold onto. Something to buy myself some time. Because I may be sick—they probably did fuck my head up in ways that will require years of therapy—but I didn't come all this way, or go through all that shit, in order to give up now. So I need something. Something that will draw him out of this sudden monologue that reeks of disclosure and put us back on track. "Christmas," I murmur, almost to myself. It's the only thing I can think of.

"What?"

"Christmas," I repeat. "I do want to go home, Ark. I do want to get past all this. But please. I love you." I climb into his lap and wrap my arms around his neck. "No matter what, I do love you. I can't just walk out. And if you love me back, neither can you. We owe each other that much. Maybe JD is gone. I don't know, he's your best friend. I don't have his secrets, only the one we made together. You have his secrets. But just because he's gone doesn't mean there is no us."

"What's that got to do with Christmas?"

"Let's just stay this way until Christmas. Can't we share one more big moment? Can't we just give this a try? And he's gonna come back—"

"No," Arks says, pushing me off his lap. "No. He can't come back. He knows he can't come back." Ark walks to the other side of the room, stops when he reaches the wall, and then turns on his heel and paces back. "I told him I'd kill him and I'm dead serious. I told him that and he knows I'd never say it if it wasn't over."

"If what wasn't over?" I do not understand.

"My protection." Ark lets out a long breath and closes his eyes. "I protected him, Blue. I didn't understand the extent of his issues at first." Ark sits back down with me. "It took a long time of watching JD's behavior before I figured out what the problem was."

"What's the problem?" My heart is racing. I want to know so bad. I don't want to know so bad.

"JD's violent. He's been violent with them before, but I've been there to calm him down. I've been there—"

My mind races to the beat of my heart. Words start coming back to me. Conversations I overheard in the beginning.

You're scaring her, JD.

Take it easy, JD.

"—when he's taken it too far. Or he's called me afterward and I got her help."

"Who?"

"Whoever, Blue. Whoever. But he was so good with you. He was so... normal."

"He never beat me, Ark. It wasn't like that."

"He did beat you. He just did it from the inside out."

And then Ark gets up and walks out of the room.

I'm not sure how much time passes as I listen to Ark on the other side of the loft. But I know he's packing a bag for JD. He talks to that Ray person they do business with. He talks to JD at one point, and even though I only hear Ark's side of the conversation, and that side is calmer than I expected, I know JD's end is not.

I know the other end is rage.

Ark walks back into the bedroom. I'm lying down, under the covers, still naked and ashamed. "We're leaving," he says.

"What?" I sit up in bed as he starts pulling clothes out of the drawers. He throws me a hoodie and a pair of jeans.

"Get dressed. We're leaving in five minutes. I know where

JD is, so it's gonna take him twenty minutes to get here. So five minutes." Ark walks out with a gym bag filled with clothes.

I get up and put on the clothes, then find my winter boots and slip those on too. Ark comes back with my fancy winter coat. "Put it on, Blue. And I don't want any bullshit about leaving this loft, you hear me?"

I nod as he holds the coat open for me and I slide my arms into the smooth satin lining the sleeves. He waits as I button it up and cinch the belt at my waist. "Where are we going?" I ask as he takes my hand and tugs me down the hallway.

My heart is pounding as I'm led through the front door and we wait for the elevator. "Where are we going?" I ask again.

"A friend's place. But she's at work, so we need to stop there first."

When we get to the garage, he stops and looks both ways, like someone might be following us. When he decides it's clear, we run towards a Jeep. He opens the passenger door and I climb in. Then he closes it up and walks around the front of the vehicle, his eyes darting around, looking everywhere he can in those few moments.

It's only when he gets in and throws something in the center console that I realize he's got a gun. "What's that for?"

He ignores me, just starts the Jeep and throws it in reverse, the tires screeching on the parking garage floor. We zoom around and hit the street. He stops before pulling out, looking left and right for what seems longer than necessary with the light traffic. Then he pulls out onto the street.

I have not been in a car since I was taken to the party the night before I escaped, and the motion makes me a little dizzy, especially since Ark is weaving in and out of traffic.

We drive for about fifteen minutes, and then stop at a Radio Shack. He grabs the gun and jumps out, leaving the Jeep running. "If anyone approaches you, honk the horn."

And then the door closes and he takes off inside.

I look around. I have no idea where I'm at, but we are a little ways out of the city. It's a big strip mall with tons of cars. We are parked right in front of the store, but honestly, how fast can Ark get to me if someone came up?

Who would try to get me? And just as I'm thinking that, I realize who we're running from.

Not JD.

The people I escaped from.

My heart starts to beat faster. Because even though I might've been holding myself prisoner in the loft with Ark and JD, I always knew I was free to go. I just didn't have the courage to walk out the door.

But if those people get me again, I'm done. They'll beat me. Rape me. And then sell me or kill me or God only knows what. I twist around in my seat, trying to see all sides of the parking lot at once, but it's too big. Several minutes go by, and I'm just about to reach for the door handle and go join Ark inside before I die of paranoia when he comes back. He throws a bag on my lap. "Open it up, Blue. Stick the SIM card in it and activate it for me as I drive."

"What's going on?"

"Just do what I say."

Inside the bag is a prepaid cell phone. Ark reaches into his pocket and hands me a knife so I can tear open the sealed plastic. I press the power button and follow the onscreen instructions for activation.

We stop in a restaurant parking lot before I can finish, but this time, Ark turns the Jeep off. "We gotta go inside."

"Seriously? We're eating? Can't you tell me what's going on first?"

But he just gets out of the Jeep and walks around to my side and opens the door. He holds out his palm, and I let him help me out, handing the phone over in the process. He stuffs it in his jacket, keeps a hold of my hand, and we trudge through the slushy parking lot to the front doors.

Once inside, he starts looking all around. "Fuck," he utters under his breath.

The hostess comes up and starts grabbing menus. "Two?" she asks.

And that word, I swear to God, gives me a little pain in my chest. *It shouldn't be two,* I want to say. JD can get help. I can get help. We can work this stuff out. But Ark is not even thinking about JD right now.

"I'm looking for a waitress named Lanie. She works breakfast and dinner."

"Lanie?" the hostess says as she tsks her tongue and huffs out a breath. "She quit ages ago. In fact, she walked one afternoon mid-shift and never came back. No one's heard from her since."

"What?" Ark asks. "When? How long ago?"

"Oh, pffft. I have no clue. Hey, Ritchie?" she yells across the restaurant. "When did Lanie disappear?"

Ark squeezes my hand when he hears the word disappear.

"'Bout six, seven weeks ago?" the cook behind the counter calls back. "She pissed me off too. I was short that night."

We are out of the restaurant before the cook even finishes his sentence. And when we reach the Jeep, Ark has the gun in his hand.

"What the fuck is going on?"

But he just blows out a breath and starts the engine. We pull back out onto the street and I know we are far from downtown, because the mountains over here are very close. "Goddamnit!" I yell when we starts weaving through side streets. "Talk to me!"

Instead, he throws the phone back at me. "Finish the activation. I need to text someone right the fuck now."

"What did JD say? Why are we running?"

But Ark ignores all my questions so I just finish the activation process and hand him the phone. He tucks it under his leg, and then reaches for the gun as he pulls up to a little house in a very nondescript suburban neighborhood.

I grab him by the coat. "Where the fuck are we?"

"Lanie's house," he says, ducking a little so he can look up at the roof.

"Who is Lanie? And what are you doing?"

"Goddammit, Blue! Shut up. I'm looking for snipers."

"Oh, my God. I'm getting out of this car—"

He grabs me by the arm and pulls me towards him. "No. You're not. I'm not fucking around right now, Blue. We are in a lot of trouble, OK? This girl, the waitress who's missing? I saw her the day JD and I met you. That's where I went that day. I needed to get two more videos for Ray to complete that week's contract, and when I'm short, I use Lanie. So I used her that day, and now I find out she's been missing all this time. Do you really think it's a coincidence?"

"I don't get it."

"Well, here's the thing, baby." He smiles at me and pulls me in for a quick kiss. "You don't need to get it. You just need to trust me."

"What about JD?"

"We're done with him, OK?"

"No! He's part of us, Ark. We can't just throw him away. We need to get him help. We need to make sure he's all right. We need—"

"He sold you out, Blue."

"What?"

"You heard me. All those films he made with you? The violent ones? He sold them today when he left. And do you know who he sold them to?"

I have to swallow very hard as I shake my head.

"The people who were keeping you prisoner, Blue. He sold. You. OK? We're fucking done with him."

"But why?"

Ark takes a long breath. "We don't have time right now. I need to go inside and see if she's in there. Maybe I'm overreacting. Maybe she's just quit her job. Maybe she's fine and this shit isn't about to blow up in my face. I don't think that's the case, but I need to go check. So we don't have time right now. You need to come with me in case people are watching her house."

I want to ask why. More and more whys. But he's out of the Jeep again. And now it's getting dark and there's no way I can let him get away. Because if I lose him—

"Come on," he says, opening my door and taking my hand again. He closes the door softly behind me, and then he leads me up the short driveway to a gate that surrounds the backyard.

He pulls the latch and we go through.

FORTY-FOUR

ARK

AS soon as I open the door, the putrid smell of a decaying body hits me. I close it back up and turn to face Blue.

"Now what?" she asks.

I just shake my head and tug her along to the detached garage and open that door with the same key I used for the house. Inside is Lanie's Toyota Camry. "Get in," I tell Blue, as I walk around to the driver's side.

"We're stealing a car?"

"Blue," I tell her calmly. "Get the fuck in the car. We're not stealing it, but I don't have time to explain what we're doing. Once we get somewhere safe, I'll fill you in. But right now, we're on the run. Do you understand? People are looking for us. Bad people. People who will kill me and take you. And if you think you get second chances to escape the kind of people who took you, you're wrong. So we need to stay focused. Now get in the fucking car."

She inhales sharply, because my rant gets louder as I talk. But she walks over to the passenger side and gets in like she's told. I get in the driver's side, start the car up, and push the button for the garage door. It rises slowly and I almost expect an army of hitmen to be on the other side waiting. But our luck holds. I pull the car out and park it behind the Jeep. Then I turn to Blue. "Stay here. I'm gonna put the Jeep in the garage to hide our tracks if anyone comes by here looking for me."

I don't wait for an answer, I just get out and climb back in the Jeep. I look at Blue's face when I pull up the drive, and she's looking around like she's expecting assassins too. She's scared. And she should be, because this is it. After four years of waiting, this is it. The moment when it all comes crashing down.

I cut the engine, grab the prepaid phone and the bag I packed before we left, and leave the Jeep behind.

"Who's after us?" Blue asks when I climb back in the Camry.

I press the button on the garage door remote and watch my Jeep disappear. I'll probably never see it again. This hits me hard. Because this life I've built over the past four years wasn't so bad as far as lives go.

"Ark," she says, grabbing a hold of my upper arm as I pull away from the house. "Please."

I turn back onto the main road, and then make a left into a bank parking lot. "Just please, Blue. In an hour we'll be settled and I'll tell you what I think. But I need to go into the bank and get something. I'll be right back."

"No," she says, grabbing my arm with two hands this time. "No, I don't want to stay out here alone."

Her fear is real and I have to remind myself that she's been locked up for a year and a half. No real outside contact at all. "OK. But don't talk. Don't ask me any questions. Don't say anything."

She nods and we both get out and walk inside the bank. I point to a sitting area near the entrance and she sits as I walk up to the bank manager's office and knock on the open door.

"I need to access a safety deposit box."

"Yes, sir, please have a seat and I'll help you with that."

I take a seat and give him all my information. He types away on his computer, frowning for several minutes, and then finally gives me his full attention. "I'm sorry, sir. But this box has special"—he squints his eyes at me as he searches for a word—"conditions attached to it."

"I understand," I tell him quickly. "I just need the box." I hold up my key on my key chain. "Now."

"Yes, sir." He clears his throat and stands, buttoning his jacket as he walks me to the back of the bank where we enter the vault.

Two minutes later, I'm staring down at the little white drawstring bag. I peek inside. New ID. New passport. Ten thousand dollars in cash to get me through. I never got an ID or passport for Blue—she never left the house, so she never needed them. But now we need them. And she doesn't have them. I close the box and walk back out of the room, fully aware that my actions here have been reported to the person who got me these credentials in the first place.

"Do you need anything else, sir?"

"No, thank you," I say, walking back over to Blue, who is wringing her hands in her lap. She smiles weakly as she rises and then I take her by the arm and we walk outside.

When we're safely back inside the car and driving north up towards Boulder, she breaks our silence. "You're not who you say you are, are you?"

"That's not entirely true," I tell her back. "I'm the guy you think I am."

"Porn king?"

"Check," I say.

"Savior of cold and shivering girls in the rain?"

"Check." I smile at that one and I can feel her relax a little.

"JD's best friend?"

"Definitely check." I look over at her as we get on the freeway, and then quickly look away. "This is real, Blue. All of it. Everything I've done with you and with JD. It's real. So no matter what happens, don't ever forget that. OK?" I chance another look over at her and she nods. But her expression is somber. Almost sad. "Hey," I say, grabbing her knee and giving it a squeeze. "Don't worry. It's gonna be OK. I swear. I know you're probably imagining all kinds of things about me right now, but I swear, it's gonna be OK."

She looks out the window at the lights of Boulder up ahead. I expected a little more confidence from her, but lying doesn't gain you trust. And even though all that stuff I just said was true, the lies are buried underneath them. I hate lying to her. Especially about JD. But I have no choice because he knows. If Lanie is dead—and she most definitely is—then I've been played. And the people playing me are playing him right now too.

"Where are we going?" Blue asks as I turn onto a street that takes us back out of town, but in a different direction than the one we came from.

"My office," I answer.

"Oh," she says softly. Like I've disappointed her again.

We drive for ten more minutes before the industrial park where I rent space comes into view.

"You own a warehouse?" she asks, as we pull into the garage after the door rolls up.

I hit the button on the keychain remote and the door closes behind us, the only light in the whole place coming from the green glow of the dashboard. "I do." I turn the engine off and the place goes dark. "Stay here until I hit the lights." She says nothing to that, just sits as I get out and feel my way over to the wall and hit the switch.

The whole place flickers to life as I walk back over to the car and open Blue's door.

"What do you keep here?" she asks as she accepts my hand and gets out. "Besides cars, obviously."

I have several vehicles. A panel van. Another Jeep, this one very well-equipped. And a little Mazda, for speed.

"Servers. For the business. You can't just put porn on a regular web host. They won't let you. So I bought this building and filled it with servers so we can be our own web hosts. Ray does it too, but he keeps his servers in his Denver building. I wanted ours to be removed from where we live. I didn't want anyone to know where they were."

"Why not?"

"Attacks," I explain, as I lead her up the stairs to the living area. "People are always trying to shut Ray down. We do it all by the book, Blue. It's one hundred percent legal."

"That doesn't make it right."

Her accusatory tone hurts more than I'd like to admit. And why should she be on board with what we do? She was held against her will by a pervert who takes pleasure from enslaving girls as baby breeders. It's not really the same. But it's not really different either.

"I know that," I reply. "I do. I just got caught up in the money and the success. But I've got my head on straight now. I swear."

"How often do you come here?" she asks, walking around the apartment, touching the leather couch, tracing a finger along the granite countertop in the kitchen. "It's pretty nice for an office."

And here we go. Lie number one, starting from the top. "I don't go out of town, Blue. So those trips you thought I was on? I was here. Working on the servers and coordinating contracts with other producers."

"I thought it was JD's job to get the producers?" She takes a seat on the couch and leans into the plush, overstuffed arm, bringing her feet up and tucking her hands under her cheek, like she's exhausted and might fall asleep at any moment.

I sit down on the opposite end of the couch, not quite sure if she wants me close or not. "He gets clients. But only the smalltime ones. He has no idea how big we really are."

"Because you lie to him?"

I don't know why I'm shocked at her audacity, but I am. "Yeah," I answer truthfully. "I lie to him. I lie to Ray. I lie to you. I even lie to me."

"Am I supposed to feel sorry for the existential struggle you wrestle with over being the bad guy?"

OK. Right to the chase. "It'd be nice if you did."

"Why should I? If you're just a liar who sells sex?"

"Because I'm asking you to trust me."

"And what about JD? Am I supposed to just forget that I love him? Have you forgotten already that you love him?"

"No, Blue." I scoot over next to her and place a hand on her shoulder. She's still all wrapped up in her winter coat, so I can't get much of a connection. But I need her to understand this part, at least. "Not at all. I'm never going to stop loving JD. And you know, I'd love for all of this tonight to be a misunderstanding." I let out a long exhale, hating myself for what I have to say next. Hating myself for the lies I have to tell her right now. "I'd love for him to tell me he was making that shit up. That he didn't sell those films to the assholes who took his kid. Took your best friend and her baby. I don't want this to end. At all. That's part of my problem, Blue. I like this life. A lot. OK? I know making and distributing porn isn't the classiest of jobs, but Ray makes it work. Ray's a good guy, you know? I love him too. He's like a father to me. Not everything about this business is bad. Not all of it is dirty."

"But it's all tainted."

"Jesus Christ, OK, yeah, I get it. It's filled with lowlifes. But—" I stop. Am I really going to defend porn as a way out? I mean, sure, some girls use it that way. Some make money, leave, go to school or whatever. Use it to create an opportunity for a better life. But most don't. Most get stuck in it. Addicted to the money, or drugs, or even the sex. The lifestyle. Most never get out until they're forced out because of diseases, or age, or addiction. "Look, I'm not going to defend what I do, and I'm not going to defend the fact that I could live like this indefinitely. I've made tens of millions of dollars in a couple of years. It's not a bad way to pass the time."

She lets out a long sigh.

"What?" I ask.

She's quiet for a few seconds and I try my best to be patient and let her think. "I want to believe you," she finally says. "I really do." And then she sits up and turns towards me, looking me straight in the face. "I love you. But I love him too. We're three, Ark. We're three and you just bailed out on that without even blinking. I can't walk out on that. Not without a conversation."

"I get it, but—"

She puts her hand up to stop me. "Just listen to *me* for once. I'm allowed to have an opinion, Ark."

"Of course you are."

"I need to see him. I need to hear his side. You two started this relationship with me. You got me all invested. I don't fault him for the rough stuff. I know it means I'm sick—"

I reach for her, because filling her with shame about that was never my intention. "Blue, if you really like it like that, it's fine. But I don't think you do. I think you're fucked up from the past year and a half of psychological sex games.'

"I know," she says quickly. "I realize that it's all tainted by my experiences. But my point is, it's not JD's fault for giving me what I asked for. Even if what I asked for wasn't good for me. And you know what? Maybe JD's way wasn't the right way. But at least he was in the game."

"What the fuck is that supposed to mean?"

"You never touch me unless he's there. When you're gone, JD can't get enough of me. And you never want more. He jokes and laughs. He smiles and makes me smile. And maybe it's not fair to compare the two of you, but Ark… he makes me feel loved."

I'm blown away. "You've got to be kidding me. After all the shit he's done?"

"He's in the game. You're avoiding it whenever you can."

"I'm the one who's here! I'm the one who's trying to protect you!"

"I know. That's all you do. Protect me. It's like… it's like I'm your job and not your girlfriend."

I laugh at that one. I scrub my hand down my face and laugh.

"You've never had sex with me alone. Ever."

"We're a threesome!"

"So now you want to be a threesome? But five minutes ago you were ready to walk away from JD and never look back?"

"It's not that simple—"

"It *is* that simple." She stands up and begins to untie her coat. "May I use your bathroom?"

And I guess she's right. It is that simple. Because just like that, she shuts me down.

FORTY-FIVE

BLUE

THE hot water washes over me as I struggle with what I'm trying to come to terms with tonight. Ark brought me here to save me from JD. Why do I have such a problem with that?

I run things through my head as the steam gathers in the shower and that takes me back to that first day when we were in the tub together. Ark left to take a phone call. JD stayed and held me.

Ark was all business back then, just like he is now. Logical. Calculating. Always keeping things at arm's length.

JD is messy emotions and heartfelt declarations. He's easy-going and friendly. And if you asked me on day one which one would hurt me more—the one who wants to slap my face as I suck his dick, or the one who wants to protect me and keep me safe—I'd never have guessed that Ark would have such power to destroy me.

Because JD might be fucked up, but I understood what he

wanted. JD shared with me. Not with words. He never told me his story with words. But he told me his story with sex.

Is that wrong?

I shut the water off and wrap a towel around myself. I don't know if Ark brought me clothes, but I figure the ones I had on are good enough, even if he did. So I put my jeans and t-shirt back on and walk back out to the living room.

Ark is still sitting on the couch, staring at me, when I walk in. He's got his leg crossed over his knee and one hand over his mouth, cupping his chin. It's a gesture that defines how different he is from JD. Because that gesture says, *How much do I tell you? How deep do I let you into my life?*

"You know what your problem is?" I ask him, taking a seat on the opposite side of the couch where I was earlier.

He shoots me a perplexed look. "What?"

"Your problem is that you're not invested."

He laughs. "Is that right?"

"Yeah. That's the difference between you and JD. You've never checked in, Ark. You never asked for the room key. You never made yourself at home."

"How do you figure? I have done nothing but help you. Nothing but support you—"

"You're right," I say, cutting him off. "You've done nothing else. Because you're not invested. I'm some kind of project to you. Or a means to an end. Or, I don't know, a distraction."

"A distraction?" he asks with one eyebrow raised. "You must be fucking with me. Because you, Blue, are the whole reason I'm checking out." And then he laughs.

"I don't even know what that means. What are you checking out of?"

"You're the one who wants me to check in. You tell me."

"I'm talking about this relationship we have. What the fuck are you taking about?"

That catches him off guard because his eyes widen and he sits back a little. And this is when I realize something.

He's lying.

Ark is lying.

I stand up, but he's got my wrist. "Please, don't," he says, pulling me back to the couch. "Please don't walk away. Because I won't be able to follow you, Blue. I won't be able to give you what you're looking for right now."

"What do you think I'm looking for? I'd really like to know, because I honestly have no idea."

"Answers," he says, pulling me closer to him. "You want answers I can't give. But I can give you reassurance, Blue." He lifts me up and places me in his lap. "I can't tell you things. But I can show you how I feel about you."

"Why now, though? Why wait until it's almost too late to show me? Why haven't you shown me this all these weeks?"

"Is this because I won't fuck you without JD?"

"That's part of it. It makes me think you're only in the relationship for him."

Ark laughs. "Blue, I'm not gay. I don't want to fuck JD. I don't want JD to fuck me. I like watching him fuck you. I like him watching me fuck you. I like him to suck my dick and kiss my mouth. I like his hands on my balls as I pound you from below. I like how he licks your clit when I have you spread open. That moment, when I'm fucking you in the ass, and we're waiting for JD to put it in your pussy. But then he leans down and licks you. And when he does that, Blue, he cups my balls and slides his tongue up my shaft. And fuck, I cannot get enough of that. But it's because of you, baby. The reason I love it is because of you. If you're not there, I'm not interested."

"And if he's not there, you're not interested in me either?"

"That's not what I said."

"I realize that, Ark. But that's how you act. When we're alone together you want to take pictures of me. Or talk about going out on a date. Or you talk about JD. Where's the part where you get invested in *me*?"

He lays me down in his lap and places his hand on my belly. It makes me think of families. Of the family I will never have. It makes me feel sad, and he sees this because he stares into my eyes. "I want you to be there *after*, Blue. When this life I'm living right now is over. When things are normal, and the filth of what I'm doing is finally washed away. I want you to be there after. I want to marry you, and be your best friend, and make love to you so that it's so much more than fucking. I want to take you out on dates and not have to worry about the people who might take you away from me. I want kids—" My face must crumple, because he leans down to kiss my lips, whispering, "We can adopt, baby. So don't worry about it. We can adopt."

I nod as the tears appear.

"I want all those things that couples have, Blue. The trinity is fun, but it's not sustainable. Not everything should come in threes. And all the shit I've done since the moment I met you was to make sure that when this fun runs out and there's only two of us left, it will be you and me, babe."

I swallow hard. "And what about JD?"

Ark sighs with a shrug. "I don't know. Maybe this threesome stuff lasts for years. Maybe tonight is a big misunderstanding. Maybe we're all gonna go home tomorrow and make up. We'll fuck till we're sore and sleep till we're refreshed, and eat and laugh, and do all the things we've been doing these past two months. And maybe we make it for a long time. But one day, Blue, he's gonna want more. I know him better than anyone alive. And when he does decide he wants more, that he wants you without the us, he will ruin everything. Because he cannot have you. I saw you first."

I bite my lip and close my eyes. "How can you say he'll ruin everything because he wants more in one breath, and claim me like property in the next? You're such a hypocrite."

"Do you want him?" Ark asks. "Instead of me? Because if you do, say so. I'll back off. But if you don't, if you want us, or even just me, then you need to trust me. Because I know him better than anyone. I know all the dark places inside his head. You see the charming smile and the playful side—"

"I see a hell of a lot more than that."

"Thanks for reminding me, Blue." Ark snarls that last comment. "What you see is the act. I know the truth."

"Then tell me what it is."

But he's shaking his head before I can finish the sentence. "It's not mine to tell."

"Oh, my God. I can't win with you. You want me to know these bad things about JD, but you don't want to be the one to tell me. You want the three of us to be together, but only under your conditions. You make no sense to me. I just want us to be perfect. I just want us to be together."

"We *are* together, Blue. He's the one who left."

"Maybe he calmed down. Maybe he came back. Maybe he's just angry about your accusations, because you know what, *I'm* angry about your accusations. You act like we don't have a say in what's normal. You act like we're the sick ones and you're the only sane person present. You act like there's only one way to exist in this relationship. And I'd just like to know, Ark, who the fuck made you the expert in *ménages à trois*?"

"OK," he says. "I think we need to take a break. Eat dinner. Watch some TV. Or something. Stop this conversation before it gets worse. Because we obviously don't see things the same way."

"You're hiding something from me. I told you why I was here. I gave up my secret. I bared my soul to you. I told you things I will never repeat again. Ever, Ark. When I finally do go home, no one will ever hear that story. You are the only one I told. And yet I know for a fact that you're keeping secrets. And probably outright lying to me."

He closes his eyes and lets out a breath of air. "I didn't really lie."

"Well, leaving shit out on purpose is the same thing. You're right. We need to stop talking because I've had enough and if we keep this going, I'm going to do something I regret."

He shoots me a hard look, his eyes narrow and his forehead creased. His jaw clenches like he's trying to control himself.

But then he gets up and walks over to the small kitchen and pulls the refrigerator door open. He closes it again, holding two beers in his hand. "Blue Moon or Blue Moon?" he asks me, twisting the caps off and handing one to me as he walks over.

I take it. Take a sip. Then another. And let the alcohol warm me for a moment.

Ark puts a hand on my shoulder. "Look, I'm not trying to manipulate you here, Blue. I'm doing my best to be authentic."

"What does that even mean?"

He takes a seat on the couch and pats the space next to him. "Come on, just relax for a second."

I scoot over and accept the offer, but I'm not done with this discussion. Because everything he's saying points to lies. Like he knows he's about to get caught in something and he's trying not to lie, but not telling the whole story at the same time.

It scares me. Because I've trusted this man with a lot of shit, and right now I feel like the clueless kid in school who is always last to get the joke.

"Let's just take a night, OK? One night away from JD. Let him have his space and do his thing. And if he was all talk, fine. We'll work it out."

Bu it's what Ark doesn't say that scares the shit out of me. "What if he isn't all talk? What if he does something?"

Ark takes a long swig of his beer and shrugs. "We'll deal with it tomorrow."

I let it go after that. I can't control Ark or JD. This is their night. This is their fight. I was fine with the way things were yesterday, but obviously we need to come to a new agreement if we all want to stay together.

The only thing I know is… I can fix this. I'll do whatever it takes. I'm not walking away from this. I'm not losing either of them.

I love two men.

My soul has two mates.

I love them equally, and with the same amount of fierce devotion.

And I'll fight to my death to have them both.

FORTY-SIX

ARK

WATCH the phone for a return text, but it never comes.

And what did I expect? That after four years people still give a shit?

I shake it off, trying to convince myself Blue is right. JD is just mad. He said things he doesn't mean. Tomorrow we'll go home, talk it out, and find a solution. In two weeks, Public Fuck will launch and we will forget all about this night.

If she has faith, I can have faith too.

We pass the night watching TV. We drop all the anger and just relax on the couch. I can feel her slipping away. I'm not sure how, but I know it. She's checking out on me. She's thinking about JD. She's thinking about the three we make, when all I see in our future is two.

My arms are wrapped around her, one hand on her belly, the other playing with the long strands of blonde hair that blow across her cheek as she breathes deeply with sleep.

THREE TWO ONE

Even though my goals have become muddied over the past four years, the no-girlfriend stipulation was something I respected. Oh, I've had fucks. Lanie at first. I liked her a lot in the beginning. She was my only contact and I needed her familiar conversation when I first got to Denver. And knowing that her body is decomposing inside her house—for God only knows how long—makes me sick.

I've had other girls too. But no one came home with me. No one came close. It was a quick fuck at their place, or in a car, or wherever. Any place but my place. Because I'm not allowed to get attached.

And here I am, very much involved in a relationship with not one, but two people. Here I am, in love with a man and a woman who make me so happy that every day for the past six weeks I had to convince myself it was real.

What are the chances a person finds their one soulmate in their one lifetime?

What are the chances they find out they have two?

Not everything should come in threes. That's what it says on my back. The two dragons fighting to claim the world. To claim what's theirs. But maybe that tattoo has been saying something else all along. Maybe the dragons aren't a team. Maybe the blue pearl isn't the world, but a girl they both want. A girl they're both willing to fight for. Fight over.

Maybe it's true. Maybe JD is right and every set of three is perfect.

But in my heart I know it's a lie—not everything should come in threes.

FORTY-SEVEN

BLUE

I WAIT until Ark is asleep and then I get out of bed and go to the bathroom down the hall from the bedroom. I'm sleeping in a pair of his boxer briefs and a t-shirt. I use the bathroom like normal and walk back to the bedroom and wait outside the door to see if he's awake.

When he doesn't ask me what I'm doing after several minutes, I walk back to the bathroom and pull on my jeans. I grab his new phone, his keys and the keys to the Camry, my coat, and my shoes, and leave the apartment as quietly as I can.

The steps are metal, something I noticed when we came, so my bare feet don't make much sound as I descend. If he wakes up in the middle of the night, he'll know where to look for me, I'm sure.

When I get to the bottom of the steps, I put my shoes on real fast, and then I get in the car and wake up the sleeping phone.

I check the call history to see if the text he sent earlier was to

JD, but it wasn't. It is, however, an area code I recognize. And that makes me stop for a second.

Why the hell would he be calling DC?

What if he called my father?

No. No, he wouldn't do that without telling me. It's got to be something else. It's got to be part of his secret and since this is the only real clue I have, I send a text to try to coax one back.

Did you get my message?

I get in the car and wait. Both texts have the little *Delivered* message below the balloon bubbles. So I know it went through.

But I didn't come down here to snoop on his phone. I came down to call JD.

I press in JD's number and count the rings, but it goes to voicemail. "JD," I say in a low whisper. "It's Blue. Please call me back on this phone. I need to talk to you."

I hang up and slump down in the driver's seat of the dead girl's Camry. Who was she? I have no idea. But it's not good when your boyfriend takes you to a girl's house and you can smell her decaying body from the back door.

The buzz of the phone in my hand scares the crap out of me, and my heart skips a beat before I realize it's JD calling me back.

"Hello?"

"Blue," he says. He sounds sad. "Where are you?"

I look around the building. "I don't know. Ark took me somewhere for the night. I'm in a big building." I leave out the rest of the info about this place. The servers. The fact that Ark has been spending a lot of time here. The lies. I just want us to make up, so that stuff will have to wait. "He said you sold my pictures. Is that true? Did you sell the videos we made?"

"I never said that shit, Blue." It comes out fast and angry. It comes out believable. "I have no idea why Ark's trippin', but this is bullshit. He thinks he owns you, Blue. He's the one who's been lying. And he's pissed off that I found out about it."

That's true. Ark admitted a bunch of lies to me and I have a feeling that's just the beginning. "I want to come home. I want Ark to bring me home. But he won't until tomorrow. Do you think I should leave?"

"Can you leave?"

"I'm in a car. But I don't know where I'm at. And I don't know how to get home."

"Does it have GPS, baby? You could program in our address and it will tell you how to get here. Do you think you can do that?"

"It does. It has a GPS. But, if I come, do you promise that we can all talk this through tomorrow? I know he's hiding things too. I can feel it. And he's admitted to some of them. They don't add up, so I'm not sure what any of them mean. But JD, I need us to make up."

"We can sort it out, Blue. I swear. And I think it's pretty fucked up that he accused me of taking advantage of you thinking you're a prisoner and then he practically abducts you."

"Yeah." JD has a point. "I know. I don't want to stay here, JD. I want to come home. Ark's scaring me. He says he's gonna call my father and make me go back to them. I can't do that, JD. I can't tell the world what I did, and the world will certainly want to know where I've been for the past year and a half."

"You're in the car right now?"

"Yeah."

"OK. Then start it up and program our address into the GPS."

I start the car and the GPS comes to life. I had one a long time ago. It feels like a different lifetime, but these steps are familiar to me. I accept the agreement that I won't mess with it while I drive, and then I punch in the address as JD reads it off to me.

"Just park in the garage and I'll be there waiting for you, OK?"

"OK," I say, pressing the button on Ark's keychain that he

used to open the roll-up garage door. "I'm on my way. Will you stay on the line with me?"

"Of course, baby. Of course. Don't panic or anything. Just follow the directions." As soon as JD says that, the voice begins to narrate the route home. "And take your time."

JD talks soothingly to me as I drive. We are far away. Past Boulder, which is miles away from downtown, where I need to be. But there's no traffic since it's late. And when I start to get nervous, JD is there in my ear calming me down.

Finally, after more than a half hour of driving. I recognize the buildings around our street. I'm starting to feel better when my phone buzzes an incoming text. I glance at it as I wait for a light to turn green.

If you went home, just let me know. Don't leave me like this. Everything I've done, I've done for us.

It's from Ark. I punch out my return message. *I'm here at home. I need JD too, Ark. I need him tonight. And not the way you think. You're lying to me.*

The light turns green and I make a left and then a right when I get to the garage. JD is waiting for me. Casually leaning up against a truck, smoking a cigarette. I drive towards him when the return text buzzes. I pull into the parking spot where Ark's Jeep was a few hours ago, and then glance down at the phone before I put the car in park.

So is JD. Be very careful. I'll be there soon.

I let out a long breath. If they're both lying, who do I trust?

JD? He is walking towards me, smiling big, the charm I love about him practically dripping off him.

Or Ark? The serious one. The one who refuses to accept that JD and I have our own special relationship. The one who refuses to even fuck me unless he has JD as a buffer between us.

I stick the phone in my pocket and open the car door. JD pulls me out and hugs me hard. "I'm so glad you came back." He kisses me on the head, and then he takes my hand and leads me to the door I came out of with Ark.

We go back upstairs in silence. I'm afraid JD's going to start asking questions, but he doesn't. And it makes me nervous. "Do you still love Ark?" I ask. "Can you guys work this out?" The elevator doors open and we walk to the loft door together.

"Of course, baby," JD reassures me as he open the door and waves me in.

I go first, so damn happy to be back here I breathe a sigh of relief. "I was only gone a few hours, but—"

I stop short as I see the man sitting on the couch in our living room.

"You were gone a lot longer than that, Star." The man tsks his tongue in that way he used to do, just before he'd beat me with a cane or cut me with a knife.

"What the fuck—"

JD grabs a fistful of hair and yanks me down to the ground, forcing me to my knees. He slaps my face. Hard. Not harder than he usually does during our ravishment sex, but this time, there is nothing sexual about his blow.

Gabriel, all dressed up in his fake priest outfit, gets up and walks towards me.

I look up at JD. "Why? Why did you do this?"

"It's you or her, Blue. And look, this is nothing personal. But my daughter is the only thing I have left of Marie."

"Marie would hate you for this!" I scream.

But JD just slaps me again. "Shut up," he growls.

"He did it, Blue"—Gabriel snarls my new name—"because I offered him something so much better than you. You're nothing," he hisses as he walks up to me. He presses his face close to mine. "You're nothing but a sick little slut who wants to be raped." And then he laughs. The stench of his breath making me want to vomit. "He told me, Star. He told me what you asked him to do." And then he pulls out a set of handcuffs and JD forces me to the ground, face first. They cuff me and then yank me to my feet. "Thank you," Gabriel says to JD.

"I want their names," JD says, yanking me away from my old master and pulling out a gun. "Now. Or you don't get her. And then we're going to take a drive and you're going to walk into their house and bring my daughter out. That was the deal. That's the trade."

"JD," Gabriel laughs. "Please. We're not going to steal your daughter back tonight, son."

JD shoots him in the leg. No hesitation. The gun goes off right next to my ear and I scream and fall to my knees at the same time that Gabriel crumples to the ground in agony.

"I'm not fucking around with you," JD says, walking forward. I'm still on the floor, so he drags me with him as he goes. And when the bodyguards appear from the hallway where Ark's bedroom is, JD shoots one in the chest, blowing him backwards into the wall. The man didn't even have a chance. His body leaves a thick streak of blood on the wall behind him as he slides down until he's just a heap on the floor.

Another gunshot blasts from that same direction, and this one grazes past my shoulder, so close I feel the sting and the gush of blood.

JD pulls me again, and then grabs my arm, yanking me to my feet. He tosses me aside as he takes another shot at the hallway, and the other guard has a giant hole in his chest. I fall forward, knocking my head into the granite countertop. The sharp blow to my temple shakes my world and my vision blurs.

"You piece of shit," Gabriel says from the floor a few yards away. He's got a gun out too, and he points it at me and fires. The stone above me shatters down, shards like shrapnel. "You'll never get her back now."

"You're going down, Gabriel. I find her and she and I will be together again. But you—you will never sell another baby again."

"That's funny coming from you."

"Shut up!" JD yells.

"I don't suppose he ever told you the truth about Marie, did he, Star?"

Bile rises in my throat from that name. But then JD pulls me to my feet once more. He shoves the barrel of the gun against my temple and I let out a sob. "You want her back pretty bad, don't you?" he asks Gabriel. "You told me earlier that my daughter is my Achilles' heel. Well, Blue is yours. And I'll take her away from you, just like you took my daughter away."

"JD! Please!" I scream. He elbows me in the side, making me gasp for air.

"Tell her then," Gabriel says. "Tell her you—"

JD shoots him again, only this time the bullet rips his shoulder apart and he is silenced.

"JD."

Ark is standing in the open doorway, a gun in his hand, but he's not pointing it at anyone. It's up in the air. "Just be calm now. OK? Think about what you're doing here. This isn't how you want it to end, brother."

"Brother?" JD spits. "You're not my brother. You're just like all the rest of them. You take. You use. You used me." He pokes the side of my head with the barrel of the gun again. It's throbbing from my fall, and my vision blurs once more.

"No," Ark says. "I've been trying to help you. All these years."

"He told you he had her. My *daughter*. The one you promised to help me find. And you walked away from those answers."

"He wanted me to fuck his wives, JD. He wanted me to give him my children too. What world do you live in where that is an acceptable trade?"

"It was a promise." JD pushes the gun into my head even harder and Ark takes a step forward.

"JD," Ark says in a calm voice that says he's the one in control. "None of this is my fault. You know that. You know the real truth. You've been hiding from it for a long time. But you know what happened to Marie and the baby."

"Oh my God," I say, the pieces starting to come together. "Oh, my God. Please tell me. Please—"

"Shut up!" JD smacks me in the mouth. "Just shut the fuck up!"

"You sold your baby, didn't you?" My disgust overshadows my fear and I wriggle in his grasp.

"Quiet, Blue!" Ark yells. "JD, just put the gun down."

But he only presses it into my head harder. "I'll kill her, Ark. Take one more step, and I'll kill her."

"You won't kill her. You love her, JD. You love her like you loved Marie."

The pressure of the barrel against my head eases a little.

"That's it," Ark says. "Just put the gun—"

"Hands in the air!"

And then all hell breaks loose. Windows crash as bodies fly through them. Red lasers are all over the place, the dots flying, one on me, then JD. I look at Ark and there's several dots dancing on his chest.

"No," JD says. "I'm not going down this way!"

FORTY-EIGHT

ARK

Denver Federal Center
Lakewood, Colorado
Present day

"**A**ND?" Matheson asks, when I say nothing. "You saw her first. What's that got to do with anything?"

I close my eyes, the scene still fresh in my mind. Gunshots. That's all I hear in my head. Nothing but gunshots. I rub my eyes, making those little pinpricks of light appear behind my eyelids. "I can't tell this story," I finally say. "It's not mine to tell."

"You bet your ass you're gonna tell this story," Jerry growls. "We've got dead bodies, asshole. Your loft was the site of several murders tonight. So we're gonna fucking sit here until you tell us—"

A knock on the door interrupts Jerry's rant. We all turn at the same time to look at the man who opens the door.

"What?" Jerry snaps. "We're in the middle of—"

"Sorry." The new guy looks at me and shakes his head.

"Someone called from DC and said they're shutting this down."

"Shutting what down?" Matheson asks. "We're in the middle of a case here—"

"Agent Matheson," the new guy says. "I realize that. But we just got orders. From DC. For me to come in here and shut you up. So get out."

There's a long moment of silence while the two assholes in front of me have a staring contest, and then Jerry starts gathering the photos, but when he tries to take the one of Blue, I hold onto it. "Fuck you!" I snap at him, taking him by surprise and making him recoil back. "I'm keeping this."

He starts to snatch it away, but the new guy interferes again. "Let him keep it, Jerry. He's gonna need it."

And then they exit the room and leave me to wonder what the fuck that means.

I stare at that picture for what seems like hours. It's one of mine. One they lifted off my computer at home.

Not my home. I need to come to terms with that. It's not my home.

I close my eyes and picture the scene when I took that photo.

Blue and JD were relaxing on the couch while I worked in my office. And they started playing around. He was making her giggle like a girl. And Blue was making JD laugh.

He started smiling again a while ago. I don't know how long it took exactly. But the past two years have been good.

No, I correct myself. Great. They were great. For him and for me.

But the laughter that day… it did something to me. It made me feel like no matter what happened, I made the right choice when I decided to help JD recover.

I look at the picture again. Blue is alone, but JD was just off to the right of her. She didn't realize I was taking pictures, so her eyes are full of two things.

Happiness. Because JD made her so fucking happy.

And surprise at the camera shutter. Because that was what I gave her.

Instead of love, I gave her lies.

The gunshots…

I want the memory to go away. But it won't. I've been here for hours. And it's still replaying in my mind like some fucked-up movie on repeat.

"You sold your baby, didn't you?"

Blue saw it in the end. She saw through my lies. And even though she was the one with the gun pointed at her head, I knew she was not the one who would end up dead.

"Quiet, Blue!" I scream at her. Please, God, just make her stop talking. "JD, just put the gun down."

"I'll kill her, Ark. Take one more step, and I'll kill her."

I zoom in on his trigger finger and his shaky hand. Please God, no. "You won't kill her. You love her, JD. You love her like you loved Marie."

And in that moment I have a glimmer of hope. Because he pulls the gun back from her head. He looks at it, like he can't believe he's holding it in his hand.

"That's it," I tell him. "Just put the gun—"

"Hands in the air!"

The FBI is everywhere. A SWAT team crashes through the terrace windows. Red laser dots are dancing on Blue, JD, me…

And then it's over.

JD points the gun at himself.

And he pulls the trigger.

FORTY-NINE

ARK

I BREAK down after that. I sit in the FBI interrogation room with my head on the cold metal table, and I break the fuck down.

I see his head exploding all over Blue. I see the horror on her face.

I feel her heart shatter. I feel her knees hit the floor. The pain that must have caused. The bruises she's probably looking at right now. Bruises I'll never see because she's gone. That call from DC was about her, I know it. Her father has surely been informed by now that his daughter is alive.

Good for him. I'm happy she'll go home. I really am. She needs to get out of this town and do whatever it takes to get her life back.

But my best friend is dead.

His life is over.

And my heart is shattered. Not in two pieces, but three.

FIFTY

ARK

FALL asleep like that, my face, wet from grief, on the cold metal table. And when I wake up, Jackson is sitting across from me, a frown on his face.

"Jacob," he says in a whisper.

I shake my head. I try to remember him the way he used to look when I last saw him, but I can't quite conjure up the image in my mind. "I haven't been Jacob in a very long time."

"Jacob," he says again. "I'm so fucking sorry. If we had known he'd do that—"

My hands are no longer in cuffs, and I pound them on the table, making the picture of Blue jump. "Where the fuck were you? I texted you! You were not supposed to send in the fucking SWAT team! The original plan was always discreet!"

"Jacob," he says again, this time with more force. "We got another text. I took that to mean it was urgent. We agreed on one text. And you sent another one."

"I didn't! Blue—Zoey, that girl we had—she sent the text when she stole my phone!"

He puts his hands in the air. "I didn't know, Jake. I didn't know. I thought you were in danger. It's been four years without contact. And I was in Nebraska, prepping a new recruit. I was hours away, I'm sorry. I swear, we didn't know it was going down until the last second and we just had to react the only way we could. I'm sorry."

I stand up and grab my photo of Blue. "I need to get out of here. Now."

"Jake," he says, standing up with me, a hand reaching out for my shoulder. "You know we have to debrief. You know this, OK?"

"My house! They're in my house, going through all our shit. I need to—"

"We already saw all the footage, Jake. We know what's been going on."

"I want it all back!" I reach out, like I'm gonna choke the life out of Jackson. But I stop when he puts his hands up to block me.

And then he steps forward, tentatively reaching. "Jake," he says. "You're Jake. Not Ark. You're Jake. My brother. We're still brothers. I'm still here."

I let him pull me into a hug, but I don't hug him back.

All I see is JD's head exploding.

Everything hurts. My mistakes. My body. My heart.

"You're Jake," he repeats. Like he needs to remind me of who I really am. Why I was really in Denver in the first place. "You're Jake and I'm Jax. And we got them, brother. We got those traffickers and we're gonna make them pay for what happened to Michael. You made that happen, Jake. You. Four years undercover. Four years and it paid off because you stuck to the plan."

I take a deep breath and my mind spins with the memories. Blue and JD. The three of us in the tub coming to terms. The three of us last night, breaking all the promises. Memories of abandoned Christmas trees and all the broken promises will haunt me for the rest of my life.

But then I picture our little brother, Michael. Where he came from. What he went through before our father took him in. How they ended his life once they found out he was still alive and no longer a controlled asset.

Sixteen years ago an assassin walked into our house and when he walked out, our little brother was dead. What kind of person kills a seven-year-old boy?

We knew who they were. My father was FBI. My uncles were FBI. And I lied to Blue about my dream job too. I never wanted to be a SEAL. I wanted to be FBI.

But I'm a fuck-up. I left Brooklyn and went to Miami when I was eighteen on a clue that the people responsible for Michael's death were based there.

I did exactly what Blue did when she went looking for her friend. Infiltrate and conquer from within.

Only I wasn't looking for a story. I was looking for revenge.

I killed a lot of people in Miami and the only reason I didn't go to jail was because of some huge shake-up in the underground organization responsible for the assassin hired to kill my foster brother. So many FBI were implicated in that bust, I was swept under the table.

But I left Miami with two things. A clue about some child traffickers that led me to Denver. And enough money to start a sting operation in the porn business so we could repeat what I did in Miami. Infiltrate and conquer. Jackson was already in the FBI when the shit went down four years ago. He was rising fast, thanks to our family connections, so we started this job looking for the scumbags responsible for Michael's death.

But what I found was JD. And Ray.

Ray knew there was a shake-up in Miami and that's why I had

to leave. He knew I killed people. He knew I was in something big. But everyone who knew me was dead by the time I bailed, so who could he ask? Who was left to point their finger and say, *That's Jacob Barlow and he's a rat?*

No one.

That's not how Denver will end, that's for sure.

"And we got another lead too."

Jax is still talking. A reminder of what we're up against. Crime pays, I know that now. It pays too well for it to ever go away. We're never going to find the people who killed Michael, even if we do find the assassin.

Because these criminals are no one and everyone all at the same time.

"A girl. She escaped ten years ago and she got out. But she knows things, Jake. She knows more than anyone we've ever had access to before. You hear me? She knows all the things, and that's who I was prepping in Nebraska."

I calm down a little. Because maybe. Just maybe—

"We're raiding homes in ten states right now. We've already found the records for the Denver sting, Jake—"

"We got them all? The parents who bought the kids too?"

"We've got hundreds of names. We'll find the one you're looking for."

And this puts one shattered piece of my heart back together. It's a small piece. Just a little sliver of hope. Hope that I can still do right by JD. Fix him. And that JD will finally be free of his mistake.

I hug my brother.

"We'll find her," Jax repeats. "I promise."

FIFTY-ONE

ZOEY

Two Years Later

THE bookstore is full of people, a fact that has had my stomach fluttering for hours. I don't like attention and I hate crowds.

My publicist can read my mind these days, because she places a hand on my arm. "Zoey, you're gonna be so great." She gives me a warm smile and I give her a weak one back.

"Why did I agree to this?" I whisper.

She just stares at me, then shrugs. "I don't know, Zoey. I was surprised myself. But you're here, and it's fine. Just read your story the way you wrote it. They're fans. They're gonna love you. They already love you. They just want to hear you tell the story, get an autograph, and take a picture."

Here is The Neighborhood Bookstore in Brooklyn Heights. That's why I said yes. But now that it's real, I feel like I might vomit. I scan the crowd, looking for Ark. Does he follow my life the way I follow his? Does he know I'm here? Will he come listen to me talk? Or stand in line to get a book signed?

My daydream is stupid and pathetic. It borders on sad.

In the two years since we parted that night, I have not even heard Ark's voice. Why would he show up now?

The store manager steps up to a small podium. She is thrilled. This is a medium-sized independent bookstore, but the crowd today is more people than they've seen in… well, ever. She taps on the microphone a few times and then clears her voice. "Ladies and gentlemen." She takes a long breath. "I'm so excited to introduce to you one of today's best new authors. You probably first heard of her from the headlines years ago when she went missing. But she was not kidnapped, as we had all feared. She was writing." The manager, whose name I don't remember because I'm too nervous to think of anything but Ark right now, turns and beams at me. "And what a book, huh?"

The audience claps. The roar echoes off the high white ceilings of the store.

I take a deep, deep breath.

"What a book," the manager repeats, trying to stop the applause so she can continue. "Filled with hope, and love." She pauses and places a hand over her heart. "And the most perfect happily-ever-after ending I've ever read. I hope that wasn't a spoiler for anyone!"

The audience laughs. Everyone has read the book.

I've been on the *New York Times* bestsellers list for almost two months. Almost a million copies sold in that time. I've been accused of plotting my disappearance in order to sell books. And while that's crazy, considering what really happened to me when I was away 'writing', it's still got a bit of truth to it. Because the only reason I wrote this book after JD killed himself and Ark was hauled away by the FBI was to find my way back again. I need to know if it was all a lie. Did Ark ever love me?

I pulled every string I could to get my story out there. I used my father. I used my disappearance. I used my Columbia contacts. I used anything and everyone I could. All for the fame. So that one person would notice me again.

My publicist puts a hand on my shoulder once more, reading my sadness as nerves and trying to give me encouragement.

"So without further ado, I'm thrilled to introduce Zoey Marshall, author of the number one *New York Times*-bestselling romantic suspense, *Three, Two, One*."

She claps her hands too close to the microphone and it creates a thunderous boom before she steps aside to make room for me.

I take another deep, deep breath and walk forward. "Thank you," I say into the microphone. I desperately search the crowd for Ark, but even though the place is packed, there's no way to miss the fact that he is not here. "I'd like to read a passage from my book, if that's OK." Chuckles all around. It's why I'm here, right? "It's my favorite part. And it's a dialog scene between Ark and Blue."

A woman in the front row actually sighs.

Yes, I think to myself. *He's dreamy. Both in the book and out of it.*

"Who is the person you love most in this world?" I ask the audience, reading from chapter twenty-three in my book. That conversation is what changed me. Changed us. Because Ark drew a line when I couldn't.

I don't look up until I'm done with the entire passage, but when I do, every set of eyes in the store are on me.

"Thank you," I whisper into the microphone.

I try to make a hasty escape, but then the store manager is back, grabbing a hold of my hand and leaning into the microphone. "Miss Marshall will be signing books at the west end of the store. Please purchase your book prior to getting in line. Thank you!"

She turns to me and the digital cameras click. Flashes flash.

My eyes see spots. And when I open them, for a split second, I think I see him in the back.

But the residual spots blind me and when they finally clear as I'm walking to the west end of the store where my signing table is set up, the apparition is gone.

I take my seat at the table and a few of the store workers are first in line. I greet them and smile. I listen for their names and then write something witty in each book, enjoying the friendly banter as I pass them back.

It's a nice feeling. But my mind is occupied with how I got here.

How did I get from where I was to where I am?

Why do I constantly have to ask myself this question?

After JD killed himself, I don't remember anything but screaming. My screaming.

And then Ark's pleading, as he rushed to JD and held him in his arms, just repeating the words, "No. No. No," over and over again.

Ark was covered in blood when they picked him up off the floor. Someone had draped a blanket over me, even though I was wearing my coat. And all I kept thinking was, *It's so hot, I think I'm in hell.*

I smile at the fan in front of me. "Yes, of course you can have a picture." I stand and she makes her way over to the photo op banner my publicist had made specifically for this event. It's a picture of the book cover and the Denver city skyline in the background.

After that I try not to think about JD too much. I still cry over him. It's hard not to. He owned one third of my heart. I don't think it will ever be possible to replace the missing piece he still holds.

I think about Ark instead. It took me weeks to get any answers, and the FBI was very reluctant. But they finally admitted

Ark was undercover. Had been undercover for four years. And that the job was over and he'd moved on.

That broke my heart again. It made me think that it was all a lie.

That's how I started to write my book. Because I needed to remind myself some of it was real, even if those parts only belonged to JD. I needed to remember Janine too, whom they never found, but her baby was in the records the FBI confiscated from Gabriel's compound up in the mountains. They said that's where I was kept too. But I have no clue. I don't think about that time. Instead I think about Janine's baby, who was reunited with her true family once they got through all the fake adoption records.

"Can I ask you a question?"

I look up at the young woman, holding out her book for me to sign. "Sure," I say back with a smile.

"Why do you call it *Three, Two, One*? I know you have a lot of references in there to the numbers. But is it like a countdown?"

"Yeah. That's all it is. Just a countdown."

Three soulmates.

Two broken hearts.

One last chance to set it right.

"Oh," the woman says, slightly disappointed. "Well, thank you so much." She takes her book and smiles at me. "I love this story. I love the fact that they all end up together. I think JD loved her more, but I'm glad she got both. They filled her up, like she said. They both completed her because they were so different."

I nod. I can feel the sting of tears. "They did," I say. "You're right."

My book is fiction. And I can end it any way I want. So JD never died. Ark never lied. And everyone lived happily ever after.

After that I keep my attention where it belongs. On the people in front of me. I still scan for Ark's face in the crowd, but by four o'clock when the last person steps up to have their book signed, I can't avoid the obvious.

He never came.

I sign the book, smile, take a picture, and then hand it back. I thank the fan for coming to see me on such a cold and wintry day, and wish her happy holidays.

And then I stand and stare out the window where the snow is falling in large round flakes. The same way it did that night everything fell apart.

I walk away from the table and grab my bag from my publicist. "Do you need a ride to the airport?" she asks me, clearly concerned with my somber mood.

"No, thanks. I can manage."

I turn and make my way towards the back of the bookstore where my coat is hanging in the employee break room. I'm just turning the corner of the hallway when a voice rings out.

"Miss Marshall?"

I turn. "Yes?"

The last girl in line is jogging down the book aisle towards me. "Sorry," she says, out of breath. "I forgot! A man was in line with me a while ago, but he said he had to leave and would I pass this along."

She holds out a sealed envelope.

I stop breathing for a moment. "A man?"

"Yes," she says. "Sorry, I forgot." And then I take it from her and she waves goodbye. "Happy holidays!"

I lose my manners and ignore her. I just stare at the envelope. And then I look around nervously. Is he still here?

I open the envelope and pull out a thick card. Not a greeting card, a two-sided card, like a glossy business card, except larger.

JA HUSS

A Private Affair
You're Invited
When: Right now.
Where: Get in the car in the front of the store.

My alarms should be going off. I've been a prisoner twice. Once by force, once self-imposed. So I should be wary. But I don't even think twice. I grab my coat and walk out the front door, searching for Ark.

The world is blanketed in white. But the car in front, with a driver standing next to it, is long and black. The driver smiles at me, then opens the door to the backseat and I get in. He walks around the front of the car and gets in the driver's side.

"It's not far," he says. Like he knows that my mind is whirling with thoughts. He looks for traffic and pulls out onto the street.

I glance down at the card in my hand. There's no artist's name or gallery listed, but my heart knows. My heart knows because Ark's got a piece of it. And the closer we get to my final destination, the more whole I become.

I got a photograph in the mail last Christmas. It wasn't of a person, but of a view through an open door of a cage. The view was from the loft terrace in Denver, looking out over California Street.

I looked at that picture every night for months and I wondered, *Why won't he come for me?*

And then I decided he was waiting for me to come to him. He was waiting for me to leave the cage and let myself be free.

When we pull up to an old building that looks like it's been rehabbed recently, my heart beats a little faster. Two Dragons Art Gallery is an urban legend in New York. People admit to having been there, but no one can tell you where it is.

When I first heard this I immediately thought they were drugged and taken somewhere in secret. But then I was told the reason no one knows where it is because the location isn't permanent. One time it's here, the next it's there. Always on the edge of things, never on the beaten path.

And somehow, that fits Ark.

The gallery changes from exhibit to exhibit. It's fleeting. Just a moment in a night. Sometimes it's in a building. A subway station. A basement room in an underused public library. Once I heard it was in a bar bathroom.

It's always in Brooklyn, though. Ark's real home town. And that's why I agreed to do the reading today. I hoped against hope he would find me and let me back into his secret world.

The driver gets out and walks around to open my door. I take his hand as he helps me out. I pull away, but he holds on tighter.

"It's icy, Miss Marshall. I was instructed to make sure you don't slip down the stairs."

I look to where he's pointing. An outside stairwell that looks like it was recently shoveled, but the snow is thick and already piling up again.

My strappy sandals were not put on with this in mind. So I keep hold of the driver's hand until we reach the bottom after a precarious descent.

He lets go of me in front of an old metal door, and then he pulls and it swings open.

I step inside and the door closes behind me.

The room seems vast and long, but it's hard to tell because there is only one small spotlight shining down from the ceiling.

I am transfixed by the image it's illuminating on the wall. I walk forward, past the darkness, and into the light. And I just stare at the picture of JD. His blue eyes. His blond hair and scruffy chin. His charming smile.

The unframed photograph is the size of a picture window. His face is so big. So happy. So familiar. And so real.

My fingers stretch until I can touch his lips. And then I

walk forward, my arms spread out, and I press my cheek to his. My hands wrap around the edges of the canvas in a desperate attempt to pull him into the hug he deserves.

And I cry.

I cry all the tears I owe him.

They fall down my cheeks in rivers.

FIFTY-TWO

JAKE

WHEN I saw the announcement in the neighborhood paper that Zoey Marshall was going to do a reading in Brooklyn, I knew it was time. I knew she was coming for me.

Two years I've watched her from afar. Two years of endless internet searches, red-eye flights to try to catch a glimpse of her in a city before she left, stalking her blog, and her Facebook, and her Twitter. I wanted to keep that connection any way I could while she healed.

I watched her story play out on TV at first. Her father did the talking, of course. Zoey Marshall does not make public appearances. At least, not until today.

Tens of thousands of people preordered the book. While she never made a public statement on TV or did a print interview, she was always a click away on her blog where she wove a story about her fictitious sabbatical at a hippy commune tree house community in the Brazilian rainforest.

JD didn't sell those films. He deleted them. No one ever came forward to say this is Zoey Marshall's real story.

And even though I know she made some of the story in the novel up to make us more romantic, all the important things are true.

We were in love.

JD is dead.

People were saved.

Lives go on.

I've been back to see Ray a few times. Jax thinks I'm crazy, but the FBI went through his records for almost a year and never found a single i undotted or t uncrossed. Ray was as up and up as a porn mogul can get. Still is.

Public Fuck America never went live, obviously. But I did get back all the videos of JD. I had to fight for the ones of Blue. Jax made sure that evidence, including the videos and contract she had with Gabriel, disappeared.

I kept everything that was mine.

We destroyed the rest.

There were lots of trials. Not Gabriel's. He bled to death on the concrete floor of my loft that night. And those trials had lots of deals. No one got off, not even the flock wives. The deals were made to keep Blue's reputation intact. And now that she wrote the book, it's sort of a cover in and of itself. A brilliant move, actually. She made our story fiction. No one will ever believe it's true.

My transient gallery has grown through word of mouth generated so as to ensure people in her circles—her publisher, her agent, her publicist, her editor—all knew about it.

I have lived every moment of the past two years with her in mind.

So when the text comes through that she got into the car, my heart beats wildly with anticipation. She is not going to a transient show in some dingy abandoned building. She's coming to my home. My personal gallery where I have labored over the past twenty-six months to create the perfect exhibit.

And not by coincidence, it's called One, Two, Three.

One lost girl.

Two best friends.

Three eternal soulmates.

The idling motor of a car outside breaks my concentration and I stand up. I straighten my suit coat, and my tie, making sure it's tight.

Her shoes tap on the concrete steps. I picture her hand being held by my driver, Matthew, and then the door opens with a creak.

She's illuminated by the outside light for a brief moment, and then the door closes behind her and she stands in the shadows.

But it only takes her a moment to see JD. It's hard not to, since I've placed a spotlight above his head. It's my favorite picture of JD, taken when he was sitting outside on our terrace when we first moved into the loft.

It was a good day. One of the best. We were rich. He was happy. I was satisfied that we'd gotten through the hardest thing he'd ever have to go through. He was better. He was whole again. He was saved.

It turns out salvation is no more permanent than anything else in this life.

But if I could save him once, I could do it again.

Blue reaches out to touch his lips and then she spreads her arms and hugs the photo. It's almost as wide as her arms, but not quite. There is just enough room for her to grab onto the edges and place her cheek on his.

"You came," I say, stepping out of the shadows.

She turns to face me, wiping the tears from her eyes. "I owed you a story. So I wrote you a story."

THREE TWO ONE

I walk forward and take her hand. "I love your story."

She starts to cry again. "Why did you leave me? After it was all over I asked them to tell me where you were, but they refused."

I take her in my arms and hold her tight. I smell her hair and close my eyes. "I left because I love you. And you were right."

She pulls back and looks up at my face, her blue eyes filled with tears. "I was wrong about everything."

"No," I whisper. "You said I wasn't invested that night. And you were right. I wasn't. I wasn't invested in anything. Not the job, not JD, not the business, not even you. So I had to let you go, Blue. Because you deserve better than that. You deserve the kind of love that has no conditions. You deserve the kind of love that's free. You deserve devotion. So I left so I could find a way to give you all those things."

And then I reach into my pocket and pull out a remote control. "Click it on, Blue."

She reaches for the little white plastic with a blinking red light. "What is it?" She looks up at me with total trust and I smile.

"My investment."

And then I press her finger and the lights come on.

FIFTY-THREE

BLUE

WE are everywhere. Our faces paper the wall, lit up like the angels we wanted to think we were, and not the demons we know we are.

Me. JD. And Ark. Three people who stumbled on each other in the rain.

Us in the tub, the mist obscuring our faces, but not our intentions. Us on the terrace, their hands between my legs, my mouth open in a moan you can hear through time and paper. Us, us, us. Everywhere.

I walk down the row of photographs, studying each one, remembering the day they were taken, the smile reluctantly coming forth with each passing moment. "We were in love, weren't we?" I ask Ark.

"We still are, baby. We still are."

My chin trembles and when I look he nods, as if to reaffirm this declaration yet again. He places a hand into the small of my back and urges me forward. I take small steps so I can see each picture. Most of them are in black and white. We are nude. We are kissing. "There are more of JD and me than with you." I sigh. "You always forgot the tripod."

"I know," Ark says. "But I don't make that mistake anymore." I give him a weird look as we take a step into the darkness. The end of the line of photos. "I can't afford to let the moments slip by. So I take pictures every day. I want to record every change."

And then he reaches for the little remote in my hand and clicks it one more time. The opposite side of the room lights up, only the photos on that wall are not of us.

They are of a little girl.

I know who she is the second I look into her blue eyes. But even if I didn't recognize her, the charm in her smile gives it away.

FIFTY-FOUR

ARK

HER name is Paige."

Blue stares at my six-year-old daughter. JD's daughter.

"Her parents went to jail, and since JD had me listed as next of kin on all his legal papers, they let me adopt her. She's my whole life, Blue. She erases all the mistakes."

Blue walks up to the largest picture and touches my little girl's face. "She's beautiful."

"She looks just like him, don't you think?"

Blue nods and then she turns. "What happened? I run that night through my head every day. Why? Why did he do that?"

I can only shrug. But it's a copout and I know it. *You're invested now*, I remind myself. "He was sick, Blue. He was sick since the day I met him. Manic-depressive. Bipolar, whatever you want to call it. And the guilt he had…" I shake my head. "He's the one who heard about the baby-sellers. He's the one who made Marie go work for them to pay for his drug habit. He's the one who handed the baby over. She disappeared the same day as the baby. And I can only assume they are the ones who killed her, but we just don't know. JD said she killed herself because he made her sell the baby. He couldn't live with the guilt."

Blue walks over to me and I wrap her up in my arms. "I couldn't save him, but I could save Paige by getting her back. I could save you by walking away and letting you figure out who you are and what you want. And I could save myself by walking away from that life and starting this one."

"I love you," she says.

I swallow hard and step back half a step. "Then stay with me, Blue. Let me love you back the way you deserve to be loved. You don't need me to save you. I don't need you to save me. She doesn't need us to save her." I motion to Paige's picture on the wall.

Blue hesitates, and then looks me in the eyes. "JD was right and you were wrong, you know."

"I'm wrong a lot. But please don't hold it against me."

She smiles and places her small hands on my rough cheeks, pressing against my skin. And then she rises up on her tiptoes and kisses me. "You were wrong about the motto on your back, Ark. *Everything* should come in threes. Especially us. Because one is where it all starts. Two is only halfway there. But three…" She rises up to kiss me again and then she whispers, "Three was always our perfect ending."

I hold Blue's hand and lead her over to the elevator. She draws in several deep breaths, betraying her apprehension. But I squeeze her hand until she brings those blue eyes up to meet my dark ones. And then I kiss her. Our mouths come together—hesitantly at first, then with more passion. I slide my hands up along her face and fold her into my embrace. She pulls back, resting her head on my chest, like she's listening for my heartbeat.

"I miss him," I say. She nods her head, but her back shakes

from the silent sobs. "But Paige... she helps. You'll see."

We ride up to the top and the doors open into my penthouse apartment. Paige waits with the housekeeper in her pajamas. You only have to look at her to know that JD is still here with us.

Paige stands up and does this little curtsy, turning on the charm she comes by naturally. "I know you," she whispers.

Blue stares at her, her sadness receding before my eyes. And then she wipes her tears and smiles. "I know you too," Blue replies back in her own hushed voice. "I know you too."

And that's how we start it. Our new life together.

One little girl.

Two soulmates.

And three mended hearts.

I'm a believer now. I can see it with my own eyes.

Everything should come in threes.

END OF BOOK SHIT

Welcome to The End of book Shit. We call them the EOBS now. I write these chapters at the end of every book. They sort of have cult status these days. Sometimes they are a little controversial, sometimes not. They are never edited. So if you see a typo, oh well. I wait until the last minute to write them—like right now it's 1 AM Monday, January 26, 2015. I have to send this to my formatter tonight. Like now. So she can get it back to me before Tuesday so I can upload with enough time to get the book live before the 28th (the official release day).

So fuck. (I swear a lot in these) I'm not sure how much I should tell you about where this all came from. It started out pretty dirty because it came right out of a porn video. I saw this video about a year and a half ago. It was a guy who made these reality videos for an online site. But that was not what captured my attention.

So here's how it went… this was in Eastern Europe somewhere, it was all in subtitles. It was the dead of winter. The guy with the camera was in a train station or something. And he must've seen this girl. She was tall, not too thin, nice curvy figure underneath her huge coat and winter clothes.

But she was very pretty. Black hair. Dark eyes. Perfect face. Beautiful actually, but in a very poor way. Like, you could tell she had normal everyday problems on her mind. Her clothes were ordinary. Nothing special. And she looked tired. She was coming home from work, I think.

So this camera guy was filming his approach to her. Telling her she's pretty, does she want to let him take her picture? She ignores him for a long time—at least ten minutes of that movie is just this guy practically begging this girl to give him some attention. He follows her all the way out to her car, and then he gets down to business. *If you show me your bra, I'll give you this money.* I don't know how many Euro he said. One hundred maybe.

Her eyes bugged out, but she said no.

But the guy knew he could persuade her if he just kept upping the amount, So he gets to five hundred Euro, holds the money out, makes her take it. And then asks her, *Where do you work?*

She's a cashier.

How much do you make in a week?

She tells him some small amount, not in Euro, some other currency. So a small amount.

And he tells her, *Just show me your underwear and that five hundred is yours.*

And you could see her face as she worked through what this money might mean.

You could pay rent with this. You could buy food. Clothes. He says all this to her as she bites her lip and takes deep breaths.

Ok, she says. *But not in public.*
He says, *OK, let's go to my place.*

So gets in his car, and he's filming this whole time. And he actually says to the camera, *I can't believe she got in my car*!

And the girl is clearly nervous, but she trusts him for some reason.

They get to his place and she lifts up her shirt and shows him her bra.

He says, *Come on. I paid five hundred Euro. Take off your clothes and stand in your underwear.*
She's got a shitload of clothes. It's like the dead of winter in some horrible wintery nation somewhere in Eastern Europe, right? She she's taking off her coat. Her sweater. Her scarf tucked inside her sweater. Her boots, her pants, her socks. Her shirt.

Finally she's in her underwear. Just some ordinary underwear.

He's like, *You're so beautiful.*

And it wasn't a lie. You could just tell in his voice (even though it was not even in English), he was mesmerized by her. Like he just met his *soulmate*.

And she *was* totally beautiful. But in a very sad way. Like her life just sucks and that beauty hasn't gotten her anywhere, so who cares. She's got problems. But she politely whispers, *Thank you.*

And then he says, *You're here. I have all this money to get girls to do things on camera for me. I'll give you all of it, three thousand*

Euro, if you let me fuck you.

And she takes a deep breath, turns around a little, like she can't believe this is happening. And then turns back and says, *OK.*

So she fucks him. She does whatever he wants, and he films the whole thing from his point of view as he comes in her mouth.

And when they're done, he gets up and looks into the camera. And in the background you see her walk into the bathroom, turn on the sink water, lean over, and spit out his come. Probably puking a little while she was at it.

And the guy, I really don't think he knew. Because he looks into the camera and says, *I have never paid so much for sex before in my life. But it was worth it.*

I was transfixed by this story. It was like thirty minutes long and only about five of it was the actual sex. But that girl's face told so much more about what was going on in her head. And the guy sorta fell in love with her for some reason. Like he wasn't after the sex, not really. You could tell he wanted *her*. He probably didn't even want to fuck her at that point. He just didn't want her to leave—he wanted a *date*. So he made her an offer she couldn't refuse.

And this guy is kinda big in the porn world. He's got a website with hundreds of videos like this, but none were like this at all.

And I thought to myself, no one who watches this video gives a shit about the fucking. It's all about this guy who buys girls for ten minutes a pop, pulling out his A-game to get this one tragically beautiful and sad girl to give him a few minutes of her time.

That's a story. And from there I started imagining who these people were. And what if there was someone else there. One guy running a camera, one guy doing the acting.

And what if... they both fell in love with her, and she fell in love with them back.

That's how Three, Two, One started.

I've been thinking about this story for over a year. I wasn't sure if I'd ever write it because it was so dirty. But the idea would not go away. The plot got more and more complicated. The characters got more and more real. And the stakes got higher and everything got darker as I imagined it all in my head.

A few things changed. Jana, my assistant, and I talked about this plot lots of times. Should it be a skanky porn piece that I use a pen name for? Should it be part of the bigger world I write in? Should I use another character from one of my other books as the girl?

But somehow I convinced myself that I could write this under my own name and even though I still think it's a big risk for me, I'm glad I did. Because I fell in love with this book just like that real life Prince of Porn did that girl he had to buy.

The early reviews are already in and so far the readers have really connected with the story and characters. So I hope that's a good sign. I hope people see past the sex and find the characters. Because no one cares about the sex *acts*. Erotic romance is not really about the *sex*. It's about what the characters are *feeling* as the sex takes place.

I didn't care about the sex in that video I saw. I only wanted to know about the people. So if this was too much sex for you, I'm sorry. But this story wrote itself once I started typing. It took me exactly forty-two days to write it. A few more days, if you add in the editing. So I basically wrote it down as it played out in my head and this is what came out.

If you want to discuss this book with me, my Street Team, and other #fans, just click this link and you'll be taken to our public 321group.

This is a standalone book, *however*, it takes place in one of my other "world's" and you will see someone from Three, Two, One in a book I'm putting out in late spring.

Up next is another standalone about a character who's been in and out of books in my Rook & Ronin and Dirty, Dark, and Deadly "worlds" for over a year now. Merc's book will be a dark erotica. MUCH darker than this. So if this was not your thing, skip that one. I will have the sexy, fun Social Media spin-offs going all summer and into the fall. So if you like that stuff more, it's all good, bitches. I can write whatever the fuck you want. Just not all the time. ;) I like the dark stuff, the twisted stuff, and the fun stuff too. So I will write them as they come to me.

If you enjoyed this book, please, do me a favor and leave your review on Amazon. Even if you didn't purchase your book from Amazon, just pop over and tell me what you think. I really rely on reviews to help get the word out about my books. People love to hear what others think and so do I.

****

If you follow me on my author page on Facebook or my Twitter account, you know I run a lot of contests. I give away a lot of signed books and prize packages. That's how I like to connect with #fans. So last fall, during one of my Social Media book releases, I had a contest and part of the prize was winning a character named after you.

My winner for that particular contest was a member of my street team, Paige. My team hardly ever wins those contests because I choose random winners using an app. But Paige was my random winner and so I named JD's daughter after her. Congrats to Paige. Thank you for playing along with me and be so supportive on the Street Team. <3

I have a really great Street Team. The best, in fact. They are awesome and we are like a family in there. I'm not taking new members, we are closed. But I do run a fan group on Facebook called Shrike Bikes. They are in there all the time, as am I. So if you'd like to hang out with us, just click the link and ask to join the group. One of us will approve you as soon as we see the request.

I also run Release Day Share Contests. If you sign up to help me spread the word about my books on Facebook and/or Twitter, you will be automatically entered to win a free copy of the book on release day. If you have already purchased the book when you are notified that you are a winner, you may choose and advanced release copy of an upcoming book instead. The next book (as I write this) is Merc's story.

If you want to be notified of upcoming books, sign-up forms

for advanced release copies (ARC's), special pre-release teasers, or how to order a signed copy of this book, you can sign up for my newsletter on my website: jahuss.com

Thank you for reading. Thank you for reviewing. And I'll see you in the next book!

Julie

ABOUT THE AUTHOR

JA Huss is the USA Today bestselling author of more than twenty romances. She likes stories about family, loyalty, and extraordinary characters who struggle with basic human emotions while dealing with bigger than life problems. JA loves writing heroes who make you swoon, heroines who makes you jealous, and the perfect Happily Ever After ending.

Other Books By
J.A. HUSS

Rook and Ronin Books
TRAGIC
MANIC
PANIC

Rook and Ronin Spinoffs
SLACK: A Day in the Life of Ford Aston
TAUT: The Ford Book
FORD: Slack/Taut Bundle
BOMB: A Day in the Life of Spencer Shrike
GUNS The Spencer Book

Dirty, Dark, and Deadly
Come
Come Back
Coming for You
James and Harper: Come/Come Back Bundle

Social Media
Follow
Like
Block
Status
Profile
Home

Printed in Great Britain
by Amazon